Shadow of Thebes

A Demon of Athens Novel

Martin Sulev

THE DEMON OF ATHENS SERIES

TYRANNY
GOD OF SPARTA
SHADOW OF THEBES
EXILE OF CORINTH (2024)

For Jun,
Message to Thebes, indeed!

MAPS

GREECE AND THE AEGEAN

Greece and the Aegean
395 BCE

BOEOTIA AND CENTRAL GREECE

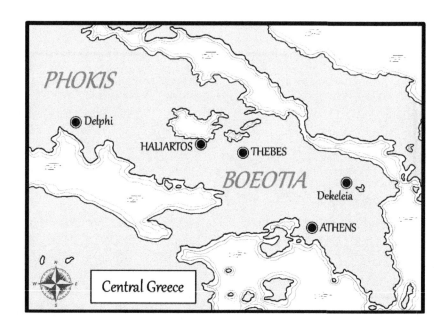

HALIARTOS AND VICINITY

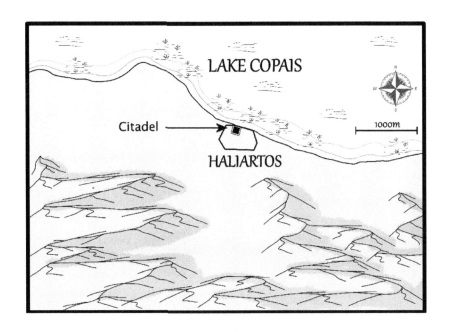

A NOTE ON SPELLING

For various reasons, transcribing Classical Greek words into English can be quite a challenge. In this book, I have used different conventions in different situations for different reasons. For familiar places such as Thrace and Sicily, I have tended to use conventional English spelling to avoid confusion. In many Greek names, however, I have used "k" instead of "c", as in Alkibiades and Perikles, to better approximate the original pronunciation or Greek spelling. In yet other cases, I made rather arbitrary decisions regarding a particular name (Thrasybulus rather than Thrasyboulos, for example) because I thought it looked nicer on the page. All that is to say, I apologize in advance if my spelling choice in a particular situation differs from what you yourself might have chosen.

M . S .

PART ONE

ΠΕΡΣΑΙ PERSIANS

CHAPTER 1

Μᾶλλον ἢ τὸ Δαρείου χρυσίον κτήσασθαι δεξαίμην
πολὺ πρότερον ἑταῖρον, ως λέγεται.

"It is better to acquire a friend than all of Darius' gold," or so it
is said.

I was not so certain. At the moment, the *peripoli* needed gold more
than friends. And our hunt for it had been an abject failure.

We had been roaming the northern part of Attica, where the pass
at Mount Parnia leads through the plains of Oropus and on to Tanagra
in eastern Boeotia. From those places and beyond, travellers and
traders go through the pass on their way south to Athens. In the past,
in more unsettled times, such merchants had often fallen prey to
bandits who made their camps in the mountains to the west. It had
been some time since the *peripoli* had patrolled there, and I had been
hoping for some good fortune.

But we had found nothing. The locals reported no attacks in recent
memory, and there was no trace of bandits in their usual hideouts in
the mountains. Except for a family of escaped slaves, terrified by the
sudden appearance of a dozen armed men in their secluded refuge,
we had seen no one but shepherds. Even the vicious packs of wild
dogs that roamed the hills had given us a wide berth. We had nothing
to show for our efforts but ten days' worth of dust.

The journey home would give me time to think. The heat of the
late afternoon sun did little to improve my mood. The lack of success
left me frustrated, but the expedition had not been completely
fruitless. It was an opportunity to train some of the younger recruits
and to build up their endurance. The veterans with us pointed out
places that were vulnerable to ambush and recounted past battles at
various sites along our route.

Mnasyllus regaled a young warrior named Taras with a tale of an
ambush from a few years past. The huge man's ridiculous
exaggeration lifted my mood. It had been a small raid, but in his
telling, twenty bandits swelled to over one hundred and we had been
outnumbered five to one. Each *peripoli* received his due moment of

3

heroism, and knowing smiles were exchanged. The wide-eyed Taras hung on every word, his jaw slack with wonder.

Mnasyllus nodded in my direction. "And the *lochagos* slew thirty men that day," he said. "His great Thracian sword went through them like a sickle through wheat!" He went on to spin a great duel between me and the bandit leader, who in his telling had been a giant whose head I cut off in a single stroke. I listened as attentively as the rest, for the story was as new to me as to the others.

Young Taras regarded me with awe. The tale done, he trotted over to my side and fell into pace with me. "Is it true, *lochagos*?" he asked. A *lochagos* is a captain. It is how my men address me. I desired no higher rank. Especially not that of commander, or *archos*.

"Mnasyllus is generous with his praise," I said vaguely, eliciting a round of laughter from the other *peripoli*. Mnasyllus gave me a surreptitious wink. Taras nodded in the way young people do when they are not sure what to believe. We trudged side by side in silence with just the crunch of the hot, rocky ground under our feet.

I liked the lad. He was twenty years old, strong and a good rider. The fourth son of a farmer, there was little prospect of his inheriting the family land, so he had shown up at the gates of the *peripoli* compound one day asking to join. Some men will never be warriors. Most can acquire a measure of skill with experience. And then there are those the gods imbue with inborn dexterity and strength. Taras was one of those rare youths with a gift for spear and sword. I could see him one day being my equal if not my better.

He was beautiful as well, smooth-cheeked and handsome like Apollo. Had he been from a wealthier class, his statuesque figure no doubt would have drawn the attention of the leering middle-aged aristocrats at the gymnasium as they ogled potential new conquests. But his skill and beauty, great as they were, were exceeded by his naive innocence. He had yet to be tested in true combat. Inwardly, I worried for young Taras. Battle was no place for kind men.

"What's that?" Taras asked, interrupting my thoughts. The pass was broad and flat for the most part, but a wide hill with gentle slopes rose before us. Taras was pointing at the long lines of crumbling stone walls at the top of the hill.

"Dekeleia," I said. "A Spartan fort."

4

Taras' eyes opened wide. "There are Spartans there?" The *peripoli* responded to the lad's question with a burst of laughter. "What did I say?" he asked, confused.

Sabas, the Cretan archer, joined in. "Use your eyes, boy!" he said. He held what looked like a staff in his hand but it was in fact his great Phrygian bow. He pointed the unstrung bow at the dilapidated walls. "That fort's a ruin. It's hardly even fit for goats anymore!"

"Then you should be happy there, Sabas!" someone else quipped, provoking another round of laughter. Taras flushed in embarrassment.

Even from a distance, it was clear that the fort was in poor condition. The Spartans had abandoned the stronghold at the end of the war. People from the nearby village and farms, not ones to waste resources, had stripped the empty fort of any valuable timber and cut stone, leaving only the reduced foundations of once imposing walls.

Staring at the abandoned fort, I felt my chest tighten. The Spartans' absence was an illusion, for their influence was ever-present. With a vanquished Athens at their mercy ten years earlier, the haughty Spartans saw a humbled Athens as more useful than an utterly destroyed one, especially as a counterweight against the growing power of an upstart Thebes. Athens' walls had to be razed and her few remaining ships confiscated, it was true, but in an act of practical magnanimity, Sparta had deigned to let defenceless Athens keep her democracy and maintain a degree of independence in her day-to-day affairs. But that was all. In reality, the heavy hand of Sparta still ruled Attica. When Sparta needed gold and silver to pay their soldiers, Athens would raid its own treasury to assist them. When Sparta requested soldiers for her distant war against the Persians, Athens could only bow meekly and accede to the Spartans' wishes. The truth of the relationship was clear: Sparta was the master, Athens the slave. I spat on the dusty ground towards the fort.

When I turned back, I found Taras waiting, his curiosity about the fort not yet sated. "Why did they build it here? Isn't it too far from Athens?" he asked.

"This is the main trade route," I explained. "They wanted to stop any food or goods coming in from the north."

Stachys increased his pace to join us. Coming from a wealthy aristocratic family, Stachys was an unlikely member among the *peripoli*, who mostly hailed from more humble origins. His clipped, educated voice stood out from the rougher speech of most of our number, but he was an adept fighter whose courage and loyalty were beyond doubt. I valued his friendship and counsel. Now that the talk had turned to strategy, his interest had been aroused.

"The Spartans didn't only use the fort to block trade," he told Taras. "They also wanted to entice slaves into fleeing from Athens."

"Did it work?" Taras asked.

"They slipped away by the thousands," Stachys said. Indeed it was true. So many slaves had run away to Dekeleia that by the end of the war there had hardly been any labour left in Attica.

"Not that it did them any good," Iollas growled. He mumbled a curse at the Spartans and spat on the dusty ground. Iollas had once been a helot, a slave of the Spartans. The tough, goat-like man's hatred for his former masters was unquenchable. Taras looked at me for explanation.

"The slaves thought they were escaping to freedom, but the Spartans just sold them on to others," I said.

"Who?" Taras asked.

I scratched at my stubbly beard. "The Thebans, mostly I suppose. It doesn't really matter if you're a slave." Taras gave another unconvincing nod. I sighed

We skirted the edge of the hill. The *peripoli* chatted and laughed, no doubt happy to be returning to the comforts of Piraeus, with its numerous taverns and brothels. Wine and women paid for with money I could ill-afford to part with. We crested a gentle rise.

And stopped. The friendly banter was extinguished like a lamp being blown out.

The gods hate me. But I amuse them, so they let me live. This is what I was thinking as I took in the sight on the road. For there, at the bottom of the slope, was a scene of violence and death.

The battle was already over. I estimated twenty attackers with horses. They had dismounted and had taken a large number of prisoners. About thirty shackled women and children of various ages stood in their ragged clothing, all joined together by a length of rope that looped around the waist of each of the miserable-looking captives.

"It looks like they've hit a slave caravan," Tibetos said in a low voice.

"I think you're right," I said.

At least the women and children were alive. The bloodied bodies of four men lay scattered on the road along with a few swords and spears. Near an over-turned cart, another victim was on his knees, his hands raised in supplication to the sword-wielding man looming over him.

I cursed my carelessness. Stealth and ambush were the *peripoli's* watchwords, but we had blundered onto the scene like blind men stepping over a cliff. But at the same time I was confused. We were well into Attica. Few bandits would be so bold as to carry out an attack in such an exposed location. And few bandits were wealthy enough to own well-kept horses of the type I saw now. It was a consideration for another time.

That the bandits had seen us was certain, for in the wide-open plain there was nowhere to hide. Our patrol only had twelve men. We were unprepared for a fight. A cautious man would have given the men a wide berth and avoided conflict. But we were the *peripoli*. It was our duty to protect the people of Athens. And I am not a cautious man.

"Mercenaries?" Stachys mused.

"On horses?" I said, keeping my eyes on the intruders. Horses were too expensive for common mercenaries. "Only one way to find out. Keep it easy," I instructed. My men were experienced and had already made their javelins inconspicuous within the folds of their cloaks. "Pick a man and be ready for my signal." I glanced at Taras. The lad was hiding his fear well. "Keep an eye on the boy," I instructed Stachys in a quiet voice. We continued walking towards the intruders at a normal pace. I raised a friendly hand. The horsemen made no move to stop us approaching. Why would they? They outnumbered us two to one and with our broad hats and thin summer cloaks we looked more like a group of harmless travellers than soldiers. If the men had been smart they would have gotten on their horses and slaughtered us. But their superior numbers made them stupid and they remained dismounted. We came to a halt a stone's throw away. "What has happened here?" I called.

The fork-bearded man by the kneeling prisoner shouted back. "It's none your affair! Be on your way!" I reckoned he was thirty years old. His well-maintained clothing and gear were not those of a common brigand. Beside him, the kneeling captive gave me an imploring look.

The bandit's unmistakable rolling accent betrayed his origins. "You are a long way from home, Theban!" I responded.

"We are reclaiming our property from this Athenian thief!" the fork-bearded man shouted back, pointing his sword at his captive.

I decided to play the role of bandit leader myself. I smiled broadly. "Then you are fortunate," I said. I swept an arm towards the terrified slaves. "It is a shame that you found them first. We have been searching for such a prize for many days!".

The Theban spat on the ground. "Then Zeus has pissed on you this day as well! These slaves belong to us!" His men laughed at our misfortune. "Now be off before…" He narrowed his eyes, inspecting me more closely, perhaps noticing for the first time the flaming red hair that poked out from beneath my broad-rimmed hat. His gaze flicked to the long hilt that peeked over my shoulder. The Theban's eyes widened as he realized who it was standing before him. I am the Demon of Athens and my reputation has spread far. And he knew that he had let me come too close.

"Loose!" I said in a low voice.

My men reacted well. In less than a heartbeat, javelins were lancing towards the raiders. Wounded Thebans were already crumpling onto the sun-baked ground when a second volley of javelins was leaving the hands of our men. To my left came the familiar whirring of a sling as my closest friend Tibetos wound up his preferred weapon. So fast did the lead bullet fly that it was shattering its victim's skull at the same time I heard the *snap* of the sling letting go its shot. On my right, Sabas had already strung his bow and was firing arrows with casual, deadly grace. Already ten men lay dead or wounded and they had not even drawn their weapons.

My men, their javelins spent, were hurrying to unsling their light, hide-covered shields from their backs and draw their swords. I had no shield, only my Thracian rhomphaia, its long, gently-curved blade flashing in the midday sun. "Kill them!" I shouted. "Kill them all!" I was already racing toward the stunned enemy, confident that Tibetos and the others would be behind me. My war-cry drowned out the screams of the terrified slaves.

The surviving Thebans lost their stomach for fighting. They ran for their horses and scrambled onto the beasts' backs. In a moment they were but clouds of dust receding to the north, the fork-bearded leader among them. The battle, if it could be called that, was over.

I surveyed the scene. Tibetos and a few others had managed to secure a few horses, but most of the animals had scattered in panic and now stood off in the distance keeping a wary eye on us. Rounding them up would be some trouble but worth the effort, for the animals would fetch enough money to pay off some of the *peripoli's* more pressing debts. And there was armour and gear to be stripped from the dead, the first plunder for my men in some time.

A few of the Thebans still squirmed and moaned on the ground, grasping uselessly at the javelins in their bodies and limbs. Some would die of their wounds quickly, but others might linger and expire in the hot sun first. I picked up a dropped spear and hurried the nearest of them on his journey to the Underworld.

A few paces away, a wounded Theban struggled to a sitting position, a javelin impaled deeply in his thigh. Taras pointed a sword at the man's chest. The Theban raised his arms in surrender, a sword still clutched in his right hand. As the man begged for mercy, Taras hesitated. His sword point dropped away from the Theban's chest. Suddenly the wounded man snarled and lashed out. Before the blow could land on the startled Taras, Stachys stepped forward and kicked the raider in the chest. As the man writhed on the ground, the aristocrat ended his life with a spear thrust through the throat.

I strode over to the stunned Taras in a fury. My heart was pounding. It was as much as I could do not to strike him. Instead I seized the frightened youth by the back of the neck bending him so that he was staring into the glazed eyes of the dead Boeotian. "Do you see that man?" I bellowed.

"Yes, *lochagos*," the young man stammered. The other *peripoli* paused in their looting the dead to observe the exchange.

"Does he have a sword in his hand?"

"Yes, *lochagos!*"

"Then why didn't you kill him?"

"I thought he was surrendering."

I yanked the boy up so that he was looking me in the eye. "If an enemy has a weapon, you kill him! Or next time that will be you!" I growled, pointing at the corpse. "Do you understand?"

The boy snapped to attention. "Yes, *lochagos!*" he said crisply.

I shoved him away and gestured at the corpses. "Go claim your share before it's gone!"

"Yes, *lochagos!*"

9

Stachys and I watched him hurry away. The lad was no doubt relieved to escape my wrath. Stachys sniffed. "You were tough on him."

"It's not him I'm angry with," I said through clenched teeth. I had done my best to train the boy, but despite his gifts I had nearly gotten him killed on his first patrol. My failure to prepare him infuriated me. His foolishness had also cost us the chance to interrogate the Theban. I closed my eyes, calming the storm of fear and anger inside me. I opened my eyes and put a hand on Stachys shoulder. "Thank you for saving him."

Stachys shrugged. "Don't mention it. But speaking of saving people," he said, redirecting my attention to the slaves at the centre of the conflict, "What are you going to do about them?"

The captive women and children cowered under my gaze. They could have come from anywhere. I held up both hands to show that I was no threat, but they only stared back in wide-eyed terror. Before I could reassure them that I meant no harm, a new voice made itself heard.

"You are the *peripoli*?" the voice said. I turned to see the source. It was the man who had been kneeling on the ground. His face was cut and bruised, and his tunic was spattered with blood. Yet his expression was one of joy. He strode towards me, his arms outstretched, and embraced me, blubbering words of gratitude. I pushed him away, but his happiness was undiminished. "By the gods!" he exclaimed, looking at the sky. "You are sent by the gods!"

"Who are you?" I asked, though I already had a good idea of his occupation.

"I was bringing these slaves to market in Athens when we were attacked," he said, confirming my suspicions. "My name is Metiochos."

A slave dealer, I thought with distaste. "And your own men?" I said, pointing at a nearby corpse.

Metiochos spat. "Worthless! They did nothing! Nothing!" That his men had died defending him meant little to the slaver. He put his arm around my shoulders. "Not like you and your men! You are *peripoli*, no? And you are Daimon of the *peripoli*, yes?"

I shrugged off his sweaty arm and pointed at the slaves. "And them?" The shackled women and children looked on helplessly while we discussed their fates. I felt too the eyes of Tibetos and the others upon me.

The slaver sniffed. "Barbarians. Poor quality merchandise. Destined for the mines, most of them. The pretty ones to the brothels. I'll be lucky to make a profit on this trip." He regarded the corpses of his mercenaries and his eyes narrowed shrewdly "Of course, I won't need to pay them anymore..." I liked the man less and less. "You will accompany me and my property back to Athens," the slaver declared. I stood as still as a statue, my eyes locked on him. "I will pay you for your protection, of course," he added hastily.

"We are not mercenaries," I said coldly.

Before the slaver could respond, one of the slave-women fell to her knees and raised her upturned hands to the sky. *"Kes Sabazitha! Akala no thrakolos mena!"* she cried. The words were twisted and warped, but I understood. She was speaking some form of Thracian.

Had I not understood her, I might have turned away. After all, the fate of these slaves was not my business. Hundreds of slaves arrived in Athens every day. But with her words, the threads that defined our destinies touched in a way that I could not ignore.

"Hisa thrakoli," I said to her. *I am Thracian.*

The desperation in her voice only grew. "You must help us! We are your people!" she begged me, hugging two children close to her.

I nearly laughed. There were hundreds of tribes in Thrace. They are often at war and kill and enslave each other as a matter of course. Though the slaver was Athenian, this woman and her children had likely been sold into bondage by other Thracians. I appraised the other slaves. "They do not look Thracian," I said.

The woman shook her head. "Skythians. Kolkhians. Others whose tongues I do not recognize." She pointed at Metiochos and the bodies of the fallen mercenaries. "They violate us, him and his men!" she hissed. "They even sate their lusts on the children!" I did not doubt her. I had seen what men did to captive women in war.

I cast a disdainful eye towards Metichios, who must have sensed the mood shifting. "What are you saying?" he asked. "I demand to know!"

"Shut your mouth," I told the slaver. Tibetos, a former slave himself, regarded me expectantly. I sighed. "Free them!" I said.

Tibetos flashed a smile. "I know you too well, Dammo!" He turned to the other *peripoli*. "You heard the *lochagos!*" Tibetos and the others began moving among the captured slaves, striking the pins from their manacles.

The Metiochos looked on aghast. "What are you doing? They are my property!"

"The Thebans stole them from you, and I took them from the Thebans, so they belong to me now."

Rage mottled the slaver's face. "You cannot do this!

My hand shot out and seized his throat. My grip tightened on his neck. His eyes bulged and a purple hue grew darker on his skin. "I don't like slavers," I finally growled before shoving him away. Metiochos fell hard on the sun-dried earth. He blinked at me in disbelief.

The Thracian woman picked up one of the dead men's spears. A few of the other women followed her lead and armed themselves. The band of haggard women and their weapons would have been comical except for the murderous desperation in their eyes. Metiochos scrambled to his feet and backed away until I was between him and the vengeful women. The cowering slave trader filled me with disgust.

"If they are your slaves, you are welcome to round them up. I will not stop you," I said.

Metiochos glowered petulantly at me. "It is true what they say of you."

"And what is that?"

"That you do not serve Athens. That you are a thief and a murderer."

I raised the tip of my rhomphaia to his throat. "If that is true, then what is to stop me from killing you now? There are no witnesses." The slaver's face paled as he realized the precariousness of his existence. I pointed the rhomphaia southward. "Athens is that way. You should leave now before I change my mind." The hot sun beat down on us.

"Can I not at least have a horse?" Metiochos begged.

"They are mine, too," I said. He opened his mouth as though to protest but seeing the small army of slaves and *peripoli* facing him thought better of it. "And Metiochos," I said. "Do you know the name Philaon of Steiria?" Metiochos' face blanched. Philaon was the slaver who had sold my sister to be worked to death at the silver mines of Laurion. His life had not ended well. "Good. I see you have. If I hear your name again, you will share his fate." I lunged at him and he leapt back with a squeak. He spun and began a shambling run south, not even daring to look back over his shoulder.

The slaver's inelegant figure grew smaller in the distance. Stachys scratched at his beard. "That was a nice bit of sophistry back there. Perhaps you have a future composing defence speeches for the courts," he said appreciatively.

"Was it a good idea to let him live?" Tibetos asked.

I let out a long breath. "Probably not." What could I have done? It was my duty to protect Athenian citizens and I had done so. But I had made another enemy. If enemies were silver, I would be the richest man in Athens. I issued commands to my men. "See the women and children are fed. Try to catch the remaining horses."

The armed women, denied their vengeance on Metiochos, hacked and stabbed at the bodies of his dead mercenaries, cursing them in their barbarian tongues. No one interfered.

While the slaves revenged themselves on the dead, I gazed west to where the Theban horsemen had fled. I wondered why Thebans were attacking Athenian slave traders on Athenian territory. Athens and Thebes were at peace, albeit reluctantly, united only by their mutual enmity towards Sparta. Otherwise, the two cities had been enemies for as long as I had been alive and long before that. I frowned. Perhaps the mauling we had just inflicted on the Theban trespassers would strain the fragile, unnatural peace beyond breaking point. If so, I would find out soon enough.

A female voice prevented me from thinking too deeply on the matter. The mutilation of the dead was completed, the Thracian woman approached me warily. "What will become of us?"

"You can come with us to Athens. You can stay with us until you have recovered."

"And if we do not wish to go to Athens?"

I swept my arm towards the horizon. "Then you are free to go."

She scanned the parched landscape around us. "We will go with you." It was a wise choice, for the unknown perils of a strange land were greater than the danger of trusting me

"What is your name?" I asked.

"Erta," she answered. My chest tightened. My reaction did not go unnoticed. "Does this name mean something to you?" she asked.

"It was my mother's name," I said.

The Thracian woman's eyes widened. "A sign from the gods! They brought you here!" I was not so sure. Erta was a common enough name among Thracian women. But the woman's conviction only grew. "*He* brought you here!" she said.

"Who?"

She reached awkwardly into the top of her tattered tunic, digging in a concealed pocket for something within. When she withdrew her hand, it was clutching something precious enough that she had kept it hidden when she had nothing else. She held it up for me to see.

It was a piece of ivory, crudely carved into the shape of a bull's horn with a hole at the talisman's base for a cord to pass through.

"Take it!" she said, pressing the charm into my palm. "You are favoured by Bassareus!"

Bassareus.

In Greece, he is known by other epithets. Bromios the Bull. Dimetor the Twice-Born. Bacchus, the god of madness and ecstasy. But most know him by his common name.

Dionysus.

The unease in my heart grew, for in uttering the deity's name, the woman had called the god's attention upon me. And it is never a good thing to fall under the scrutiny of the gods.

CHAPTER 2

Slaves are not human.

That is why we call them *andrapoda* — things with feet — for to speak otherwise would be to acknowledge they are something more than livestock. Yet even animals are worth more than slaves. A good horse costs seven hundred drachmae and an ox three or four hundred. A healthy male slave may set the buyer back a mere two hundred drachmae. Women and children can be had for even less. This is because animals are valuable and hard to replace. Slaves are not.

My Thracian mother had been a slave. She was more fortunate than most, for she had become a servant girl to an aristocratic woman, my father's first wife. The drudgery of washing, cooking, and weaving was never-ending, but in that her life was not much different from that of any other woman. When the great plague killed my father's first wife, he caused something of a scandal by taking my mother as a wife in deed if not in law. My father had been a *strategos*, — a general — but was never again elected to that post. He did not care, for he adored my mother, and she him.

My sister Melitta and I had inherited our mother's green eyes and copper hair, which are so common among the Thracians. This reminds other Athenians that we are not citizens, for only a person with both an Athenian mother and father can claim that right. So, though my ancestors fought at Marathon and Salamis, and though I have defended Athens all my life, my mother's origins give many Athenians an excuse to despise me, for Athenians are always eager to take down their betters. Stealing the haggard slaves from Metiochos would further erode my reputation, I knew. But it was done.

Back in Athens, I watched grimly as Erta and the other rescued slaves were led away to the women's quarters of the *peripoli* compound. The slave women and children – most of them, in any case, for some had fled on our journey home – still required food. And each bite of food the hungry slaves gobbled down would cost me drachmae I could ill-afford to part with. A low rumble of frustration built up in the back of my throat.

The problem, as always, was money.

The *peripoli* did not live in the crowded, haphazard streets of Athens but in the well-ordered port of Piraeus a few miles away. The *peripoli* compound was enormous. At one time, the complex must have consisted of separate warehouses and private homes that line the grid-like streets of Piraeus. Over time, successive commanders of the *peripoli* had acquired and joined the various parts together until they formed the great walled warren of buildings and workshops that the compound is today, almost a separate village of soldiers, women, and children. And I was responsible for all of them.

Maintaining soldiers is expensive. I needed to pay my warriors. Feeding the men, women, and children of the compound was a constant struggle. I was besieged by never-ending demands for other prosaic necessities such as wool for the looms, pots to cook our food in, and oil for the ever-thirsty lamps. Weapons needed to be repaired or replaced. The dozen or so horses stabled outside Piraeus were becoming an unaffordable luxury.

I am Daimon, son of Nikodromos. In the agora of Athens, I was feared. Women would make a sign to ward off the evil eye as I passed and their children would hide in the folds of their mothers' skirts. Crowds would part to let me pass and not a few men would turn their heads rather than meet my green-eyed stare. They were fools, but sometimes it is better to be feared.

The merchants and traders of Piraeus did not fear me, though. When they saw me approach, they smiled like wolves and their eyes sparkled with greed, for they scented the profit I brought with me. No enemy has fought me as viciously and tenaciously as a merchant trying to extract every last drachma from my purse. I had learned from bitter experience to play the merchants off one another, but the haggling exhausted me and despite my best efforts, the purchases ate through my funds faster than I could replenish them.

I had a few sources of money. Thrasybulus, the first man of Athens, wielded enough influence in the assembly to wring a few drachmae out of the treasury for us. The wealthy aristocrat also granted me the use of one of his many farmsteads. I, in turn, rented the land out for a small but steady source of income and a portion of the crop.

But our main source of income — plunder — had been depleted. During the great war between Athens and Sparta, the pickings had been rich as we feasted on the enemies encroaching on our lands. Even after the war, many mercenaries and other desperate men had turned to banditry, and we hunted them down and stripped their bodies of whatever they had, keeping what we needed and selling the rest. But we had been too successful. Peace was not good for business.

We had caught nine of the Thebans' horses, a good profit even if we kept a few horses for ourselves. But the *peripoli* were bleeding money, and the money from our raid would do little more than staunch the gushing wound for a short time. The rumble in my throat grew even louder.

Beside me, the raw recruit Taras cleared his throat. I turned my frustration on him. "Is there a problem, farmer's son?" I asked sharply. Exhaustion was creeping over me and I had little patience for his reticence. The young man flinched under my gaze. "Out with it, Boy."

Taras found his resolve. "Why did you take the slaves if not to sell them, *lochagos*?"

It was a good question. The slaves were worth the value of at least a few horses. "Who's to say I won't?" I asked. Beside me, Tibetos scoffed, for he knew my heart well.

Taras glanced at Tibetos and back to me. "You said they could stay if they wanted."

"And so they can," I said.

Taras frowned. "But they're *slaves*."

I nodded towards Tibetos, who was listening with a bemused expression. "He was a slave," I said. "And I am the son of a slave. In any case, the women are slaves no more."

"Can you do that?" Taras asked.

In truth, I wasn't sure. But I had claimed them as my property and I had freed them. Anyone who wanted to dispute that would find themselves at the wrong end of a spear. Tibetos interjected before I could answer. "I believe what the *lochagos* is trying to say is that he doesn't abandon women and children to Theban bandits or turd-sniffing slavers like our friend Metiochos."

Taras looked over at me. "I understand," he said, nodding slowly. He did not understand.

I sighed. "Go get something to eat, Boy," I said, dismissing him with a wave.

Taras snapped to attention. "Yes, *lochagos*!" He scurried off.

"He's a good lad. Maybe too good."

Tibetos knew me well. "That's why you like him, I reckon."

I became more serious. "What do think?" I asked, staring in the direction of the women's quarters. "Should I have handed the slaves back to the slave-dealer?"

"If I had said yes, would you have done it?"

"No."

"Then there you go."

"What *have* I done then?" I asked.

Tibetos gave a tired smile. "I think you've done what you always do: poke at a sleeping viper with a stick."

I shrugged. "Vipers are small."

"Maybe," Tibetos said. "But they can kill you all the same."

A FEW DAYS LATER, the vipers were still lurking under their rocks. But the world would not give me any peace.

Taras poked his head inside the office. He coughed to get my attention. Annoyed at the intrusion, I stayed hunched over the sheet of papyrus I had been scrawling on. "What is it?"

"There's someone here to see you, *lochagos*," Taras said hurriedly.

I stopped scratching and looked up. "Who?"

Before Taras could answer, a barrel-chested figure strode past him into the room. "Daimon!" boomed the great voice.

I narrowed my eyes at the visitor, who stood awaiting my response. "*Strategos*," I said at last with a cautious nod.

Thrasybulus.

He was at the height of his influence then. He was the first man of Athens, much as Perikles had been in my father's time. He had been elected as *strategos* every year since he led the revolt that restored democracy almost ten years earlier. Like any great man, he had his political enemies and did not always get his way, but the average Athenian loved him, which meant he usually had enough support to win a vote in the assembly.

He was an aristocrat, of course, and a wealthy one, with property all over Attica. He had even granted a parcel of land rent-free for use by the *peripoli*. The income from the farm was modest but essential. Part of me was resentful of his generosity, for it made me indebted to him. He knew this and he used it.

18

The burden of obligation was mutual. I had served him loyally for many years. I had saved his life on the battlefield many times. I had also saved his family on more than one occasion, which weighed heavily on his honour.

But whatever loyalty he felt towards me, it was exceeded by his desire to free Athens from Spartan hegemony and restore the city to her former glory. Thrasybulus could not oppose Sparta openly, for to do so would be to invite harsh repercussions. When he needed dangerous business done in secret, he would often seek me out. He had not made a trip to Piraeus out of friendly interest. I was wary, for I knew the general's pleasant demeanour hid a mind like a dagger.

"Bring the *strategos* some wine, Taras," I said. The young man hurried off to his task while I indicated that Thrasybulus should take a seat across the table from me. He almost hid his frown as he fetched a nearby stool and sat down opposite me.

"How is your son, Daimon?" he asked. The question caught me off-guard.

"He is well, *strategos*," I responded without elaboration. My son Nikodromos was almost ten years old. He lived with my old tutor Iasos in the city. I saw him perhaps once per month, but our meetings were awkward. The boy was excited by mathematics and music and the other odd Pythagorean ideas Iasos stuffed into his head. Niko showed little interest in the wooden training weapons I brought him. I could have brought the boy to Piraeus, but he preferred the company of Iasos and his models and scrolls. I did not blame him, for I was not a good father. "And your family, *strategos*?" I asked, changing the topic.

"They are well, though the children wonder why it has been so long since you last visited."

I waved at the ever-present clutter of administrative documents on my table, all of which concerned matters requiring my attention. "Tell them I am a prisoner in Tartarus being punished with never-ending torture."

Thrasybulus permitted himself the trace of a rare genuine smile just as Taras returned with a jug of wine. We regarded each other like two boxers before a bout while the young man poured us each a cup. Taras, whose social graces were even worse than mine, excused himself with a mumble and hastened to leave my visitor and me to our business.

Thrasybulus came out with another question I would have rather left alone. "Have you considered the matter we discussed the last time we met?"

I knew of what he spoke. Thrasybulus had been pushing for me to take up the mantle of commander of the *peripoli*, a notion that I had already rejected. "Stachys would make a better *archos*," I said evasively.

Thrasybulus brushed off my suggestion. "He is a fine man, but the *peripoli* already has a leader. It just needs to be made official."

I shook my head. "The assembly will never vote in favour of appointing a non-citizen as *archos*," I countered.

"The assembly will vote as I wish," he said with an impatient wave of his hand. The arrogant streak that underlay his confidence vanished as quickly as it had come, replaced by a look of exhaustion. "Not that you make it easy, Daimon." I knew the admonishing look he was giving me well enough. I crossed my arms and stared back at him. He sighed. "Have you had dealings with a man named Metiochos?" he asked.

The ungrateful slave-dealer had not heeded my advice to stay quiet. I shrugged, keeping my expression neutral. "I might have, but I don't remember the name. Should I know him?"

Thrasybulus ran his finger around the edge of the full cup of wine, but abstemious as always, he did not drink. "He says you and your men attacked him on the Dekeleia road and stole his shipment of slaves."

I barked a laugh. "If I had attacked him, he wouldn't be alive to spread his lies," I said.

Thrasybulus acknowledged the truth of this with a shrug. "Should I even ask about what happened to the slaves?"

"They fled. It is not my responsibility to round up escaped slaves," I lied. Most of them were a mere shout away in the women's section of the *peripoli* compound, costing me money with every bite of food they ate.

Thrasybulus raised a dubious eyebrow but did not challenge the claim. "Be that as it may, the slave-dealer has been accusing you of robbing him of his merchandise."

I scoffed. "I offered him the chance to take them back, but he refused."

Thrasybulus continued as though I had not spoken. "Now he is threatening to bring a lawsuit against you."

"He's a brave man if he does," I said, wondering if I should pay Metiochos a visit.

Thrasybulus knew me well enough to know what I was thinking. "Indeed," he said wryly. "Nevertheless, it might be better for you to leave the city for a time."

There it was. Thrasybulus did nothing without a purpose. The questions about my becoming *archos* of the *peripoli* and my dealings with Metiochos had only been devices to lead up to the true intentions of his visit. "What is it you want me to do, *strategos*?" I asked, failing to mask my irritation.

The corners of the general's mouth bent upwards in the barest of smiles. We understood each other. Then he reached into his robe and pulled out a leather cylinder. The message case was stamped with an intricate geometric pattern, not Greek work by the look of it. Thrasybulus placed the cylinder on a bare patch of wood on the table.

"Daimon, I have a mission for you."

CHAPTER 3

"Cavalry," I said.

Sabas shielded his eyes against the midday sun and peered towards the shimmering horizon. "It's just the heat," he said dismissively.

"Look again."

Sabas squinted. "Damn the Fates!" he exclaimed.

"The riders worry you, old friend?" I asked, raising an eyebrow in surprise.

"No," Sabas said with a resigned breath. "It's just that I bet Tibo that I would be the first to spot the enemy!" The Cretan dug a silver drachma out of a pouch at his side and flipped it to Tibetos.

Tibetos deftly swept the coin out of the air. He winked at Sabas. "You shouldn't bet against a sure thing!"

"I was distracted!" Sabas protested in defense of his honour.

"Maybe it's just age," I suggested.

"You're one to talk!" Sabas sniffed. As if to prove his point, I shifted on my horse's back to ease a persistent cramp in my back.

In the meantime, the cloud of dust had grown larger. "Are they Spartan, do you think?" Tibetos asked, trusting my sharp eyesight.

I considered the approaching riders. Dark shapes danced in the centre of the dust-cloud. A flash of metal glinted in the sun. Was there a glimpse of Spartan red cloaks? "If it is, then we're dead," I said.

This had been the fate of our predecessors, according to Thrasybulus. The Spartans had caught the two ambassadors and promptly executed them as spies. Athens denied any knowledge of the men's mission, claiming they had travelled to Asia on their own initiative.

That is why Thrasybulus had asked me to cross the sea to Ionia. I had brought Tibetos and Sabas as my only companions. As *peripoli*, we were adept at evading Spartan patrols, something we had been doing for two days. The second reason, although Thrasybulus had been tactful enough not to mention it, was that we were expendable because none of us were Athenian citizens. Some Athenians might even welcome our deaths.

I suddenly wished I had brought more men. The three of us, alone on the plain with our guide, would be no match for the approaching cavalry, whoever they might be. The presence of the hulking Mnasyllus and a dozen more *peripoli* with their javelins would have been reassuring. I let out a long breath, knowing that success was more likely with smaller numbers, despite the protests of my churning guts.

Our guide, Babak, felt otherwise. He turned towards me, his eyes wide with fear. "We must flee!" the Phrygian urged in his lightly accented Greek.

"We wait," I said flatly.

"They will kill us!" Babak protested.

"If you try to run, Sabas will shoot you down first," I said, lifting my chin towards my long-time comrade. The Cretan archer bared his teeth in a hungry grin. Babak swallowed hard but made no move to escape. Not that I disagreed with the Phrygian, for there was a chance the riders would cut us down anyway. Sometimes it takes more courage to keep one's weapon sheathed.

As the riders drew nearer, my initial fears ebbed, if only by a hair. There was red, but the profusion of other colours revealed the horsemen's true origins. "They're Persians," I reported.

I had only ever seen Persian cavalry but once in my youth, and that was at a distance. Our army had watched helplessly as the brilliantly-coloured horsemen streamed out of the city of Ephesus, their banners flapping. The Persian riders had disappeared over a distant rise before going on to slaughter scores of our soldiers. The men bearing down on us now reinforced the memory of those beautiful, deadly horsemen.

"They will kill us!" Babak moaned again, his voice quavering. The Phrygian shrank under my baleful stare and had the good sense to cease his whining. Inwardly, however, I shared his fears. As Greeks in Persian lands, a hostile reception was likely. I felt the hands of Lachesis pause over the thread of my life as the immortal weaver of Fate considered the best way to compose the pattern of my destiny. Her sister Atropos' merciless shears hung close, ever ready to sever the filaments of life. Outnumbered as we were, our fate would be decided in the next few moments.

Then, the Persians were there. With admirable precision, the dozen or so horsemen formed a perfect half-moon around our small party, the arc of polished spear-tips pointing inward like a lion's teeth. We countered the hostile stares of the newcomers with flat-eyed curiosity.

The most colorfully-dressed Athenian could not compete with even the lowliest among the Persian cavalrymen in resplendence. Corselets of burnished bronze scales overlaid tunics of deep green, shining yellow, and magnificent purple. Like the horse-riding Thracians and Skythians, the Persians wore breeches, but in bright hues never seen in those harsh lands. Even the Persians' leather boots, with their oddly upturned toes, bore swirling patterns on their sides. Their caparisoned horses, too, put our rustic mounts to shame, for their beasts' decorated halters glinted with accents of silver and bronze. But the Persians were hard-looking men, despite their finery.

The leader, his garb grander than the others', spurred his horse forward with a jerk of his heels. A high, red crest crowned the open-faced helmet. Thin silver cheek plates framed a veteran's face, with a nose flattened by countless battles and a pale scar across the darker, leathery skin under one eye. His brilliant scaled corselet was overlaid by a green tunic with billowing sleeves. A light, half-moon shield protected his left side, while his right hand sat lightly on the golden pommel of his sword. His black eyes took in each of our party before finally coming to a rest on me. He scowled at me. I stared back.

The silence stretched out. The Persian captain's pointed beard twitched. At last he could bear the stand-off no longer and assaulted me with a string of Persian invective.

"*Darust dar wey*," I responded with a memorized Persian greeting. I hoped that I had wished him good health and not mistakenly called his mother a whore. The captain sneered and spat on the dusty ground. I glanced at our trembling Phrygian guide. "Babak," I said, giving the man his cue to earn the silver we were paying him.

The Phrygian swallowed deeply before dipping his head low towards the Persian captain. The words tumbled from his lips like a gurgling spring as he hurried to explain our trespass in the Persian satrapy of Phrygia. The unfamiliar babble could have been Aegyptian or Phoenician for all I knew. Babak finished his prepared speech, and his head dropped even lower. The cavalry captain barked another unintelligible stream of Persian at Babak, who cowered under the verbal onslaught. The Phrygian guide, his fragile nerve strained to the breaking point, sputtered a response in fits and starts. His trembling hand rose and pointed at me. The Persian glared at me.

With deliberate slowness, I pulled a long object from the satchel at my hip and held it aloft. It was not a weapon but the embossed leather cylinder that Thrasybulus had shown me in Piraeus. The cavalry captain's eyes flicked to the case and back to me. A corner of his thick moustache rose as his lip curled in contempt.

"*Hasak!*" he snapped, and in an instant an arrow appeared on the bow of the rider next to him. In one fluid motion, the horse-archer drew and released, and the leather case was torn from my grasp.

The captain shouted another command to his men. I did not need our Phrygian guide to translate. As one, the Persian soldiers cocked their weapons and a dozen arrowheads and spear-tips were ready to pierce our chests.

We had only set foot in Asia two days earlier.

Already we had failed.

CHAPTER 4

The Persians are barbarians.

That does not make them special. We Greeks call all foreigners barbarians, for their odd exotic speech all sounds like *barbarbarbar* to Greek ears. It is the nature of men to thus lump all outsiders together with a single convenient term of disdain. I am descended from Athenians from the time of Theseus, but many Athenians call me a barbarian, for I am Thracian in appearance. The Thracians, for their part, call anyone from beyond their borders *alakaban*, and I have been called that as well, for the Thracians see me as Greek. Barbarian, *alakaban* — I am sure there are as many such words as there are races of men. And so, we Greeks call the Persians barbarians, for it makes us feel superior to them.

Sometimes we also call the Persians Medes. The histories tell us that the Persians and the Medes are two separate peoples and the former conquered the latter, but we Greeks cannot be bothered to learn the difference, so we use whichever word suits our mood. Even so, when Greek cities submit to the Great King of Persia by offering earth and water, we call them "Mede-izers."

The Great King himself lives in a city so far to the east that it would take months to travel there from the coast of Ionia. From that capital, the Great King's vast empire stretches a thousand miles in every direction and encompasses a hundred different nations. That one man could rule such an empire seems impossible, and so it is. Instead, each region is administered by a satrap, one of the Great King's brothers or cousins or some other powerful nobleman. The Great King is content to let these satraps rule their regions almost as kings themselves, as long as they provide the Great King with money, goods, and soldiers.

So, that is to say, whether the horsemen surrounding us were Persians or Medes or some other people, I do not know, but I will call them Persians, for they served the Great King of the Persians. More precisely, they served Pharnabazus, the man who had sent a secret summons to Thrasybulus in Athens. I knew little of Pharnabazus, save what Thrasybulus had told me. Pharnabazus, Thrasybulus had advised me, had been satrap of Phrygia for more than twenty years, an astounding accomplishment given that most satraps found themselves assassinated by ambitious relatives or recalled by the Great King when they fell out of favour, which was often. A man who had survived the vicissitudes of Persian politics for so long was not someone to be underestimated.

The satrap's soldiers took our weapons but not our lives. The captain, it seemed, thought it better to confirm our story rather than slaughter us outright. Surrounded on all sides by our escort, we proceeded eastward across the plain, a monotonous landscape marked only by the appearance of small villages or symmetrical, flat-topped mounds that marked the tombs of long-forgotten heroes. A hard ride took us to a walled city by the edge of a vast lake. The main gates opened at the Persian captain's command and we entered the barbarian city.

Barbarians the Persians might have been, but I swear to you, Athenian, that you would hesitate to call them that were you to see their cities. As the Persians led us through the streets, I was struck by what I saw. The city was smaller than Athens but gave the impression of being richer. We passed brightly-painted houses decorated with flowers. There were well-maintained workshops of every kind, with their wares of pottery and textiles neatly displayed. I noticed something else. Every district seemed to have a small, open temple in which burned a well-tended fire. I asked Babak about them.

"They are *atashgah*," the Phrygian guide whispered. "Temples to Ahura Mazda and his..." he fumbled for the right word, eventually settling on *angelloi*. "His messengers." I had heard that the Persians call Zeus *Ahura Mazda*, but I did not know the names of their other gods, his *angelloi* as Babak had called them. The Persian captain shot us a baleful look and Babak retreated into silence.

Evening was falling fast and there were few people in the streets, but those we saw appeared healthy in body and mind. Nowhere to be seen were the beggars or madmen who were such a common sight in Athens. There was no sound of drunken revelry or heated debate. Nor did prostitutes solicit customers from their doorways, though I do not doubt such places existed. Sabas had his own opinion. "What a lifeless place," the Cretan archer muttered. But the grand sight awaiting us as we emerged from a bend in the road made even Sabas let out a low whistle of admiration. "Not bad for foreigners," he said.

It was an understatement. Though a high wall concealed much of the palace complex, what was visible radiated wealth and refinement.

The central building atop the low hill blazed in the evening sun. The roofs of numerous other structures peeked over the top of the wall, as did the crowns of a small forest of trees, promising the respite of cool shadows.

The buildings disappeared from view as the Persians led us to the palace gates. Six guards with spears and shields blocked the way forward. The Persian captain exchanged words with the leader of the guards, a broad-torsoed bull of a man who eyed us suspiciously. The captain handed my leather scroll case to the frowning guard. He barked a command and one of his charges stepped forward to take the message before scurrying into the complex.

While we waited for the messenger's return, the palace guards stared at us with a mixture of curiosity and disdain. We bore their scrutiny patiently, for there was little else we could do. The bull-like leader approached me. He peered at my corselet. My armour was made of overlapping black scales made from the hooves of horses. The makers of the corselet, barbarians from the far north, had subjected the scales to some secret treatment that turned them as dark as night and as strong as iron. The armour was light and flexible, allowing me to move fast, but it could turn away a sword edge or arrow's tip. The Persian reached out and tapped one of the black plates. He shook his head and said something over his shoulder and the assembled guards laughed.

The guard leader moved on to examine my two companions. Next to the brawny Persian, the wiry Sabas looked like a reed next to a tree-trunk. I knew this to be misleading, for the Cretan was as tough as any man and fast with a sword or spear. Not that he often used those weapons, however, for his bow would drop most opponents before they ever got near him. He was also gloriously mad, a trait which now manifested itself in a wide grin. The Persian muttered something into his beard and continued his inspection, stopping in front of Tibetos.

The man squinted at Tibetos. *"Persela ekba? Medona?"* he said. Tibetos turned to Babak for help.

Our Phrygian guide, having done his best to remain inconspicuous, flinched as all attention focused on him. He cleared his throat. "He wants to know if you are Persian or a Mede," he translated. With his wide, dark eyes and olive skin, Tibetos could have put on the cavalry captain's uniform and passed as a Persian with ease. But Tibetos had grown up with me in Athens and knew not a word of Persian.

Tibetos looked the guard in the eye. "I'm Athenian," he said with deliberate slowness. The guard snorted and said something to his Persian audience, eliciting a round of cold laughter. Tibetos looked at Babak. "What did he say?"

"You don't want to know," the Phrygian said, flushing.

Tibetos curled his lip at the guard. "Perhaps I do," he said. The stout guard understood the challenge well enough and grunted like a boar preparing to charge.

The arrival of some newcomers from within the complex snuffed the flame of conflict before it erupted into a violent conflagration. The guard gave Tibetos a final glare before stepping aside for the delegation. Four soldiers in immaculate kit accompanied a man in simple but elegant Persian robes. He took us in with his cunning, slightly protuberant eyes.

"I am Tolmides," the man said with a dip of his head.

Despite the man's Persian dress, his name and perfect Greek betrayed his origin. "You are Greek?" I asked.

"I am from Melos," he confirmed.

I could not hide my surprise. "Melos?" Melos had been destroyed by Athens nearly twenty years earlier, its men executed and its women and children sold into slavery. The man opposite me was my age, more or less. He would have been around ten years old when Athenians razed his city.

For an instant, the Greek's eyes took on a cold hardness, but he blinked and the anger was gone. He smiled. "I serve my lord Pharnabazus, who rules here in the name of the Great King."

"This city is Daskyleion?" I asked. Daskyleion was the main Persian city in Phrygia.

The man Tolmides nodded. "In Greek, yes. In Persian it is *Dashmedar*."

"And the satrap, Pharnabazus. He is here in the city?"

"My lord Pharnabazus is here," he confirmed.

Weary relief surged through me. For once, my mission would be simple. I was already calculating how long it would take before I was back in Athens. "I have come here from Athens at the request of Pharnabazus. I am the ambassador for Thrasybulus, son of Lykos," I said. Ambassador. It was strange to hear the word falling from my lips, for I had been a warrior, a spy, a smith, but never anything as august as an ambassador.

Tolmides accepted my claim without comment. "My lord Pharnabazus knows of the deeds of Thrasybulus. He brings honour to Athens. My master has always been a friend of your city."

I raised a doubtful eyebrow. Persia had ever been the enemy of Athens. In the great war against Sparta, it had been Persian gold and silver that had paid for the Spartan ships and the men to oar them. Without Persian support, many believed, Athens would have emerged the victor, not Sparta. But I ignored the interpreter's blatant falsehood, as a good ambassador should.

"Let me take you and your men to your quarters," Tolmides said, extending an arm towards the interior of the compound.

"We are staying inside the walls?" I asked, surprised.

Tolmides gave an apologetic smile. "It would be difficult to guarantee your safety otherwise. There are many people who see all Greeks as enemies. They are raised that way, and not a few families have lost sons and fathers to Greek spears."

"But you are Greek," I said.

"And I am careful to stay inside the walls," he responded. "Now come with me."

We left the cavalry captain and the surly guards at the gate. Inside the walls of the palace compound, a wondrous scene revealed itself to us. The tantalizing hints we had glimpsed before lived up to their promise. Trees lined pathways paved with perfect squares of limestone. White swans glided idly across the surface of a walled pool, while unseen songbirds bade farewell to the setting sun. Above it all towered the main palace, like Zeus's hall looking down on his creation. Broad steps led up to a portico with rows of blazing red columns that stood like ranks of soldiers guarding the entrance. It was meant to impress, and it succeeded in this goal. I had often seen young farmers come to Athens for the first time. The residents of the city would poke fun at the rustic bumpkins as they gawped at the temples on Acropolis and the public buildings around the agora. I was a child of the city and had done the same in my time, but now it was we who were playing the role of an unrefined yeoman.

There was little time to marvel at the grandeur of the palace, for Tolmides led us to a smaller building in one corner of the compound. "This is one of the residences for visiting ambassadors and other delegations," Tolmides said as two of the soldiers opened a pair of ornately-carved wooden doors that were half as tall again as a man.

"*One* of the residences?" Tibetos asked.

Tolmides gave me a diplomatic smile. "My lord Pharnabazus is an important man. Many ambassadors come to seek his blessing for various enterprises." He stepped aside to let us enter. "The accommodations are simple, but I trust you and your men will be comfortable enough."

Simple! The residence was more opulent than that of the home of the wealthiest aristocrat in Athens. The main hall was replete with reclining couches covered with colorful cushions. Trays of fruit and other food beckoned temptingly from the tables. More discreet were the slaves who stood in the shadows.

I turned to Tolmides. "Please express our gratitude to your master Pharnabazus," I said. "We do not need the slaves."

Tolmides gave me a patient smile. "Do not mind them. They are here to serve you." And to spy on us, no doubt, I thought. "My lord Pharnabazus would be upset to know that his guests were not being looked after," he said. His tone made it clear this point was not negotiable. But I did not let the matter drop completely, for I was still curious as to the interpreter's origins. And his condescending manner irked me.

"And you, Tolmides? Are you a slave?" I asked bluntly.

Once again, the Greek's veil slipped and hidden fire flared in his eye before his sense of diplomacy won out and his neutral expression reasserted itself. "My lord Pharnabazus is generous and rewards me for my service." He held out his arms, displaying his fine Persian robes. "I am a wealthy man. I owe my position to my master and the Great King."

"I understand," I said, noting that he had not answered my question. Another matter concerned me much more than the status of Tolmides. "When can I meet with your master Pharnabazus?" I asked. I did not want to idle days away in a luxurious prison.

"My lord Pharnabazus is a busy man. You are not the only petitioner to deal with. You will wait until you are summoned."

"And when might that be?" I asked.

"When you are summoned," the Greek repeated.

"Then we will wait," I said, swallowing my impatience.

"You must be tired from your journey," Tolmides continued. "And dirty," he added with a sniff. Beside Tolmides and the immaculately outfitted guards, we were conspicuous in our rough tunics and armour with their stink of sweat, dust, and horse. "You will find that the Persians attach great importance to cleanliness. Your attendants," he said, with a nod to the slaves, "will help you wash and dress. I will return when my master has sent for you." He gave a curt bow and left us, followed by the two guards. The double doors closed with a thud.

Our quarters were luxurious by any standard, but one thing was clear.

We were prisoners.

CHAPTER 5

Two youthful servants trailed us at a discreet distance as we explored the premises. Exquisite furniture and ornate items adorned every room. Our guide Babak seemed almost fearful of the ostentation surrounding him.

Sabas lay down on one of the plush beds and sighed. "By the gods, this is like the caress of Aphrodite! I am suddenly realizing that our accommodations in Piraeus leave something to be desired.".

"This kind of living will make you soft," I warned.

"That is a risk I am willing to take," Sabas replied.

The residence even had its own bathing chamber. In the centre of the room was a bronze tub large enough for a man to sit in. Smaller basins sat on marble pedestals in the corners. Sluices in the stone floor led to holes in the wall where the dirty water could drain. It was similar to some of the public baths in Athens, though more luxurious by far.

One of the house slaves cleared his throat, and we turned to look at him. In a soft voice, the young man said something in Persian. Seeing my incomprehension, the slave gestured at his tunic. I looked at Babak for help.

"He wishes you to strip down so that they can bathe you," the Phrygian translated.

I scoffed. "I can wash myself. Tell them to go away."

Babak told the slave what I had said. The slave glanced at me with concern in his eyes and said something in a hurried whisper. Babak turned to me. "He said that if they do not carry out their duties, they will be beaten."

"Then tell them to lie," I said. "I won't give them away."

Babak winced. "For that, O Athenian, they would be worse than beaten."

The slaves stood ready, unable to hide their fear. I sighed. "Tell them to get on with it, then," I said, untying my corselet. "Sabas!" I shouted. "Wake up! Time for one more service you won't find at home!"

With obvious relief, the slaves set about their unenviable task of removing the layer of grime that we had accumulated on our journey. Our armour and clothes were whisked away, much to my consternation. "Make sure they bring those back!" I told Babak.

The Phrygian, obviously uncomfortable with his public nakedness, gathered what dignity he could and relayed my concerns. "He assures me it will be cleaned and returned to you," Babak said. "He asks that you remove your necklace as well," the Phrygian added, pointing to the thin gold chain around my throat. Tibetos and Sabas could barely suppress their smiles.

The necklace in question was a recent purchase from a Thracian goldsmith in Piraeus. It was not vanity that had led to my buying it but rather the freed slave Erta. The Thracian woman had insisted that I wear the horn-shaped amulet she had given me lest I offend the god. The leather cord I had been wearing soon became frayed and rough and after a few days I took it off, much to the irritation of Erta who had loudly berated me in the *peripoli* courtyard like a disobedient child. My public chastisement was a great source of hilarity for my comrades, though they knew better than to mention it in my presence. The fine chain satisfied the Thracian woman as suitable respect for the god, though I still found it irritating. I fixed the slave who had asked me to remove it with a hard stare. "It stays on." No translation was needed. Tibetos and Sabas exchanged a knowing look.

With resignation I submitted myself to the slaves' ministrations. Scented oil soon covered my body. It did not remain there long, for the slaves scraped off the oily film with practiced strokes of their strigils, each gentle motion of the curved blades leaving a clean streak in their wakes. Tibetos bore his treatment with amused patience. Sabas, sitting on his own stone stool, was more receptive.

"This is something else we need at home," the Cretan said, his face a picture of blissful peace.

"I think you are in danger of Mede-izing," I said as a slave flicked grimy oil from his strigil.

The archer cracked open one eye. "I'm considering it," he said. I laughed and felt some of my tension ease. Perhaps he was right. Sometimes it was easier to accept one's fate than to fight it.

The strigils having done their work, a succession of slaves bearing enormous jugs filed into the room. Standing behind us, the slaves raised the jugs above our heads, and streams of heated water hit our scalps and cascaded over our bodies. Sabas let out a sigh of pleasure. Even the tense Babak, water streaming off the ends of his thick moustache, seemed to have accepted his comfortable fate.

The slaves patted us down with soft cloths and I rose to my feet, but the slaves gestured that I should remain seated. Their attentions had not yet ended, it seemed. I bore the unpleasantness as a slave combed out the knots and tangles of my long copper hair. The slave's labor evoked the memory of my mother doing the same for my sister Meli. I smiled to myself, for I knew my sister's unruly hair surely would have defeated the slave's efforts. The slave, satisfied with his work, combed in a few drops of fragrant oil and tied my hair back. Four more slaves appeared, each bearing a stack of neatly folded clothes. Our own clothing gone, we had little choice but to don the Persian garments offered to us.

We assessed each other's Persian outfits with amusement. We Greeks do not wear breeches, sneering at them as an affectation of less civilized peoples, especially the Persians. I have noticed that breeches are the clothing of choice among horse-riding peoples, for they protect a rider's legs from being rubbed raw by his horse's rough hide. I was comfortable enough in breeches, having worn them often when I was living among the Thracians. In his pants and belted robe, Tibetos could have passed for a Persian. "I think we're all in danger of Mede-izing," Sabas observed, and we laughed. Out confinement would be comfortable at least.

That we were prisoners rather than guests, I had little doubt. Every morning the immaculately uniformed cavalry captain who had brought us to the city arrived at our residence to take us out for our daily exercise wandering among the ornate gardens and discreetly positioned guards. The captain's constant scowl on his face made it clear that he felt the task demeaning and beneath his rank. We barely had a chance to loosen up before he barked at us to return to our quarters. There we would idle the day away in our luxurious prison. Ever-present slaves made sure our cups and bellies were full and took away our chamber pots. After a night's sleep on beds that were too soft, our daily routine repeated itself.

This life of Persian idyll ruled our days. The boredom of it grated on my nerves. Pacing about in my Persian clothes, I felt a keen sympathy for the colourful caged birds that one could buy in the agora. Even Sabas grew restless, his appetite for luxury sated after a few days.

On the fifth day when the doors swung open, the Persian captain was not alone. The Greek Tolmides had returned.

"My lord Pharnabazus wishes you to dine with him this evening," he stated.

So the satrap had deigned to receive us. "All of us?" I asked, indicating my companions.

"Only you," the Greek responded curtly. Sabas shrugged. Tibetos looked relieved, as did Babak.

I nodded at Babak. "And my interpreter?" The Phrygian froze.

"He may accompany you," Tolmides confirmed. Babak's shoulders fell. "I will fetch you later when it is time," the Greek said. He turned and began to stride towards the open doors, followed by the Persian captain.

"When?" I asked towards the functionary's back. Tolmides ignored me and kept walking until the twin doors swung shut behind him.

"Looks like you'll have to wait," Tibetos said.

"Something I've grown used to," I growled.

We whiled away the day. I tried to rest, but sleep would not come to me. My thoughts were unsettled by the looming meeting with the Persian satrap. I was ill-suited for diplomacy. The prospect of a prolonged feast with much talking and drink was more daunting to me than battling an army of Spartans. More frustrating was that my purpose was still a mystery to me, for the satrap's message was little more than a summons. Perhaps I was a mere messenger. The more I considered the matter, the more I resented Thrasybulus for sending me on this fool's errand in the first place. Perhaps, I thought, lying on the soft bed, I was just angry at myself for being foolish enough to have accepted it.

A small cough interrupted my reflections in self-pity. Another nameless slave stood at the door of the room, a stack of folded, brilliant robes lay on his outstretched arms. "Time for supper, is it?" I asked. The slave smiled mutely and extended the clothing towards me. I sighed and rose to my feet. "Let's get dressed then."

The clothes were extravagant. In addition to vibrant ochre-coloured breeches, the first layer included a shirt, whose sleeves also would have offended any tunic-wearing Athenian as much as the barbarian pants. A rich green robe with billowing sleeves and flower-patterned hems formed the outer layer of the outfit. The robe was held closed by a row of horn-shaped buttons, and a patterned leather belt with a silver buckle cinched the outer garment at the waist. The costume was completed by a pair of handsome sandals. I attempted to salvage some dignity by waving away the insistent slaves and tying them myself. I stood up. The clothes felt light and cool, despite the layers, They were also, as far as I could tell, new, and the entire ensemble fit so well that I suspected they had been made just for the occasion.

My comrades met my Persian transformation first with wide-eyed disbelief and then howls of laughter. Even the fearful Babak, who was dressed in simpler garb, cracked a grin. I felt my face reddening.

"What have you done to my friend, Evil Spirit?" Tibetos said with an actor's dramatic flair. "I demand you return him at once!"

I held out my arms, showing off the voluminous sleeves. "Not very good for fighting," I said.

Tibetos came close and wrinkled his nostrils. "You smell like a *hetaira* courtesan at a symposium," he said.

Sabas stepped forward and took a sniff. "Or an aristocrat's favourite bum-boy," he suggested.

Before I could respond, another voice saved me from my comrades' teasing. "I see you are dressed, Athenian." It was Tolmides, escorted by his two Persian soldiers. "My master Pharnabazus awaits." The interpreter stepped aside and extended an arm towards the door.

I turned to bid farewell to my friends. "I leave for battle," I said in a weak jest.

"You are well armoured!" Tibetos said, pinching the fine robes. He leaned in close, his eyes more serious than his tone. "Be careful, Dammo."

"What trouble could I get into?" I asked. My friend responded with a look that suggested it was the maddest thing I had ever uttered.

Tolmides led us through the compound, the two soldiers a few paces behind us. We ascended the wide steps of the palace and passed through a colonnaded portico. The sentries at the gilded entrance moved aside to let us pass.

The hall before me made our residence look like a fisherman's hut. Light from a hundred torches reflected off the gleaming marble floor. Pillars of red and gold lined both sides of the vast chamber. In front of each pillar stood a soldier in the same kind of scaled bronze armour that the Persian cavalry captain had worn. A painted wall relief of figures in profile wrapped around the entire perimeter of the huge room. The figures marched one after another towards a larger figure on a throne at the centre of the back wall of the chamber, the Great King himself. And below the image of the King of Kings was my host.

Pharnabazus sat at the end of a long table bedecked with platters and cups of silver and gold. Seeing us approach, the satrap rose and began to walk towards us, his arms spread wide as if one of the carved figures had come to life and stepped down from the wall. His black hair and beard were tight, coiled cylinders aligned as regularly as soldiers in a phalanx. How long it had taken a slave with a hot iron to achieve such a look I could only guess. A profusion of gold necklaces, bracelets, and rings complemented elegant purple robes that could not completely hide the figure of a once-powerful body going to fat, his belly bulging slightly over his wide jewelled belt. His broad smile was welcoming but I had known too many politicians in Athens to be fooled, and his eyes radiated a powerful, calculating intelligence.

The satrap addressed me in a voice both strong and deep. When his speech was done, he nodded to Tolmides.

"My lord Pharnabazus bids you welcome to Daskyleion," Tolmides began to translate. "He begs forgiveness for the simplicity of the accommodation he has provided for you. He invites you to enjoy the hospitality of his table this evening." I stumbled through a prepared greeting, wishing the satrap good health from Thrasybulus and the people of Athens. I hoped that Babak conveyed the message with more eloquence than I had delivered it.

Tolmides gave a brief bow to his master before turning towards me. "Please excuse me while I attend to another matter. I'm certain your Phrygian will prove an adequate translator until I return," he said, casting a doubtful look at the terrified Babak.

Pharnabazus smiled as the Greek hurried off to his mysterious duties. Not knowing what to say, I commented on the impressive nature of the colorful reliefs that adorned the walls. With a grin, Pharnabazus warmed to his task as host and took me by the arm. His lecture came out in a constant stream, but Babak, staying by my side, translated a beat behind the satrap's own words. We paused before the various figures as the Persian explained how each represented an ambassador from assorted tribes bringing tribute to the Great King. Most of the gift-bearing subject hailed from lands unfamiliar to me. Pharnabazus paused at one whose origin I did recognize.

"Greeks, too, pay homage to the Great King," Babak translated. Pharnabazus pursed his lips slightly as he awaited my response to the provocative statement.

"Not all Greeks," I said. Babak flinched slightly. Pharnabazus looked at the Phrygian, who offered a belated translation.

Pharnabazus laughed and clapped me on the shoulder. "*Tar'ov!*"

"Not yet!" Babak said.

There was an awkward pause. Pharnabazus regarded me expectantly. I glanced at the enormous table and its many chairs. "Are you expecting more guests, O Pharnabazus?" I asked, seeking to fill the silence.

As if he understood my question, Pharnabazus smiled his politician's smile. He looked past my shoulder to the entrance of the great hall just as the echo of many footsteps reached my ears. I turned to look at the new arrivals. Tolmides had returned. The Greek led half a dozen armoured men and the same number again of servants bearing small wooden chests.

The six men were not Persian. Their burnished armour glinted in the torchlight, but their crimson cloaks appeared darker, like blood that has begun to dry. I could have recognized the men just as easily by the casual arrogance in their walk or by the long oiled braids that their warriors wore as a badge of honour. I cursed under my breath. The Spartans had arrived.

One of the Spartans had eschewed the long braids of his countrymen for shorter hair. Fine dark curls framed a face that was more severe than handsome. The Spartan's sword-sharp eyes flashed in angry recognition.

"It is my master's understanding that you two are already acquainted," Tolmides said by way of introduction.

Instinctively I reached for the sword that normally hung at my hip, but I found only my ornamented Persian belt. Had the Persians not taken our weapons, I would not have hesitated to murder the Spartan then and there. As it was, all I could do was utter the bastard's name.

"Lysander!"

CHAPTER 6

Lysander and I glared at each other.

The Spartan general's bodyguards advanced on me, reaching for their swords, but of course they found none, for like me, they had surrendered their weapons to their Persian hosts. The Persian satrap's personal guard, however, were still armed and their swords grated menacingly as the soldiers drew them halfway from their scabbards.

The voice of Pharnabazus cut through our hostile stares. Tolmides translated. "My master Pharnabazus reminds you that you are all under his protection as his guests and it would be a terrible discourtesy to violate the trust he has extended to you. He says that the Great King wishes that past hostilities be put aside." *For the evening, at least*, I thought.

I turned my back on Lysander's delegation and faced the satrap. "I offer no hostilities, O Pharnabazus," I said.

Lysander's voice came from behind me. "Nor I," he said before proceeding to slander me. "This man is a known mercenary with a reputation for treachery. My men reacted accordingly. But I will put my enmity aside, for I have more pleasant tasks to attend to. You see, O Satrap of the Great King, that I bring you gifts." The slaves accompanying Lysander's party had stepped forward, each holding a wooden chest. "Treasures from distant lands." The Spartan general gestured and the slaves flipped open the lids of their chests to reveal the valuables within.

I almost laughed at the gall of it. The opulence of Pharnabazus surrounded us, yet Lysander sought to win the satrap's favour with some trinkets. But to my astonishment, Pharnabazus did not scoff. Instead, he approached the first slave and reached inside the chest. When he withdrew his hand, it was holding a wreath of delicate golden leaves.

Lysander smiled. It did not suit him. "The crown of a Makedonian king. I have heard of your passion for collecting such curiosities, O Pharnabazus." Tolmides whispered a translation in his master's ear. Lysander swept his arm towards the other chests. "And there is more, if you wish to see." Pharabazus arched an eyebrow and said something to Tolmides.

"My lord Pharnabazus wishes to see what you have brought him," Tolmides said.

Lysander's false smile widened. "It would be my honour, O Pharnabazus." My lip curled in disgust at Lysander's obsequiousness. Yet Pharnabazus was pleased enough. The men turned their backs to me. Tolmides stood close to Lysander, switching from Greek to Persian with ease as he kept up with the animated discussion of the gifts. I was alone.

My distaste for Lysander's fawning turned to grudging respect as Pharnabazus gave a cry of delight at another bauble. I stared at Lysander. The Spartan approached diplomacy with the same cold logic as he did military matters. Now his strategy of deference had left me isolated. Thrasybulus, wise in many things I reflected, had made a poor decision in sending me as an ambassador.

I had little time to regret my lack of diplomatic skills. One of Lysander's party detached himself from the general's retinue and sidled my way in a very un-Spartan-like manner. The man lacked a Spartan's long oiled braids, opting instead for hair and beard hacked short. I knew him, too. Only with great effort did I restrain the violence in my heart. A ruffian's grin of yellowed teeth split his scarred face.

"If it isn't my old Thracian whore-son," he said, slapping my shoulder and ignoring my stony stare.

His name was Orchus. He was not a Spartan but an Andrian mercenary. He must have been nearing fifty years of age, but he was still as tough and lean as an old wolf. Our paths had crossed many times over the years, but somehow the vile Andrian always seemed to cheat death. He was one of the few men I instinctively feared, more for his feral cunning than his fighting skill. He was a dangerous man.

Orchus cast a jaded eye over my Persian dress. "I wouldn't have taken you for a Mede-izer, Boy."

"Better Persian dress than Spartan," I replied.

He glanced at his crimson cloak and shrugged. "I wear the clothes of whoever pays me," he said.

"And Lysander pays you well?"

Orchus glanced at his employer, who was still engaged with the animated satrap. "Indeed he does, Boy!"

"To lose battles? Like in Thrace?" I had last seen him dragging himself from a river like a half-drowned dog after we had handed Lysander a humiliating defeat.

Orchus reddened, his mouth tightening. "I've fought more battles than you'll ever know, whelp!"

"Running away from battles, more likely," I goaded.

He bared his teeth like a growling dog. His body tensed, as though he were about to lunge. It was hardly a place to fight. Orchus must have realized this as well, for his grimace softened back into his habitual leering smile. He reached out and gently adjusted a crease in my robe. "Good soldiers like us know when a fight is lost. That's why you and me are still breathing while others are naught but ashes and bones. You and me, my Thracian whore-son, we're survivors." The offending wrinkle gone, he patted my chest and pinched his face in an exaggerated wink, the two halves of his scar joining across his closed left eye. It was a truce, then. For the moment at least.

"What is Lysander doing here?" I asked.

Orchus turned his head and spat on the polished floor. "The same as you, whore-son: begging the barbos to part with some of their gold." He regarded the occupied Pharnabazus with a look of genuine loathing. "Fucking perfumed Medes." Orchus looked at me. "You Thracians may be horse-humping barbos, but you're tough," he conceded.

"Gold? What for?" I asked innocently.

Orchus peered at me through narrowed eyes. "Stop playing the fool, Boy. It doesn't suit you," he said. I felt myself flush, for the barb was well deserved. Orchus gave a happy grunt at my embarrassment. He glanced at Lysander. "Gold and silver are always useful for ambitious men like our god-like friend over there, or for old Thrasybulus back in Athens. It's all the same to me. As long as I get my share," he said with an avaricious grin.

"I'll gut you like a pig before you ever have a chance to enjoy it."

The Andrian's dog-toothed grin grew wider. "How many times have you tried, boy? It's just not on." He leaned in conspiratorially. "The Pythia told me so." The confession caught me off-guard. The Pythia was the seer of Delphi. Orchus had been in Delphi a year earlier with Lysander. It was revealing that he had asked who would kill him but perhaps not surprising. Soldiers are superstitious as a rule. His faith in oracles exposed a weakness I could exploit.

"That's not what my sister said," I replied. It was a lie, for my sister had told me no such thing.

The mercenary's eyes flickered with fear. "Is the little bitch here?" he hissed. His hand reached instinctively for his sword, not to draw it but to touch iron and thus ward off the evil eye. But his weapon had been confiscated, and his fingers, finding nothing, twitched with agitation.

Having gotten under his skin, I twisted the knife further. "She said your end is coming soon, Orchus," I said in barely more than a whisper.

The Andrian's eyes darted about nervously, but then steadied themselves as the obnoxious yellow-toothed smile returned. "You had me going there, you did, my whore-son!" He exhaled in relief. "Still, a corpse don't bite, I reckon." He glanced towards his employer and the Persian satrap as Pharnabazos marvelled at another wonder. "What gifts did you bring for the barbos?" Orchus suddenly inquired.

"Nothing," I said, feeling foolish.

Orchus chuckled. "You'd think the silver-mad Athenians would know you've got to spend money to make money. I'd wager the race is already lost, my old whore-son. As much as I'd like to rub your nose in the shit," he said, nodding towards Lysander and Pharnabazus, "It looks like the boot-licking's coming to an end." Indeed, the satrap had moved away from the Spartan general and was issuing directions to his servants. Orchus slapped a rough hand on my back and strode back towards his employer.

Pharnabazus turned and extended his arm towards the enormous table. "My lord Pharnabazus bids you to join him for a humble meal," Tolmides said.

Pharnabazus took his place at the head of the table, his jewelry jingling with the movement. Neither I nor Lysander moved, watching to see what the other would do. Pharnabazus smiled and gestured that we should be seated. "Please," he said in Greek, revealing that he knew at least something of our language. Lysander took the seat closest to Pharnabazus on one side of the table. The Spartan soldiers followed his lead, sitting stiff-backed as though the fine chairs had poison on them. I sat down opposite them with a casual air and leaned back, returning their murderous stares with a calm smile. Orchus, annoyingly, chose to sit beside me.

The staring contest gave me a chance to inspect the glowering Spartans. Though weaponless, they were kitted out in breastplates and skirts of metal-reinforced leather strips. Their long oiled braids marked them as Spartiates, the elite class of pure-born Spartans. "Do I know you, Spartans?" I asked. I frowned in concentration as though trying to recall their faces. "Did we meet in Thrace last year?" I scratched the stubble on my chin. "Or perhaps in Piraeus a few years earlier? I don't know many Spartan faces, for I usually only see Spartan backs as they run away."

As one, the Spartans growled and began to rise, but were checked by Lysander. "Sit!" the former hegemon of Greece hissed. His men lowered themselves back down. Pharnabazus, with Tolmides whispering in his ear, was following the exchange with a look of amusement.

I turned my smile to Lysander, whose own jet-black eyes were fixed upon me with an eagle's cold focus. "Your Spartiate dogs are well trained," I said.

If the implied insult pricked him, he did not show it. Unlike his men, Lysander himself was not a pure-born Spartiate; his mother had been a helot slave. It spoke much of his ability in war and politics that he had risen so high among the rigidly traditional Spartans. His power had once eclipsed that of the two Spartan kings as he became the hegemon of all Greece. Some cities had even proclaimed him a living god. Lysander had tried to usurp power and claim the kingship of Sparta for himself. His secret plot failed, however, because I defeated and humiliated him in the wilds of Thrace a year earlier. Despite Lysander's attempts to cover up the debacle, whispers of his failure had spread. His reputation of invincibility lay in tatters and his power and influence were but a shadow of what they once were. He was a god no more. Because of me.

Lysander retaliated with an insult of his own. "You are one to speak of dogs when you are still begging for scraps at the table of Thrasybulus," he observed. It was a sore point in my pride and Lysander knew it. "Or," he continued, eyeing my Persian robes, "have you gone over to the Medes?"

I laughed. "Even if it is true," I said, straightening out one of my voluminous sleeves with exaggerated care, "I reckon I could humiliate you and your men again, even in these robes." The Spartan warriors opposite leapt to their feet with a growl. Beside me Orchus chuckled, delighting in chaos as always.

Lysander flicked his hand up. His Spartans froze, like dogs straining against a chain. Slowly they lowered themselves back onto their finely carved chairs. Lysander spoke. He kept his voice even, despite the rage that burned in his eyes. "You are bold for one so outnumbered, Daimon."

Before I could provoke the Spartans further, the mellifluous voice of Pharnabazus floated over the table. "My lord Pharnabazus," Tolmides translated, "feels that he has been a poor host to let such conflict flare." The satrap's shrewd expression suggested he felt otherwise. I wondered what other traps he had set for us that evening. "Perhaps some food and drink will soothe tempers still inflamed by the heat of the day," Tolmides continued.

"It is we who have been poor guests," Lysander said with the barest bow of his head. Pharnabazus accepted the apology with a gracious nod.

The feast arrived, first in a trickle and then in a flood. Slaves bearing food and drink came in a steady stream. First came gilded cups filled with water scented with roses and orange blossoms. Then came silver platters of dainty morsels that tasted of odd foreign spices. Orchus sniffed suspiciously at the exotic offerings. He shrugged and tucked in like a man who had not eaten for days.

In truth, I was out of my depth. I could only watch with grudging respect as Lysander effortlessly engaged Pharnabazus on matters of trade and war. My only solace was that the remaining Spartan soldiers were struggling with the occasion more than I, sniffing and picking at their food as if it might be poisoned. Rather than compete with Lysander for the attention of Pharnabazus or join the Spartans in their bad manners, I focused on my food.

A soldier eats when he can, and I did not spurn what was placed before me. I ate with interest if not pleasure, and I confess that the food was delicious. New flavours delighted and surprised at every turn. My throat tingled from the spiced wine that accompanied the meal. I helped myself to another tasty orange-tinted cake, something that did not go unnoticed by our host, whose attention had wandered away from his conversation with Lysander, much to the latter's obvious annoyance.

The satrap said something in Persian, but no translation came. Pharnabazus cast an irritated glance at Tolmides, but the Greek, bending down to listen to something Lysander was whispering in his ear, had not noticed his master's need of him. Pharnabazus flicked a finger at Babak, who had stood stiffly, almost invisibly behind me the entire evening. "My Lord Pharnabazus says it is called '*sappor*,'" the Phrygian translated nervously. "It comes from the centre of a flower and is worth ten times its weight in gold."

I had seen such a luxury at a spice trader's stall in Athens and knew its value. "It's a marvel," I said with a nod to Pharnabazus, and the satrap beamed as Babak translated my words.

"My Lord Pharnabazus says he will be sure to send some back with you to Athens," Babak said with greater confidence. I voiced my appreciation for the gift. Tolmides, belatedly realizing his duty as interpreter had been usurped by Babak, scuttled back to his master's side, giving the Phrygian a murderous look as he did so.

But Pharabazus was not done with me. Ignoring his wayward official, the satrap continued to address me through Babak. "My Lord Phranabazus," Babak said, "would like to know if you were at the battle of Piraeus with the *strategos* Thrasybulus." The Spartans across from me froze. Lysander's cheeks flexed as he clenched his jaw. The satrap's eyes flashed with calculated mischief.

"I was," I said. "I was one of the *strategos'* captains."

"My Lord Phranabazus has heard of this battle, but has never spoken with someone who was present at the event. It would give him great joy to hear you speak of it," Babak said.

"It would be my pleasure," I said, ignoring the seething Spartans across from me. Lysander's face tightened even further.

I have always had a bit of the rhapsode in me, and I rose to the occasion. I spoke of how, outnumbered and poorly armed, the small army of Thrasybulus had defeated the combined forces of his puppet tyrants and the Spartan garrison on the Munychia hill in Piraeus. Pharnbazus listened intently as I told of how I cut down the Tyrant Kritias and then watched the defeated Spartans and their allies flee down the slopes of the hill. I explained how a reinforced Spartan army besieged us in Piraeus until I helped lure them into the narrow streets of the port, where we slaughtered them and I slew a Spartan *polemarch* by my own hand. But nor did I omit how our victory almost turned to defeat when enthusiastic soldiers led a reckless charge in pursuit of the fleeing Spartans and how they were only saved from annihilation by the inspired generalship of Thrasybulus. All the while, the Spartans opposite me stewed in their seats, powerless to interrupt me.

At the end, Pharnabazus clutched his hands together and expressed his wonder at the story while Lysander fumed. But I was wary of the satrap as well. He was sowing seeds of discord for more than just amusement. He beckoned to Tolmides, the Greek's previous lapse of attention apparently forgiven. Tolmides received the satrap's whispered instructions. Without a word, the Greek strode with determined purpose from the great hall.

I could only consider the matter as more platters heaped high with spiced meat found their way to the table. Beside me, Orchus grunted with contentment as he stripped bone after bone of roasted flesh. As the meal progressed, we were entertained by a succession of dancers and acrobats while musicians played in accompaniment. Even the humourless Spartans could not ignore the lithesome beauties who leapt and spun in their seductive costumes. Orchus leered, transfixed, with only the occasional gulp of wine or belch to distract him. Lysander feigned interest, leaning over occasionally to say something to the hulking Spartan on his right. I sipped at my wine, watching those around me rather than the dancers and musicians.

Pharnabazus caught me observing him and smiled a fox's smile. He turned his attention to the returning Tolmides. The Greek, reaching his master's side, bent down and whispered something in the satrap's ear. Pharnabazus nodded and clapped his hands three times. The music stopped mid-phrase and the dancers froze with military discipline. Pharnabazus looked at me and spoke. Tolmides cleared his throat. "My Lord Pharnabazus wishes to know if his entertainment bores you, Athenian." The Greek's voice echoed in the now silent hall.

The Spartans, sensing my discomfort, leaned forward with hungry anticipation. I bowed my head as my mind groped for the right words. "Forgive me, O Pharnabazus. I am overwhelmed by your hospitality. I am a simple warrior, unaccustomed to such things. Everywhere I look is a wonder to the eyes, and as a result I can focus on nothing." Lysander's lip curled at my fumbling attempt at honeyed words.

Pharnabazus, regarding me coyly, stroked the tight curls of his beard. At last he raised a finger, as though something grand had just occurred to him. He spoke with a broad smile. "My Lord Pharnabazus has something that might be entertaining to a warrior like yourself." Tolmides turned to Lysander. "My lord Pharnabazus says that perhaps Spartan honour was challenged earlier in the evening with no chance to respond. My lord would very much like to offer your men the opportunity to demonstrate their famed martial prowess."

Suspicion rippled across Lysander's face, but he was trapped by the demands of honour. "We would relish such an opportunity, O Pharnabazus." Pharnabazus nodded as though he had expected no less.

The satrap of Phrygia flicked an idle hand. At the gesture, one of his guards barked a command towards the front of the hall. At once two lines of soldiers entered the chamber and marched towards us. Between the two ranks of Persians was a shackled figure in a simple tunic tied with leather cord at the waist. The broad-shouldered prisoner was barefoot but stood taller than his Persian captors. Most striking, however, was the man's hair. It was disheveled and loose from captivity, but there was no mistaking the long black braids that hung down the man's chest and back.

Across from me, Lysander and his men erupted from their seats as one, their voices raised in anger.

The prisoner was a Spartiate.

CHAPTER 7

Lysander and his men erupted at the sight of their countryman in chains. I took this as anger towards the Persians for their ignoble treatment of an elite Spartan warrior. But as my gaze slid over to the captive Spartiate, it was clear that I had misread the situation, for the prisoner's stare radiated hatred not at his Persian captors but at Lysander.

"My Lord Pharnabazus wishes to know if you are acquainted with this man," Tolmides said, addressing Lysander.

Lysander replied through gritted teeth. "He is a traitor."

The prisoner spoke for the first time. "You conspire with the Medes now, *mothax*?" he asked, his rough voice dripping with contempt. A *mothax* was a half-breed Spartan.

Lysander's eyelid twitched at the insult. He turned to Pharnabazus. "What do you plan to do with this villain, O Pharnabazus?"

"He is a foreign invader, and as such should be executed for his disrespect of the Great King," Tolmides translated.

"Sparta does not object, O Pharnabazus," Lysander said coolly.

I shifted in my chair to afford myself a better view of the prisoner. The sound attracted the captive Spartan's attention and he noticed me for the first time. Confusion flashed across his face. "You!" he hissed. I frowned, trying to place the man's face. I had never set eyes on him before. His perplexed gaze darted back and forth between me and the grimacing Lysander. If he wished to say more, the chance vanished, for Pharnabazus began to speak.

"If you wish it, O Lysander, one of your men can face him in combat here and now," Tolmides said. "If any of your men are up to the task," he added. Pharnabazus smiled like a wolf. Phrased thus, the satrap's challenge to Spartan honour left Lysander little room to manoeuvre.

The odds were not in the prisoner's favour. Lysander's men were clad in breastplates and armoured skirts. The prisoner, barefoot and wearing only a coarse tunic, was as vulnerable as a hog in a butcher's slaughterhouse. And while Lysander's men looked fresh, the lean prisoner moved with the stiffness born of long captivity.

And yet I saw the uncertainty in the eyes of Lysander's men and Lysander himself. Even the bothersome Orchus had withdrawn into a wary silence. I reappraised the prisoner in a new light. For someone listening to others negotiating the manner of his impending death, his demeanor was that of cold stone. Underneath his haggard appearance lurked the confident strength of a lion. I made a sniff of derision at the Spartans' hesitation.

Pharnabazus seized on my disdainful gesture. "Do you have an opinion, Athenian?" the satrap inquired through Tolmides.

I cursed inwardly for having drawn attention to myself, but I trusted the feeling in my guts. "The prisoner will win," I said, fixing my gaze on Lysander. The Spartan general clenched his jaw even more tightly.

Pharnabazus responded, putting on a doubtful expression. "Are you certain of this?" Tolmides asked.

"I am."

"My Lord Pharnabazus wonders if you would both care to wager on that outcome?" Tolmides inquired. Pharnabazus leaned back in his ornate chair, awaiting our response.

We were being manipulated, Lysander and I both. Pharabazus had planned everything, from having me and Lysander together at the same table to asking me to relate the battle at Piraeus for his amusement. Lysander knew it too, and could not hide his displeasure. But we could only play his game.

Lysander spoke first. "What are the stakes, O Pharnabazus?"

Tolmides listened closely as Pharnabazus explained the terms of the contest. "You have both come to me seeking the same thing: gold from the Great King to support your respective causes. If Lysander's man prevails, the money will go to him. If the prisoner is victorious, the gold will be awarded to the Athenian."

A wager always has two sides, a fact not lost on Lysander. "And what shall we risk in return, O Pharnabazus?" the Spartan general asked.

"Should you lose, you will have lost a valuable man, O Lysander. That is enough to satisfy my lord," Tolmides said.

Lysander glanced my way. "And the Athenian? What thing of value does he put on the table?"

All eyes turned my way. I was at a loss. "I have nothing of value to wager," I said, which was true enough.

Tolmides translated, though by now I reckoned the Persian satrap could understand every word that passed my lips. Pharnabazus gave a secretive smile and raised one hand. At his signal, a servant entered the hall carrying a long object laid across his palms. My heart fell.

Her name was Whisper. The Persians had confiscated her along with our other weapons. She was as much a part of me as one of my limbs. She was a Thracian *rhomphaia*, a gently-arcing blade as long as a man's leg. She had been forged by a half-mad smith, so I had been told, and I only knew that her unnatural strength was related to the smoky ripples that played across the blue-tinged metal. Her silent cuts had sent many men to the Underworld. She was one of a pair, the other belonging to the Thracian prince who had gifted her to me. There were no other weapons like them in the world.

Pharnabazus gripped the long hilt with both hands. His stare drifted greedily down the length of the glimmering blade as though admiring a sensuous woman. "My Lord Pharnabazus says that he would accept this unique weapon as adequate compensation," he said in lightly accented Greek. I recalled the satrap's apparent passion for rare treasures.

I fixed the satrap with a flat stare. Whatever game Pharabazus was playing, I was losing. But what could I do? There was little stopping Pharabazus from taking Whisper from me if he had so wished. Fate and honour forced my hand. "I accept." The prisoner had watched the entire exchange with dead eyes as we bargained away his life in gold and prizes.

The terms of the contest decided, Pharnabazus clapped his hands and a brigade of palace slaves scurried into activity. The table and remnants of the feast were hastily carted away as the musicians and dancers vanished through doorways set in the side walls. Slaves set up seats for us on the raised dais at the rear of the hall so that we would have a good view of the spectacle. Thirty or so Persian soldiers formed a ring around the prisoner.

The prisoner's guards freed him of his fetters. Barefoot and in his threadbare tunic, the prisoner massaged his chafed wrists. Pharnabazus nodded at one of the soldiers, who unsheathed his sword and tossed it towards the haggard-looking Spartan. The clattering ring of the sword against the marble floor echoed in the high-ceilinged hall. The Spartan held the stare of Pharnabazus for a few heartbeats before limping over to the weapon. He bent down and retrieved the blade at his feet.

The straight-edged Persian sword was longer than either a leaf-bladed *xiphos* or the forward-curving *kopis* favoured by the Spartans. To balance the additional length, the hilt terminated in a heavy pommel. The prisoner held the unfamiliar sword uncertainly, almost gingerly.

Tolmides addressed Lysander. "Have you chosen your man?" Beside me, Orchus stiffened.

One of the Spartans stepped forward, shedding his crimson cloak. "I will kill the traitor!" He looked to be the youngest of Lysander's bodyguard.

Lysander hesitated, his gaze still locked on the mysterious prisoner. To deny the young Spartan now would be to dishonour him, especially against so decrepit an opponent. Lysander acceded. "Pittilakos! Put this dog out of his misery!" Nodding to Lysander, the Spartiate made his way to the circle of combat. Beside me Orchus let out a long, relieved breath. The Spartan Pittilakos took the sword offered to him and shoved past the Persians to face his waiting opponent.

Lysander's man whipped his sword in a cross-cut pattern as he tested the blade's weight. In contrast to the haggard prisoner, the muscular young Pittilakos radiated dangerous strength. He pointed his sword at the prisoner. "Prepare to die, traitor!" he spat. The dull-eyed prisoner remained motionless, his sword held loosely by his leg. My confidence in the prisoner's ability wavered.

"Begin!" came the order from Tolmides.

Pittilakos raised his sword to a fighting position. The prisoner shuffled back a step. Pittilakos sneered. "You are a coward as well as a traitor!" The prisoner bore the taunt impassively. Pittilakos tried again to provoke some reaction from his opponent. "Will you not even defend yourself?" The prisoner edged back one more step. Pittilakos' fellow Spartans jeered. Except Lysander, I noticed, whose intense stare was fixed on the prisoner.

Pittilakos' patience was at an end. "Bah!" he grunted, advancing on his spiritless victim. Suddenly he dashed forward and swung his blade down towards the crook between the prisoner's neck and shoulder. There was a flurry of movement and a sword skittered across the stone floor. But it was Pittilakos who was stumbling back, his hands clutching at his throat. The prisoner, lifeless no more, stood in a fighting stance, his hard eyes fixed on his dying opponent.

It had been as fast and violent as a serpent's strike. The prisoner had exploded into movement, stepping under the hacking blade of Pittilakos and lancing his sword tip into the base of the Spartan's neck. Pittilakos' eyes bulged in disbelief as his lifeblood ran out between his fingers. He took a few more drunken steps before his eyes rolled back in his head and he collapsed in a heap. Stunned silence filled the hall. Relief flooded through my body.

Lysander's Spartan honour guard sprang from their chairs, clamouring for the prisoner's death. Orchus alone stayed seated. "Should have just executed him," the Andrian muttered. Seeing me looking at him, Orchus nodded towards the still-warm body of Pittilakos sprawled on the cold stone floor. "A corpse don't bite," he offered, as though that explained everything.

I glanced at Pharnabazus. Along with Orchus, he too seemed unsurprised by the outcome. He gestured for Tolmides but once again the Greek was attending to Lysander, who was whispering furiously in the official's ear. Pharnabazus frowned. "*Bandaka!*" the satrap snapped. Tolmides flushed and hastened to his master's side.

While the Persian noble spoke to his wayward Greek, I leaned back to address Babak, who had not budged from his space behind me. The Phrygian interpreter had done an admirable job at remaining inconspicuous throughout the evening. "What does '*bandaka*' mean*?*" I asked in a low voice.

"'*Slave,*'" Babak whispered hurriedly.

A chastened Tolmides raised his hands in the air. "Attention!" he called out. The Spartans continued their angry protests. "Attention!" the official repeated. Lysander gave the faintest of nods and his men ceased their shouting. "My Lord Pharnabazus says that the contest was poor entertainment, He suggests that perhaps two Spartans should face the prisoner instead of one. He will double the stakes. He will offer twice as much gold to the victor."

Twice the gold! Surely it would be enough for Thrasybulus to secure allies and launch his war to free Athens from Spartan domination. I exchanged a hateful stare with Lysander. It was also more than enough for Lysander to finance another attempt to seize power in Sparta, I thought. If he were successful, he would raze Athens to the ground and sell the population into slavery. Of that I had little doubt.

Lysander rose to his feet. "And what can I offer against these increased stakes, Persian?" he challenged.

Tolmides swallowed. "Should you lose, you will leave this place immediately and have half a day before my lord Pharnabazus sends his men to hunt you down. We are at war with Sparta after all." Lysander shot a baleful glare my way before nodding in agreement to the terms of the wager

"And what of the Athenian?" Lysander said, pointing at me. "What more can he offer besides a barbarian weapon?"

Pharnabazus regarded me with the smile of a man who knew he could not lose either way. Tolmides continued. "My Lord Pharnabazus says that the talents of such a renowned warrior should not go to waste. Should the prisoner fail, Daimon the Athenian will remain here in the service of the Great King. Are the terms acceptable, Athenian?" Tolmides asked.

There it was. I would join the satrap's collection of unique items. *In service of the Great King.* Just another slave, in other words. I glanced at the Spartiate prisoner. It is a difficult for a lone man to defeat two opponents at the best of times. It helps if the enemy are inexperienced or foolish. Lysander's men were all Spartiates who had done little but hone their fighting skills since they were children. I would have said my wager was already lost, except for one thing. The prisoner himself, a witness to the conversation, displayed a total lack of concern for his fate. He exuded not the despondent resignation of a doomed man but an aura of disdainful confidence. Sometimes we must wager our lives on little more than instinct and experience. "It is acceptable," I said.

A new voice echoed in the hall. "And if I am victorious, Persian? What is my reward?" called out the prisoner in a voice like rough stone.

Pharnabazus scowled and spewed forth a stream of angry Persian. "My Lord Pharnabazus," Tolmides translated, "says that for such impudence he should have you crucified at the city gate and let you bake in the sun while the ravens pick at your still-living flesh. But your insolent Spartan hide will stay on your body in the unlike event you emerge victorious."

The Spartan prisoner grunted. He pointed his sword at Lysander. "Then choose your men, *mothax*," he said. "Or face me yourself if you are not a coward."

Lysander brushed aside the prisoner's challenge. "Aktis! Matelos! See to it!"

Two more Spartans doffed their crimson cloaks and approached the ring of Persian soldiers. The two men were older than the unfortunate Pittilakos. Their scarred faces and arms testified to their combat experience. They accepted two of the straight Persian swords as their weapons and tested their weight as two Persian soldiers dragged the body of the unwise Pittilakos from the fighting area. A congealing pool of the Spartan's blood stained the patterned white tiles.

"Begin!" Tolmides said.

Lysander's two Spartans, unlike the cavalier Pittilakos, were wary of their opponent's skill. They spread apart so that they and the prisoner were like the three corners of a triangle. The prisoner could not isolate one of them without exposing his flank to the other.

The two Spartans advanced on their quarry with caution. The prisoner took two steps back, maintaining the distance between him and his would-be executioners, but taking him closer to the cordon of Persian guards. Then, in an explosion of movement, the prisoner spun around. His arcing sword buried itself in the neck of a Persian soldier, whose eyes opened wide in disbelief. The prisoner ripped the sword free and a plume of blood spouted from the Persian's wound. As the unfortunate Persian soldier collapsed, the prisoner seized his victim's spear and in one fluid motion pivoted and hurled it at one of Lysander's men. The Spartan soldier grunted as the long spear-tip took him under the sternum and drove through his breastplate right up to the wooden haft. His borrowed Persian sword clattered to the white marble floor. He clutched the spear and tried to withdraw it, but his energy drained and he fell to his knees. There was a hiss of disgust from Lysander as his man toppled over, still grasping the spear in his chest. The prisoner, his sword back in his right hand, had already dropped into a defensive stance facing the remaining Spartan. It had all happened in the space of a few heartbeats.

The remaining Persian soldiers, finally recovering from their shock, belatedly pointed their angry spears towards the prisoner. They drew back their weapons in preparation to skewer the prisoner, but an angry shout froze them in place before they could strike. Pharnabazus, his eyes blazing, berated his men in Persian, who shrank before the torrent of abuse from their lord.

Lysander beckoned towards the Greek Tolmides, who stepped away from his master's side. "What is he saying?" Lysander asked.

"He told them to stand down," the interpreter said. "He said that the man was careless and deserved to die. He said he promised the man a chance to fight and he will honour that promise." Pharnabazus glared at his official's turned back.

As Tolmides moved back towards his master, he was met by a ferocious blow from Pharnabazus. The Greek fell sprawling to the ground. "You interpret when I tell you to do so!" the satrap shouted in accented but fluent Greek.

Tolmides, dazed from the blow, instinctively touched the growing welt on his cheek. Recovering enough of his wits to know he had erred, he crawled towards the Persian satrap, prostrating himself before his master. "My deepest apologies, my Lord Pharnabazus," he mumbled.

"Resume your place!" Pharnabazus snapped.

"Yes, my lord Pharnabazus." Tolmides struggled back to his feet and took his place by the satrap's side.

Lysander's previous warmth towards his Persian host had evaporated like morning mist. He shot Pharnabazus a murderous look before turning his attention back to the contest at hand. "Kill him!" he shouted at his remaining fighter.

The prisoner sneered at the Spartan general. "Are you afraid to meet me yourself, *mothax*?" Pharnabazus laughed, amused when the prisoner's impudence was aimed at someone other than himself.

The insult stoked Lysander rage. "Kill him!" he yelled again, urging his man on. The prisoner glanced my way and our eyes met. I gave him the barest of nods, willing him to victory. His lip curled and he turned away to face his remaining opponent.

The two men circled each other. The prisoner kept the body of the impaled Spartan between him and his remaining enemy, for without any armour he was still at a great disadvantage. Suddenly he reversed his direction so that the body of the impaled Spartan was no longer an obstacle. With open space now between him and Lysander's man, he lunged in for a strike. I inhaled sharply, for the prisoner had miscalculated, his strike falling short of its target. Overextended and off-balance, the prisoner made a frantic leap back, exposing his side to a counterattack. Lysander's Spartan, seeing his chance, sprang toward the prisoner, his sword pulled back to deliver a killing blow.

And he died for it, for like those watching the contest, he had failed to see the trap the prisoner had set.

The Spartan's sandaled foot skidded in the congealing pool of Pittilakos' blood. The small slip sealed his fate. The prisoner, his bare feet firm on the stone floor, snapped a straight-armed thrust at the Spartan's face. The tip of the sword took out the Spartan's eye. Lysander's man only grunted as half his sight was stolen from him, a testament to his Spartan training. The half-blind Spartan lashed out with a wild cut, trying to catch his opponent in a quick counterattack, but the prisoner crouched low and propelled himself forward, dragging his blade across the Spartan's leg just above the knee, severing muscle and tendons. The wounded leg buckled and Lysander's man dropped to one knee. He struggled to rise but the prisoner rose up behind him, his reversed sword held high in a double-handed grip. Showing emotion at last, the prisoner screamed as he plunged the sword deep down between the kneeling Spartan's shoulder and neck. The Spartan shuddered and keeled to one side and was dead before he hit the ground.

The prisoner straightened up and stared at Lysander. The Spartan general's face was taut with rage and disbelief. His remaining captain grimaced with shame and helplessness at the fate of his two comrades lying dead on the floor. Pharnabazus clapped in appreciation for the unexpected but not unwelcome entertainment. Only Orchus showed no surprise.

"A corpse don't bite," he mumbled to himself.

CHAPTER 8

The prisoner stepped forward. "I have won. You will free me now, Persian."

Pharnabazus shook a finger at the victorious prisoner. "I promised you your life, not your freedom," he admonished in Greek. "Why should I let you go just to have you kill more of my soldiers on the battlefield? You will stay in your prison."

"It is said that your people pride truth above all other virtues. But you are a liar, Persian," the prisoner said through clenched teeth.

Pharnabazus brushed off the insult. "And you Spartans pride your fighting skills and are unmatched in this regard. I concede this. But in negotiations you would be bested by any Persian child. I told no lies. I promised to spare your life and I will hold to that promise, but no more." He switched to Persian and his men surrounded the prisoner. I thought the Spartan would resist, but I was wrong. The prisoner, resigned to his fate, let himself be shackled. In a moment, the mysterious captive and his escort were gone, leaving many of my questions unanswered.

Pharnabazus turned to Lysander. "You have lost the wager, Spartan. You have half a day before I send men in pursuit of you. I have the fastest riders in Asia. I suggest that you not squander the time granted to you."

Lysander, his eyes blazing, took a half-step step towards the satrap. In an instant, a dozen spear-points were aimed at the Spartan general. Lysander's chest heaved with suppressed wrath as he stared at the calm Pharnabazus. Lysander's gaze flicked my way and I winked at him. I could only hope that he was foolish enough to lash out. Alas, Lysander was no fool.

"How do I know you will honour your word?" Lysander asked.

"I am a faithful follower of the prophet Zarathustra. As such I must adhere to my word, as distasteful as that may be. Tolmides will see that you are escorted to the city gates without incident."

"Yes, my lord Pharnabazus," the Greek said with a bow. As the interpreter turned, our eyes met. He looked away quickly, his face flushed with shame. With a frustrated growl, the Spartan general pivoted towards the hall entrance. "Come!" he ordered his remaining men.

Orchus brushed past me as he moved to join Lysander. "Until next time, my Thracian whoreson," he said with a nose-clearing sniff. Led by Tolmides and surrounded by two dozen soldiers, The Spartans strode past the still-warm bodies of their comrades. They passed through the high double doors and were gone. I was alone with Pharnabazus and his Persian guards.

The satrap turned to me. "Your weapon will be returned to you when you leave the city," he said regretfully. He cast a longing look at Whisper. "It is a shame, for I would have very much liked to possess such a fine weapon for my collection." He raised a suggestive eyebrow, letting the statement hang in air that stank of spices, wine, and death.

His meaning was not lost on me. He wanted me to offer Whisper to him as a gift. I could almost hear the blade calling out to me, begging me not to abandon her. Yet on the battlefield, if I had to lose the rhomphaia to save Tibetos or Sabas or Thrasybulus, I would do so without hesitation, for a weapon is a tool, no matter what virtues we ascribe to it. Was I not now on a battlefield of a different nature? My path was clear if painful. "May you wield her with honour, O Pharnabazus," I said, forcing a smile while my soul wept.

Pharnabazus clapped his hands with genuine joy. "You bless me with your generosity!" Realizing he had let his air of dignity slip, he put on a more haughty tone. "As for your gold, it will be delivered before you leave," he said, dismissing me with a casual wave of his hand.

But I ignored his dismissal. Gold or not, I was unwilling to let Whisper go so cheaply if I could exact a higher price. "I confess, O Pharnabazus, that I will miss her," I said glancing at Whisper.

The satrap's eyes sparkled with amusement. "What is it you wish to ask, Athenian?"

"A mere favour. It will cost you nothing."

The satrap's eyes narrowed. "Yet such favours often cost the most in the end. But name your wish, Athenian."

"I wish to speak to the Spartan prisoner, O Pharnabazus."

Pharnabazus narrowed his eyes even further, calculating what my request might cost him. Apparently it was very little. "Granted!" he said.

THE PRISON WAS A STONE BUILDING near the city walls. The dark-skinned prison overseer scrutinized the satrap's orders and wax seal for a long time before grunting and handing the papyrus back to Tolmides. He motioned for us to follow him and he led us to a cell door at the far corner of the courtyard.

I glanced at Tolmides. The bruise on the interpreter's cheek had darkened since the banquet. I did not especially like the officious Melian slave, but he was a fellow Greek after all. "Your master should not have struck you," I said.

His lips tightened and his eyes regarded me with a mixture of shame and contempt. "Go see the Spartan. I will wait here," he said, averting his gaze to stare past my shoulder. I considered saying something more, but at last I shrugged and turned away.

The cell door was solid wood except for a small square to admit air and a little light. The heavy iron locking-bolt grated against its housing, and the door groaned in resistance as the overseer pulled it open. He handed me a torch from a bracket and stepped aside to let me enter the cell. I ducked through the low door into the Stygian gloom beyond.

The weak light from the sputtering torch barely illuminated the cell. Nor could the smoke overcome the odor of stale sweat and old piss that permeated the small room. The Spartan was there, squatting beside the rear wall. He stood up with a metallic clinking, and I saw the chains that bound his manacled hands to the stone behind him. He squinted against the light that had disturbed his dark world. Seeing it was me, he gave a dismissive grunt and sat back down. He leaned against the wall and watched me with an intense, eagle-like stare.

"What is your name, Spartan?" I asked him. My question was met with silence. I tried a different tack. "What are you to Lysander?" The Spartan's mouth twitched at the mention of the Spartan general's name.

I stepped closer and the prisoner sprang to his feet, his eyes wary. I raised my hand to show I meant no harm. Then I reached into my other sleeve and withdrew some bread I had slipped into my voluminous robes from the satrap's table. I extended the round loaf towards the Spartan. Hunger defeated suspicion, and the prisoner took the peace offering. "Gratitude," he said.

"I have known a prisoner's hunger," I said. The Spartan grunted and sat back down. He tore off a bite of the Persian bread and chewed. I let him eat half the loaf before I spoke again. "What is your name?"

The Spartan brushed some crumbs from his unkempt beard. "I am Neon, son of ..." He hesitated. "I am Neon."

I patted the stone wall of the cell. "And how do come to find yourself in such circumstances, O Neon?"

He shrugged. "The Persians captured me," he said simply.

"From what I have seen, you would not be taken prisoner easily," I said.

"A slinger's stone knocked me senseless," he said bitterly. A stone from a whirling piece of leather could take down the mightiest soldier. It was why I employed so many slingers in the *peripoli*.

"Why did they not just kill you?" I asked.

"A full-blooded Spartiate prisoner is a rare prize," he said. "And a rare shame," he added more softly.

I let the comment pass, for there were more important things I wished to know. "You seem to know me, O Neon," I said. "But I do not know you."

The Spartan's expression did not change. "Yes." Like many Spartans, he was parsimonious of speech.

"We have met before?" I pressed.

The corner of the Spartan's mouth flexed in the barest hint of a smile. "'Met' is an exaggeration," he said without elaboration.

"When?"

"Last year. In Thrace." he said. I tensed. His answer, though short, revealed much. The previous year I had sent a score or more Lysander's Spartans to a watery death at the bottom of a river in Thrace.

"You are Lysander's man?"

The Spartan's stern facade cracked, and he gave a mirthless laugh as he rattled his manacles. "What do you think, Athenian?"

"But you fought for him in Thrace?"

"I was Lysander's man, yes. One of his most trusted captains. But no longer."

"You left him?" I asked, beginning to understand the source of the enmity I had seen in the palace of Pharnabazus.

"Yes."

"Why?"

The Spartan dropped his head. "He promised me many things, but I saw at last that he had played me false. The chains that bound me to him were broken and I was free of his lies, his ambition. Now we are enemies. I have you to thank you for that, I suppose," he said, looking back up. For a Spartan, the response would be reckoned as a long speech. He narrowed his eyes and regarded me. "I thought you were his enemy too, Athenian. So I did not expect to see you in barbarian robes sharing a table with him in a barbarian palace."

I scowled at my luxurious clothes. "Know that I am no Mede-izer, Spartan. And know that Lysander will ever be my enemy," I said, unable to hide my bitterness.

"I jest, Athenian," he said. "I saw the hatred with which you two regarded each other."

"No less than you, I think." I thought back to the contest in the satrap's great hall. "You fought well tonight, O Neon."

"Not as well you did in Thrace, Athenian."

I brushed aside the compliment. "You should have thrown the spear at Lysander," I reflected.

"I wanted to, but I was facing the wrong direction."

"It would have served both our purposes," I said.

Neon arched an eyebrow. "And what is your purpose here, Athenian?"

I ignored the question. "The Persians are at war with Sparta, yet Lysander dines with a Persian satrap. Does Agesilaus seek peace with the Great King?" King Agesilaus of Sparta had been at war with the Persians in Asia for more than a year.

Neon snorted. "Agesilaus did not send Lysander. Of that, I am certain."

"Then what was Lysander's purpose here?"

Neon shrugged. "Lysander serves Lysander. That is all you need to know, Athenian."

"Why are sure he does speak on behalf of King Agesilaus?" I asked.

"Lysander has lost favour with the king," Neon said.

"How do you know this?"

"I went to Agesilaus when I left Lysander's service. I was fighting with the king's forces when I was captured by the Persians."

"I had heard that Agesilaus was Lysander's creature," I said, choosing my words carefully.

Sparta is an oddity among the Greek poleis. It is ruled by not one but two kings, each descended from a different family line. In theory, each king was a check on the other's power, though the practicalities of the arrangement were more complicated in reality. Of the current kings, Pausanias was the senior monarch, intelligent, level-headed, and ruthless when he needed to be. I had met him twice, the last time a little more than a year earlier when I had driven him defeated and humiliated from the fields of Thrace.

Of the second king, Agesilaus, I knew little. It was said that he was small and lame, and had only been spared the fate of being exposed as an infant because his father was king. Now forty or so years of age, it was long rumoured that Lysander had dominated the king from a young age. And, if the stories were true, the relationship was an intimate one.

Neon shook his head. "Once it was so, but no longer. Agesilaus has grown into a man of some ability and independence, much to Lysander's surprise, I think. Whispers of Lysander's activities in Thrace reached the king's ears," he said with a nod my way. I had thwarted Lysander's plot to overthrow the Spartan kings in Thrace a year earlier. But Lysander's secret attempt to secure gold from Pharnabazus made it clear that his ambitions were far from dead.

"Why does Agesilaus not have him killed?" I asked.

"Agesilaus has grown wary and suspicious, but has no proof of his treachery. Lysander's power has been greatly diminished, it is true, but he still commands the loyalty of many men. Agesilaus cannot dismiss him outright."

"How does Agesilaus keep Lysander in check?"

A wry smile cracked through Neon's Spartan demeanour. "The king sends Lysander scurrying about like the weasel he is, collecting troops, delivering pay. No task is too small. He is a mere messenger now. I think the king just wishes him to die in some skirmish and be done with it." He tore off another chunk of bread and stuffed it in his mouth. He watched me carefully as I considered his words.

The motives of Pharnabazus were clear enough. For the past year, Agesilaus and his army had been liberating the Greek cities of Ionia from Persian rule. Bested on the field of battle, the Persians would strike back not with soldiers but with money. The Great King could finance a rebellion by Athens and other Greeks against Sparta. Or, Persian gold could support Lysander in his bid to seize the Spartan throne. In either case, Agesilaus would be forced to leave Asia to deal with matters at home. More importantly, all of Ionia would come back under Persian control. All for a few hundred talents of silver and gold.

Neon swallowed his last piece of bread. Then, as if hearing my thoughts, he spoke. "Pharnabazus is using you for his own ends. Mark my words, Athenian." I knew the truth of what he said, but the noise of the cell door creaking on its hinges behind me cut me off before I could respond. The relative brightness of the torch-lit courtyard cast my shadow over the sitting Neon. The silhouetted figure of Tolmides stepped into the doorway.

"The prison warden says you have had enough time," the Greek said, but the scowling face of the Persian over his shoulder did not need to be translated.

I turned to Neon, but there was little comfort I could offer him. "Farewell, Spartan."

"May the twin gods protect you, Athenian," he said.

Returning to the residence under armed escort. I reflected on the odd meeting. The Spartan Neon had earned my respect, He demonstrated his skill as a warrior, but even more, he was thoughtful and forthcoming, not at all like the arrogant Spartans I had encountered in the past. The Spartans had been the bitter enemies of Athens for generations. But before that, the two powers had been allies in the war against the Persian hordes. Seeing Neon locked in a barbarian prison, I regarded him not as an enemy but as fellow Greek abandoned by the gods and his countrymen. Had my life not been the same?

There was nothing I could do for him. On the great loom of destiny, our threads of fate had drawn near, touched, and now would part once more.

But I was wrong, as I often was.

CHAPTER 9

"Hunting?" I asked.

Tolmides dipped his head in acknowledgement. "That is correct. My master Pharnabazus is going hunting in his game park today and wishes you to join him." The Greek's mask of inscrutability had returned, with only the purplish bruise as a reminder of the indignity he had suffered at the banquet.

It was a command rather than a request, despite the polite phrasing. But I would not go alone if I could help it. "And my companions?" I asked, gesturing towards Tibetos and Sabas, who were looking on with interest.

"They are welcome to join you, if they wish. I will return to collect you soon," Tolmides said before leaving us to muse over our upcoming excursion.

"Thank the gods!" Sabas exclaimed. He scooped up an apple from a silver bowl and took a bite. "I don't know how much more of this luxury I can stand," he said through the mouthful of fruit.

I took his meaning. Tolmides' appearance that morning was the first time I had seen the Melian since the banquet three days earlier. We had been confined to the opulent residence, attended to by the silent slaves who came and went with ample quantities of food and drink. It was a luxurious existence, but a prison nonetheless.

Prison had been much in my thoughts. I had related the events of the banquet to Tibetos and Sabas, as well as my meeting with the Spartan prisoner, Neon. They did not share my interest in the Spartan warrior. "How many Athenians has he killed?" the Cretan archer asked. "Safest thing is to let him rot there." Tibetos agreed.

My conversation with the Spartan warrior had left me less certain. There were not a few men — cruel, ambitious men like Lysander — that I would have happily left festering in a Persian prison cell. Neon the Spartan was not among their number. But there was a little I could do to alter the destiny the Fates had woven for the unlucky Neon.

A contingent of Persian guards came to collect us, led by the same gruff captain who had intercepted us on the Phrygian plain. If his opinion of us had improved, his manner did not reveal it, for his instructions were as brusque as before. The captain and his squad of eight men led us to the main gates of the palace compound, where Pharnabazus awaited us with his retinue.

The satrap had eschewed his formal robes but was no less elegant for the change. Embroidered flowers patterned his pale green breeches and sleeved tunic. Gold and silver accented the fringes of his clothing. But my eyes were drawn to Whisper's familiar oversized hilt poking over his shoulder. Seeing where my gaze fell, Pharnabazus turned to talk to his captain, though his true purpose was to show me his recently acquired treasure. In the three days since the banquet, the satrap had commissioned an ostentatious jewelled scabbard for the rhomphaia. I frowned to see her treated thus. She was like one of the gaudy courtesans at an aristocrat's drinking party, their natural beauty hidden behind golden baubles and garish cosmetics. Tibetos and Sabas watched me intently, waiting for me to do something rash. But I disappointed them by maintaining an air of civility.

Having given me a view of his new toy, the satrap turned to me with a wide grin and put his hands on my shoulders. "A fine day for hunting, is it not, Athenian?" he said in his accented Greek.

I could not disagree, for the sky was clear and the air cool. "I look forward to the opportunity," I replied. "I have heard that the boars of Phrygia are fearsome."

Pharnabazus warmed to the subject. "It is true! You have experience hunting boars?"

I grew up in the streets of Athens and hunting had played no part in my youth. Such things were the pursuits of the wealthy. I was a *peripoli.* I pursued a different quarry. "I have more experience hunting men. But my friends," I said, indicating Tibetos and Sabas, "are skilled with sling and bow. They could defend the honour of Athens, if only they had their gear."

But Pharnabazus had anticipated this. He snapped his fingers, and two slaves approached us. In their hands were Sabas' great Phrygian bow and Tibetos' sling, both of which had been confiscated upon our surrender to the Persian soldiers.

"It will be amusing to test your comrades' skill against that of my men," Pharnabazus explained, pleased to be able to demonstrate his magnanimity.

"And me?" I inquired. Pharnabazus pointed at one of the horses. The animal had a leather holder for a bow and arrows hung over its shoulders. "I have no skill with a bow," I said.

"Then we shall teach you, for no one surpasses Persians in archery," he said proudly. Sabas, with obvious effort, held his tongue. As Tibetos took his sling, the satrap peered at him intently. "You! Are you Athenian?"

"Of a sort, O Pharnabazus," Tibetos answered. "I was a slave once but I am a free man now."

Pharnabazus nodded as though his suspicion had been confirmed. "You have a Persian look about you. I have a cousin in the Great King's court who could be your twin."

"Others have said the same, O Pharnabazus."

"Then let us see today if you have the skill of your ancestors!" the satrap challenged.

Sabas, still piqued by the Persians' assertion of archery supremacy, stepped in. "I am Cretan by birth, O Satrap," he said, raising his chin slightly. "We are also renowned for our skill with a bow!"

Pharnabazus, perhaps unaccustomed to being addressed without permission, frowned at the slight, wiry figure of Sabas. Then he smiled coyly and spoke in Persian, evidently translating the *peripoli* archer's boast. The Persian soldiers broke into laughter. Sabas flushed, his pride pricked. I had never seen my long-time comrade and friend so irritated. It was going to be an interesting day.

The satrap seemed pleased to demonstrate his authority. With practiced competence, he directed his guards and attendants. Soon the hunting party was underway. Pharnabazus led the small procession through the streets of the city. As an ambassador, I was permitted to ride. Tibetos and Sabas were content to walk and chat with Babak. With some surprise I saw that Tolmides would be joining us. The Greek was also on foot, along with the foot soldiers and slaves. The small humiliation was deliberate on the part of Pharnabazus, no doubt. Tolmides trudged in expressionless silence, ignored by Pharnabazus and the soldiers, but too important to mingle with the slaves.

We wound past homes and shops and several of the square-columned shrines dedicated to their god Ahura Mazda. Residents in our path were sure to stop their business and step aside to allow the horses to pass, bowing their heads in deference to the satrap. "What would happen to Thrasybulus if he rode like this through Athens, I wonder?" muttered Tibetos, who was walking beside my horse. It was a fair question. In Athens, men were free to voice their opinions, right or wrong. Thrasybulus, or any other powerful man, would be met by greetings and jeers both, but mostly by indifference.

Outside the city walls, signs of habitation grew sparse and then vanished completely. In the forested hills, there were no glimpses of foragers or even the odd traveller. It was something I commented on to Pharnabazus, who rode beside me. "This is a *paradiso*," the satrap explained. "The game park is for the exclusive use of the Great King and members of the royal family. It is forbidden for others to hunt here."

"It is hard to enforce such a decree, especially when people have hungry families to feed," I said.

"You cannot feed your family at all if your corpse is hanging outside the city walls," Pharnabazus responded with a casual shrug. He spurred his mount forward to speak with his captain, leaving me to consider the sight of my rhomphaia slung across his back in its ridiculous new scabbard.

Cresting a rise, we were met by the sight of a vast lake. We gazed out over the coruscating surface at the distant hills on the opposite shore. A plain of reeds near the foreshore rippled in a cool breeze off the lake that fought back the growing heat of the day. The marsh teemed with songbirds and waterfowl. A small army of ducks erupted from the reeds, beating their wings madly to become airborne. The birds grew ever smaller as they headed out over the water. The richness of the area was a striking contrast to the rocky, hardscrabble land that surrounded Athens.

The lake disappeared from view as we descended into a broad valley. The forest broke up into copses and groves separated by wide areas of brush and grasses. Pharnabazus dropped back so that he was riding beside me. "This area is rich in game. Let us see what we can flush out," the satrap said, his dark eyes sparkling in anticipation of the sport ahead. "Perhaps even a boar or two?"

The riders spread out, their bows in hand, while the slaves with the boar-spears walked behind us. Tibetos twirled his sling lazily. To my left, an eruption of beating wings broke the calm as a rider disturbed a partridge in the brush. I heard the familiar whir of Tibetos' sling, and the partridge met its end in an explosion of feathers. Even the Persian soldiers cried out in admiration of the fine shot.

"A reward for that man!" Pharnabazus exclaimed as a slave scurried to retrieve the fallen bird. "I see that Athens has not diluted the blood of your homeland!" the satrap called out to Tibetos. I raised an eyebrow at my friend, who gave me an exaggerated bow.

It was only the first success of the day. As Pharabazus had promised, game was indeed abundant on the plain. A line of beaters shouted and thrashed the vegetation with sticks to flush out hares and game birds from their hiding places, and soon more than a dozen had fallen victim to the Persian archers. Pharnabazus, too, showed his skill, hitting a young fallow deer in the neck as it bounded across our path. A competition of sorts arose between the Persian horse archers, with their shorter, more highly curved bows, and Sabas, with his long Phrygian bow.

Pharnabazus, beaming after taking a long-tailed pheasant, called over to me. "And what about you, Athenian? Do you not shoot?" The satrap pointed to the unused bow resting in its case next to my hip.

Pharnabazus found an unexpected ally in Tibetos. My friend, having enjoyed success with his sling, seconded the satrap's suggestion. "Show us your skill, Dammo!" I shot him an irritated look, but my friend just grinned when Sabas joined the chorus.

In the churning carnage of a phalanx, where endurance and luck count as much as skill, I fight as well as any man. With a javelin, I am competent. But with a bow I am a poor shot, and with a sling I am more a danger to myself than my enemies. With great reluctance I lifted the bow from its pouch and nocked an arrow.

I did not have to wait long. Pharnabazus put a finger to his lips and then pointed at a clump of brush. A hare cowered there, motionless and almost invisible. An easy target. I raised my bow and drew the fletching to my cheek. The bow-string twanged as I loosed my shot. The arrow clattered on the ground behind the hare, which sprang into motion and bounded away. Pharnabazus and his men laughed at my poor marksmanship, and I felt a warm flush rising up my neck.

"It is fortunate you wagered on the Spartan's fighting skills rather than on your prowess with a bow!" the satrap joked. Even Tibetos and Sabas grinned at my failed attempt. I sighed and joined in their laughter, for I knew that they would gleefully share the tale with our *peripoli* comrades in Athens at every opportunity. Pharnabazus was graceful enough to save me from my embarrassment. "Perhaps we would do better to find a boar or some deer." He pointed to a densely wooded area farther ahead. "I have had luck in that area before."

As we drew near, Pharnabazus signalled for a halt. The beaters advanced to encircle the wooded area and flush out any large game that might lie concealed within. Men reached for their water skins to slake the built-up thirst from the morning's hunting. The Persians talked amongst themselves, as did Tibetos and Sabas a stone's throw away from me. Tolmides was near me and I shifted to speak to him. I checked my tongue when I saw that Greek was peering intently at the wooded area ahead.

I wondered what had captured the Greek's attention. What I lack in an archer's skill I make up for with an archer's eyesight. A tiny movement caught my eye. Not the flash of a bird or the flutter of leaves in a gust of breeze. Something else. My warrior's sense flared in warning. With the *peripoli*, I had lain hidden in forests and gullies too many times not to recognize an ambuscade. But it was too late. The enemy were already erupting from the trees when I called out.

"Ambush!"

CHAPTER 10

Ten or more barbarian horsemen burst from the woods with twice that number of bowmen and foot soldiers. Their leader barked something in his foreign tongue and half a dozen archers loosed their arrows.

I launched myself at Pharnabazus. My momentum drove the Persian from his mount just as a hail of arrows ripped through air and horseflesh. The satrap bore the brunt of the impact and he gasped as his breath was knocked from his lungs. Too late the satrap's men reacted as another volley of arrows from landed among the soldiers and the shouts turned to screams.

I scrabbled to my feet. Several of Pharnabazus' bodyguards lay on the ground, clutching at the arrows embedded in their bodies. Riderless horses ran amok, most with arrow shafts protruding from their necks or haunches. As more arrows fell, the Persian captain was still astride his mount, screaming at his remaining men to defend their fallen lord. Through the chaos I caught sight of Tibetos and Sabas. Tibetos' whirling sling loosed a stone at the attackers. An enemy horseman dropped his spear and clutched his shattered face before tumbling from his mount. Another enemy was knocked back as one of Sabas' arrows took him squarely in the chest. The enemy, now under attack, were charging at the fallen satrap. Cursing the gods, I seized the prone Pharnabazus.

The dazed satrap, misunderstanding my intentions, raised his hands weakly to ward off an attack. I swatted away the Persian lord's arms and roughly rolled him over. I seized Whisper and tore the rhomphaia violently from the flailing Pharnabazus, snapping the strap that bound her to him. I freed her from her garish prison and tossed scabbard aside. Rising up with Whisper in hand, I loomed over the paralyzed Pharnabazus, his eyes wide with fear. I growled and spun away from the Persian noble to face the horsemen pounding towards us.

There were three of them. The number dropped to two as another one of Sabas' arrows toppled one attacker from his horse. The Persian captain, an arrow protruding from his left shoulder charged into the attackers. Blood sprayed as his sword hacked into an enemy rider's neck. The remaining horseman was still galloping at me, his short cavalry spear levelled at my chest.

My instinct screamed at me to flee. But to run from a horseman is death either from a spear-thrust to the back or a sword-cut to the head and neck. When facing a rider, it is best to attack the horse, for it is a large target, and despite its great bulk, vulnerable, This is what my arms-master Neleus had drilled into me as a youth, and was something which I forced myself to do now. Whisper quivered in my hands. The rider tightened his hold on his spear and leaned out as he prepared to impale me.

I spun across the charging horse's path, dropping to my knees as I did so. Whisper trailed behind me, and as I came around I twisted my body forward, accelerating the blade in a wicked arc. The rhomphaia hacked into the horse's foreleg, the impact of the blow sending a shock through my wrists and arms. The beast screamed in pain and terror as its wounded leg snapped beneath its weight on the next stride, and the crippled animal collapsed in a skidding heap, sending its rider sailing through the air. The assassin crashed into the ground a few strides and lay motionless, his neck bent at an unnatural angle. Pharnabazus, who had managed to get to his feet, blinked at the dead man in disbelief.

I scanned the field for new threats. Half of Pharnabazus' men lay wounded or dead. The remaining soldiers, scattered and outnumbered, fought valiantly to protect their lord. Four of the enemy foot soldiers breached the loose defense and were rushing towards the vulnerable satrap. I was all that stood between the assassins and their prey. Screaming a Thracian battle-cry, I sprinted towards them.

The rhomphaia is an odd weapon. The four-foot, gently arcing blade takes two hands to wield properly. In the crush of a phalanx, it is almost useless. But in the open space like the one I now found myself in, it is deadly, combining the advantages of spear and sword and axe. The assassins had likely never even seen such a weapon, so rare was it at the time. They pulled up in the face of the copper-haired, screaming Thracian who was running at them.

I charged the nearest assassin. The leather-armoured warrior planted his feet and thrust his spear at me, but I twisted at the waist and guided the spear-tip harmlessly past me. Plunging forward, I twisted back, letting the power build from my waist to my shoulders and into my now extended arms. The rhomphaia's horizontal blade chopped through the man's cheek-guard to bury itself half-way into his skull. He was already dead as I ripped the weapon free and pivoted to face my next attacker.

The next warrior, armed with a straight Persian-style sword, fared little better. Before he came close, Whisper sliced off his ear and continued down to cleave through his collar bone at the neck. I jerked the blade free and dodged to my right to avoid the spear thrust of another attacker. My leap took me away from him but there was still a target. I hacked inelegantly but my aim did not need to be perfect. My blade scraped along the spear's shaft towards the man's forward hand. He screamed as Whisper severed his fingers. The spear dropped, and I slashed across the the spear-man's thighs. The rhomphaia's tip raked through the flimsy pants and thick muscle like a metal claw, and the man collapsed over his mutilated legs.

The mauled man had not even hit the ground before I pivoted towards the last attacker, another spear-man. I pulled up, giving the assassin a tempting stationary target. The spear-man took the bait, aiming a thrust at my chest. I parried the attack and flipped my right hand up to grasp the spear's shaft. I jerked the spear back. Instead of letting go as he should have, the spear-man maintained his firm grip on his weapon. Already off-balance from his attack, he fell towards me as I extended Whisper in front of me. The blade's point punched through the soft point at the base of his throat and out the back of his neck. His eyes widened in shock as I withdrew the blade and he released his spear at last to press his hands to his throat. The dying man fell to his knees as his fingers failed to dam the torrent of blood pumping from his wound. He toppled on his side, convulsing as the Underworld pulled his soul from his protesting body.

I sought new enemies, but the battle was over. The Persian captain and his three remaining soldiers now formed a screen in front of the recovered Pharnabazus, who was shouting orders at his men. I noted with surprise that Babak the Phrygian stood with them, a bloodied spear in his hands. The bodies of Pharnabazus' guards and those of the unknown attackers lay scattered about the plain. Riderless horses wandered here and there, seemingly oblivious to the carnage around them. Tibetos and Sabas trotted up to where I stood.

"There's one more," Tibetos said, pointing.

A lone horseman remained, surveying the results of the failed ambush in disbelief. The surviving rider wheeled his horse away and spurred the beast into a gallop. Pharnabazus, disheveled but alive, screamed at his remaining men to pursue, but no horse was without at least one arrow protruding from its flesh. The Persian captain shouted an order, and his men drew their bows and fired at the rider. But the enemy horseman was beyond the range of the Persian bows, and the arrows fell harmlessly to the earth.

Sabas stepped forward. The Cretan archer shut his eyes and inhaled deeply. Then in one motion, he raised his great Phrygian bow to a steep angle and drew the string back to his ear. He narrowed his eyes and lowered the bow by the breadth of a finger. The string thrummed and he arrow sailed in a high arc towards the fleeing assassin. It reached its apex and began its downward trajectory. A heartbeat later, the distant rider jerked and tumbled from his horse's back. There was an appreciative gasp for the *peripoli* archer's feat. Sabas did his best not to look smug.

I squinted. In the distance there was one more horseman, almost invisible against some high brush, an observer rather than a participant in the attack. Even at the great distance, I recognized the figure by his bearing, its having been seared into my memory since my youth. Orchus. Lysander, denied his gold, had also been denied his revenge. I blinked, but the Andrian mercenary had already vanished like smoke, escaping justice as was his way. I looked about at the others. No one else had seen him. I inhaled deeply, letting the blood-rage of battle and murder subside into the depths of my soul where they would rest until they erupted anew.

I surveyed the survivors. A few strides away stood Tolmides, whose shocked gaze moved from corpse to corpse. His eyes met mine and I saw fear there. Not a survivor's fear but a fear born of guilt. I recalled how the Greek had been staring at the woods before the attack. I levelled Whisper at Tolmides. "What did you know, Melian?"

The functionary's eyes widened. His mouth opened, but for a heartbeat no words came. I could see his mind racing and in that instant I knew that my suspicion, cast without proof, had struck the truth.

Too late, Tolmides denied the accusation. "I know nothing of this!"

The rhomphaia did not waver. "They knew we would be hunting. They knew where to wait."

The Greek's eyes darted between me and Pharnabazus. He pointed at shaking finger at me. "It was the Athenian!" he protested. "He is accusing me to draw attention away from himself! He must have been in league with Lysander!" Tolmides clamped his mouth shut, realizing too late that in accusing me he had revealed too much.

"How long have you been in Lysander's pay, Melian? How long have you been his spy?" I demanded.

Pharnabazus stepped forward. "You will regret your betrayal!" His voice seethed with cold fury. "You will wish for death a thousand times before my torturers are finished with you!" The satrap flicked his chin towards his traitorous interpreter, indicating that his men should seize him.

Trapped, Tolmides stepped back and let out a frustrated snarl. From within the folds of his cloak, a dagger appeared in his hand. Like a cornered dog, Tolmides attacked, lunging towards Pharnabazus.

I was faster. Whisper chopped down across the Greek's outstretched arm, cutting through sinew and bone. The severed hand fell to the ground still clutching the dagger. Tolmides blinked at the stump of his forearm.

The Persian soldiers, reacting at last, seized the bleeding Tolmides. Other Persians pointed their spears and swords uncertainly at me and my comrades. Pharnabazus scolded his men in a torrent of harsh Persian. With sheepish expressions, the soldiers lowered their weapons.

The satrap, glaring at the now ashen-faced Tolmides, barked an order in Persian. I thought the Greek would be executed on the spot, but I was wrong. Instead, the captain tore a strip from the interpreter's garment and tied it tightly around the disgraced official's bleeding arm. Tolmides shrieked in pain and then passed out.

The satrap surveyed the scattered dead before turning his gaze on me. "You spoke the truth before, Athenian."

"The truth?" I asked.

"You said you are a hunter of men." He smiled grimly. "I believe you now."

I still had Whisper. Holding the rhomphaia with an inverted grip, I offered the hilt to Pharnabazus. "Your weapon, O Satrap," I said flatly.

Pharnabazus stared at me. His fine hunting robes were dishevelled and sullied with dirt and blood. He turned his gaze skyward for a moment and then back to me. "Keep it, Athenian. I would be a fool to ignore such a clear rebuke from Ahura Mazda. I was wrong to have taken it from you."

Relief flooded into my heart. It was like a lost limb had suddenly been returned to me. "You are generous, O Pharnabazus," I said, being careful to hide my joy. "What will happen to him?" I asked, glancing at the unconscious Tolmides.

Pharnabazus' expression became as hard and cold as stone. "He will be dealt with."

He issued some more orders and the surviving soldiers began rounding up the few surviving horses for the journey back to the city, leaving the dead where they lay. The satrap had promised an eventful day.

He had not been wrong.

THE PERSIAN CAPTAIN ARRIVED at our residence the next morning. His new helmet bore a green crest and I wondered if he had been promoted. He still spoke in gruff, unintelligible Persian. We had been summoned to an audience with Pharnabazus, Babak explained. All of us were to attend. Tibetos and Sabas exchanged a curious look. The captain was our only escort, a change from the usual bevy of guards.

Pharnabazus, reclining on his throne-like chair, had regained his splendid opulence. I bowed to the Persian noble, a lead followed by Tibetos and Sabas. Beside me, a quivering Babak prostrated himself before his lord.

The satrap rose to his feet, his grin wide and his arms wider. "Come to me, my friend!" he boomed. He crushed me in a powerful embrace. Stepping back, he regarded me appreciatively before turning his attention to TIbetos and Sabas. "Let it not be said that Pharnabazus is ungrateful or ungenerous. I reward you both for your service to the Great King." He beckoned two slaves, who brought forth gifts for my friends. Each received a small box filled with silver and something more. "For you, Cretan, the finest bow from my armoury. You have shown yourself worthy to wield it."

Sabas was uncharacteristically humble. "You honour me, O Pharnabazus," he said, admiring the beautifully wrought bow. "Never have I held such a weapon."

Acknowledging the archer with a beneficent nod, the satrap addressed Tibetos. "And you, Tibetos. Though you return to Athens, you must not forget your Persian soul. I grant you your true name, *Artabanu*." Another slave came forward bearing a chest. They laid it down and opened the lid to reveal a sumptuous set of Persian robes.

Tibetos bowed. "I will treasure both these things, O Pharnabazus," he said, his voice cracking with emotion. I was surprised, for my friend was not one to wear his feelings openly. The satrap beamed.

There was another who had helped me in his own small way. I made a quiet cough. Pharnabazus turned to me. "There is something else, Athenian?"

I glanced down at Babak. The Phrygian guide had not moved from his prostrate position. "May my guide rise?" I asked Pharnabazus.

"He may."

I gave Babak a small kick. The Phrygian reluctantly left his place of safety on the floor. Pharnabazus looked at him like a man buying a sheep in the market. "Is he a good man?" the satrap asked.

"He has done well by us," I answered honestly.

Pharnabazus sniffed. "What languages do you speak?"

Babak nearly jumped. "Greek, Persian, Phrygian, Thracian, Kolkian, Phoenician, and some Aegyptian, my lord," he managed to stammer.

Pharnabazus arched an eyebrow. "Where did you learn?"

"My father was a trader, my lord," Babak said, staring at the floor.

"What is your name?"

"Babak, my lord."

Pharnabazus pursed his lips. "I find myself in need of a new interpreter, Babak. Ahura Mazda smiles upon you this day."

"Yes, my lord," Babak said. Pharnabazus pointed to a spot on the ground next to his chair. Babak scurried from my side to take his position beside his new master.

"And you, Athenian," Pharnabazus said to me. "It is no small matter to save the life of a satrap," Pharnabazus said. He settled back in his seat and waved an idle hand. "Name your favour and it is yours if it is in my power to grant it."

"What I want will cost you nothing, O Pharnabazus," I said.

Pharnabazus sighed. "Yet somehow I sense that the price will still be high."

"Merely a life for a life, O Pharnabazus," I said.

The satrap knitted his brow. "What is it you want, Athenian?"

I took a deep breath. "The Spartan. Neon. Free him from his prison and I will take him back to Athens with me." Tibetos gave me a curious look. To this day I do not know why I asked such a thing. Neon was a Spartan, an enemy. But he was an enemy of Lysander as well, something that raised my estimation of him. He had also, in his own unexpected way, helped me succeed in my mission. Like Pharnabazus, I felt a sense of obligation to those who did me good.

Pharnabazus' frown deepened. "He killed many men before we captured him," he said. "*Many* men," he repeated more softly.

"Yet it is in your power to free him," I reminded him, holding the Persian noble's stare.

Pharnabazus broke first, spreading his hands in concession. "Athenians have never lacked for boldness. I grant you your request." He raised a finger. "On the condition that the Spartan swears an oath never to return to the lands of the Great King."

"Done, O Pharnabazus" I answered.

The satrap cleared his throat. "Speaking of the Spartan, there is also the matter of the money I owe you from our wager." He clapped three times and the great doors of the hallway groaned open. I do not know what I had expected. Perhaps a parade of slaves bearing chest after chest of money. The satrap had shown himself fond of such grand gestures. But no heaps of silver or piles of gold were forthcoming. Instead, a small man dressed in Greek-style robes strode across the hall to stand expectantly before us.

I blinked in confusion. "I don't understand."

Pharnabazus chuckled at my perplexity. "Here is your gold, Athenian!"

The slight man cleared his throat to draw my attention back to him. "Perhaps I should explain. I am Timokrates," he said, as though this would make things clear. "Timokrates of Rhodes."

CHAPTER 11

Timokrates was not made of gold but he may have well have been.

The Rhodian would accompany the shipment of gold back to Athens with a message: this was just the first of many such payments if Athens and her allies would make war on Sparta.

"It is a small amount," Pharnabazus sniffed. "A gesture of goodwill from the Great King."

A small amount! I shook my head as I watched dozens of chests being loaded onto a Persian trireme, each weighty box filled to the brim with Persian *darics*. Each gold coin was stamped with an image of the Great King wielding a bow, leaving no doubt to the Athenians as to who their benefactor was.

Soon I would follow the precious cargo up the gangplank, a thought that sent a shiver of dread up my neck. I am a poor excuse for an Athenian, for unlike most of my countrymen I fear the sea. I would rather stand in the front ranks of a phalanx three times than board a ship. But board the trireme I would, unless I wanted to travel overland for a month or more. To distract myself from the looming voyage, I spoke with Babak.

"You have done well for yourself, Babak," I said. It was true. The Phrygian's hair and beard were now styled in the Persian fashion and he wore the colorful garments favoured by those people. There was even a flash of gold from a few pieces of jewelry.

Babak beamed. "Sraosha has answered my prayers!" he said.

"Sraosha?"

"A servant of Ahura Mazda," he explained. A look of resolve told of him. "I will serve my lord Pharnabazus as Sraosha serves Ahura Mazda. I will bring honour and wealth to my family!"

"Don't let it go to your head," I warned him "Remember what fate befell Tolmides."

Babak's dark complexion paled slightly, for he too had seen the Greek's flayed body tied to a post outside the city walls. "I will serve with humility... and caution," he said, amending his previous declaration. "In fact," he said, glancing uncertainly at the setting sun, "Perhaps it is time for me to return to my lord Pharnabazus."

He communicated this desire to the Persian captain, who had accompanied us from the satrap's palace with a small army of soldiers. The captain nodded and turned his grim gaze on me with his teeth bared. I tensed, expecting some harsh words, but then realized the grimace was in fact the soldier's version of a grin. We shook hands, warrior to warrior. No words were needed. He turned to bawl another stream of commands at his troops.

As the Persian soldiers made ready for their departure, the trireme's captain strode down the gangplank. His wavy hair and thick beard had gone to grey but he moved with the strength and grace of a younger man. His dark, leathery skin attested to many years of weathering by sun, wind, and salt-spray on the open sea. His simple clothing was Greek in style, a thick gold chain the only indication of his rank. He stopped in front of me, his deep-set, intelligent eyes sizing me up.

"The cargo has been loaded," he said in a clean Athenian accent. "We can embark as soon as you're on board." It was a voice of a man comfortable with wielding authority. Even as he spoke, crewmen with their oars, cushions, and their kit-bags of provisions were marching up the gangplank like ants returning to their nest.

"We will not wait until morning?" I asked, surprised.

The captain looked unconcerned by the prospect. "The Hellespont is patrolled by Spartan ships during the day. I'd rather avoid the wolves if I can. We can slip by the ports at night. The current is strong and will take us to the sea by morning, by which time it will be too late for the thick-headed bastards to do anything."

I regarded the sleek Persian trireme sceptically. "The ship is up to the task?"

The captain scoffed. "It is called the *Arstibara*. Pharnabazus' pride and joy."

"The *Arstibara*?" I asked, my tongue experimenting with the unfamiliar Persian word.

"It means "Spear-Bearer," he explained. "Flies almost as fast as a spear, too."

There was another thing I had noticed. "You have taken down the mast?"

"Leaving it behind," the captain said. "And no marines either. Your cargo is heavy and I have to compensate if we're to stand a chance of outrunning any wolves we come across. The sooner we get to Athens, the better." He said the name Athens as though it left a bad taste in his mouth despite his Athenian accent. I was curious.

"You are from Athens?" I asked.

A wary edge crept into the captain's sharp gaze. "Once, perhaps."

I pressed on. "I would know your name, Captain, if we are to sail together."

The man weighed me with his stare before answering. "I am Konon, *admiral* of the Great King's western fleet."

Konon. It was a name that every Athenian would recognize, but a name that carried with it both honour and disgrace. He had been a *strategos* during the war with Sparta. Then came the disaster at Aegospotomi when Lysander captured the bulk of the Athenian fleet, a defeat that forced Athens to its knees in humiliating and absolute surrender. Konon had been one of the few to escape the trap, fleeing the debacle with ten ships. But instead of returning to Athens, he had gone to Persia and done quite well for himself, judging by his current rank. It had been an understandable choice. Had he returned to Athens, he most likely would have been blamed for the disaster and executed, even though he had not been in command of the fleet. I did not blame him, but many in Athens would hold a different view. He was no doubt aware that I knew this, and his expression dared me to challenge him.

I held out my hand. "We place ourselves in your hands, Admiral."

Konon shook my hand. "You are Athenian as well, by sound if not by appearance," he said, glancing at my odd armour and weapon.

"I am Daimon, son of Nikodromos," I confirmed.

Konon's expression softened a touch. "I know of you. I knew your father. He was a good man."

"I serve Thrasybulus, son of Lykos," I added.

Something rippled under the flat expression on Konon's weather-beaten face. "A more... complicated man," was all he said of Thrasybulus. Whatever he felt about Thrasybulus was a discussion for another time, for the last of the rowers had boarded. The Great King's admiral extended an arm towards the gangplank. "Poseidon waits for no man."

The Rhodian Timokrates greeted Konon as he passed. "I trust this journey will be as uneventful as the last one?"

"By the will of the gods, it will be so," said the erstwhile Athenian *strategos*. I could not help notice that he touched the iron hilt of the sailor's knife at his belt as he said this to ward off ill fortune. Konon nodded at Sabas and Tibetos as they followed Timokrates onto the ship. As Neon approached, Konon moved to block his path. "I'll have no Spartan on board my ship," he said, eyeing Neon's distinctive braids.

"He is my charge," I said. "I guarantee his good conduct."

"A prisoner?" Konon asked suspiciously. "If so, he should be bound."

I glanced at Neon, who stared ahead, expressionless. Was he my prisoner? "An ally. Without him, there would be no gold bound for Athens," I said, jerking a thumb towards the trireme.

Konon was unmoved. "I've never met a Spartan I could trust."

I tried another tack. "I watched him kill two of Lysander's men, and would have cut down Lysander in a heartbeat had the opportunity arisen. He is our enemy's enemy."

Konon narrowed his eyes, reappraising Neon. "An exile, then?" Neon's cheek twitched. "Not only a Spartan but also a traitor?" Konon prodded, not trying to hide his disgust.

Neon's face tightened and he fixed his flat stare on Konon. "You may bind me if you fear me, Athenian," he said.

Konon scoffed. "It sounds like a Spartan trick if even I heard one!" He frowned, coming to his decision. "You may board. But," he said, poking a stiff finger in the Spartan's chest. "If you cause even a single hair on my neck to stand on end, I'll have you tossed overboard to feed the fish, by Poseidon!"

The Spartan acknowledged the threat with the barest dip of his head. Konon moved aside to let him pass. Neon paused. "I am grateful for your generous hospitality," he said and strode up the gangplank.

Konon watched the Spartan's back with a curious stare. "I think that Spartan just made a joke, by Zeus."

"He's not your typical Spartan," I confirmed before ascending the gangplank myself.

We cast off under a darkening sky. Dock-workers pushed against the trireme with stout poles and the warship drifted away from the wharf. At Konon's command, nearly three hundred rowers extended their oars and dipped the blades into the calm water of the harbour. The slow pulse of the drum began and the oars moved in gentle unison with the beat. Like a great beast awakening from its slumber, the

Arstibara lurched into motion. The experienced sailors manoeuvred the trireme through the narrow entrance of the harbour and into the open water beyond. Soon we were in the narrow strip of the Hellespont, travelling south to the open sea.

OUR PARTY SAT ON THE FRONT DECK OF THE SHIP. The Spartan Neon found a space away from the rest of us, covered himself with his cloak, and promptly fell asleep under the light of the waxing moon. Sabas sat at the very prow of the ship, his feet hanging over the edge as though he were riding a giant horse. The mad Cretan sang to himself in the odd dialect of his home, a sailor's song from the island he had left so long ago. Some of the rowers below-decks, Cretans themselves perhaps, had joined in the gentle tune as they matched the easy stroke Konon had set for them. Tibetos and I watched the darkening silhouette of the western shore slip by, each of us lost in our own thoughts. I shifted my position for the hundredth time.

My discomfort drew a sympathetic chuckle from my friend. "I think you're getting better at sea travel, Dammo. You're as pale as a corpse, but that's an improvement from how you usually look when you're on a ship."

I forced a wan smile and waved weakly at the calm sea. "As long as the water stays like this, but Poseidon is capricious." I shuddered at the thought of rougher seas.

Tibetos knew the reason for my fear. We had once spent a night in a raging tempest lashed to the shattered wreck of a half-sunken trireme. Tibetos showed no ill effects from the storm, but then again he had been unconscious for the better part of it. I had been awake for all of it, listening as the fury of the sea god tore our ship to splinters. Since that time I could hardly set foot on a ship without feeling the cold touch of fear on my neck.

My friend put a reassuring hand on my shoulder. "Maybe we'll be lucky and get in a battle," he said dryly.

I grunted. "You know me too well. At least that's something I could control."

The sea may not have troubled my friend, but some thoughts rippled even his calm soul. Beyond the western shore lay Thrace. Tibetos gaze lingered. "What do you think she's doing right now, Dammo?" he asked at last.

He did not need to name the person of whom he spoke. Somewhere inland from the coast, deep in the wilds of Thrace, was my sister Melitta. She had heeded the call of the Thracian gods of our ancestors and was learning their mysteries. She had been gone for more than a year. I missed her. But Tibetos missed her more, for he loved her.

"I'm sure she is safe," I said. I did not doubt it, for my sister was a formidable woman. She possessed a hidden sight and could perceive the will of the gods. She was skilled in secret spells and curses, but was not above burying a knife in a man's ribs if necessary. "And causing trouble," I added. Tibetos allowed himself a sad smile.

"She comes to me in my dreams sometimes," Tibetos said. "But not for some time. I wonder if she has forgotten me."

"You are a fool for thinking so, Tibo. The acropolis will crumble before my sister's loyalty ever will!" I had faith in my assertion, but I knew how doubt infected the heart of a man in love. Such thoughts were a pale memory for me, for love's madness was something I had not suffered for a long time.

That is not to say I did not suffer other things. As if hearing our musings, the old gods of Thrace responded with a cool wind from the north. As such things are reckoned, it was merely a breeze, but it was enough to set the ship rolling gently from side to side. Tibetos secured me as I retched over the side of the ship for the third time since our departure. My stomach had long since emptied itself of its contents. The Spartan Neon had roused himself to witness my ordeal, his face betraying neither sympathy nor amusement.

Perceiving my misery, Konon strolled up the length of the trireme from his position at the stern of the ship to where I sat, hunched over and trying to focus on the wood of the deck. Sparing a suspicious glance at Neon, the admiral stared down at me quizzically. "You have not often been to sea?" he asked.

I wiped some sour spittle from my cheek. "More often than I'd like."

He took a deep breath of salt air and scanned the horizon. "This is nothing. In the autumn, especially, storms can appear from nowhere, as if driven by the Furies themselves!"

"I know," I said, calming my guts with a deep breath.

Konon raised an eyebrow. "You speak from experience?"

"I was at Arginusae," I said. Even uttering the name of that accursed place was enough to wake terrors that were best left sleeping. I shuddered.

Konon pursed his lips. He knew what I had left unsaid. "You survived the storm?"

I nodded. "And Tibo, too."

Tibetos scoffed. "I was unconscious for most of it, thank Bendis," he said, invoking the Thracian goddess, a habit he had picked up from my sister. "Dammo held me the whole time. Otherwise I'd be down there," he said, glancing at the sea.

"It was a terrible thing," Konon said simply. "Try to get some sleep tonight. Tomorrow I might have something that will cure your ills."

KONON WOKE ME AT DAWN. "We have exited the Hellespont," he informed me. Konon was not the only one awake. Some of the rowers had come on deck to stretch and take their morning piss off the edge of the ship. I groaned as I rose unsteadily to my feet. In the morning light I saw that we had indeed left the narrow confines of the Hellespont.

Konon handed me a wineskin. "Drink this," he ordered. The spicy liquid coated my mouth and throat, masking the taste of stale vomit.

I wiped some wine from my chin. "The rowers must be tired," I said, jerking a thumb at the rowers on deck.

Konon shook his head. "The current did most of the work. They rowed in shifts while the others snatched some sleep." I imagined that a space on a rowing bench did not make for the most pleasant sleeping berth.

"And no attention from the Spartans?" I asked.

Konon touched the iron pommel of his knife to ward off misfortune. "Not yet, by Zeus, and I'd like to keep it that way!" The delicately balanced ship rocked as resting oarsmen walked to and fro on the deck. My stomach churned the recently swallowed wine in protest. Konon gave me a knowing look. "Still haven't gotten your sea legs?"

"You mentioned a remedy yesterday?"

The admiral's eyes glinted with mischief. "Just come with me." Supporting me, he led me back towards the stern of the warship. He stopped at an open hatch and pointed at it. I took his meaning.

"You want me to row?" I said incredulously.

Konon winked. "In my experience, a good remedy for seasickness is to impose a greater discomfort!"

I was dubious. "Curing a headache by cutting off your head?"

"Something along those lines." Konon extended an arm towards the open hatch. I resigned myself to my fate and descended into the bowels of the trireme.

Bowels was an apt description, for the air reeked of piss, sweat and the stale breath of the labouring rowers. Some light and air managed to penetrate the space through the gap between the top of the hull and the raised deck, but it was not enough to conquer the darkness and stink of the Stygian place.

Nearly three hundred men packed the trireme's interior like so many salted fish in a clay pot, but the clever seating arrangement made it so. On either side of the narrow central aisle were three banks of rowers almost stacked one on top of the other. The topmost bank sat beside the open gap above the hull, their scalps barely a hand's breadth below the deck overhead. For the precious air and the view, it was a coveted position, though more vulnerable to missiles during a battle, even with the tough leather battle flaps lowered for protection. The cheeks of the next row of men were at the level of the hips of the men above them. Below them even further, hugging opposite sides of the keel were the poor souls condemned to breathe the farts and stale air of their comrades above them.

Only about half the men were rowing while the others rested themselves for the hard day ahead. As one, the active rowers bent forward, pushing their oar handles with extended arms. Then, with a collective release of breath, the men leaned back and drew the oar handles to their chests. The sheen of sweat made their flexing backs and shoulders appear more like cut stone than human flesh. Again and again the rowers swept through the oar-stroke with perfect coordination. It reminded me more than anything of some great galloping horse, its lungs working like some great bellows as its churning muscles propelled it ever forward.

As if reading my thoughts, Konon cupped a hand to his mouth. "It is like a living beast, is it not?"

Before I could respond, the light from the hatch above dimmed as another figure descended into the depths of the ship. It was Neon. "I would join you," he said. "My imprisonment has stolen my strength and I wish to regain it. And," he said, fixing his flat gaze on Konon, "I would earn my passage on your ship alongside the Athenian."

Konon's face tightened at the Spartan's presumptuousness. I thought he would deny Neon's request but the Athenian admiral relented with a grunt of acquiescence. Konon sized us up. "You're both big — too big to be real rowers, by Zeus! Best take the middle row or else you'll be banging your heads against the underside of the deck.

Konan stepped down a level and put his hands on the shoulders of the two rearmost rowers. "Agros! Eubonides! The gods smile on you today! Give your oars to these men and go up above!"

The two rowers stopped and leaned on their oars to keep them from blocking the strokes of their fellow rowers in front of them. The bare-chested men regarded Konon suspiciously. "Will we still get our pay?" one of the pair demanded, a square-headed man with close-cropped black hair.

"These men will earn your day's wages for you," Konon confirmed. It was a reminder that the men were not slaves but paid labourers.

The rowers' demeanour changed instantly. "In that case, have at it," the short-haired man said. Konan shouted for the other oarsmen to stop rowing. There was a clatter of scraping wood as men pulled their oars in to take advantage of the moment of respite. Curious stares turned to smiles and laughter as Neon and I stripped down and awkwardly exchanged places with the two rowers. The Spartan's stony glare dampened the spectators' amusement, but only somewhat.

"We will slow the pace to start with. Agros will instruct you until you get the rhythm of it. Eubonides will call the stroke." With that, he left us under the tutelage of the veteran rowers.

The focus required to stay in time with the other rowers demanded all of my concentration. The heavy blade was counterbalanced by a block of wood and a lead weight just beyond the handle, but the motion was awkward. At first our oars clipped those of the rowers around us or skipped above the water, and I could see that Neon's frustration matched my own. Soon, though, under the exasperated direction of Agros, our technique improved. My heart flickered with pleasure as the unseen blade of the oar bit into the surface of the invisible sea on the other side of the hull. My muscles responded to the task, loosening with every stroke. Konon was right. Without knowing it, the sickness that had been plaguing me dissipated as new forms of discomfort manifested themselves.

I was no stranger to exertions, yet the simple, repetitive act of sweeping the heavy oar was punishing. My hands were calloused from wielding sword and spear but the oar somehow found new places to raise angry blisters. Years of riding had toughened my backside, but soon I was as sore as a first-time rider despite the the thin cushion between me and the beam on which I sat. As the day wore on, each stroke seemed to edge closer to pulling my arms from their sockets. But it was pain honestly earned and I felt better for it. I glanced at Neon. The Spartan, sensing my eyes on him, grimaced as he doubled his effort. I grinned and shook my head. I was labouring in the guts of a semi-dark warship like a shade enduring eternal punishment in Tartarus, but I was happy enough. So I began to sing.

It was an old song. My father had sung it, and my grandfather before him, and back even farther than that, or so my father had told me. I barely finished one verse before more of the rowers joined in. Soon the men's ringing voices lit up that shadowy place and lightened the rowers' toils, if only by a little. I glanced at the Spartan Neon, catching a hint of a smile that flickered and vanished.

The rest of the day passed both quickly and slowly in that odd way that mindless labour robs us of our sense of time. In the evening, we arrived at a small island. The beat of the oars slowed and then came a shout from above. "Oars out!" We drifted a moment until I felt the gentle crunch of the ship running up on the shingle of the beach. The rowers Agros and Eubonides came to reclaim their equipment.

"We'll make rowers of you yet!" a well-rested Agros grinned.

Every muscle in my body protested as I rose from my bench for the first time since the morning. "If I'd known it was so easy, I would have taken it up years ago," I said, massaging my cramped hands. Neon gave a grunt that might have been a laugh.

CHAPTER 12

Tibetos greeted us as we emerged on deck from our day's confinement. "You look like you've risen from the dead!"

"More than you know," I said, giving him a haggard smile. Rowers streamed past, sparing us a curious look before clambering down to the beach.

Sabas chimed in. "You've missed your true calling, Boy!"

I flexed my aching arms. "Why not? I'm an Athenian after all! And you, O Neon?" I said, addressing the dour Spartan.

Rolling his stiff shoulders, Neon grimaced. "I am no Athenian!" We laughed at his proclamation and went to gather our gear before disembarking.

We joined the entire crew, Konon included, in hauling the trireme ashore. "There's a fishing village on the far side, but they'll be no bother," Konon explained once the ship was secure. "And there's a spring just up the hill."

"You've been here before?" I asked, surveying the deserted beach.

Konon scratched at his ear. "I know every rock and cove in the Aegean," he said. "I'd be a poor admiral if I didn't."

Timokrates fretted over the safety of the cargo. "We are vulnerable here. What if we are attacked?"

"Better here than Lemnos," Konon said, pointing at a large island in the distance. "Too many Spartan ships there. In any case, we'll leave at sunrise tomorrow well before anyone gets it in their heads to investigate."

The local islanders discovered us soon enough, bringing all manner of food and drink. The haggling was intense, but the locals were at advantage, for we had little to eat. Provisioned and a little poorer, the rowers broke off into their accustomed groups and began to set up camps scattered along the beach. We did the same, gathering some firewood before night fell. Timokrates stayed with Konon, and I saw the two deep in conversation, the agitated Rhodian and the calm Athenian. I shrugged, for it was not my affair.

Later, our bellies satisfied if not full, we began to talk, as men do around a fire. The long-simmering thoughts of the day found their voice as we drank the piss-poor wine purchased from the islanders.

"I do not understand Tolmides," I said, prodding the fire with a stick. The Greek's grim fate had played in my mind as I toiled at my oar. "He had prestige and wealth, yet he betrayed Pharnabazus. For what? What could he have gained?"

Tibetos snorted. "It's because you have never been a slave, Dammo."

"What do you mean?"

Tibetos was silent for a moment as he collected his thoughts. "You don't know the humiliation of it, Dammo. To be insulted all the time. To be struck like a dog but be unable to fight back. That stays with you like a scar on your soul. You know, there is hardly a day that I don't think of that shit-eater Adrastos at least once." There was a bitter edge of vehemence to my friend's voice that surprised me, for he was by nature gentle and thoughtful. My older brother Adrastos had enjoyed tormenting Tibetos when we were children, especially when I was not there to defend him. But I had not realized the depth of hatred that still lingered in my friend's heart.

"But he's dead now," I said, for I had slain my treacherous sibling. Tibetos had spat on his corpse.

"Not to me," Tibetos said. An uncomfortable silence settled over the campfire.

Sabas addressed Neon. "So what is your story, Spartan?" the Cretan asked. Tibetos relaxed as the scrutiny shifted to our unexpected companion.

Neon had not uttered a word the entire evening, The Spartan kept his gaze fixed on the fire. "Did your friend not already tell you?"

"Only that you hate Lysander and killed three of your countrymen," Sabas said.

Neon grunted and drained his cup, his fourth by my reckoning. He cast a look my way. "Is that not enough, then?"

Sabas was not to be put off. "But what is the reason for Lysander's grudge against you?"

"I left his service. Lysander is not one to forgive such a betrayal."

Sabas scoffed. "What does one less soldier mean to someone who commands thousands?"

"I was his *aitas* once."

The eyebrows of Tibetos and Sabas rose in unison. In Athens, it was not uncommon for older men, especially among the wealthy, to pursue a handsome youth as a lover. In Sparta, however, a young Spartiate was expected to become the *aitas* of a older man, accepting the senior warrior as both lover and mentor. That Neon had been

Lysander's *aitas* explained a great deal. In Sparta, the bond of loyalty between *aitas* and his senior was a sacred one, continuing even after the youth became a man himself. The rift between Lysander and Neon would have to have been deep indeed to destroy such a relationship.

Sabas pressed on. "But now Lysander's star has dimmed. What does it matter if you leave his service? Go serve King Pausanias! Go serve King Agesilaus!"

Neon fixed his interrogator with a long stare. "It is not so simple, Cretan."

"Then serve no one! Go back to your lands and raise a litter of Spartan pups!" Sabas said, baiting the Spartan. It was a dangerous game.

Neon's face tightened. "I have no lands to return to. My father disinherited me." The fire snapped and crackled while we considered the Spartan's statement.

Sabas' adversarial tone softened. "Tell us your tale, O Spartan, and I promise our ears will sit in fair judgment of you."

For a long time Neon stared at the fire. I thought Sabas had pushed him to silence, but at last the Spartan spoke. "Who lost the great war? Athens or Sparta?"

"Do you seek to shame us?" Sabas retorted.

Neon held up an appeasing hand. "Just a simple question."

Sabas, as quick to humour as he was to anger, laughed. "Now the Spartan plays Sokrates with us!" Tibetos and I laughed, and the tension subsided. "Since you ask, O Sokrates," Sabas said. "Sparta won. Athens lost."

Neon snorted. "Did you? Lose the war, I mean? By the twin gods, I'm not so sure!"

Sabas shook his head. "The walls of Athens are torn down. She has been stripped of her navy. She has lost her empire. All her former subjects now pay tribute to Sparta. So, yes, Spartan, I would say that Athens lost the war!"

"Things are not always as they seem, Cretan. On the outside, Sparta looks strong, but inside her guts are decaying," Neon said.

"What do you mean?" I asked.

Neon gave a bitter laugh. "It is just that in the end, by losing your empire, you Athenians may have succeeded in destroying Sparta."

Sabas was having none of it. "Win by losing? Now you go too far, by Zeus!"

"Did the gods not punish Athens for her arrogance by spreading plague amongst you?" We knew of what he spoke. At the beginning of the war, before I was even born, the sickness, the *vosos*, had cut through the city like a scythe through stalks of grain, filling the streets with corpses and the air with the smoke of funeral pyres. My own father had survived but bore the scars of the illness for the rest of his life. Neon looked at us in turn. "Now the gods curse Sparta with a plague of sorts."

Sabas made a sign against the evil eye. "There is plague in Sparta?" he asked, a touch of dread creeping into his voice.

Neon gave the Cretan a feral grin. "Of sorts. The tribute that once flowed to Athens now pours into Sparta. But the wealth is tainted. It is like a disease has infected the soul of my people. It harms us more than any spear or sword."

Sabas snorted. "A disease I would suffer with pleasure!"

Neon shot the Cretan a scornful look. "You do not understand. In the past, Spartans respected the laws of Lycurgus. Money was forbidden. Men possessed only what they needed and nothing more. Men distinguished themselves by their deeds and their character, not by their wealth."

Tibetos was quick to interject. "*Spartiates* were equal, you mean. Not the helot slaves who tilled your lands and fed you," he said pointedly.

Neon allowed himself the hint of a smile. "You have no slaves in Athens? Do slaves not toil in your silver mines and quarries? Does not every farmer have slaves to help him gather his crops?" I sensed my friend's hackles rising.

I intervened for the sake of peace. "No slaves serve the *peripoli*. Every man, woman, and child in the compound is free." I looked at Tibetos, who just sniffed and turned his gaze back towards the fire. "But continue your story, Spartan," I said, for in truth I was curious about what had befallen the exiled warrior.

Neon picked up his tale. "My father and I have always quarrelled. He believes that it is Sparta's right to rule over all of Greece, a view shared by too many of my countrymen. But there are others, like me, who believe that Spartans should mind our own affairs, as our ancestors did. The gods will punish us for our arrogance," he said, looking at me, "Just as they punished Lysander in Thrace."

"You had a falling out with your father?" I asked.

"In a word, yes, but it was my brother Kleagoras who turned the old man against me. The snake!" Neon exclaimed with sudden ferocity.

"How?"

Neon reined in his anger. "According to the ancient laws, my father's lands would have passed on to me, the oldest son."

"And what of your brother?"

"He could acquire land by marrying into a family with no sons. It is common enough, for many Spartans have died fighting on foreign soil. This is as it has always been, until recently."

"But your brother did not accept his lot, I take it?" I asked.

"My brother has a talent for acquiring wealth," Neon said. "On campaigns, I fought for Sparta. My brother fought for treasure. There was no battle that he did not profit handsomely from. While I followed the ways of my forebears, my brother's hoard of wealth grew and grew."

"What did your father think?"

Neon's upper lip curled in disgust. "My brother's wealth impressed him. He scolded me for not bringing my own plunder. Kleagoras brought honour to our family, my father said, while I brought nothing. I accused him of abandoning the Spartan way and our relationship grew ever more fraught. It was what my brother had been waiting for. He offered all his wealth to my father if only my father would make him his heir. My father asked me if I could outbid my brother, but I refused, for the inheritance was my right. My father disagreed and gave Kleagoras what he wished."

The Fates are cruel, I thought, but many had suffered worse. "Can you not mend the relationship with your father?" I asked.

Neon grunted. "Only if I venture to the Underworld. My father died soon after he made Kleagoras his heir."

"How?"

"He died in his sleep, or so I was told."

"You believe your brother had a hand in it?" I asked.

"I would not be surprised. But whether or not it was so, my brother saw his opportunity to harm me further. His serpent tongue spread rumours that I had murdered my father with poison. Men cast suspicious eyes my way because of my brother's slanders against me." Neon's voice flared with unexpected anger. "My fellow Spartans! I fought beside them! Many of them now live only because my spear saved them!" He remembered himself and let his tone subside back to Laconic flatness. "I was landless. I could not afford my place in the mess hall. My poverty made me an outcast."

And I began to understand. "And Lysander?" I prompted.

"Lysander promised to restore my property." Neon hung his head. "I am ashamed to say I believed him, so desperate was I to retake my place among my fellow Spartans. But the longer I was in his company, the more I saw him for what he truly is. He has no honour. Only ambition and malice. Like my brother. Then in Thrace, when you defeated him," he said, sweeping a hand towards us, "I saw that the gods were punishing him for his hubris. I told him as much before I left his service to join Agesilaus in Ionia." Neon lifted his head and regarded us, his eyes flashing. "I don't think Lysander has forgiven me."

"Why did you not go to Pausanias?" I asked.

Neon's expression turned to distaste. "Pausanias prefers my brother's company. Kleagoras has poisoned the king's mind against me. This is no great accomplishment, for the king is weak of character." He cocked an eyebrow at me. "And I have heard it rumoured that you gave Pausanias a thrashing in Thrace last year?"

"I had a small part in it," I conceded.

Neon gave the barest of smiles. "I have heard differently." He leaned forward. "Is it true you killed a Spartiate with your bare hands? While Pausanias and his army looked on and did nothing?" he asked in a low voice. The question hung in the air. My companions knew that Neon's question brought forth painful memories.

I looked into my cup. "I am not proud of it."

"His name was Gorax — the man you killed. A good man to stand beside in the phalanx, but cruel in nature. It is no great loss. I only wish it had been my brother! He was there, cowering beside Pausanias. Alas, he lived to slink back to Sparta with the king." Neon shook his head with regret. "He is protected by some god, that is certain!" He tipped his head back and drained his cup.

Perhaps the wine had loosened his tongue, for Neon was not yet finished. "Now," the Spartan said, pointing the empty cup at the black shape of the beached trireme, "Pharnabazus sends that disease among the men of Greece, men of Athens and Sparta alike. Athens needs it to fight my countrymen. And what of the Thebans? The Corinthians? It is like dropping a chunk of meat among a pack of hungry dogs!

94

Mark my words, that cursed gold will send as many men to Hades' gates as any plague, all while the Persians take back Ionia and watch the chaos from afar."

"And Lysander?" I asked. "What would he do with the gold?" I had been wondering about this. Pharnabazus' gift of gold was grand indeed for a poor man like myself, but enough to field an army? Armies eat money like a fire burning through dry grass. The money in Konon's ship was enough to gather an army and pay it for a month I reckoned, perhaps two, but nothing more. Lysander must have another plan. Neon confirmed my suspicions.

Neon snorted. "Lysander wants it to contend with Pausanias and Agesilaus. Not to pay for soldiers, as you think, but to bribe the *gerousia*." The *gerousia* was the ruling council of Sparta. "And believe me, now that they are infected with the gold plague, those greedy old men will gladly accept Lysander's bribes and proclaim him the sole King of Sparta. Are the leading men of Athens any less corruptible?" No one answered, for we all knew the truth of the Spartan's words. It was much simpler, and cheaper, to bribe a few dozen key men than to defeat ten thousand on the field of battle. At one time the Spartans were as incorruptible as mortals could be, but that time had passed, if Neon could be believed.

Sabas tipped the amphora over his cup, looking despondent as the last dregs dribbled out. "That is a sign from the gods if I ever saw one," he quipped before lying down on the shingle and covering himself with his cloak.

With the soft groans of tired men, Tibetos, Neon, and I followed the Cretan's lead and lay down around the glowing embers. Soon the others' deep breaths of slumber were lost in the night breeze blowing in off the sea. My thoughts fended off unconsciousness for some time while I pondered Neon's words. I knew the Spartan was correct. But the Persians were a distant threat in the haze of the future. Sparta's hegemony over Athens and the rest of Greece was in the present.

The persistent pressure of fatigue overcame my restless mind and I succumbed to a fitful sleep haunted by ghosts of those lost on the plains of Thrace.

CHAPTER 13

We rose with the growing light of dawn. My body ached from the exertions of the previous day. After a hurried breakfast, the men set about preparing the ship with a practiced efficiency that even impressed the Spartan Neon. Soon the small island was receding behind the *Arstibara* under the synchronized beating of nearly three hundred oars, the glistening blades flashing like the morning sun with each stroke.

The benefits of my previous day's labours persisted into the new day. My stomach stayed calm as the warship cut through the sea. On uncertain sea-legs I hazarded the journey to the stern of the ship. I held on to the edges of the deck as I groped my way through the recessed walkway along the central axis of the trireme. Some of the rowers crammed below decks called out to me, inviting me to take their place for the day,

At the stern, I climbed back up on the deck, keeping my eyes on Konon so that I could avoid looking at the discomforting sight of the sea moving by. Konon raised an amused eyebrow. "We'll make a sailor of you yet."

Timokrates, who was standing with steady confidence next to the captain's chair, shared in Konon's amusement. "You are the first Athenian I have met who doesn't take to the sea!" he joked.

I scowled at him. "And I am curious to find out if you are the first Rhodian I have met who doesn't know how to swim!" I said, jerking a thumb at the wine-dark water. Timokrates wisely placed himself in a safer position behind Konon's seat.

I gripped an overhead rope to steady myself. "When will we arrive in Athens?" I asked.

"The sea is calm and our pace is steady. Two days, if the weather holds. Once we pass that cape, we'll turn south," he said, pointing to a spit of land that jutted out from the large island ahead of us.

"Where are the rowers from?" I asked.

Konon gave a shake of his head. "Athenians, Argives, Corinthians, Megarians, Phoenicians… Even a few Aegyptians." Many of those men would have been enemies a few years before, and I said so. Konon laughed off my concern. "They get along well enough because their livelihood depends on it! I'll say one thing for the Persians: they pay their rowers well — half as much again as anywhere in Greece

— so I can attract the best rowers in the Aegean, no matter where they're from!"

I was about to respond when a movement by the distant cape caught my eye. I have always been able to see farther than most men. With the motion of the ship and the sparkling sunlight on the waves, I did not trust my own eyes. I peered more intently.

And I saw them.

"What are those ships?" I asked, pointing at the distant cape.

Konon squinted. "I see nothing!"

"They are there! Look again!"

The admiral was about to admonish me but then his expression became grave. "Hades!" he said bitterly.

Konon's previous calm evaporated. A flurry of commands flew from his lips, ordering the steersman and the rowers to come about. Three triremes were emerging from behind the rocky promontory. The warships turned towards us, their banks of oars flashing in the morning sun as they beat the water at a blistering pace.

They were attacking.

THE TRIREMES WERE BEARING DOWN on us at full speed, the warships' pipers pulsing out a furious pace for their rowers. By the time we turned and built up speed, they had cut the distance by half. In a steady voice, Konon ordered a moderate pace. "Let them tire themselves out," Konon said as the gap shortened even further. I trusted the man to know his business.

I focused my attention on the pursuing ships. I could see them more clearly now. The decks bristled with marines, more than the usual complement found on a trireme. There was a familiar flash of white at the stern of the lead ship.

"It's Lysander," I informed Konon.

"That was my guess," Konon replied dryly. I stared at Lysander's ships. How had he found us? The sea was a big place and our mission was secret. I said as much to Konon. The Athenian admiral shook his head. "Lysander's reach is long and his spies are many. Someone from the village likely set out to inform him as soon as we beached. He knew roughly where we were going as well." Konon let a loud curse push through his outward calm. "Even so, by Poseidon's balls! That bastard Spartan has Hermes' own luck!"

How the Spartan leader had found us may have been a mystery, but his aim was not.

"He wants the gold!" Timokrates exclaimed.

Konon concurred. "He means to board us rather than risk sinking us," Konon said, pointing at the marines on the enemy decks. "Gold's no good to any man at the bottom of the sea." Konon squinted at Lysander's small squadron. He nodded to himself and I knew his decision had been made. "You and your men are proficient with javelins, no?" he asked. I nodded. He pointed at the step. "There are weapons and shields under the quarterdeck." Then he told me what he wanted us to do.

I hailed the others, who made their way to the stern.

"We're going to board them?" Tibetos asked incredulously as we hauled up the weapons.

I gave him a condemned man's grin. "Not quite," I said, explaining as I handed up a bundle of javelins.

Tibetos shook his head as he hefted a shield. "He's almost as mad as you," he said, glancing at Konon. Beside him, Neon grunted and extended a hand.

I hesitated. Circumstances forced my hand. Without marines, every man was necessary. "You know what to do with these, Spartan?" I asked.

Neon snatched the javelins. "Since the day my mother bore me!" He took the gear and moved off.

Sabas was last. The Cretan shoved an axe in his belt but held up a hand when I offered him a brace of javelins and a shield. "This is my shield," he said, stringing his recently acquired Persian bow. I knew better than to argue.

We lay prone on the deck. The familiar thrill and fear that anticipated battle boiled up inside me, waiting to erupt. I suddenly laughed and Tibetos glanced my way. "I don't feel sick at all, Tibo!" I said. My friend grinned.

Seeing us prepared, Konon bellowed a command from his captain's chair. "Hard to starboard!" With practiced precision, the starboard oars lifted out of the water while the port rowers beat a furious stroke, all as the steersman pulled the rudder as far as it would go. The ship lurched into a sharp turn and the deck sloped. Even lying flat, I felt the desire of the ship to fling me from her deck. The timbers groaned with the effort of the tight manoeuvre. The ship became level again. We had completely come about and were charging Lysander's squadron head on. "Full speed!" Konon shouted. The boatswain called out a rapid stroke and the oar blades churned the sea with unified purpose.

Too late the enemy ships saw what Konon was up to. Pursuing a lone ship, the three triremes had adopted a loose formation. Now, the *Arstibara* was charging them head on, aiming for the gap between the ship in the centre and the one to its port side. The enemy forgot their purpose. They should have presented their sides, inviting Konon to ram them. If Konon had done so, the *Arstibara* would become trapped, allowing the other ships to hem us in and board us. The loss of one ship was a low price to pay for the treasure we carried.

Lysander must have realized this too, for the central Spartan warship belatedly began to angle away, but our prow had already found the gap between the two Spartan ships. Konon shouted down to the boatswain. "Oars in!"

The rowers hastily retracted their oars with the efficiency born of hundreds of drills. The vertical edge of the *Arstibara*'s bow scraped along the port side of the central ship like a blade, shearing off the enemy oars as though they were mere twigs. Now was the moment of greatest danger. The enemy could not be allowed to recover and board us before we made it clear.

While Timokrates crouched behind the captain's seat, the *peripoli* and Neon stood up. We hurled our javelins at the chaos on the enemy deck as the Spartan ship ground past. Sabas fired his arrows with rapid, deadly accuracy.

Some of the enemy marines had kept their wits enough to counter-attack. Javelins clattered on the deck, but the hasty throws missed their mark. A lone crewman managed to hurl a grappling hook, but the rope went limp as one of Sabas' arrows pierced the unarmoured man in the chest. More missiles came. An enemy javelin arced towards the unprotected Konon. Neon dove in front of the Athenian admiral, shield aloft. The iron javelin head drove through the shield and Neon hit the deck hard. There was no time to check him. We were almost clear.

Then I saw Lysander, his white cloak marking him out.

I reached back, cocking my arm. In a blink, my mind took in the speed of the passing boat and the distance to the shouting Lysander. His eyes met mine. I loosed the javelin with a grunt. As soon as the javelin left my hand, I could see that the throw was perfect. Lysander saw it too. The white-cloaked Spartan seized a sailor and wrenched the man in front of him. The hapless human shield jerked as the javelin punched through the chest. Lysander thrust the dying man aside, glaring at me. And then we were past.

"Oars out!" Konon bellowed. The retracted oars shot out once more and chopped into the sea. I gazed back at the confusion Konon had sown. Lysander's ship drifted uselessly, remnants of its splintered oars bobbing in the water around it like stalks of straw. The remaining two triremes were themselves in disarray, their oars entangling with each other as the warships attempted to turn and pursue our vessel. With each stroke we drew farther away from the failed ambush.

Neon was on his knees, shaking off his dizziness. Konon extended a hand and helped the Spartan to his feet. The Athenian admiral frowned. "I never thought I'd owe my life to a Spartan!" Tibetos and Sabas ambled up the deck to join us.

Tibetos pointed at Neon's shield. "That was a near thing!"

Neon held up the round shield. The fateful javelin had pierced it a foot deep just above his arm. Neon loosened the shield's arm-strap and it dropped to the deck. "The Twin Gods smile upon me for once," he said. He gave a curt nod to Konon and walked away towards the prow of the ship.

"He has a Spartan's manners, by Poseidon!" Konon observed.

I glanced behind us. Lysander's floundering trireme grew ever distant. His two remaining triremes were now in pursuit. "The manoeuvre was well done, *strategos*," I said, addressing Konon by his former Athenian title. "But could we not have simply outrun them?"

His eyes narrowed as he peered at his enemy. "I owed the bastard Lysander something, after what he did to us at Aegospotomi," he said bitterly. Despite his victory, there was dissatisfaction in his voice.

Timokrates had risen from his hiding spot. "And Lysander's ships?" he asked, watching the pursuing triremes.

Konon barked a spiteful laugh. "Let us see what kind of rowers a mere drachma a day has bought for the God of Sparta!"

Konon's confidence proved well-founded. Lysander's remaining triremes fell farther and farther behind until they were only specks on the horizon. By evening, they were nowhere to be seen. Konon laughed, sweeping an arm towards the oarsmen below deck. "The most expensive rowers in the sea! And worth every drachma!"

"Will we beach the ship tonight?" I asked, squinting at the setting sun

Konon looked back towards the stern. He had bested Lysander today, but did not want to tempt the Fates. "I think not," he said at last. "It's going to be a tiring night."

The sun sank below the horizon and night came fast. Under the jewelled night sky, the ship skimmed over the ink-black sea.

Towards Athens.

Towards Home.

CHAPTER 14

We rowed through the night. Neon and I took our own long shifts at the oars. One small lamp at the prow let us know that we were still in the world of men and not in the Underworld.

By the next afternoon, our destination was in sight. With an exhausted stroke, the *Arstibara* limped towards the main harbour of Piraeus. In the distance the temples atop the acropolis beckoned to weary mariners arriving at the humbled but still great city of Athens. I joined Konon at the helm.

Konon stared wistfully at the city. "It has been many years since I laid eyes on that sight." His voice was suffused with an exile's longing.

"Is it wise for a Persian ship to dock in Athens?" I asked.

"I would say no, but one trireme looks much like another. Besides," he said, nodding towards Neon. "We'll make sure your Spartan is seen standing on the deck so we look like a Spartan ship. And you have your letter from Thrasybulus. By the time anyone starts getting suspicious, we'll be gone." I hoped he was right.

The trireme slid through the defensive mole into the main harbour. A lone warship was no threat to the port but still merited caution. A contingent of twenty soldiers backed up the customs officials waiting at the wharf. A crowd of onlookers was gathering, eager to see what tidings the warship brought. "Let me deal with them," I advised Konon.

The first step on the solid earth of the Piraeus wharf was a reassuring sensation. My appearance caused a rumble of voices among the crowd, for my face was well-known in Piraeus if not always welcome. The customs official, a man named Anaxibius, pushed his way through the throng to meet me.

"I never expected to see you aboard a Spartan trireme," he said, squinting at the warship from under the wide brim of his straw hat. Neon stood at the stern, his Spartan braids visible to all. Konon was nowhere to be seen.

"Nor will you ever," I said ambiguously. Anaxibius regarded the ship with new interest.

Before he could indulge his curiosity, I handed him a document case. He uncapped the leather tube and removed the document within.

He unrolled the papyrus. His lips moved silently as he read. I helped speed up the matter. "It is the seal of Thrasybulus with the authority of the council. There will be no inspection of the cargo aboard the ship, nor will any duties be levied," I said. I held out my palm for the return of the scroll.

Anaxibius pulled the papyrus closer to his chest. "It is an irregular request. This could be a forgery, for all I know," he said with an air of smugness.

I was tired and begrimed with dried sweat and salt. I bolstered my patience with a deep breath. Thrasybulus may have been the most influential person in Athens, but he was far away. Anaxibius, despite his limited power, was present before me and could make my life difficult. I chose the Persian path to resolution. I counted out ten silver coins from a pouch at my waist. Anaxibius coughed. I sighed and counted out another ten coins.

"Far be it from me to challenge the word of Thrasybulus," the customs officer said, stepping aside.

"If you ever tire of your occupation, you have a great future in banditry," I growled.

Anaxibius grinned. "Why go chase travellers when they come to me?" He chuckled as he ambled off in search of someone else to extort.

The crew disembarked, groaning as they stretched out their cramped limbs for the first time in almost two days. The rowers dispersed throughout the port, looking to make the most of their short leave by spending their generous wages on food, wine, and women, all of which were in great supply in Piraeus.

As the stream of sailors and rowers passed by, I gave instructions to Tibetos and Sabas. "Get the *peripoli* to bring some carts," I said to Tibetos. "And take Neon with you before someone notices him." Athens may have been under Spartan control, but a lone Spartan warrior walking the streets of Piraeus might suffer a beating or worse. Memories were long and a desire for revenge against the hated Spartans could flare up in an instant. Tibetos and Sabas disappeared with the cloaked form of Neon.

Soon a familiar figure emerged from behind the far end of the customs building. Even at a distance, the strapping bulk of Mnasyllus was easy to pick out among the crowd. And he brought with him a dozen *peripoli* and several donkey carts scrounged from somewhere. I could not help smiling as the big man approached.

Mnasyllus grinned. "Dammo!" He nearly crushed me in his embrace.

I led Mnasyllus and the other *peripoli* aboard the *Arstibara* to unload the gold. I pointed at the diminutive chests and Mnasyllus laughed. "You needed us to carry these?" he asked with a dismissive shake of his head. He bent over and seized one chest by the bronze handles on either side. He grunted in surprise the chest resisted his effort. I felt the corners of my mouth creeping upward. Mnasyllus straightened himself up and regarded the chest as though it had just insulted him.

"There's more than four talents of gold in each one of those chests," I said. Mnasyllus' eyes widened. Four talents was more than a skilled craftsman might earn in a lifetime. It also weighed as much as a fully-armoured hoplite. Undaunted, the brawny warrior took a deep breath and bent down once more. His muscles tautened as he raised the offending weight off the ground. We shouted encouragement as he shuffled up the steps and placed the chest on the upper deck. His shoulders heaved as he caught his breath to much back-slapping and words of admiration.

Still breathing hard, Mnasyllus gave us a sheepish look. "A little help might be appreciated." With good humour and not a little sweat we managed to get the carts loaded, with Timokrates fretting over the cargo like a mother hen looking after its chicks. Before we departed, I ascended the gangplank one last time to bid farewell to Konon, who had changed into the unremarkable garb of a common sailor.

"Tell Thrasybulus that Pharnabazus has pledged more aid when the war starts," he said.

"I will tell him." I held the admiral's eye. "And you? Will you return?"

"I am Athenian," he said. "Not a day passes that I do not wish to serve my polis and redeem myself in Her eyes. May the gods grant you success in your endeavours, Daimon, son of Nikodromos."

"And you, O Konon."

We shook hands and I left the enigmatic admiral to his business. The *Arstibara*'s crew were mustering as we left with the gold, for it was dangerous for Konon to tarry in Piraeus. I pushed through the returning sailors to join my companions.

The creaking carts trundled through the streets of Piraeus. Timokrates, a stranger in a foreign city, shot fearful glances at any passing group larger than three or four men. For my own part, I worried more about the carts collapsing and spilling Persian coins all over the road. I eyed the groaning carts with concern, but whatever craftsman built them knew his business, for the carts arrived at the compound no worse for wear.

Taras, shifting nervously on his feet, greeted us at the gate. "*Lochagos!*" The din of raised voices drifted out from the compound into the street. Taras anticipated my question. "It's the Spartan, *lochagos*. Some of the men are not happy."

Beyond the main gate was a courtyard, a gathering place for meetings and training. The *peripoli* were crowded there now, arguing and cursing. I shoved my way through the barrier of angry men to the centre of the storm. Neon stood impassively, absorbing the abuse directed his way. His only shield was Tibetos and Sabas, who were fighting a losing battle to quell the unrest. Every mob has a leader, an instigator, and now was no exception. The captain of the discontent was apparent, for he stood toe-to-toe with Tibetos, hurling abuse at Neon over my friend's shoulder. It was the last person I would have expected.

Iollas.

He was a former helot, a Spartan slave. He was a small man, but with ropey, lean muscles as tough as iron. He had the stamina of a mule and the agility of a goat. His age was uncertain, and he looked much the same as the day I first saw him, but he might have been close to his fiftieth year. He had made a home with us, and even had a wife of sorts, an equally tough widow named Aiode. His love of her was matched only by his fierce loyalty to the *peripoli* who had freed him from bondage.

By nature, Iollas was frugal of speech, rarely speaking unless spoken to first. His rustic Messenian accent gave the impression of his being stupid, but he was a keen observer with clever hands and an almost uncanny talent for sensing danger. But now the normally reticent Iollas was on the edge of rage. The presence of the Spartan Neon had caused long-dormant feelings in the former slave to erupt.

"A Spartan should not be welcome in this place!" Iollas cried. Many in the crowd echoed this sentiment. "He is the enemy!" Iollas hissed, the hundreds of years of brutal Spartan enslavement and oppression of his Messenian people dripping like poison from every word. It served to further stoke the hostility towards the black-braided Neon.

I forced myself between Tibetos and the irate Iollas. "Enough!" I shouted. The thrum of angry voices ebbed only slightly. "Enough!" I glared at the men around me. Their voices subsided to resentful muttering. "This man," I said, pointing at Neon, "is my *xenos*. He is under my protection." A *xenos* is a guest-friend. The mutual obligations between host and guest — *xenia* — were known to all present.

My declaration failed to dissuade the implacable Iollas. The helot unashamedly hiked up his tunic, revealing his buttocks and lower back. He turned slowly to let the assembled *peripoli* view the fishnet pattern of white scars that crisscrossed his flesh. "This is what his kind did to me. Many more — my wife! My brothers! — suffered worse before they died!" The sight of their comrade's scars was like blowing on embers, and I felt the mood growing hot once more.

"Enough, Iollas!" I snapped. The helot looked at me as if I had betrayed him. It could not be helped. I addressed the men of the *peripoli*. "It is true that Sparta is our enemy, but this man," I said, pointing at Neon, "has earned my trust. He is the enemy of Lysander and an exile. I have just returned from Ionia," I said. There were some surprised expressions among the men, for the purpose of my absence had been a secret. "Without this man, I would not have succeeded in my mission. He has helped Athens."

But I was not done. I turned to Neon. "We are the *peripoli*. We are rogues. We are thieves. We are hunters. Some are citizens, some are foreigners, and some are former slaves. But we are all free men who have earned their place here by their worth. Know that you are my guest-friend here, Spartan, and under my protection. But know, too, that to disrespect the people here is to violate the laws of *xenia*. What do you say, O Neon?" I could only hope that the Spartan would play his part.

He did. Neon stepped forward into the small space formed by the circle of *peripoli*. His thick, Spartan accent filled the courtyard. "I am grateful for the hospitality of the *peripoli*. I swear by the twin gods, that I will abide by the rules of this place. And I swear," he said, turning his eyes towards Iollas, "that I am the enemy of no man here." Iollas, his face taut with anger, shot Neon one last murderous glare before spinning on his heel and pushing his way through the gathered *peripoli*. I let out a long breath. The fire was controlled, at least for the moment.

"There are carts outside that need to be brought in and unloaded. Mnasyllus will direct you." Mnasyllus nodded and began to enlist the strongest men for the task of storing the gold safely away in secret caches within the compound. The men began to break up, casting a few last curious glances or hostile stares towards Neon. I turned to the Spartan.

"You will be welcome here," I said.

Neon regarded the dispersing *peripoli* doubtfully. "Your comrades do not share your sentiment."

"Not yet, perhaps, but what I said is true. A man's worth is all that is important here. They will accept you in time."

"And the helot?"

I cast a glance around the courtyard, but Iollas had disappeared. "That might be another matter."

THRASYBULUS PAID A VISIT to the compound the next day.

The First Man of Athens spread his arms wide when he saw me enter the courtyard with Timokrates at my side. "Welcome home, *lochagos*!" he said in a booming voice that could likely be heard all the way up in the streets of Athens. He leaned in close and in an only slightly lower voice added, "I was right to put my faith in you, Daimon."

"*Strategos*," I answered more curtly than I had intended. My apparent coldness provoked a twinge of hurt in the general's eyes.

I did not let the awkward silence linger. "This is Timokrates of Rhodes." The two men greeted each other with proper formality. I pulled a gold coin from a pouch at my waist. "We have brought you a gift from the Great King," I said. I handed the Persian daric to Thrasybulus, who inspected the image of the bow-wielding Great King of Persia on the coin's face.

"We will beat the Spartans with ten thousand Persian archers, it seems!" Thrasybulus said with a wink. Timokrates coughed and threw a wary eye about at the men milling around the courtyard. Thrasybulus took his meaning and slipped the gold coin into his belt.

"Let us speak in a less public location," I said.

The celebrity of Thrasybulus hampered our progress through the compound. The younger *peripoli* goggled at the great man, for his military victories were legendary. Many of the veterans had met the *strategos* before, but they still came under the spell of Thrasybulus' aura. He was one of those leaders who exuded a balance of natural authority and approachability, equally at ease with a rustic farmer's son as he was with aristocrats of his own class. It was why men followed him.

After Thrasybulus had seemingly greeted each *peripoli* in the compound, we found ourselves alone in the spacious room that served as my administration office. On a large table lay a pile of rolled documents that had accumulated during my absence in Phrygia. I sighed. "It seems I cannot escape this prison."

Thrasybulus gave me a sympathetic smile. "Administration is the bride of leadership, Daimon," he said, taking a seat on a stool. I gestured at another stool and Timokrates sat down.

The Rhodian's fingers twitched impatiently. "What are your plans now that the gold has arrived, O Thrasybulus?"

"I will dispatch messengers to our allies inviting them to come to Athens to discuss the matter."

Timokrates frowned. "The fewer who know, the better."

"We will be discreet," Thrasybulus assured the Rhodian.

"And the gold?" Timokrates asked. Thrasybulus looked my way.

"It is hidden in our compound's weapon caches," I said.

Timokrates was unconvinced. "Would it not be safer in the treasury atop the Acropolis?"

Thrasybulus pursed his lips. "It is as safe here as anywhere, and transporting it to Acropolis would draw unwanted attention from Spartan informers. Better to let it stay with Daimon. The fewer who know, the better," he said, echoing the Rhodian's earlier words.

With some reluctance, Timokrates agreed to leave the gold in my care. He and Thrasybulus spoke some more on which allies would be invited to Athens and what the Great King had promised in terms of further aid. I said little.

At last, Thrasybulus straightened up and cracked his shoulders. "There will be plenty of time to discuss these matters at my home, O Timokrates. But we should depart immediately if we are to reach the city before nightfall." Thrasybulus looked my way. "Will you come with us, Daimon? I wish to hear more of your mission." It was as close as he would come to giving me an order.

I nodded. "As you wish, *strategos*."

As Thrasybulus, Timokrates, and I left through the main gate, I took Tibetos aside. "Keep the peace and make sure Iollas doesn't kill Neon in his sleep," I told him.

Tibetos cast a worried look back towards the compound. "I can't promise anything."

I trudged with Thrasybulus and Timokrates up the long, straight road connecting Piraeus to Athens. The road had once been protected by high walls, but now only rubble of the former defences remained, a requirement that ensured Athens' continued servitude to Sparta. The overgrown heaps of tumbled stone cast long stabbing shadows in the setting sun. The journey gave me ample time to recount our adventures in Phrygia. Lysander's desire to acquire the gold elicited little comment, as did the machinations of Pharnabazus. Only when I spoke the name of Konon was Thrasybulus unable to contain his surprise.

"Konon!" He turned and gazed back towards Piraeus and the sea. "Athens could use his skill now!"

"He longs to return here, I think, but fears punishment for the defeat at Aegospotomi," I said.

Thrasybulus frowned. "His fear is not without reason. Perhaps it is good he has the ear of the Persians. Sometimes a distant ally is worth a thousand hoplites at home."

I mulled over this as Thrasybulus and Timokrates discussed schedules and strategies. Night had fallen and I insisted on escorting Thrasybulus and Timokrates to the *strategos*' home. The streets of Athens were a dangerous place after dark at the best of times but I was well aware of Lysander's fondness for using assassins. I stayed alert for ambush in the dark streets, but we encountered only stray dogs and the occasional drunk sleeping off his wine.

"You will not stay with us tonight, *lochagos*?" Thrasybulus offered at the door of his home.

I knew that the offer was sincere. I sometimes stayed with the *strategos* and his family when I was in Athens. But something drew me away that night, a need for solitude and reflection. I thanked Thrasybulus for his invitation and bade him and Timokrates farewell. I would navigate the dark streets of Athens to my own home.

The house was a convenient place to sleep and little more. My son Nikos lived with my old tutor Iasos. I granted myself the luxury of a rare smile. The boy was thriving, at least in his own manner. Iasos told me he was clever and excelled in his studies, a talent from his mother. I worried sometimes that the boy was too enamoured with his letters and mathematics. When he was older, I would take him to live with me in the *peripoli* compound and he could learn the skills of a warrior. I would face opposition from Iasos, I was certain, but that was a matter for another day.

I made the last turn and came to the door of my house. Most non-citizens could not own property in Athens, but Thrasybulus had worked to earn me the permission to do so. The house had been in my family since before the time of Homer, or so my father had told me. I rarely spent time there, for if I was not in Piraeus I was away on a mission for Thrasybulus.

That was not to say the house was empty, nor was it left unguarded in my absence. Robbers could easily cut a hole through the mud and plaster walls if they so wished. As it was, would-be thieves knew whose property this was and that restless spirits lurked within, and that was enough to make superstitious robbers move on to less risky targets, not that there was much of value inside in any case.

The click of the heavy iron lock cut into the silence of the deserted lane. The heavy oak door swung inward with a creak. At once I knew I was not alone in the house. I unslung Whisper from my back.

A lamp burned softly in the centre of the courtyard, dimly illuminating the figure who sat cross-legged behind it. It was a frightening sight. The figure's untamed hair was like a lion's mane, wild and powerful. Arcane markings swirled about the creature's face, framing emerald eyes that stabbed into me like spear-points. The visitor rose, and the swish of her barbarian cloak caused the lamp flame to ripple. It was an *empousa*, a servant of Hekate.

I knew many veterans of fearsome battles who would have turned tail and run into the street like frightened dogs at the sight before me. The braver ones, standing their ground, would have touched trembling fingers to iron to ward off the evil eye.

I neither ran nor trembled from the creature, nor did I fear her. I loved her, for she was my sister.

"Hello, Meli."

PART TWO

ΘΗΒΑΙΟΙ THEBANS

CHAPTER 15

"Greetings, Brother."

Melitta was as tall as most men. Her dark cloak only augmented her presence, its arcane symbols rippling with their own life as she took a few gliding steps towards me. She stopped a few paces away and stared at me. In the weak light of the lamp, her fey green eyes appeared black. Like Lysander's, I thought.

My joy at seeing her was diluted by a measure of caution. My sister was playful and mischievous by nature, but darkness lurked in her soul. Sometimes madness gripped her and she could turn as cold and hard as mountain ice. I did not know which Meli was before me now.

"I am happy to see you, Meli," I said gently. "I thought it might be many years before I laid eyes on you again."

"The gods told me it was time to return to Athens."

My smile faded as a chill passed through me.

Many men claim to speak to the gods. There are the priests in the temples who collect the offerings and make the sacrifices on festival days, chanting their prayers with great pomp. There are the *mantises* who tell the generals whether it is an auspicious day for battle by reading an animal's entrails or interpreting the gods' wills in the flight of birds. There are the unctuous soothsayers and fortune-tellers who prey on the superstitious in the marketplace.

Priest, *mantis*, fortune-teller. They are all frauds, seeking only to eke out a living by separating the gullible from their silver. The gods, for the most part, do not talk to men.

Women are another matter. Perhaps it is recompense for the other hardships that women bear, but the gods really do speak to them. In homes and villages, women commune with the gods in secret rituals away from the prying eyes of men. The witches of Thrace hear the gods in their dreams. And there is a reason why the Pythia of Delphi, the greatest oracle in the world, is always a woman.

So when my sister said she had returned at the gods' behest, I believed her. And when the gods spoke, their words brought ill omens more often than not. I shivered again.

But a warm smile spread across my sister's face, blowing away the chill of my premonitions. She leapt at me and wrapped her arms around my chest as she had done since she was a child. "I missed you, Dammo," she whispered into my shoulder.

We stood there holding each other for some time in that courtyard full of ghosts. I gently pushed her away. "Let me look at you, Sister." She stepped back with her hands on her hips, striking a confident pose. The curling tattoo on the right side of her face had lightened since I last saw her. Beneath the cloak, she was garbed in the patterned pants and sleeved tunic of the Thracians. At each hip a sword hilt peeped out from inside the cloak. I nodded with approval. "You look like a proper Thracian *hurisa*," I said. A *hurisa* was a Thracian warrior woman. Meli beamed at my praise, for since she was a child she had yearned to be like an Amazon from the old tales. I gestured towards the swords. "Do you know how to use those?"

Meli gave me an enigmatic smile and reached towards her hip. Instead of drawing one of the swords, she pulled a long cloth-bundled shape from within her cloak. "This is for you. A gift from Zyraxes." Zyraxes was a Thracian prince, son of King Medokos. He was my brother in spirit if not in blood.

I took the proffered bundle. It was heavy. I unwound the wrapping to reveal the treasure within. I took a deep breath. Zyraxes honoured me too much.

It was a spearhead. Longer than my forearm, the flat blade flared and tapered to its deadly tip like an olive leaf. I turned the spearhead over in my hands, admiring its craftsmanship. Mysterious symbols like those on Meli's cloak circled its base. Even in the dim light I could see the smoky ripples on blue-tinged metal, just like those on Whisper. Prince Zyraxes employed a mad Persian smith who jealously guarded a secret to making iron stronger than normal. He had made my rhomphaia, and I knew at once that it was the same master who had crafted the blade before me.

"It is beautiful," was all I could say.

"Zyraxes knew you would like it. But what is its name?"

The Thracians have a practice of naming their weapons. They believe that doing so imbues the blade with life and gives it power. Meli peered into my eyes as though willing me to hear her thoughts. A name came to me, as though from a forgotten dream suddenly remembered. "*Psychokleptis*," I said. *Soul-Thief.*

Meli clapped her hands in delight. "Zyraxes called it *Denakokra!*" *Denakokra* meant "Soul-stealer" in Thracian. "It is its true name, then!" she said with a wide grin.

Her smile brought joy to me. "I have missed you, Sister." But there was another who missed my sister even more. "Tibetos would like to see you, I think. He speaks of you every day."

My sister's sharp features softened. "I have missed him, too."

"We can leave for Piraeus now, if you wish, and be there before he wakes up," I suggested. Like me, Meli was more a creature of the night.

Meli shook her head. "No, we will surprise him tomorrow evening. I have other business in Athens."

"Business?" I asked, surprised. I could think of no one in Athens Meli would need to see. But of course there was, for she had other family here besides me.

"I would like to meet my nephew."

MY SON NIKODROMOS lived with my former teacher Iasos. It was not an ideal arrangement. I had offered to bring the boy to live with me at the *peripoli* compound. There were plenty enough women there to take care of him. I could also begin to train him with shield and spear, something that had been neglected in my view.

But Iasos had rejected my suggestion. "This is the only home the boy has known!" he declared. "It would serve no purpose to take him away!" The truth of this pricked at my heart. Iasos was more of a father to the boy than I had ever been. "Besides, I would trust no one else with his education!" Iasos remonstrated. So my son remained with Iasos, something that seemed to suit them both.

I hammered my fist on the door of my tutor's house. Meli and I waited for an age. "Perhaps Iasos is not home?" she suggested.

I knew better. "Wait."

Another age passed before we heard the muffled clink of the lock being undone. The door creaked open to reveal a tired-looking face. The grey-haired man looked at me as though he had never laid eyes on me before. "Yes?"

"Xanthias, let us in, by Zeus!" I said impatiently.

The slave stepped aside and let us pass. In my whole life I had never known the slave to do anything with haste. But he was unswervingly loyal to Iasos.

Xanthias dipped his head towards my sister. "It is good to see you, young Melitta."

Meli stepped forward and embraced the old slave before he could move. "Xanthias!" Xanthias stood stiffly, his eyebrows raised. It was more emotion than I had ever seen from him. He relaxed visibly as Meli parted from him.

"Come with me," he said, turning away. Meli and I exchanged a glance and followed the stoop-shouldered slave.

As usual, the courtyard was filled with the clutter of Iasos' innumerable investigations. In the light of the open space I saw Xanthias more clearly. A weariness beyond his normal lassitude lay on him like a wet cloak, "You look exhausted, Xanthias," I said. The elderly slave's eyes flashed with sadness. He opened his mouth to speak but clamped his lips tight as Iasos entered the courtyard.

"Daimon, my boy!" Iasos said, his arms held wide.

I was shocked by my old teacher's appearance. Iasos had been one of those rare men who never seems to age. He had looked the same at sixty as when he had been beating me for shirking my lessons as a boy. He was an avowed Pythagorean and he proudly ascribed his youthful vigour to the cult's strict vegetarian diet and life of moderation. But since I had last seen him, it seemed as though years had ravaged him all at once. His limbs had lost flesh and his robe hung on him like a shroud. His pale skin was stretched thin over his face and bald skull. Only his eyes gleamed with their characteristic intelligence.

"Teacher," I managed to stutter, stepping forward to embrace the old man. I felt the ridges of his ribs under my hands. We separated and he turned to my sister.

"You have changed much and not so much, I think, Melitta!"

"I would say the same to you, O Iasos!" she replied warmly.

"And as beautiful as your mother!" Iasos said, causing Meli to blush uncharacteristically. Both of us towered over the old man, but we would always be children in his eyes. "But I think it is not me you have come to see!" He turned his head and called over his shoulder. "Nikodromos!"

The slapping of sandals on the packed ground brought my son into the courtyard. He came to halt beside Iasos.

My son was almost ten years old. There was little Thracian to see in him, for his hair and eyes were raven-black like his mother's had been. But his face had the same sharp features as Meli's, and he was tall for his age, a legacy of mine. Seeing me, he addressed me formally. "*Pater*," he said.

Our relationship had settled into awkward familiarity. I was not a good father. I visited him when I was in Athens, but was often absent for months at a time when my duties took me elsewhere. When I was with the boy, he spoke endlessly about the mathematics and philosophical matters that Iasos filled with his head with. I could only nod dumbly as he deftly leapt from topic to topic with hardly a breath in between. He was at an age when he should have been learning to hold a spear or learning to fight, but he showed little interest in these things.

"*Pai*, this is your Aunt Melitta."

He peered at Meli intensely. "Aunt," he said at last with a small bow.

Meli held out her hand as though she were a man. "I have not seen you since you were a baby, Nikodromos. I see much of your mother in you, *pai*."

A flicker of emotion passed over Niko's face at the mention of his mother, whom he had never known. He took Meli's proffered hand. "You have come from Thrace," Niko declared.

Meli smiled. "And what do you know of Thrace, *pai*?"

Niko glanced at me before answering. "The Thracians are great warriors but they often fight amongst each other. Their king is Medokos and his son is Zyraxes. Right now they are at war with Seuthes, who also wants to be king. Thracians wear pants instead of robes and tunics like Greeks. The women sometimes fight alongside men." He looked back at me and I nodded. It was as good a summary as any.

Meli switched to Thracian. "*Manisara thraki re?*" *Do you speak Thracian?*

Niko looked my way once more. "*Onsika manisavi,*" he said awkwardly. *I speak a little.* "*Pater* taught me some."

Meli smiled warmly and switched back to Greek. "Good! You must remember your ancestors! Now," she said, taking the boy's hand. "Show me what Iasos is teaching you today." Niko looked to Iasos for permission.

"Go, *pai*, whilst your father and I talk," Iasos said. Niko grinned and led Meli to the nearest table, the words already spilling from his mouth like the waters of a swollen winter river. Iasos gestured at another table that was relatively uncluttered by contraptions and rolls of papyrus.

Iasos winced slightly as he sat down. Xanthias and I exchanged a glance before the slave shuffled away. "Are you ill, Teacher," I asked.

Iasos waved away my concern. "Something I ate doesn't agree with me," he lied. He recovered his composure and with a thoughtful expression regarded Meli and Niko, who was showing my sister an odd-looking device. "She was always clever, that one," Iasos observed appraisingly.

"Your lessons would have been less wasted on her than on me," I said. Iasos chuckled but did not disagree. I looked at his frail body and a great shame came over me. "I am sorry I was such a disappointing student to you, Teacher."

Iasos held up a hand. "No, *pai*. It was I who was wrong to think I could change who you were! A stubborn mule does not become more obedient when you beat it! True wisdom comes too late!" he said with a sigh of regret. "Tell me where you have been, *pai*. I get out so rarely these days that I have lost touch with the goings-on of our great city!"

While Niko continued educating his aunt, I spoke to Iasos of my secret journey to Phrygia and the shipment of Persian gold. He listened intently with his hands held together touching at the fingertips. He leaned back. "So it is to be war again?"

"So it seems."

Iasos frowned. "Sparta will not spare Athens a second time if we are defeated."

"Thrasybulus believes we will be victorious if Thebes joins our cause."

"And will they?" Iasos asked, raising an eyebrow.

I shrugged. "We'll know soon enough. Thrasybulus is inviting ambassadors from Thebes and elsewhere to hear his proposal."

"And Thrasybulus will want you by his side," Iasos said.

"He wants me to become *archos* of the *peripoli*," I confirmed.

Iasos, always perspicacious, asked, "And you do not wish this?"

The very question made me weary. "I am not an administrator," I said.

Iasos pursed his lips, considering this. "Yet the *peripoli* have risen from the ashes under you. The compound has been rebuilt. Your numbers are growing. That suggests that you are a better leader than you give yourself credit for."

"I am skilled at sending other men to dine with Hades. That is all."

Iasos gave a laugh of concession. "There is that, too! But hear me; Thrasybulus is a keen judge of men's worth. Daimon, my boy," he said, taking my hand in both of his. "It is foolish to try to make someone into something they're not, but it is also a fool who squanders the gifts the gods have given him!"

"I will consider it, Teacher," was all I was willing to commit to.

The return of my sister and Niko saved me from discussing the matter further. As they approached, Meli leaned towards Niko and whispered something in the boy's ear, causing him to break out in laughter. He looked so much like his mother then. My own smile was as much to hide the sudden ache in my soul as it was from the joy of seeing my son and my sister enjoying a measure of happiness.

I stared down at my son. "You were polite to your aunt?"

Niko pulled himself tall, like a soldier. "Yes, *pater*."

"And what did you talk about?" I asked. Niko hesitated. "Well?" I pressed. Niko glanced at my sister uncertainly, looking for guidance.

Meli rescued him, her eyes flashing mischievously. "I was telling him what you were like when you were his age." I frowned. When I was Niko's age, I was shirking my lessons, prowling the streets of Athens, fighting with other boys, and stealing when I could, all of which earned me plenty of thrashings from both Iasos and my father. I looked at Niko, who was regarding me with what might have been wide-eyed admiration. I let out a resigned breath. In the time it had taken to drink a few cups of wine, Meli had gained from the boy more respect for me than I had managed to earn in almost ten years.

I shifted my interrogation over to my sister. "And what did you learn of my son?"

"He is clever beyond his years, thanks to you, O Iasos," she said.

Iasos rested a gaunt hand on Niko's shoulder. "'A smith cannot forge a strong blade with poor metal,'" he said modestly, though his face shone with pride.

"We must return to Piraeus," I said.

"Ah, the burden of leadership," he said, giving me a knowing look.

I leaned down and Iasos embraced me. When we parted, he grasped my forearm. "You have grown into a good man, *pai*," he said. "Your father would be proud of you." He released me and turned to my sister. "And your father would marvel at you, young Melitta!"

"Farewell, O Iasos," Meli said. She held him as if it would be the last time she saw him. She was always wiser than me.

"Remember what I said, *pai*," he said, watching us depart.

Xanthias saw us out to the street. My teacher's ill health weighed heavily on my heart. I turned to bid farewell to Xanthias to meet an unprecedented sight.

The old slave was crying. I knew why.

"Iasos is not well," I said.

Xanthias shook his head. "There is a pain in his belly. He was taking a draught to ease the discomfort, but it has lost its efficacy of late."

I thought about my son. Caring for the boy must have drawn deeply from my old tutor's limited well of energy. "I should take Nikodromos. It would give Iasos time to rest."

Xanthias clutched my wrist with surprising strength. "No!" he said, his eyes wide with pleading. His grip loosened. "The joy he gains from teaching the boy is the only thing keeping him in this world!"

I put my hand on his. "Then I will leave him, O Xanthias," I said.

"Thank you, *pai*! Thank you!" The slave shuffled back into the house and the door shut behind him with a dull thud. Meli and I walked through the streets of Athens in our own silent worlds. There was no rush to speak, for the long walk to Piraeus would give us plenty of time to talk.

Only when we set foot on the long, straight road to the port did I at last speak. "Iasos will die soon," I said. I spoke in Thracian, as I often did when I was with my sister.

My sister did not argue otherwise. "Yes."

We trod on. So absorbed in my own thoughts was I that I hardly noticed how other travellers on the road went out of their way to give us a wide berth. Iasos was the last of my mentors still surviving from my childhood. I sought to stave off the tightness in my chest with idle chatter. "I have never seen Xanthias act in such a way," I said distractedly.

Meli sighed. "You are a fool, Brother."

I cocked an eyebrow at her. "I never claimed otherwise."

"Do you not know the source of Xanthias' tears?"

I did not. Xanthias, though sullen and insolent by nature, had proven his loyalty to Iasos beyond doubt many times, and I said as much to Meli. My sister regarded me as if I were one of the half-wit beggars in the agora. "They are lovers," she said.

I came to a sudden stop. "Iasos and Xanthias?" I exclaimed.

"Do you not see it now?" Meli asked. It was something to ponder as we resumed our journey to Piraeus.

Iasos had never married, it was true, but it was something that I had always attributed to his ascetic Pythagorean habits. I wondered how I could have been so blind to such a thing, but my sister often saw in people what was invisible to others. It was common enough for older men to pursue a pretty youth, but a relationship between older men was likely to be regarded with some degree of disrepute, more so in Athens than it might in Thebes, where such things were more common, or so it was said. But Meli was rarely wrong about such matters.

Unable to say more, I changed the topic. "I'm happy you got on with Niko. It is more than I have ever achieved," I said, unable to hide a touch of envy in my voice.

"Your son will be a great man," Meli declared. "Greater than you even."

A hopeful pride welled up inside me. "He will become a warrior?" I asked.

Meli stopped in the middle of the road and fixed her piercing green gaze upon me. "You *are* a fool," she admonished me again.

"What now?" I replied, exasperated.

Meli shook her head at my obtuseness. "People do not decide what talents the gods give them. They can only make the best of what they have."

"Iasos was saying much the same to me," I said, recalling my conversation with my old tutor.

"And," Meli said, holding up a finger, "It is foolish to try to be something you are not."

"You are beginning to sound like Sokrates!" I laughed.

But my sister was not finished with her Sokratizing. "Would you use a fine cavalry horse to pull a plough in the fields?" she asked.

"Of course not!"

"And would you ride an ox into battle?" she continued.

I could not help smiling at the absurd image. "No!"

"Then you should not force Nikodromos to be a warrior."

"What is the boy's talent then?" I pushed back.

"He is a philosopher by nature."

"A philosopher!" I snorted. I thought of the unkempt gadflies who lounged about the agora arguing nonsense with each other, playing with words day and night but ultimately saying little. Like that shit-eating Plato. I scowled.

"It is his *arete*," Meli insisted. "His excellence."

"What kind of excellence is that?" I said a little harshly.

Meli jabbed a finger into my chest. "The kind that makes Iasos a wise and good person," she said, and I felt some shame for impugning my former teacher if only by association. But Meli was not done. "And I tell you this, Brother. The work of Nikodromos will live on when memories of our deeds are but shadows of shadows." She pulled herself up to her full height, daring me to contradict her.

I let out a long breath. It would do no good to argue with my sister when she was in such a mood. I let the corner of my mouth curl upwards. "We are like a pair of debating philosophers, are we not?"

Meli could not suppress a smile. "Not that they would know it," she said, waving at the curious passers-by. They must have wondered at what the barbarian Thracians were arguing about with such passion.

"And what is my *arete*?" I asked jokingly.

Meli's face, however, became serious once more. "You are Daimon by name and a *daimon* by nature. You are a protector. You exact justice that is due. You are vengeance."

"It is a lonely calling," I said.

Meli raised her hand to my cheek. "Others will help you bear your burden, Brother."

"That is enough," I said.

Our talk moved on to other things, flitting from the situation in Thrace to the state of the *peripoli*. Sometimes the tone was serious, sometimes we laughed. Mostly we enjoyed each other's company, for we knew each other's hearts as only close siblings can.

In the late afternoon we arrived at the *peripoli* compound. Those who knew her — Sabas, Mnasyllus, Stachys, Iollas — greeted my sister as if she were their own sister. More recent members crowded around us, curious to see the odd-looking warrior woman they knew only by her fearsome reputation. Meli bore their scrutiny with equanimity until Tibetos, drawn by the commotion, appeared in the gateway. His eyes widened when he saw Meli standing at my side.

Meli pushed through the throng and wrapped her arms around my stunned friend, eliciting a hearty cheer from those assembled. Tibetos held her close, unashamed of the stares he drew from the others in the compound.

For a moment, it seemed the gods and Fates had blessed us with a measure of peace and harmony.

But it was an illusion.

The gods are cruel.

CHAPTER 16

Thrasybulus moved fast to convene a meeting of potential allies.

The gathering was an unofficial one, taking place in the privacy of Thrasybulus' home only a month after I had returned from Phrygia. I studied the seated attendees who ringed the courtyard. The largest group was the Thebans and their Boeotian allies. Smaller delegations from Corinth and Argos sat far apart from each other, the lure of the chance to rid themselves of Spartan control tempting enough for the two cities to overcome their ancient acrimony. A scattering of other delegates from lesser players had formed a loose confederation on the east side of the chamber. I sat alone.

I suppressed a yawn, struggling to focus on the self-important blustering of the various ambassadors. A faint scuffle from the upper floor landing drew my gaze. Thrasybulus' young son and his daughter were peeping over the railing to spy on the goings-on below. They caught me watching them and I flashed my teeth at them in a playful, silent roar. Their stifled giggles stopped abruptly as their mother Astera loomed up behind them and pinched their ears. Hissing at her disobedient children, she began to pull the two spies away. The refined Astera, who had once regarded me with ambivalence at best, was now a firm ally. We exchanged a knowing look before she disappeared with her reluctant children, leaving me bored once again.

Timokrates had risen to speak. In a surprisingly rich and confident tone, the Rhodian communicated the pledge of the Great King Artaxerxes to support the struggle against Spartan hegemony. He praised, cajoled, and admonished his audience in turn as he took on the daunting task of uniting the disparate cities against the common foe of Sparta. With deft skill he answered or deflected questions from all parties, always dangling the promise of further payments of gold from the Persian treasury.

While men of influence argued about how to best use the Persian gold hidden away in the *peripoli* compound, my wandering thoughts were occupied with other matters.

My sister had reclaimed the house in Athens for herself, much to the chagrin of the locals. Thracian traders were common enough in Piraeus, but my sister reinforced every prejudice Athenians held of the savage, mysterious barbarians from the north. The sight of the unaccompanied tattooed woman striding confidently through the agora with her swords and flowing green cloak was almost a scandal. Meli's reputation as a gods-touched soothsayer spread, and soon our home was a place of secret visits for citizens high and low who wished to know what the gods had in store for them.

Gods-fearing citizens were not the only visitors. Tibetos spent many days with Meli at our old home. It did not bother me, and I delighted in their happiness together. The three of us passed some evenings together in the house of our childhood, finding joy in each other's company.

More often, however, I made the lonely trek journey back to Piraeus, for there were always duties to attend to. One such matter was Neon. The Spartan had asked to stay longer, which had surprised me. His presence in the compound was tolerated if not welcomed. He repaid the forbearance of the men by helping drill the younger recruits. Iollas gave him a wide berth and the peace had held.

I put thoughts of Neon aside as my attention wandered back to the debate at hand. Timokrates had finished responding to the barrage of questions and Thrasybulus took the floor. His booming voice filled the small space of the courtyard. Thrasybulus abandoned any claim to the Persian gold. The money would be of more use to Athens' allies, he declared, in the upcoming struggle to shake off the heavy yoke of arrogant Spartan rule.

With this appeal, Thrasybulus adjourned the formal meeting. House slaves appeared bringing refreshments to the guests. The visiting ambassadors and their Athenian hosts mingled in the courtyard, sounding each other out. Thrasybulus moved about from one knot of people to another, making introductions and bringing people together. I found as inconspicuous a spot as possible, admiring how the *strategos* was weaving a web of alliances before my very eyes.

I was still very much an outsider. Thrasybulus had requested my presence, but I could contribute little, for I possessed neither official status nor a politician's slippery tongue. I rose from the bench with the intention of making a quiet exit.

My escape was thwarted by Thrasybulus. He beckoned me to join him and a group of men I recognized from the meeting as the Theban delegation. Unable to flee, I threaded my way through the crowded courtyard. The Thebans regarded my approach with restrained curiosity.

Thrasybulus greeted me with a diplomatic smile. "*Strategos*," I said, ignoring the Thebans' scrutiny.

"*Archos*," he replied, addressing me by the title I neither possessed nor desired. He turned to the Thebans. "Allow me to introduce you to Daimon, son of Nikodromos, Commander of the *peripoli*."

I am not a man without a reputation. The Thebans' reactions upon hearing my name were a reflection of how that reputation varied in the minds of men. The man I took to be the leader of the delegation, a grey-beard with short-cropped hair, raised an eyebrow in surprise, while the face of another older man in a deep-red robe stiffened as though he had seen a dog eating a corpse. The jaw of one young man dropped in astonishment. The final Theban's lip curled in a sneer.

This last one was richly dressed. Gold threads were woven into the hems of his delicately patterned robe, and a chain of thick silver links hung around his neck. His black curls were well-kept and his beard oiled into a stylish point. I reckoned he was my age more or less. "He is an Athenian?" he asked. His gaze moved up from my simple garb and ended on my thick copper hair. His brown eyes met my green ones. "I mistook him for a barbarian slave!" He laughed and turned to Thrasybulus. "I have heard that in Athens it can be difficult to distinguish between slave and citizen. I see that it is true!" I disliked him immensely.

The strained air of cordiality was on the verge of shattering. The corners of my mouth edged up in condescension. "No insult taken. Many men of poor judgment have made the same mistake, but never twice." The man's smirk vanished and he took a step towards me, only to be stopped by the older man in the deep red robe. There was a resemblance between the two.

The short-haired grey-beard intervened. "I am Ismenias. I, for one, welcome the aid of the *peripoli*."

I dipped my chin in acknowledgment. "*You* are gracious, O Ismenias."

The red-robed man cut in before Ismenias could respond. "It is well-known that the *peripoli* are little better than bandits. Bandits, whose predations too often take them into Boeotia, I might add."

"I would know the name of my accuser," I said, meeting the man's stare. He was slender with a long, hard face. His thinning black hair and full beard were streaked with grey. His eyes were cold, calculating, and filled with cunning intelligence.

Thrasybulus introduced the red-robed man. "This is Leontiades, son of Eurymachus, of Thebes."

I brushed off Leontiades' attempt to goad me. "I'm afraid you are mistaken about the *peripoli*, O Leontiades. We guard our borders but do not venture beyond them." My measured response brought about a look of relieved approval from Thrasybulus."

The man Leontiades continued to provoke me. "It is also rumoured that Daimon the Athenian defiled the temple of Delphi and did great evil there little more than a year ago."

"I have never even been to Delphi," I lied.

"It was Daimon and the *peripoli* who brought the gold safely from Phrygia," Thrasybulus interrupted.

The young man who had insulted me earlier snorted. "Is such a simple task worthy of praise?"

I looked at him as one would regard a warm pile of donkey dung in the street. "You should show more respect when you address your betters."

His eyes widened at the insult. "You? My better! A bold claim from a Thracian, by Herakles! " He looked at Thrasybulus. "Was it wise to trust that task to a thieving Thracian? How much of the gold has disappeared into his pockets already?" The other young man in the party, almost hidden behind the rest, winced at his companion's rudeness.

When I was a young man, the little turd-sniffer's barbs might have provoked me to violence. But with years I had learned that words could often wound more deeply than fists or blades. I appealed to Ismenias. "Are all Theban children so insolent?"

"I am Eurymachus, son of Leontiades," the man proclaimed, confirming my earlier suspicion. *Eurymachus, son of Leontiades, Leontiades, son of Eurymachus.* A family that alternated names between generations, I surmised. The latest scion needed a check on his pride.

My gaze drifted to Leontiades and back to Eurymachus. "I do not see the resemblance," I lied. "Are you certain *he* is your father?"

"My father is the wealthiest man in Thebes!" Eurymachus growled. "He could buy an army to crush the *peripoli* if he so wished."

I turned to Leontiades, ignoring his son. "If that is true, O Leontiades, why are you here at all?"

"The Great King's money," Leontiades said through gritted teeth, "makes us beholden to the Persian barbarians. But it is here now and we must make use of it."

"I would have thought conspiring with the Persians is something you Thebans have much experience with," I said. Leontiades began to turn red again.

The insult was an ancient one but it still stabbed deeply at Theban pride, for the Thebans were Mede-izers. When Xerxes and his Persians had ravaged Greece, Thebes had submitted, giving the Great King gifts of earth and water. At Plataea, when Athens and Sparta had stood together to drive Xerxes' armies from Greece for good, the Mede-zing Thebans had not fought for the freedom of Greece but rather had stood alongside the Persians in order to subjugate their fellow Greeks, to their everlasting shame. My allusion to their past treachery was undiplomatic, to say the least. Thrasybulus shot me a warning look.

Ismenias intervened before the situation deteriorated further. "It is neither Athens nor Persia nor Thebes that is arrogant: it is Sparta. Our common cause makes us allies now, whatever the past has been." The Theban ambassador's voice was infused with the same idealism that drove Thrasybulus. I accepted his gracious offer at peacemaking.

"The *peripoli* are ready to serve this cause, O Ismenias. But I am just a solider. I will leave important matters to wise men like yourself," I said. I glanced at Thrasybulus before turning to leave. He looked relieved.

One of Thrasybulus' house-slaves opened the front door. I emerged into the street, angry at myself for letting Thrasybulus persuade me to come to the political snake-pit in the first place. Robes and debates were not for me, I thought. I strode with purpose, seeking to put some distance between myself and the home of Thrasybulus. The sound of running footsteps made me halt.

"Wait!" a voice called. I turned to see the quiet young Theban approaching. He stopped and paused to catch his breath, giving me a chance to study him more closely. His dress and appearance suggested that he was from an aristocratic family. His well-muscled body spoke of many hours training at the gymnasium with other young men of wealth. Yet there was a roughness about him as well.

A broken nose had healed poorly, marring his otherwise handsome face. His patterned robe, though fine, was faded with age and fraying at the edges. Likewise, his black hair and beard were rough-cropped like those of a labourer, eschewing the fashionable styles popular among other young aristocrats like the haughty Eurymachus.

"Have you pursued me to insult me further?" I asked dryly.

He shook his head. "You must excuse Eurymachus. He and his father do not speak for all Thebans."

"You are not a relation then?" A thought occurred to me. "You are the son of Ismenias?" I ventured.

The young man looked embarrassed. "No, I am Epaminondas, son of Polymnis." He hesitated "My sister is to marry Eurymachus," he offered by way of explanation.

I scoffed. "That is unfortunate for her."

The Theban raised his chin. "Leontiades is the wealthiest man in Thebes. My family —" He hesitated. "My family enjoys great esteem. We are descendants of Cadmus himself," he said, naming the legendary founder of Thebes.

I sensed what was left unsaid. "In other words, the marriage will bring your family much needed money," I ventured, glancing at the frayed collar of the Theban's robe, "while Leontiades basks in the glow of your family's honour."

My accusation, cast uncertainly, struck flesh it seemed. "It is a union that benefits everyone," he said defensively.

I recalled my encounter with the odious little turd Eurymachus. "Except your sister," I observed.

Epaminondas flushed. "She will do as she's told," he said in a tone that suggested otherwise.

But Theban political marriages were not my affair. "Surely you have not chased me outside just to speak of weddings and family finances."

The young Theban relaxed, evidently relieved to be speaking of other matters. "I wanted to meet you."

"Me?" I said, frowning.

"I have heard of your exploits. It is known even in Thebes that you slew the tyrant Kritias and the Spartan *polemarch* Chairon. Many Thebans hate the *peripoli*, it is true, but I think there is much to learn from their tactics."

I fixed him with a hard stare. "Perhaps you have heard of other deeds of mine, deeds less worthy of praise."

Epaminondas did not flinch. "It is true that there are rumours. But they are hardly to be believed. Men often slander their enemies to conceal their own fear of them."

"You see me an enemy, then?"

The young man pulled himself taller. "No, but I would be your *xenos*, if you would have me as such."

I nearly laughed aloud. A young man I had just met asking to be my guest-friend! But the words of Thrasybulus came back to me: *Sometimes a sympathetic voice in another city is worth a thousand hoplites.* I considered the young Theban's request in a new light. There was an audacity to it, if nothing else. To be the guest-friend of the hated Daimon of Athens! And this Epaminondas had an earnestness about him that won me over. "When do you return to Thebes?"

The young man's face brightened with hope. "The others are to depart tomorrow or the next day, but I can remain in Athens. Provided that I have somewhere to reside," he added.

I could have walked away. Instead I made one of those capricious decisions upon which our fates so often turn. "You can stay in the *peripoli* compound in Piraeus if that is what you wish."

Epaminondas grinned with gratitude. "Thank you, O Daimon!"

I nodded towards the home of Thrasybulus. "The others will not object to your remaining in Athens?"

"Ismenias will support my decision, I have no doubt. His aims align closely with those of Thrasybulus."

"And Leontiades?"

Epaminondas' face darkened. "Ismenias is the ranking ambassador. Leontiades will follow his lead." I did not press the issue, for there would be more time to interrogate the young Theban about the politics of his home city if he remained in Athens.

"Then it is settled," I said. "Present yourself at the *peripoli* compound in Piraeus tomorrow. You will live and train with us as long as you wish."

Epaminondas beamed. "I will be there, O Daimon!"

I watched him hurry back to Thrasybulus' home. Epaminondas, son of Polymnis. A poor aristocrat from Thebes. Another young man seeking glory but who would likely amount to nothing. I shook my head and began the long walk back to Piraeus.

Of course I could not hear the gods laughing at me.

CHAPTER 17

Epaminondas, son of Polymnis, presented himself at the *peripoli* compound the next day, a spear in his hand and a canvas kit-bag slung over his back. He had swapped out his worn-out robes for a more practical tunic and footwear. A plain but well-crafted sword hung at his belt.

"I want to train with your men," he declared. "I want no special treatment."

"It is easy enough for me to give you nothing," I said. "But do not complain when nothing is what you get." Epaminondas accepted my terms with a nod. "Give me your hands," I told him. Confused, the Theban did as I asked. His hands were calloused and muscular, not the soft flesh that one often found among the aristocratic classes. I grunted my approval. "You train in arms?"

"I train at the *gymnasion* every day," he said with a hint of pride.

"That is good, but you will find the training here a bit rougher than what you are used to, I expect."

"I am here to learn," he said without hesitation.

I led Epaminondas into the main compound. Neon was drilling the younger men in close combat. The Spartan warrior took us in with a glance. As always, some of the older men sat on benches, cheering and betting on the sparring matches.

The Theban's eyes grew larger at the sight of the black-braided warrior. "Is that a Spartan?"

"Another guest-friend of sorts," I said. I gestured at the sword at his hip. "Do you know how to use that?"

"I practice with spear, javelin, and sword," he said briskly.

I pointed at the young men training in the yard. "Show me."

Epaminondas blinked in surprise but recovered quickly. "Of course!"

His willingness to get stuck in pleased me. "Good! Neon!" I called to the Spartan. "Here is one more to put through his paces! Try him on Taras."

Neon barked at the recruits. "That's enough! Zenon!" he barked at a young man wearing a battered helmet so old that it might have been from the time of Homer. "Lend your gear to the newcomer."

Neon's five sweaty, red-faced charges gladly accepted the chance to recover their wind. That there was the chance for some entertainment while they did so was just an added windfall. The veterans, too, became excited at the prospect of the unexpected contest. They made space for me on their bench as Epaminondas donned the proffered gear.

"Who's the puppy?" asked Stachys.

"A Theban. He'll be staying with us for a time."

Stachys made a face of disgust. "A Theban?" The other *peripoli* murmured their disapproval. They had barely accepted Neon the Spartan, but antipathy to Thebes was bred in the bones of many Athenians.

I shrugged. "He seems a good lad."

Stachys looked doubtful. "Can he fight?"

I nodded towards the pair of young combatants. "We're about to find out."

"Begin!" Neon commanded.

The two fighters tapped wooden swords and separated. They circled each other warily, each seeking gaps in the other's defences. Taras struck first with a flurry of thrusts and cuts. Epaminondas, hard-pressed under the onslaught, fell back. Taras let loose a swipe at the Theban's head but checked the blow, giving Epaminondas room to duck down and drop into a roll. The Theban came up with a slash at the younger man's legs that Taras easily leapt clear of. The exchange elicited a murmur of appreciation from the spectators. I was not pleased, however, something that did not go unnoticed by Neon, with whom I exchanged a knowing look.

The contest continued in much the same frustrating manner with Epaminondas acquitting himself well enough and Taras holding back. "Halt!" I cried. The *peripoli* applauded the young combatants. Taras shrank under my icy stare.

Epaminondas, still breathing hard, removed the old helmet from his sweat-drenched head. "Have I lived up to the standard of the *peripoli*?"

"Your foundation is adequate," I said. The Theban's face dropped at the underwhelming appraisal. I turned on young Taras. "And you! Have you learned nothing?"

"Yes, *lochagos!*" he stammered. "I mean, no, *lochagos!*" The *peripoli* burst into laughter.

133

"If you hesitate, you will die," I said, glaring at him. "If you do not kill your enemy, he will kill you and your brother *peripoli*!" I said, sweeping an arm towards the gathered fighters. Taras blinked at me, his face tight. "Is that what you want, Taras the farm boy?"

"No, *lochagos*!"

"Go!" I said, waving him away. "You will help the woman empty chamber pots every night. It will give you time to think whether you want to remain here or go back to your brothers' farm and raise pigs!" It was a shameful task, but I wanted to prick his pride. Taras' eyes sparked with anger, and for a heartbeat I hoped he would defy me.

But his kinder nature won out. His shoulders slumped. "Yes, *lochagos.*" He trudged dejectedly from the courtyard.

I turned around. Epaminondas had not moved. "What do you want, Theban?" I growled, still irritated by Taras' performance.

"Tell me why I am merely adequate."

"Did you win?" I asked.

"No," he said.

"And Taras held back. You are competent. That is all."

"Show me," he said, slipping the helmet back on. He stepped back and waited expectantly. I measured up the young Theban, looking for arrogance, but I saw nothing but an eagerness to learn. The *peripoli*, young and old, looked on with anticipation to see what I would do. I glanced at Neon, who shrugged. The challenge issued, the lesson would have to be given.

"Very well," I said. An excited chatter filled the courtyard as I relieved another young recruit of this wooden practice sword and shield. I gave the weapon a few practice swings, feeling its familiar weight. I extended it towards Epaminondas, who tapped it with his own weapon. The contest had begun.

With a roar that could have been heard by all in Piraeus, I charged at Epaminondas. The wide-eyed Theban had no time to brace himself before I threw my shoulder into him, sending him flying onto his back. The *peripoli* laughed at his sprawling figure. I stood motionless while Epaminondas scrabbled to his feet.

I waited for him to come to me. He approached with caution, sensing a trap. At last he attacked. I redirected the blows with my shield, edging back with each blow. I dropped my shield a fraction, leaving an opening for him. Epaminondas took the bait and sliced towards my head, but I was not there. His momentum exposed his flank and I drove my shield into him. He stumbled away, flailing to keep his balance. Again, I waited for him to recover. Blinking furiously, Epaminondas raised his guard and planted his legs like tree stumps, challenging me to break his defence. I smiled.

I did not attack. Instead I began to lope around him, like a shepherd's dog circling a wayward sheep. He pivoted to keep his guard towards me. The *peripoli* laughed even harder as Epaminondas shifted and spun like a dancer at a festival. His embarrassment grew as I ran around him. At last he could bear it no longer and he lashed out at me in frustration. The attack was desperate and off-balance. I stepped into the thrust and the wooden sword skimmed past my ear. I planted my right foot behind his legs and shoved his chest with my sword hand. His back slammed into the dusty ground and his breath exploded from his lungs. He hastened to rise, but the blunt tip of my practice sword pushed into the divot of his throat. The spectators gave a hearty cheer, for it pleased them to see a Theban so easily bested.

I tossed the wooden sword aside and extended my hand. Epaminondas grasped my forearm and I hauled him to his feet. Far from anger, he was grinning sheepishly.

"I have much to learn," he said. "Your skill greatly exceeds mine."

I chuckled. "It is not so much skill as experience. It was not a fair contest."

Epaminondas frowned. "What do you mean?"

"I cheated," I said simply.

"You beat me fairly," the young Theban insisted.

"I changed the rules," I said. "You expected me to fight like Taras, or like we were sparring in the *gymnasion*. Instead I attacked you like a Thracian on the battlefield. That is the lesson. If you follow the rules in a battle, you will die." Epaminondas nodded like an obedient child. "Come," I said, putting my arm around his shoulder. "It's past time I introduced you to the others."

IN THE MONTH THAT FOLLOWED, Epaminondas made his presence felt. The Theban's curiosity poured forth from him like water from a gushing spring. He observed everything and peppered the other *peripoli* with questions at every opportunity, nipping at their heels like a puppy. I feared they would tire of his pestering, but they bore his constant interrogation with surprising patience.

He even questioned my sister when she was in Piraeus with us. He asked her about the Thracian gods, of all things, insisting that they were just the Greek gods by another name. Sometimes Meli and I would watch him train with the other *peripoli*. "There is a greatness about him," she said once as we watched Taras knock him to his backside yet again.

"You might be mistaken, Sister," I said doubtfully as Epaminondas clambered to his feet and rushed forward to receive another beating.

Meli shot me the same impatient stare I had seen a thousand times from my mother. "You must guide him, Brother, as Lykos once guided you." I remained silent, promising nothing.

But for all the disruption he caused, Epaminondas was a likable fellow. He was not the most gifted of warriors, yet he drove himself relentlessly, joining Neon's training sessions every day, despite being older than the younger recruits. When not drilling with Neon, he would enlist a veteran to spar with him while the others shouted out advice from their benches. He accepted without hesitation my suggestion that he join a patrol with Sabas to the borders of Megara and Boeotia. I had hoped the strenuous journey would sap him of some of his energy, but instead the entire patrol came back singing the Theban paean.

But above all, he was interested in tales of battle. Many of us had fought with Thrasybulus on Munychia and in Piraeus, but the collective experience of the *peripoli* was broad and varied. They spoke of battles against Spartans and Thebans, victories and losses, and the great grinding mass of metal and flesh that is the phalanx.

The front rank of a phalanx is a terrifying place. Every breath is an effort. Not only do the heat and weight of your armour stifle your lungs, but your enemy pushes against you from the front while a hundred of your own men crush you from behind. Yet still you scream for the death of your enemy to quell your own fear. All the while you thrust your spear over your shield, under your shield, again and again, hoping to find a gap of flesh. Skill counts less than courage and stamina, and the best soldier can be slain by a random blow from an unseen enemy. I told Epaminondas so, but he was unconvinced.

"There is strategy to the phalanx," he insisted. We were sitting around a fire pit in the rear courtyard of the compound, fighting the early winter chill with flames and wine. The men of the *peripoli* were enjoying the debate.

I shook my head. "You choose your ground, and then it is up to the gods."

"What about the arrangement of the hoplites? And the skirmishers?" he asked. There was a moan from the *peripoli*.

I waved him off. "When you are a general in charge of ten thousand Thebans, you may deploy them however you wish!" I retorted. There was some laughter and the young Epaminondas was gracious enough not to press the question. I took advantage of the young Theban's rare silence to conduct my own interrogation so that I might have something to report to Thrasybulus. "Do you think Thebes will join Athens to defy Sparta?"

Epaminondas was cautious in his response. "If Ismenias and his faction have their way, then yes."

"And what of the other Boeotian cities? Will they follow the lead of Thebes?"

It was an important question, for Thebes was not like Athens. The polis of Athens encompassed all the land of Attica. Every man of proper birth in Attica from the wealthiest aristocrat to the lowliest labourer was an Athenian citizen.

The relationship between Thebes and Boeotia was different. Boeotia is similar in size to Attica, but it consists of dozens of independent cities, of which Thebes is merely the most powerful. When Thebes is strong it can impose its will on the other Boeotian cities. But many of the cities resent their subservience and defy Thebes whenever they believe they can get away with it. In the coming conflict, if those cities remained neutral, or worse, allied themselves with Sparta, it would almost certainly doom Thrasybulus' rebellion to failure.

"Most of the cities will go with Thebes," Epaminondas declared.

"'Most' means not all," I said.

"Orchomenus openly supports Sparta," Epaminondas confessed. That was no surprise, for the Orchomenenians had ever been an obstacle to Thebes' wider ambitions. "And there are other cities with strong pro-Spartan factions like Chaeronea and Haliartos," he added. "But Ismenias will persuade them to stand with Thebes."

"Bribe them with Persian gold, you mean," Stachys interjected.

In Thebes too, I suspected the situation was more fraught than Epaminondas had let on. "And what about the faction of Leontiades?" I asked, recalling the adversarial Theban aristocrat.

All eyes were on Epaminondas. I could see him struggling between truth and loyalty to his future in-laws. He chose truth. "Leontiades favours peace with Sparta."

"Do many share his view?" I asked.

"Many of the old families of Thebes, yes."

"You mean the wealthy families," I said.

"Yes," he admitted.

I sighed. It was the same old story in every polis in Greece. The wealthy aristocrats favoured the Spartan hegemony, while those with democratic leanings chafed against it. "And how wealthy is Leontiades?" I asked.

"The wealthiest family in Thebes!"

"What is the source of their wealth?"

"There is land of course, but their wealth is built on slaves."

I had disliked Leontiades and his arrogant son before, and this new information did nothing but confirm that my instincts had been correct. Another thought occurred to me. "Is your family wealthy, Epaminondas?"

"My family is held in great esteem in Thebes," he said evasively.

To my left, Stachys let out a derisive snort. "A Theban family with esteem! By the dog, that would be a first!" he exclaimed. Others murmured their agreement. How many men had lost relatives in battles against the Thebans? Athens and Thebes were not natural allies and mutual suspicion born of generations of conflict ran deep. Thrasybulus was overly optimistic to think they would work together against Sparta, I thought.

"Thebans are an honourable people!" Epaminondas said, rising to his feet.

"The Thebans are Mede-izers," someone mumbled.

"Yes!" said Stachys, taking up the role of prosecutor. "Everyone knows that the Thebans fought with the Persians not against them!" The murmuring grew louder, like a thunderstorm that was drawing near. The young Theban was a guest. Enough was enough. I shifted to rise but caught Meli looking at me from across the fire. She gave a tiny shake of her head and I knew her meaning. *Let him defend himself.*

"Not all of them," Epaminondas said, looking Stachys in the eye. "Some Thebans fought against the Persians rather than join them. My family never bowed to the barbarians."

Stachys scoffed. "Thebans who refused to Mede-ize! Is there such a thing?"

"Ask the Spartan," Epaminondas said, pointing at Neon. All eyes turned to the taciturn Lakedaimonian.

Neon nodded. "It is true. Some Thebans fought and died beside King Leonidas at Thermopylae."

"And Leontiades' ancestors were not among them," I ventured.

"They were among the oligarchs appointed by the Persians," Epaminondas confirmed.

"So Leontiades wishes his son to marry your sister so that the sweet scent of your family's reputation masks the stink of his family's treachery?"

Epaminondas tightened his jaw and said nothing, perhaps realizing that the wine had loosened his tongue too much. I felt some guilt at the public airing of Epaminondas' history. It had raised his esteem in the eyes of the *peripoli,* but not enough.

I rose to my feet. "Brothers! Do we *peripoli* judge a man on his birth?" I asked. "If we did, there would be many of us found wanting, myself first among them!" A chuckle broke the chill that had been building. "And," I asked, looking at Stachys, "Has young Epaminondas not shown himself to be worthy of respect? Never have I seen a man knocked down so many times without complaint!" The chuckle turned to laughter and I knew I had won them over. Epaminondas smiled sheepishly. Stachys, looking abashed, stood and offered the young Theban his hand. There was a drunken cheer as they clasped hands.

When the mood had settled, I offered Epaminondas some more recompense for his trouble. In the month that he had been with the *peripoli*, the Theban's days had been occupied with training. There had been little time for talk, and on the rare occasions we spoke, Epaminondas had been almost deferential to me. Yet sometimes his curiosity drove him to the verge of asking me something before thinking better of it. I knew what he wanted to ask.

"We were talking of battles, O Epaminondas, before other matters pulled our discussion elsewhere," I said. "But you have not asked me of my battles! Are my deeds not worthy of telling?" I asked, feigning a hurt expression to the amusement of the men.

All eyes turned to Epaminondas, whose face had taken on a serious cast. "Your name is not unknown in Thebes," he said, choosing his words carefully.

"And what do the Thebans whisper of Daimon of Athens?" I prodded.

Epaminondas hesitated but at last gave voice to his doubts. "They say that you have done terrible things," he said.

The audience shifted their gaze back to me. I shrugged. "Maybe I have. Tell me what they say of me, Theban." I poked the fire with a broken javelin shaft.

"They say you and you men come in the night to murder farmers and pillage their farmsteads."

I laughed out loud at that. "I have nothing against farmers. They have nothing to fear from us! What else do your countrymen say, Theban?"

Epaminondas pressed onward. "It is said that you have put entire villages to the sword, sparing no one!"

"I have slaughtered bandits and tyrants and enemies on the battlefield, I confess, but that is all. What other slanders against me have you heard in Thebes?" Epaminondas was building towards something.

"They say the year before last you murdered the Pythia in Delphi!" he said. There it was.

I continued to poke at the fire. "Do they?" A cold silence descended on the gathering like winter mist.

He was committed now. "They say you murdered a prophet of Apollo — a boy! — and there was a great battle in Thrace!"

I did not deny it. "A battle?" I asked, my attention focused on the burning wood.

His irrepressible curiosity bested his sense of propriety. "It is said that you and a Thracian horde had routed the combined army of Lysander and Pausanias!"

Smiles appeared among the men, for they knew the truth of it. I glanced at Neon. His face was impassively Spartan. I raised my gaze towards Epaminondas. "Like all rumours, there is a seed of truth to it, but with each telling the story drifts farther from what actually transpired." I waved towards one of the younger *peripoli*. "Break out another pot of wine from the stores! Let me tell young Epaminondas what happened in Thrace!" The men cheered at the prospect of wine and the entertainment of the story to come.

I sometimes wonder about my life. If Nemesis, the goddess of retribution, had not claimed me as one of her own, I might have happily become one of the storytellers who wander the world collecting tales and spinning them out for food, wine, and a night's shelter. I have always had something of the rhapsode in me, and that night I was in fine form for my Theban guest. "It was not I who murdered the Pythia," I began.

It was a good tale, one that Epaminondas took in with the rapt attention of a child listening to stories of Herakles or Achilles. I described how Lysander's assassin had murdered the Pythia and how we had kidnapped a prophet from Lysander's camp, escaped from the Thracian war-lord Seuthes, and lured Lysander's Spartans into a trap. Neon followed the tale with long pulls from his cup but did not dispute my telling. But the Spartan leaned forward with interest as I described how we battled the army Pausanias, for he had not been present there.

The Muse filled my soul that night. Like all good storytellers, I played up the heroic deeds of Sabas, Tibetos, Stachys, and the mighty Mnasyllus, who blushed under the hearty wine-driven praise of his comrades. The men had heard the tale before, but they still cheered for the feats of their fellow *peripoli*. Tears were shed when I honoured the names of the fallen veteran *peripoli* Telekles and the Thracian captain Basti. I did not mention the horror of men choking on their own blood or slipping on the spilled entrails of their comrades, for veterans knew of these things well enough. Nor did I speak of boy Sosias, who the gods slew to spite me, and whose death haunts me still.

My story done, I drained my wine and tossed the empty cup into the fire. "Do you believe it, Theban?" I asked Epaminondas.

"It is no wonder Lysander hates you," he said.

"Lysander would cut my guts out and feed them to the dogs while I watched," I confirmed.

"But now his power is diminished," Epaminondas said.

I shared a long look with Neon across the fire before responding. "Here is another lesson for you, Epaminondas. As young Taras has learned, an enemy is dangerous until he's dead. And Lysander is very much alive. It would be good for both Athens and Thebes to remember that."

The combination of wine and thoughts of Lysander brought on a wave of fatigue. I rose from the bench and bid the others good night.

That night I did not sleep well, for the shadow of Lysander pursued me even in my dreams.

CHAPTER 18

As the rains of winter ebbed, Thrasybulus' preparations for war expanded.

Corinth, Argos, and other potential allies had already claimed their share of the Persian gold. The bulk of the money was still cached in the *peripoli* compound, waiting to go to Thebes. The only question was who was going to deliver it.

"The Thebans insisted on escorting the gold back to Thebes themselves," Thrasybulus informed me.

"How many?" I asked.

"They have sent thirty soldiers and horsemen."

I shook my head. "That is not nearly enough. Gods! Even a bandit gang would give them trouble!"

"I'm told that the small number is to avoid attracting the attention of the Spartans," Thrasybulus said, keeping his tone neutral.

I scoffed. "If that is the case, then let the *peripoli* take responsibility. We could have the gold in Thebes with none the wiser."

Thrasybulus gave me a long look. "The Thebans specifically demanded that the *peripoli* not be involved."

"At the request of Leontiades and his faction, no doubt," I said dryly.

"I am not privy to the internal matters discussed by the Theban council, but Leontiades was likely behind it, yes."

I scratched at the stubble on my cheek. "The strange thing is," I said, "I may soon be making a trip to Thebes in any case."

Thrasybulus' thick eyebrows rose slightly. "Oh?"

"A messenger arrived from Thebes yesterday bearing a message from Epaminondas," I said. The young Theban had returned to his polis a month before. "He has invited me to be his *xenos* in Thebes," I added casually.

Thrasybulus pursed his lips. "And you wish to go?"

I gave a noncommittal shrug. "It was not my wish, but now I am reconsidering the matter. I could accompany the messenger back to Thebes. With some of the *peripoli*, I added. "And horses. And pack-mules. After all, it is a long journey to Thebes and I don't know how long I'll be staying."

Thrasybulus knew me too well. "Tell me what you have in mind."

And I told him.

A DAY AFTER THE THEBANS LEFT with the locked chests of Persian gold, we made our own departure. The messenger sent by Epaminondas, Malkos, agreed to accompany us at my invitation.

"Why are we not taking the Eleusis road?" Malkos asked in a thick Theban accent. The Eleusis road led northwest to the broad valleys that connected with the plains of Boeotia. From there Thebes was an easy trek north. The route was well-travelled and level, which is why the Thebans and the gold would go that way. And why we would not.

"The *peripoli* never take an easy route when a hard one is available," Stachys said, checking the panniers on a mule one last time.

Malkos craned his neck to peer over Stachys' shoulder. "Why do you have so much baggage?" he asked. Stachys shifted slightly to block his view.

Tibetos put his arm around the Theban's shoulder, turning him away from the mules. "The *peripoli* never travel light when they can haul a heavy load," he said, echoing Stachys.

Malkos frowned. "That is not your reputation," he said.

I redirected Malkos to his horse. "Thrasybulus sends gifts to the people of Thebes," I explained. "Bronze ingots and spear-points for the war ahead." I locked my fingers to provide a step for the Theban to mount his horse.

Atop his animal, Malkos was unconvinced. "There must be easier ways of transport such a gift!"

"Thrasybulus thought it would improve my reputation among the Thebans. I am not well-loved there, I understand."

"That is an understatement," he confirmed. "But it is an odd gesture, nevertheless."

I smiled sympathetically. "I said the same. But politicians like Thrasybulus think differently from us," I said, tapping the side of my head. "He is a *strategos* and I am a wool-headed soldier. Who are mere mortals like us to argue, eh, Malkos?" I slapped his horse's rump and the beast trotted away before her rider could pry further.

Our expedition had thirty men and horses, as well as a dozen mules and donkeys. At a steady pace, we could be in Thebes in three days. Neon had asked to be part of the expedition. The request surprised me, for the Spartan asked for little while contributing much to the operations of the compound. I let him join us. I sensed some unease among the others, but no one openly objected to my decision. I wondered if my trust in the Spartan went too far, but I valued his experience. In the end we agreed that he would accompany us as far as the border. "I reckon Spartans are not very popular in Thebes these days," I observed.

"Thebans are not my favourite, either," he said in a flat tone. It was always difficult to know if he was joking.

My sister had also declared her intention to accompany us. "Bassareus' presence is strong in Thebes. I will search for him there," she said, using the Thracian name for the god Dionysus. Where I spurned the gods, Meli sought them out. I knew better than to argue with my sister, but I did not begrudge her desire to join us. After more than a year with the horsemen of Thrace, Meli was the best rider among us.

As odd as it was to have a woman among our number, none of the *peripoli* dared object. The veteran *peripoli* regarded my sister with a mixture of awe and love, but also looked upon her with barely-concealed fear, for they had heard terrible tales of what happened to those who crossed the Thracian witch-woman.

I spent much of the first day interrogating the messenger Malkos. The Theban confirmed that the political rifts in Thebes ran deep and the commitment of many Boeotian allies to a war with Sparta was halfhearted at best. The great alliance that Thrasybulus was building rested on weak foundations.

I mulled over what Malkos had told me. Even as Thrasybulus plotted, the enemy too advanced their goals unseen. I turned my attention upwards. Heavy clouds scudded across the late winter sky, a reminder that winter rains still might hinder our journey. As we travelled through the plains north of Athens, I could not but feel our band of soldiers was a scar on the land, bringing with it the rumblings of war that disturbed the serenity of the place. The grapevines were bare, and next year's wine was already fermenting in buried vats all over Attica. Even to my untrained eye it was apparent the vines were still young, replanted less than ten years earlier to replace those destroyed by ravaging Spartans during the war. The farmers' hope for future harvests might soon be dashed once again by the fires of an invading army, I thought.

At mid-day, we stopped in an olive grove to rest while we fed and watered the animals at a nearby spring. Down the slope was a well-tended vineyard. Mnasyllus, a farmer's son, expounded on all things agricultural to the lounging *peripoli* while sheep bleated in the distance. Taras, not long gone from his own family farm, added his own insights.

While we rested, I interrogated Mnasyllus. "Do you miss this life then?" I asked. I knew that Mnasyllus' family, though not wealthy, had a productive farm a day's ride east of Athens.

Mnasyllus was uncharacteristically philosophical. "If the gods will it, I will be a farmer again one day. My brothers are taking care of our family's land. For now, the gods have made me one of the *peripoli* and I am content with that."

Sabas chipped in from where he was lounging under an olive tree. "What are your brothers like?"

"Let's just say I'm the smallest one," the ox-like Mnasyllus said, grinning.

"Gods help us! I'd hate to see what your father looked like!" Tibetos exclaimed.

"Or your mother!" Sabas joked. The others laughed.

I noticed Taras staring out the vines, lost in his own thoughts. "And what about you, young Taras?" I asked, snapping the lad from his daydreaming. "Would you rather be tending vines or fighting with the *peripoli*?"

"I want to be a *peripoli*," he responded with a little too much alacrity

I grunted. "A good choice. Farming seems a dull life," I said, plucking a leaf from an olive tree. There was a murmur of agreement from the dozing *peripoli* lying sprawled about the orchard.

Taras disagreed. "It is a hard life, *lochagos*, but a peaceful one. To harvest the fruits of your land and labour is the greatest freedom," he said a touch wistfully.

Mnasyllus sided with Taras. "Don't mind the *lochagos*, Boy. He grew up in the city and wouldn't know a plough from an olive press." The two of them wandered off to inspect the vines more closely, leaving the rest of us to idle.

A little later, our beasts rested and watered, we prepared to set out once more. Mnasyllus approached me as I reloaded my horse. "You will always be welcome on my family's farm, Daimon," he said seriously. "You will find peace there, I think." Meli, within earshot, tended to her horse, but I knew she was listening.

"If the gods will it, I will be there," I said. That seemed to satisfy the big man, who ambled off to help the others with their packs. As I looked at his broad back, a shadow passed over my soul, for I knew the gods would never grant me the peace of rustic domesticity that he and Taras longed for. I know moments of joy and laughter and the comfort of friendship, but enduring happiness, if it exists, I have not discovered, even to this day.

The gods had made me for other purposes.

ON THE SECOND DAY we ascended into the mountains. The veteran *peripoli* knew the passes and valleys well, but for the younger men like Taras it was unfamiliar terrain. "You will learn these paths well," I told them, "for your knowledge of them will help you defeat the enemies of Athens who trespass here." During the great war, countless Spartans and Boeotians had met their doom in *peripoli* ambushes.

Iollas gave a derisive snort. "Then are you wise to be revealing such things to a Spartan?" he challenged. I would not have thought it, but I had begun to miss the freed helot's customary reticence.

"This route is hardly a secret," I said. Indeed we had passed several travellers that day.

Iollas grunted and stayed silent for a time, but only to let his bile build up. "Do you know," he said, raising his voice to address everyone, "what happened on the other side of that ridge?" he asked, pointing to the west. I narrowed my eyes at him, for I knew where he was heading. "It was there that I was freed!" he proclaimed. "And where young Daimon killed his first Spartan! The first of many, praise the gods!" There was a murmur of approval from the others. I glared at Iollas but he wanted to fight. "What was the Spartan's name?" he asked, though he knew perfectly well, for the Spartan had been his master. "Kalchas, wasn't it?"

"You know it was," I said, irritated.

Iollas glanced over at Neon. "Was he a relative of yours, Spartan?" Iollas asked hopefully.

"I do not know the name," Neon said, his eyes steady on the road ahead.

Iollas' disappointed frown was short-lived as his eyes flashed with malice and he continued his tale. "And Lykos was there! The great Lykos, son of Lykos, brother of Thrasybulus himself!" This elicited a greater reaction from the *peripoli,* for Lykos was a hero whose reputation nearly eclipsed that of Achilles. Most of those present did not know my mentor — he had died long before they joined our ranks— but a few of us had, including Sabas, Mnasyllus, and Tibetos. And my sister.

Meli had been Lykos' lover. The scars on her soul grew thicker with each year, but I knew that old wounds could still tear open. Meli's green eyes revealed little. I exchanged a concerned glance with Tibetos, but said nothing, for my sister was quite capable of dealing with Iollas if that was what she wished. Instead she surprised both of us.

"Tell us, O Iollas," she said in a strong, clear voice, "what happened that day. I don't think I have ever heard your version of events." Iollas, in his zeal to antagonize Neon, had forgotten the presence of my sister. The former helot, superstitious to a fault, touched his iron buckle to ward off my sister's evil eye. Meli assuaged his fear of divine punishment. "Please, O Iollas. Entertain us with a tale to soothe sore backsides."

Iollas, cautious at first, eyed my sister warily as he began his tale. Seeing that he was not struck dead or blind, his confidence grew and his guttural Messenian voice took on a bardic quality as he recalled how the *peripoli* had trapped and slaughtered a troop of Megarian soldiers led by their Spartan commander Kalchas. He recounted how I, an outmatched lad whose beard was but a future promise, had run to face the Spartan Kalchas in single combat. The helot's description was thrilling and comic in turn, and even Tibetos and Meli cracked a smile. But Iollas saved his greatest enthusiasm for describing how Lykos had strung up the Spartan's spread-eagled corpse on a frame of spears as a warning to those who would follow him. "There was a man who knew how to deal with Spartans!" he finished, aiming each word at Neon like an arrow.

All eyes turned to the Spartan exile, but Neon disappointed them. "A fine tale, O Iollas," was all he said.

Neon's muted reaction denied Iollas the effect he had been seeking. The former helot grimaced. "Remember Kalchas," he declared to all.

"*That* is what should be done to Spartans." He wheeled his pony around to join some of his fellows at the rear of our column.

Tibetos brought his horse beside Neon's. "I would sleep with one eye open if I were you, Spartan" he advised.

CHAPTER 19

My hope that matters would simmer down was a vain one. Setting up camp and preparing the evening meal kept Iollas too busy for conflict, but when the meal was done, the Messenian fanned the embers of discord anew.

"Have you heard of the *krypteia*, brothers?" he asked those gathered around the central fire. Most had, of course, but that did not stop Iollas from explaining. "It is a secret Spartan cult. Only the finest — the purest! — young Spartans are deemed worthy to join, those destined for great things. But the initiates still have to prove themselves," he said, staring at Neon across the fire. Iollas shifted his attention to Taras. "Do you know what they have to do, young Taras?"

Taras, wide-eyed, shook his head. "No, O Iollas!"

Iollas flashed a jagged smile. "They kill helots." He looked back at Neon. "Is it true, Spartan?"

"It is," Neon said impassively.

Iollas reacted as though he had caught a thief red-handed. "You see! He does not even show shame!" The mood was shifting in favour of Iollas, who seized the moment. "They come in the night, seeking the strongest helots, the most outspoken. They murder them in their sleep with their wives and children, leaving their corpses to be found the next morning as a warning. My brother's family fell to them. The *krypteia* killed them all, even his daughter and two-year-old son." Iollas turned an accusing stare at Neon. "I have watched this Spartan. And I know a member of the *krypteia* when I see one." All eyes turned to Neon to see how he would respond.

"I was many things once, Messenian," he said, not denying Iollas' accusation. "For many years, I have questioned what I was taught. It has cost me much. My inheritance. My reputation among my comrades. When I was rotting in a Persian dungeon, I thought much on what I had been. I confess there was much to regret. But I am not the same man."

"Once a Spartan, always a Spartan!" Iollas sneered.

Neon rose to his feet and walked slowly around to where Iollas sat. The *peripoli* watched entranced, like an audience watching a tragedy. Neon held out his wineskin to Iollas. "I swear by the twin gods I am no longer your enemy, O Iollas."

Iollas leapt to his feet with a snarl, swatting the wineskin from Neon's hand as if he had been offered poison. "Do you think my friendship is bought so cheaply, Spartan?" He pivoted on his heel and stomped off to his sleeping spot at the edge of camp.

Neon calmly retrieved the wineskin, most of whose contents had drained out onto the rocky earth. He retook his place near Tibetos, unaffected by the stares that followed him.

"You should sleep with *both* eyes open," Tibetos advised, amending his earlier warning. *To protect himself from whom*, I thought, wondering how much Iollas' words had stirred up the suspicion among some of the men towards Neon. It was a good time to remind them that Neon was my guest-friend and protected by my guarantee of safety. But my sister pre-empted me by speaking first.

Meli rose to her feet. "Iollas is our brother and his hatred of Sparta is a just one," she said. Many of those present nodded in agreement. "But I have seen no evil in Neon, though he is a Spartan. Know that I have even asked the gods about him, and they have told me that he is our ally, not our enemy." She sat back down.

It was a gesture that did much to blunt the accusations of Iollas. It seemed better to let the men sleep with my sister's words in their minds rather than those of Iollas. "We have an early start if we are to arrive in Thebes before evening," I announced. "I will take the first shift of sentry duty." The men took their cue and shuffled off to claim their piece of ground for the night. Neon found a place far from the others. It was not long before the snapping of embers was joined by the droning snores of tired men.

A shiver vibrated through me and I pulled my cloak tighter. I had something to do before I settled down for my watch. Picking my way through the sleeping *peripoli*, I made my way to the edge of camp where Iollas had made his sleeping spot for the night. I squatted down.

"Iollas!" I said softly. The cloak-covered lump did not move. "I know you are yet awake, Iollas!" I whispered, giving him a shove. The helot remained stubbornly silent. "I have come to speak to you about Neon," I said. Silence. "If you want me to send him away, I will do so, O Iollas."

At last the lump shifted. "You are wrong to trust him."

"I have watched Neon closely and I believe him to be an honourable man."

Iollas sat up with a start, his face close to mine. "He is a *Spartan!*" he hissed.

"We cannot choose our fathers anymore than we can command the weather. We can only choose our actions. Neon has chosen exile." *Though he has yet to admit it to himself*, I thought.

Iollas gave a disapproving grunt. "How do you know he is not just Lysander's spy?" It was an intelligent question. The enmity I had witnessed between Lysander and Neon seemed genuine enough, but Lysander wielded deception like a knife and no ruse was impossible for him.

"I don't," I said honestly.

"Yet you value him," Iollas said, a touch accusingly.

"Yes."

"Then why would you send him away?"

I put my hand on his shoulders. "You are my comrade, but more importantly you are my friend. His presence causes you pain. I will tell him to find his own destiny."

Pride and the desire to see the back of Neon battled across Iollas' face. Pride was the victor. "You've extended the protection of *xenia* to the Spartan. The gods will punish you if you violate your oath," he said sagely. He sighed. "We cannot fight the gods." He reached for his spear and rose to his feet. "I cannot sleep. I will take the watch with you," he said, resting his spear on his shoulder. His lips parted in a feral sharp-toothed smile. "And I will keep an eye on the Spartan, in case you are wrong."

"I often am," I said. Iollas shambled off towards the other side of the camp in his odd, bow-legged gait. Like me, he preferred to be alone.

I found a boulder down the slope from the camp and sat down. I shut my eyes and pinched my temples. The uncertain politics of Thebes and Boeotia. The hidden machinations of Lysander and the Spartans. The internal divisions that were eroding the *peripoli* as fast as I could build it up. I felt like a man groping about in a black forest on a moonless night. I opened my eyes.

Under the starlight the blackness of the forest turned into a shadow world of greys and blues as my vision adapted to the night. I reached out with my senses, searching for enemies seeking to infiltrate our camp but only heard the occasional rustle of an animal going about its business. I adjusted my cloak and settled in for my watch.

And I began to search for a way back to the light.

WE LEFT NEON AND TEN MEN encamped in the foothills along the Boeotian border. Iollas, true to his word, volunteered to stay with Neon.

"We will be back in a few days. Try not to start a war with Neon in the meantime," I warned Iollas.

"The oath of *xenia* binds my hands," he said with a hint of regret. I narrowed my eyes at him and he shrugged. There was nothing to be done. It was time to set out.

Our train of horses and pack animals descended onto the broad plain that comprised most of Boeotia. As much as rich harvests, the flat land bred skilled horsemen and even tougher hoplites. For this, many Athenians regarded the Boeotians as little more than unrefined swineherds, but I saw only well-tended farms and prosperous villages. The Theban messenger Malkos was proud to point out the various temples and sights along the way, brightening as his home drew nearer. "I have been away too long!" he said.

"It has less been than ten days," Stachys observed.

Malkos grinned. "Like I said, too long!" he said, pointing at the city in the distance. "Look! The city of Herakles!"

Thebes is situated atop a ridge of low hills. Above the imposing city walls was the elongated acropolis of the Kadmeia, its temples already visible. Our approach no doubt drew interest. Upon our arrival at the commanding southern gate, a squadron of grim-looking spear-men with shields and helmets blocked our path. Their captain, a warrior with a high horse-hair crest on his helmet, stepped forward. "What business brings you here?" he demanded, his thick Theban accent full of suspicion.

"Ah! The vaunted Theban hospitality!" Stachys said dryly.

Malkos, casting Stachys an irritated glance, dismounted and strode up to the burly captain. The Theban captain's suspicion hardly seemed assuaged by Malkos' explanation of our mission, judging by the glances he directed our way. The conversation complete, the captain disappeared into the city and Malkos returned to report. The soldiers, I noted, still barred our way. "We have to wait to enter the city," Malkos explained.

"Are the guards usually so strict?" I asked.

Malkos shrugged. "These are tense times," was all he could offer.

We were content enough to dismount and stretch out our limbs. We idled about for what seemed an age, checking the pack animals' panniers and checking them again. Even Malkos was growing frustrated by the officiousness of his fellow Thebans. At last the tough-looking captain returned. If anything, he looked even less welcoming than before. But at his command, the city guards stepped aside. "You may enter," the captain said, waving his spear. Permission granted at last, we led our caravan into the open area beyond the gate.

"Something isn't right, Dammo," Tibetos whispered to me.

"We are here at the invitation of Epaminondas," I said.

"And how much weight does the word of Epaminondas carry in Thebes?" my friend muttered.

"I think we're about to find out," I said, pointing at the fifty or so fully-armoured soldiers awaiting us. Behind us, the guards had formed a line of locked shields, barring any exit from the city. We were surrounded.

Some of my men reached for their swords. "Do not draw your weapons!" I ordered.

Now even citizens were thronging to our location, men and women both, shouting and hollering abuse. Tibetos dodged a clay tile that was hurled his way. Meli, delighting in the chaos, grinned at the growing mob like a hungry fox. Then a welcome face appeared.

Epaminondas shoved his way forward, his hands held high. "I am Epaminondas, son of Polymnis. This man is my guest-friend!" The din of the threatening crowd almost drowned him out. The young Theban recognized one of the soldiers and approached him. They huddled close in intense discussion. The soldier nodded and pushed his way into the mass of angry Thebans. Epaminondas hurried over to where I stood with Malkos, who was at a loss to explain the hostile reception.

"What is happening?" I asked.

Epaminondas was grim. "The soldiers escorting the Persian gold from Athens were ambushed two days ago. The men were slaughtered. The gold is gone."

"That doesn't explain this," I said, glancing at the mob howling for our blood.

"There is a rumour that it was Athenians. They say it was Daimon *O Phobomenos* who carried out the attack."

O Phobomenos. The Feared. It was an epithet I had not heard before. Daimon the Despised would have been more suitable. Soon it would be Daimon the Flayed if the mob were not brought under control. "That's absurd," I said, cupping my hands to my mouth so that Epaminondas could hear. "Malkos has been with us the past three days. He will attest to our innocence."

"I know, but the rumour has already spread throughout the city," he shouted back. "The magistrates are coming."

I regarded the surging crowds doubtfully. "They might be too late to save us from being torn apart."

"I will defend you with my life, even against my own people," Epaminondas avowed.

"We may still hope that the Fates have not woven that destiny for us," I said.

The cordon of soldiers parted to let the newcomers pass. Ismenias was among them, as was Leontiades and his turd-sniffing son Eurymachus.

Leontiades glared at me. "You dare show your face in Thebes!" Beside him, Ismenias was grim. It was not a good sign.

"I am the guest-friend of Epaminondas, son of Polymnis," I said.

Epaminondas stepped forward. "This man is under my protection," he confirmed. Eurymachus scowled at his future brother-in-law.

Leontiades ignored Epaminondas and pressed on with his attack. "The soldiers bringing the gold to Thebes were ambushed near the border," he said, his voice dripping with venom.

"And the gold?" I asked.

Ismenias stepped in. "Stolen. All of it," he said dejectedly. I scratched at the week's growth of beard on my cheek.

Leontiades pointed an accusing finger at me. "You do not seem surprised, Athenian!"

"I did warn of such a possibility," I said. "You might as well as have sent a messenger to Lysander for all you did to keep it secret."

Leontiades swatted away my statement. "It is convenient to have someone else to blame."

I laughed. "You believe I am responsible?"

Leontiades' eyes flashed as though I had fallen into a trap. "There was one survivor. He said they were attacked by the *peripoli*! He said Daimon of Athens led them!" he said triumphantly.

"*Your* man, no doubt," I said casually

"That matters little!" Leontiades snapped.

I swept an arm towards my men. "The *peripoli* are here!" I tapped my chest. "I am here! Why would we come to Thebes if we had just massacred your men?" Leontiades seemed perplexed by my lack of concern.

Eurymachus stepped in for his father, stabbing a bejeweled finger at me with a rhetorician's flair. "To throw off suspicion! But Thebes will not be fooled by your schemes, Athenian!"

I barked a laugh. "You say I attacked your men?" I asked, still grinning.

"There are witnesses," Leontiades repeated.

I pointed at Malkos. "The Theban herald Malkos accompanied us from Athens. With the help of one of your own, I did this?"

The aristocrat, committed to his accusation, did not relent. "You have tricked him in some way! Your evil ways are well known!"

I looked at Tibetos, who shrugged. My sister floated to my side. Her hungry smile matched my own. Leontiades flinched under her green-eyed stare. "And the gold is gone?" I asked.

"Into the hands of thieves!" Leontiades said.

Without another word, I turned to the nearest mule. I detached one of the leather packs hanging over the beast's shoulders and returned to the waiting Thebans.

I turned the pack over. A tinkling stream of coruscating gold coins poured out onto the ground. The last coin fell into the metallic pool at my feet with a clink. I pointed at the gold at the Theban aristocrat's feet.

"If the Persian gold is gone, then what is that?"

CHAPTER 20

Leontiades was quick to recover from his state of stunned incomprehension.

"You see!" he cried, pointing at the scattered gold coins. "The Athenian reveals his guilt!"

Ismenias saved me from further slander. "Don't be a fool, Leontiades," he said with some exasperation. "It is unlikely that he stole the gold only to bring it here. Besides," he said, gesturing toward Malkos. "The herald accompanied him all the way, no?"

"Yes, O Ismenias," Malkos confirmed.

Epaminondas frowned in confusion. "But what of the escort? What were they transporting if not the gold?"

"The chests were packed with iron," I said.

Leontiades tried to salvage some dignity. "We should have been informed!"

"There was no time," I lied. "In any case, secrecy was better protection than spears."

"Loyal Thebans died for iron!" Leontiades said accusingly.

The wealthy Theban was irritating me. "Only because you refused to send enough of them. Had you done so, I would be in Athens right now instead of standing here with an empty belly and a sore arse arguing with a turd-sniffer like you." The *peripoli* laughed.

Ismenias stepped in before a brawl broke out. "And how much gold did you bring?"

"One hundred talents' worth, more or less" I confirmed. "I trust *you* to make a proper accounting of it, O Ismenias," I said. Leontiades and his son glared at me.

Leontiades knew the battle was lost. He shifted his position with a politician's oily ease. "Then Thebes should be grateful for your foresight. I will see to transporting the gold to the treasury immediately," he declared, trying to regain some of his damaged authority.

Before I could protest Leontiades' proposal, Eurymachus waved a dismissive hand our way. "And what of the Athenians? If the money is here, they are no longer needed. It is hardly past midday. They should return to Athens at once."

Epaminondas objected. "Daimon is here at my invitation. He is my *xenos*."

Eurymachus' lips tightened as he restrained himself from criticizing his future brother-in-law. His gaze landed on the rest of the *peripoli*. "Surely your invitation did not extend to this entire rabble?"

Ismenias chose his words carefully. "The Athenians have done us a great service. Accommodation will be found," he said. "Should they wish it," he added.

Tibetos, reading Ismenias' cue, cast a wary eye over the mob of grim-looking Theban citizens surrounding us. "I think willing hosts might be hard to find," he said. "We can get back to Iollas and the others before evening if we set off now." It was the sensible solution.

A woman's voice cut into the discussion. "I will stay with my brother in Thebes, Tibo," my sister said, putting her hand on my friend's forearm. "With the permission of Epaminondas, of course," she added, making a slight bow towards the Theban.

I shot Meli an irritated look, for she had not forewarned me of her intentions. If my Theban host was surprised, he hid it well. "You honour us, O Seeress," Epaminondas answered graciously before I could contradict her. Unlike me, Epaminondas was reluctant to cross a witch. Meli avoided my glare.

"Then it is done," Tibetos said, a little regretfully.

With angry mutterings, the crowd began to disperse. Leontiades and Eurymachus, denied the bloodletting of the *peripoli,* took charge of enlisting the gathered soldiers to load the bags of gold onto hastily obtained carts. While the other *peripoli* readied the horses and donkeys for the return journey to Athens, Tibetos joined Meli and me where we stood with Epaminondas.

"You don't mind being in charge while I'm gone, Tibo?" I asked.

"Mnasyllys will keep troublemakers in line," Tibetos said, jerking a thumb towards the huge farmer. Mnasyllus grinned.

"Then I know things are in good hands," I said.

Tibetos cocked an eyebrow at Meli. "You will keep *him* out of trouble?" he said, glancing my way.

"You should be asking me to keep an eye on *her*," I said.

Tibetos looked skywards. "Gods help us!"

While Tibetos and Meli shared a few more quiet words, I spoke with Epaminondas. "I feel we are imposing on your hospitality."

"Nonsense! I have already sent a slave ahead to notify my father of your arrival and that your sister will be joining us. Let Bulis carry your things." He beckoned a tunic-clad man of middle years who had been standing discreetly a short distance away. The slave Bulis hurried over and moved to take the kit-bag slung over my shoulder.

I held up a hand. "There is no need," I said. At a loss, the slave Bulis appealed to Epaminondas with a confused look. Epaminondas hesitated before giving a brief nod. "As you wish. But let Bulis take your horses to be stabled at least," he said. I nodded and Bulis scurried off and set about his task.

"It does no good to have idle slaves," Epaminondas said sagely. I said nothing.

Epaminondas led us through Thebes, taking us away from the hostile mood around the Kadmeia. He spoke incessantly, his restless mind jumping from topic to topic, though neither Meli nor I paid much attention. My sister had never set foot in Thebes. Her curious gaze darted about, taking in the sights of the city. I was reacquainting myself with a place I had stayed in only briefly.

Besides the Kadmeia, there were several other long hills within the walls of Thebes. As in Athens, the roads and lanes had no sense of planning, but the buildings and houses were less crammed than in my home city, leaving space for small gardens and livestock. Pigs, goats, and chickens wandered about, left to their own devices by the residents. A huge sow snuffled across our path and Epaminondas dodged it as a matter of course, his patter not missing a beat.

The thick Theban accents of the locals filled the air. Vendors hawked their wares, customers argued about the prices, and layabouts chatted and gossiped, gazing idly at passersby. It was much as in Athens, save for the fact that there were many more women about, and not only slaves. Women of all stations were visible, including merchants as hard-nosed and shrewd as any man, or so I had heard. The sight of so many women going about their business in public would have offended the typical Athenian male.

Suspicious stares followed us as we wended our way through the streets. Our decidedly Thracian appearance did not help matters. Thebes was not Piraeus with its abundance of Thracian traders. Meli, with her tattooed face and patterned Thracian cloak, and myself, oddly-armoured, copper-haired, and a head taller than most men, found no concealment from curious Theban eyes.

It was a relief then when Epaminondas came to a halt in front of a sizable if somewhat run-down house. "Welcome to my home," Epaminondas said, extending an arm towards the open door.

The door was flanked by two small altars, each adorned with the image of a god. On the left was a small statue of Apollo. The god of doorways was no ally of mine. I turned my attention to the unfamiliar god on the right-hand altar. The image was simple in style and worn with age, its distinguishing details eroded by generations of sun and rain. I would have to ask my sister, for she was knowledgeable of such things. Even now she was staring at the strange idol.

A fresh offering of wine and figs sat at the deities' feet. Epaminondas came from a pious household. My father would have approved of such piety. "May our ties of friendship deepen," I said formally. Epaminondas beamed. We stepped over the threshold.

Like Epaminondas' worn clothes, his family home hinted at having seen better days. The house boasted a spacious courtyard with a stone altar, but was like an aging matron who tries to mask her age with poorly-applied cosmetics. The paint on the columns had faded or even peeled off in places to reveal bare wood underneath. Many flagstones were cracked or uneven. I was strict about the maintenance of the *peripoli* compound, and now by habit I mentally ticked off a list of posts and beams in need of mending and patches of wall requiring repair.

"It is a fine home," I told Epaminondas.

A stout older man in a faded blue robe stood in front of the family altar. In bearing and appearance, the similarity to Epamaminodas was striking.

"This is my father, Polymnis," Epaminondas said.

"My sister and I are grateful for your hospitality, O Polymnis," I said.

Polymnis stepped forward and extended his hand in greeting. "No need to dwell on formality. My son speaks highly of you and that is enough for me. You and your sister," he said, smiling at Meli, "are welcome to stay as long as you wish." Polymnis acted as if having a tattooed Thracian soothsayer before him was the most natural thing in the world.

Meli bowed. "You are a gracious host, O Polymnis." My sister could be very charming when she wished.

Polymnis accepted the praise with a genuine smile. "Let me introduce you to the others." He clapped and three figures emerged from the back rooms of the courtyard. "This is Manus, our head slave," he said, indicating a balding man of middle years. "Speak to him if you need anything."

The slave gave a courteous if slightly stiff bow. "Greetings, *despote*," he said. I could not say where he was from, for Manus was a common enough slave name. From the look of him, he could have been from one of the barbarian tribes beyond Makedon. The other two slaves, a waifish young girl with short black hair and a hard-looking, thickset older woman with greying hair, were similarly hard to place. They regarded me with the practiced blank stares of slaves everywhere. With the other slave Bulis, Polymnis owned four slaves, a small number for an old aristocratic family.

"Thank you, O Polymnis. But I fear my sister's presence will be an inconvenience," I said, casting an irritated look at Meli.

"She will be welcome in the women's quarters," came a female voice. "The seeress Melitta of Athens is known even in Thebes. We will be honoured by her presence." Two women were descending the stairs from the apartments above.

"My wife Iokaste and my daughter Althaia," Polymnis said.

In bearing, Polymnis' wife was tall and comely. Iokaste's clothing and jewelry were modest but refined. Her elaborately coiled braids framed an intelligent, aristocratic face graced by age rather than diminished by it. But whatever the older woman's charms, she was eclipsed by her daughter.

When Epaminondas told me his sister was betrothed to Eurymachus, I had imagined a girl of fourteen or fifteen years old, the age at which most girls wed, but Althaia appeared to be closer in age to Epaminondas himself.

A sculptor would have wept to see her, for the finest statue would have paled in comparison beside her. I had always doubted that men went to war over Helen's beauty, but I found that conviction dissolving like mist in the morning sun. There was no artifice about her. A simple braid about her crown held back thick black hair that cascaded over her neck and shoulders. The only element out of place was a chain of thick gold links about her throat. That and the frown with which she regarded me. After a moment that seemed both eternal and instantaneous, the two women were at the side of Polymnis.

Fumbling for words, I managed to utter some pleasantry or other. The look of obvious disapproval from Epaminondas' sister did not help. Meli saved me. "May Bendis bless you for your kindness, O Iokaste," she said.

"The followers of Bendis are always welcome in this house," Iokaste said. If I thought my discomfort had gone unnoticed, I was wrong, for Epaminondas' mother turned towards me. "Do I make you uneasy, Daimon of Athens?"

I felt myself turning red. "Not at all, O Iokaste," I said.

Iokaste chuckled. "It sometimes disturbs Athenian men to be addressed directly by women. In Thebes, our women are not immured in their rooms like birds in cages when strangers come to visit!" That Iokaste had apparently misunderstood the reason for my embarrassment filled me with relief.

"My sister," I said, recovering, "has taught me not to underestimate the strength of women. In Thrace, I have seen women fight alongside their men as equals."

Epaminondas' sister Althaia interrupted. "By his looks I would not judge him Athenian," she observed. Her voice was as clear as ice. Epaminondas shot her a warning look and she raised her chin in defiance. I was not the only one with a strong-willed sister, it seemed.

Perhaps sensing the underlying tension, Polymnis stepped in and admonished his wife and daughter. "You pester our guests. They have travelled far and surely in need of refreshment. Manus," he said, calling his head slave. "Bring some food and drink to the salon. We will dine early tonight."

DINING WITH IOKASTE AND ALTHAIA was a novel experience. It was not that women never joined male guests in Athenian salons. Female entertainers, refined *hetairai* courtesans, mistresses, and common prostitutes were welcome additions to aristocratic drinking parties. But it would be shameful for the host's daughters and wives to dine with outsiders.

Despite Iokaste's assertion of Theban women's independence, in Polymnis' salon the men and women still sat at separate tables. I kept one ear on the women's conversation, but talk with Epaminondas and his father engaged my attention. Polymnis went to some effort to provide a good meal, sending Manus and the young female slave to the market to fetch good wine, sausages, and a chewy, oily fish of some kind.

"Grilled eels," Polymnis explained. "They are brought fresh from Lake Copais every day. They are a delicacy," he added proudly. I dutifully voiced my appreciation, for I sensed that he had spent money he could ill-afford to part with to impress us.

The conversation turned to other things. "You come at an interesting time," Polymnis said.

"War will come soon," I confirmed, sopping up some oil with a chunk of heavy bread.

"Yes, yes," Polymnis said distractedly. "But I am speaking of local matters. *Family* matters."

"My sister's wedding is in seven days time," Epaminondas clarified.

"To Eurymachus, son of Leontiades," Polymnis added. The astringent oil scratched at my throat. I glanced at Althaia, whose hand had moved to the heavy gold chain around her neck. Polymnis, oblivious of his daughter's unease, took a long pull of wine and sighed with satisfaction. "It is a good union," he declared proudly. "It will bind our family to that of Leontiades. It cannot come too soon." Althaia clutched at the chain as though it were choking her.

"My congratulations to you, O Polymnis," I said awkwardly.

"There have been plenty of suitors, to be sure, but none of good standing. They got it into their heads to marry above themselves just because my daughter is a widow!" *Widow*. That explained Althaia's age, I thought. Polymnis made a derisive snort. "Even that rogue Kepheos had the gall to approach me!" I looked to Epaminondas for explanation.

"Eurymachus' right-hand man," he said. "He handles the day-to-day business at the slave market. A man with a nasty reputation," he said. He washed away the distaste of the name with a generous mouthful of wine from his cup.

Polymnis shook his head. "Three times he came to ask! Marry my daughter to a mercenary like Kepheos? I would sooner sell her to a Thrac—" Polymnis caught himself too late. An embarrassed silence filled the salon. "My apologies," Polymnis said. " 'The reins of my tongue slipped my grasp,' as we say in Thebes."

I raised my cup to my host. "No offense taken, O Polymnis." Athenians who hated me, and there were many, often called me *Thrax*

163

— The Thracian — in an attempt to insult me. But Athenians, on the whole, were practical above all else, and old prejudices were easily put aside if there was money to be made. So many Thracian traders had set up shop in Piraeus that there was even an altar to Bendis in the port. Some Athenians even worshipped the goddess and offered sacrifices at her festivals. And more than a few Athenians counted Thracians among their ancestors though they were loath to admit it. But among the Thebans, I had sensed the ill-feeling towards my mother's people ran deeper than the prejudice I was accustomed to in Athens. I said as much now.

Epaminondas and his father exchanged a look. "The memories of Mykalessos linger," Epaminondas said.

"Mykalessos?" I asked.

Epaminondas explained. "A small city to the east. Athens set an army of Thracian mercenaries upon it during the war. They slaughtered every man, woman, and child. Even the livestock was not spared the sword. I was only a few years old when it happened but I have heard the tales."

"I saw it with my own eyes. The men tied to trees, their ribs cut open and their guts spilled on the ground," Polymnis said, his face grim with the memory. "I was part of the force sent to hunt them down before they did more damage."

"Did you find them?" I asked.

Polymnis nodded grimly. "Indeed we did. By Ares, they fought like men possessed by the Furies themselves! But we sent hundreds of them to Hades and the rest scurrying back to Thrace!"

"Then they suffered the fate they deserved," I said. I was beginning to realize that as an Athenian and a Thracian, I was guilty twice over in the eyes of many Thebans.

A new voice, clear and strong, chipped in. "Do you not stand by your countrymen?"

I shifted on my chair to face the speaker. Althaia regarded me with the same haughty stare as when I had first seen her. "I am Athenian, O Althaia, despite appearances," I said. "I have spent time among the Thracians. I count many among them as my friends. There are many tribes and I fought against them as often as not. But I do not condone cruelty by anyone, be it barbarian or Greek."

"That is not your reputation," Althaia said in a tone both defiant and challenging.

Meli came to my defence. "It is a reputation created by his enemies, who fear him. But your brother, I think, knows differently." Althaia looked sceptical but held her tongue. An awkward silence filled the salon.

"I'm sure my sister will tell you more of Thrace, if you wish, O Althaia," I said.

Althaia did not pursue her questioning further. "I am always eager to learn," she said curtly.

Polymnis wrested the conversation back onto safer ground. "You should be thinking more of your wedding, Daughter!" he said with an edge of reproof. Althaia's face tightened. Polymnis turned to me, seeking to draw me into a conversation I wanted no part of. "It should have happened a long time ago. There have been too many delays!"

"Delays?" I asked.

Polymnis looked at Iokaste. "It is at my wife's insistence. She did not want the marriage to happen before the *Dionysia.*"

"*Dionysia*?" I asked. Every city had its own celebrations to honour the gods, but I was not familiar with the festivals of Thebes.

"To honour Dionysus. It is like your *Anthesteria* in Athens," Epaminondas said. The *Anthesteria* was a three-day festival to welcome the arrival of spring during which honouring the gods came second to revelry and drunken debauchery. That the Theban festival was named for Dionysus suggested that it was much the same in Thebes.

As if sensing my thoughts, Iokaste spoke. "Dionysus has long favoured our city. Perhaps you too will receive His blessing while you are here, O Daimon," she said, dipping her head towards me. Epaminondas' mother rose to her feet. "We will retire to the women's quarters," she announced, "to discuss our preparations for the festival. Melitta has expressed an interest in learning more about our ways."

Althaia and Meli took their cue from Iokaste and stood to join the older woman. As the women departed, Althaia passed me without a look but stopped to give her father a dutiful kiss on the cheek. Meli was last to leave, a coy smile playing on her lips.

The women's footsteps faded away, leaving an awkward silence behind them in the salon. Epaminondas and his father peered into their wine cups uncomfortably. "The women of Thebes —," Epaminondas said, pausing to find the right words, "— celebrate the *Dionysia* with particular devotion."

My hosts' faces filled with palpable relief when I changed the topic of our discussion. We spoke of the upcoming war, the politics of Athens and Boeotia, and other great matters. I cannot remember any of it.

I could only think of Althaia.

CHAPTER 21

I was awake and stretching in the courtyard when Epaminondas descended the stairs from the upper storey of the house before dawn the next morning.

"You slept well, I hope?" he inquired.

"As fine as anywhere I have been," I responded. My sister had stayed with the other women upstairs. I had been given a hastily-converted storage room on the west side of the courtyard, well away from the women's quarters. Guest though I might have been, hospitality had its limits.

In truth I had slept poorly. The pallet bed was too short for my tall frame and I had spent much of the night trying to find some comfort on the thin mattress. Incessant thoughts about the previous day had not helped my efforts to fall asleep. The hostility of the Thebans, understandable as it was, was a sign that the alliance of Thebes and Athens rested on fragile foundations. The tension I sensed in the home of my host was another matter. Polymnis was amiable, but I was less certain about Iokaste's feelings about my presence, though she had taken to my sister well enough. I did not know what I had done to earn the disdain of the haughty, beautiful Althaia. Epaminondas and his father had insisted we stay for her wedding to the arrogant Eurymachus, to my great regret. I was more eager than ever to return to Athens.

Besides the two of us, the only other person awake was the slave Manus, who brought us two steaming bowls of porridge. As we spooned up the barley and onion gruel in the courtyard, I periodically glanced at the stairway to the upper floor, wondering if the rest of the household would soon descend. *No*, I admitted to myself. *I am waiting for Althaia to come down.* By the gods, Aphrodite herself would have been jealous of the woman's beauty! I exhaled deeply at my foolishness, something that did not go unnoticed by Epaminondas.

He paused mid-spoonful. "Something worries you?"

"I was just thinking about our arrival yesterday," I lied. "Perhaps it was a mistake to come here."

Epaminondas reprimanded me with a shake of his spoon. "Nonsense! Without your ruse, the Persian gold would be gone. You're a hero!"

"Leontiades might disagree with you. As well as your sister's future husband," I added. "It is more than likely that they were involved in orchestrating the ambush on the caravan in some way."

Epaminondas' eyelid twitched. "Your suspicions are unwarranted. There are those, like Leontiades and his faction, who are wary of Athens' motives. But they are Thebans first and foremost."

I grunted vaguely and focused on finishing my pottage. We spoke little before setting out onto the waking streets of Thebes.

Althaia's absence in the morning still lingered in my mind as we headed to our destination. "You will like the gymnasium," Epaminondas said with an enthusiasm I did not share. In Athens, the gymnasium was the enclave of the wealthy. Aristocratic youths did calisthenics and other drills to strengthen their bodies, while older men honed their skills at javelin or other military skills. The more vigourous among them tested their mettle in wrestling matches and the toughest engaged in boxing contests. The ostensible purpose of all this jumping and running and throwing was to toughen up the men for the rigours of battle, but it was as much for bragging rights or a chance to win glory at the countless games around Greece.

Older men frequented the gymnasium as well, though they exercised less and chatted more, lounging about while casting a lascivious eye over the taut naked bodies of the young men as they leapt and dashed, seeking a youth to seduce with wine and scented oils later in the evening.

As a youth, I had escaped the old men's lustful stares. As the son of a slave, I was not welcome at the gymnasium, no matter my father's status as a *strategos*. When other boys were running lengths of the track or hurling the discus, my arms-master Neleus had me performing more strenuous if mundane tasks. His favourite was to make me haul a cart-load of rocks around the Acropolis, but standing in the hot sun with a heavy shield performing spear thrust after spear thrust was not far behind. Neleus, a man of more humble origins and a practical soldier above all, had no truck with the refined world of the gymnasium. "The gymnasium only teaches them to run away faster," he often observed. The backbone of the phalanx, Neleus insisted, was in the hardened farmers and craftsmen in their beaten-up armour passed down from their fathers and grandfathers, not the "strutting ball-ticklers in their shiny new breastplates," he sneered. I miss him still.

Memories of my mentor brought a smile to my face as we passed through a city gate on the western side of the city. The gymnasium was next to the river that followed the line of the substantial city wall. The river also served as a convenient place for men to rinse off the sweat and grime of their exertions.

Epaminondas swept his arm towards the gymnasium. "What do you think?"

The complex was impressive. The temple's colours gleamed in the morning sun. The long stadium and its stands matched anything I had ever seen and spacious athletic fields allowed plenty of space for javelin or discus practice. The social nature of the gymnasium was evident too. Stone benches under the broad canopies of plane trees provided a shady refuge for relaxation and idle gossip, and a porticoed stoa allowed vendors to set up their stalls for food and refreshment.

"Herakles himself would stand in awe," I said.

Epaminondas beamed with pride. He pointed to the stadium. "It's been too long since I've done some running."

We stripped down, leaving our clothes near the edge of the track. After stretching the morning stiffness out of our muscles, we took some laps of the track at a half-sprint. Soon a thin sheen of sweat covered our skin and our breathing settled into a bellows-like rhythm that matched the crunching of our footsteps on the gritty surface of the track. After twenty lengths, we drew up to catch our wind. Epaminondas grinned. I nodded, feeling my strength coming back. Despite my misgivings, I had to admit the mindless exercise was invigorating.

The simple joy of exertion was short-lived. When we arrived, few others were present. I thought we might take our exercise and escape the notice of Epaminondas' fellow Thebans. It was a vain hope. A fair number of locals had come since our arrival and more were trickling in. More than that, judging by the number of people staring and pointing in our direction, we had attracted their attention.

"Perhaps coming here was a mistake," I observed as we slipped into our tunics.

"Can you blame them for their curiosity?" Epaminondas said.

"It is not their curiosity that worries me."

"Come! I will introduce you," he said, waving a hand. I followed reluctantly.

By now, the newcomers had aggregated into a small crowd. At the centre of the murmuring throng stood a scowling Eurymachus, his arms crossed in disapproval. Unpleasant as that was, more surprising was the familiar face standing beside him. The man's forked beard had not changed since the I interrupted his Theban raiding party's attack on the Athenian slave caravan half a year earlier. I pointed at him, anger rising in my chest. "You there!" I called, striding towards him. The man's lip curled at my approach.

I seized the man's tunic and yanked him so that my forehead ground into his. A cry rose up from the Thebans and hands pushed roughly at me, but I held the man close. "Your men are not welcome in Attica," I said before shoving him back. The fork-bearded mercenary smoothed out his rumpled tunic, smirking as I was assailed by angry shouts. Only the intervention of Epaminondas saved me from a physical attack from his fellow Thebans.

Eurymachus stepped forward. "What gives you the right to assault this man, Athenian?"

I regarded the Theban aristocrat as though he were a piece of sheep dung. "You know this thief?"

"Kepheos is in my employ. Any quarrel with him is a quarrel with me."

Kepheos. Not only a bandit but the failed suitor of Althaia. And he was also the lackey of Eurymachus. Epaminondas had told me that the slave trade was the main source of Leontiades' wealth. The attack on the slave caravan made more sense now.

"Your *servant*," I said, causing the man Kepheos to bristle, "attacked a slave merchant in Attica." I turned my gaze on Kepheos. "Your men's bones still lie on the plain near Dekeleia. If I ever see you within the borders of Athens again, you will join them."

Eurymachus shrugged off my accusation. "You must be mistaking him for someone else."

"Your family deals in slaves, does it not?" I said.

"We have a hand in many businesses, but we are not bandits," he sniffed. "Besides," he added, gazing pointedly at Epaminondas. "To let this misunderstanding fester would not bode well for upcoming events." Epaminondas frowned at his sister's future husband, but, caught between his duty to his guest and his family, was clearly in an awkward situation.

I narrowed my eyes at my adversaries. There was nothing to be gained beyond what I had already learned. "Perhaps I am mistaken. After all, the man I saw was fleeing so fast that I only saw the back of his head." There was a chuckle from some of the Thebans. The man Kepheos flushed but wisely held his tongue.

Eurymachus gave an insincere smile. "Then the matter is settled." He glanced about at our surroundings. More Thebans had arrived for their morning training and were going about their business. Eurymachus turned back to me. "I suggest a friendly contest to show there are no hard feelings? A javelin competition?" he said, gesturing at some human-shaped bundles of straw far out on the training ground.

I peered at the distant figures. "The targets I'm used to rarely stand still and they're usually throwing something back at you." I glanced at the fork-bearded Kepheos. "When they're not running like frightened sheep, that is," I said, taking another dig at the mercenary. More Thebans joined in the laughter this time, confirming my suspicion that Eurymachus and his mercenary Kepheos did not enjoy universal admiration.

The lack of absolute solidarity from his fellow Thebans irritated Eurymachus. "Then something more challenging. A boxing contest. Nothing too violent," he added hastily. "The first to knock his opponent to the ground three times will be declared the victor."

"Or the first to knock his opponent unconscious," I corrected him.

"Of course," Eurymachus said. He put his hand on Kepheos' shoulder. "Do you think you can beat a true Theban, Athenian?" he asked.

I appraised Kepheos more closely. He had the kind of hard body forged by a life of soldiering. He looked like the type of fighter I would have gladly welcomed into the ranks of the *peripoli*. He met my stare unblinkingly. But I am larger than most men, and I stood a head taller than the mercenary and outweighed him by a hefty margin. Good fighter or not, I reckoned I would pound him into the grit of the athletic field, a small measure of payback for his incursion in Attica. I looked back at Eurymachus. "I do," I answered,

Eurymachus' smile told me immediately that I had made some error. He cupped his hand to his mouth and called out to a recently-arrived group of men stretching near the temple steps. "Thaletos!"

A burly figure detached himself from the cluster of men and approached us. A twisted nose and scarred face spoke of many bouts in the boxing circle. Only a hands-breadth shorter than me, he had the advantage of weight and brawn, with a neck hardly visible for all the muscle of his upper back and shoulders. His eyes, though, glinted with lambent intelligence as he took me in at a glance before addressing the man who had called him over. "Eurymachus," said the newcomer in a tone that was polite rather than friendly.

Eurymachus extended a hand in my direction. "Thaletos, this Thracian goat-shagger claims he could defeat a true Theban like yourself in boxing. What say you to that?"

The man Thaletos sized me up. "I think he is wrong," he said, staring flatly at me. Whatever his opinion of Eurymachus, the honour of Thebes was more important, it seemed.

"Would you be willing to test his claim, O Thaletos?"

"I would."

Eurymachus, his expression victorious, turned to me. "You seem surprised, Athenian. Do you wish to withdraw your challenge?"

I had grown up fighting in the streets of Athens. There was no honour there, only victory or shame, and no dirty trick was too low. I fought often, losing sometimes but also winning fights against larger boys. Like every good fighter, I learned to gauge my opponents, assessing their strengths and weaknesses. With sword and spear, few were my equal and even fewer could best me. In a brawl, I could mete out and take punishment in equal measure. But assessing the muscle-bound Thaletos, I knew at once that I was not his match. Eurymachus had set me up and like a fool I had blundered into his trap. There was only one sensible answer to Eurymachus' question.

"I will fight."

Eurymachus clapped his hands. "Then let there be no delay!" Beside him, the fork-bearded Kepheos smirked.

Word spread quickly. No one at the gymnasium wanted to miss the chance to watch their man lay a beating on an upstart Athenian, particularly one of my reputation. The crowd of expectant Thebans ringed the contest ground. On opposite sides of the circle, Thaletos and I stripped down in preparation for the bout. The horn amulet at my chest caught the attention of Eurymachus.

"I did not take you for a superstitious man, Athenian!" he called out, indicating the charm. "But then again, the simple-minded take comfort in simple beliefs! It may be time to pray to your god, for all the good it will do you!" There were knowing smiles and laughter, though not from Thaletos, who had seemed not to hear. I ignored the goading of Eurymachus, slipping the gold chain over my neck and placing it in Epaminondas' outstretched palm.

I slipped on a pair of fighting gloves that someone had scrounged up for the contest. The leather bands across my knuckles were more to protect the fighter's hands than to soften a blow to his opponent. Epaminondas briefed me on my opponent. It was not good news. "Thaletos is the best boxer in Thebes. He is twice champion of the Pythian Games and once at the Nemean games. He is beloved here." Even Epaminondas could not hide a note of pride in his city's glorious son. "They call him the Breaker of Men," he added unhelpfully.

"So you have seen him fight before?" I asked.

"Many times!"

"Have you ever seen him lose?"

"Never."

I clenched and unclenched my fists in the unfamiliar gloves. "You are familiar with how he fights?"

"I have paid close attention to his technique and form," confirmed the ever-studious Epaminondas.

I eyed Thaletos, who was rolling his massive shoulders to loosen up. "Does he have any weaknesses?" I asked.

"None," Epaminondas replied without hesitation.

"No habits or preferred attacks?"

Epaminondas thought carefully. "He mostly leads with his left, but will switch suddenly from time to time.When he does, he often follows with a left hook. He conceals it well and it has laid out not a few good fighters."

"And if he doesn't use his left hook?" I asked. Epaminondas shrugged apologetically.

Eurymachus, his eyes bright, repeated the rules of the contest. "The first man to knock his opponent to the ground three times or unconscious will be the victor."

The Theban and I stepped forward and a murmur of excitement rose from those gathered round us. As I raised my hands, I dipped my head towards my opponent. Thaletos nodded in acknowledgment.

"Begin!" Eurymachus shouted.

A boxing match differs little from the street brawls of my youth. Anything is permitted save eye-gouging. Kicking, head-butts, and grappling were fair game, and Thaletos looked like a master of all of them.

Thaletos and I circled each other. As Epaminondas had predicted, Thaletos led with his left side. The Theban boxer sized me up. I let him see my flaws, staying flat-footed and leaning forward too much. I dulled my expression. I wanted him to see a brute who depended on strength rather than technique. Thaletos sniffed, having taken his measure of me. His eyes narrowed.

Suddenly he made a quick shuffle step and his left hand snapped out towards my face. I stepped in, deflecting the blow with my forearm and countering with a kick at his midsection. My foot found only air as the Theban danced out of range with an agility surprising for such a large man. He appraised me again, a hint of a smile playing on his face. The first exchange had been a test to draw me out. I was more skilled than I had let on and now he knew it.

I had little time to reflect on my mistake. Without warning, he lunged at me. I surged to meet him and we collided like a pair of bulls. As we grappled I drove a knee up into his midsection. His body was as solid as a horse's hindquarters and the blow only elicited a small grunt from the Theban. Suddenly, a short punch from nowhere caught my cheek and stars filled my vision. Instinctively I shoved the Theban away but his foot slammed into my mid-section, sending me sprawling onto my back. The ringing in my ears faded only to be replaced by the cheering of the Theban spectators.

"First fall to Thaletos!" Eurymachus declared. Thaletos stepped back. My cheek was throbbing and my chest felt as if it had been kicked by a horse. I rolled onto my hands and knees and pushed myself back up, glowering at the gloating Eurymachus. Turning away from the grinning aristocrat, I lifted my hands and nodded to Thaletos. The big Theban nodded back and the contest resumed.

We exchanged a few glancing blows. The Theban connected with a rib-shaking hit to my flank, but it left him open to a solid punch that thudded into the left side of his mouth. Before I could pull back my hand, his left arm snaked out, wrapping itself around my extended arm and holding me close for a counterattack from his right. A fist as dense as iron pounded my ribs again before flicking up in a fast uppercut that caught me under the chin. Tyche, the goddess of luck, favoured me that day, for I had been moving away and the punch only clipped me. Even so, the power of it sent me to the ground once more, my eyes filled with white light.

"Second fall to Thaletos!" called out Eurymachus. The Thebans jeered as I pushed myself to my feet, blinking away the flashing stars.

Across from me, Thaletos touched his split lip and then spat a gob of blood onto the ground. The Theban regarded me with annoyance. This was not a match at Olympia. Thaletos had come to the gymnasium for his morning exercise, not a bloody brawl. He would want to finish the fight quickly and be done with it.

I rubbed my aching jaw while I tried to ignore the protests of my bruised ribs. Eurymachus and the Thebans jeered. The fighting circle was Thaletos' domain. If I fought by the rules, few as they were, I would suffer a humiliating defeat. So I would not play by the rules.

I let Thaletos attack, but I did not fight back. Instead I danced about, just staying out of range of his punches and grasping hands. I trotted about the space, making him chase me. Once or twice he almost engulfed me in his massive arms, but I slipped out of the trap. Thaletos grew visibly frustrated at my refusal to engage him. The spectators, impatient for a victory, mocked my evasiveness and their champion's inability to land a blow.

And then my opportunity came. Frustrated fighters will often fall back on old tricks when pressed. Now, as Epaminondas had predicted, Thaletos stepped back, shifting awkwardly into a right-leading stance and inviting an attack while he feigned being off-balance. It was well done, and if I had not known better, I would have believed it. But I knew the shift was a feint meant to draw me in. I let him think he had succeeded, leaping forward to the opening he had left me. With wicked ferocity, Thaletos sprung his trap, pushing off his back foot and swinging a massive left hook to where my head should have been.

But I was not there. I had not tried to hit the Theban. Instead I had bent down, twisting my body under the punch. It was a risky manoeuvre, for I was looking straight at the ground instead of my opponent. Thaletos' fist brushed the back of my head. I let my power build through my hips and shoulder and into my swinging fist. My punch was blind, but I put everything into it. If it missed, I was done for. But Tyche, the goddess of luck, was still with me. My fist slammed into the massive warrior's left cheek, the shock of the blow numbing my arm.

The Theban champion spun from the impact, tottered, and slammed front-first into the dusty ground of the exercise yard. He lay there unmoving, his eyes closed. The spectators gasped and stared dumbly at their fallen champion. I glared at them, my fists tight at my sides.

Epaminondas, thank the gods, seized the moment before Thaletos regained consciousness. "Thaletos is knocked out! Daimon is the victor!"

"Any other challengers?" I growled, fixing my gaze on the shocked Eurymachus and Kepheos. The Theban aristocrat's face was taut with thwarted anger. The Thebans, let down by their champion, began to disperse, led by Eurymachus and his henchman.

"Kepheos!" I called out. "I can see why Polymnis considered you an unworthy suitor for his daughter!" The mercenary flushed with hateful shame. "And I am not sure what he sees in you either, Eurymachus, son of Leontiades!" None of the Thebans leapt to the defence of Eurymachus. Before either Eurymachus or Kepheos could respond, I turned my back on them to tend to my fallen opponent.

Thaletos groaned. He managed to prop himself up on one elbow and was shaking off his dizziness. I extended my hand towards him. He hesitated but then accepted my offer. I hauled the brawny Theban to his feet, letting him hold my shoulder until his sense of balance returned.

"You hit like a hammer, by Zeus!" he said, massaging the darkening bruise on the side of his face.

"A lucky punch, O Thaletos," I offered. It was the truth after all.

The Theban appraised me through narrowed eyes before giving me a shame-faced look. "You played on my impatience," he observed shrewdly.

"Fighting you honestly was not serving me well," I admitted, rubbing my own bruised cheek.

Thaletos shook his head. "The gods punished me for my arrogance." He glanced at Epaminondas. "I have never known young Epaminondas to be anything but a good judge of character, Athenian." Epaminondas swelled with pride. Thaletos extended his hand. "Thaletos, son of Rhexenor."

I shook his hand. "Daimon, son of Nikodromos."

Thaletos chuckled. "Your name is not unknown in Thebes, Athenian."

"So I have learned," I said.

Thaletos looked towards the already distant figure of Eurymachus and frowned. "A man's enemies seldom cast him in a good light." He turned back and shook his head ruefully. "Still I would like another match with you sometime for the chance to chance to regain my honour, by Herakles!"

I held up a dissuasive hand. "It's not something either I or my ribs look forward to, Theban!" I said, wincing as I took a breath. His eyebrows rose in surprise, and the three of us laughed. I knew I had at least one more friend in Thebes.

CHAPTER 22

"You should have seen it, Father!" Epaminondas exclaimed.

Epaminondas recounted the tale of the bout at the gymnasium for his family. The house slave Manus brought out chairs from the salon into the courtyard so that the family could listen in comfort. I could only stand silently in tight-lipped embarrassment as Epaminondas told an exaggerated and misleading version of events. To hear him speak, it was a battle between Achilles and Hector.

Polymnis was suitably impressed but could not hide his hurt Theban pride. "Thaletos is a good man!" he offered.

The women's reactions varied. My sister kept looking my way, her eyes twinkling with amusement at my discomfort. Iokaste listened with aloof detachment with a barely raised eyebrow. Althaia was another matter. Throughout the tale, her disapproving frown remained constant.

Epaminondas, almost breathless, finished his report. Polymnis clapped his hands. "It is a rare achievement!" he declared. "One deserving of some refreshment, at least." He ordered the short-haired slave girl to fetch some wine and barley cakes to celebrate the occasion.

The slave girl soon returned. She had unwisely loaded a single platter with a jug, stacked cups, and a heap of cakes. Her brow was knitted in concentration as she balanced the precarious load. I stepped forward, raising my hands to take the tray from her. The movement distracted her and her gaze flicked upward and met mine. Her eyes widened in surprise to see me towering over her and she came to an abrupt halt. The jug of wine teetered on the edge of the tray. The girl let out a shriek. In her effort to save the wine, she only succeeded in tipping the tray further in the other direction. Cakes, cups, and wine tumbled to the ground in an explosion of food and pottery. Cool wine splatter my shins and feet. One determined cake rolled across the courtyard to the household altar.

I loomed over the slave girl. She was a slight thing, hardly fourteen or fifteen by the look of her. She looked up at me, her blue-grey eyes wide with terror.

"You foolish girl!" Polymnis snapped. "What god has cursed me with you!" The girl flinched as though she had been whipped.

"It is nothing, O Polymnis," I said, shaking off my wine-drenched feet.

"Leontiades sent her a month ago as a gift for my daughter before the wedding," Polymnis explained, scowling at the cowering slave. "But the girl is as clumsy as a drunken Thessalian. She has already cost me more in spilt wine and broken pottery than she's worth!" He gestured at the broken wine jug impatiently, and the slave girl hastened to gather the scattered pieces. I stooped down to help her. Polymnis objected. "Leave it to her, O Daimon."

I waved him off. "It is nothing, O Polymnis," I said, kneeling to help the slave girl pick up pieces of the shattered jug, piling them on the largest fragment. I was glad to have something to do rather than listen to Epaminondas sing his praises of me.

I glanced at the girl. Her brown hair had a reddish tinge and I wondered if she were Thracian. "*Manisara thraki re?*" I asked her. The girl looked at me dumbly. I sighed. On our hands and knees, the two of us gathered up pottery and sticky cakes. Rising to my feet, I handed the heaping tray to the slave girl.

"Thank you, *despote!*" she spluttered in heavily accented Greek.

"I'm not your master, Girl," I said.

"Yes, *despote!*" she said quickly. She turned on her heel and scurried away, nearly colliding with Epaminondas as she did so.

Only when she had vanished into the larder did I become aware of the awkward silence in the courtyard. Polymnis cleared his throat. "If I may offer a word of advice, young Daimon: one should not become too familiar with slaves. It only breeds laziness and insolence."

My opinion of Polymnis diminished somewhat. But his attitude was not an unusual one, and he was my host. "I will remember that, O Polymnis," I said evenly. Polymnis grunted, apparently satisfied that the matter had been put to rest. The slave girl reappeared carrying another jug of wine with extra care. Polymnis waved her towards the salon and turned to say something to his son and wife. The slave girl glanced my way and I winked at her. She flashed a shy whisper of a smile before disappearing into the salon.

My silent exchange with the slave girl had not gone unnoticed. Althaia and Meli had been watching. My sister, her eyes still on me, whispered something in Althaia's ear. The Theban woman's brow creased.

Iokaste's voice interrupted Althaia's thought. "We will take our refreshments in our quarters," she announced. "I do not wish to listen to men going on about brawling in the dirt." She acknowledged me with a small dip of her chin and swept towards the stairs with a graceful elegance. Her daughter and my sister, taking their cue, followed her up, but not before Althaia threw one last curious look my way.

THE BAREST HINT OF DAWN was scratching the sky when I awoke.

Epaminondas and I, we agreed, would train in his courtyard rather than at the gymnasium. My Theban host was still asleep in his chamber. I wanted some time to myself before he joined me, for it was my habit to run through my drills alone. I stood in the centre of the silent, empty courtyard, Whisper's gently arced blade held out before me in a two-handed grip. I began.

The rhomphaia sliced through the air and cut down invisible enemies. My aching ribs screamed from the punishing blows Thaletos had landed the day before. I ignored their protests. My muscles loosened, leading my mind to do the same. I dropped into a roll, and the rough grit on the ground bit at my bare skin like a hundred tiny teeth. The pain was good. It made me forget. My awareness stretched out, filling the space and seeking out enemies. There was a presence behind me. I spun, bringing the rhomphaia above my head, ready to strike down whoever was there.

Althaia let out a squeak of surprise. She stood at the base of the stairs with Epaminondas, who was smiling sheepishly.

"My sister wished to watch us train," he explained. "If it is not too much of an imposition," he added.

I was naked to the waist and barefoot, with only a belted skirt. Despite the damp spring chill, a thin sheen of sweat already covered my arms and body. There was nowhere to hide from Althaia's scrutiny. "It will be dull entertainment, I'm afraid, O Althaia."

She regained her habitual aloofness. "I wish to see what my brother has learned," she said, brushing aside my weak objection.

Epaminondas sniffed. "You will see, Sister! Just sit on the step and hold your tongue!"

Althaia accepted her brother's chastisement with a polite smile. "Of course, Brother." She sat down on the bottommost step and wrapped herself in her blanket. Epaminondas, rolling his eyes, gave me an apologetic shake of his head.

Another figure descended the stairs. Meli, wrapped in her patterned Thracian cloak, sat down beside Althaia, who greeted my sister like an old friend. My sister, at least, had overcome Althaia's dislike of Thracians. I had heard their muffled voices and occasional laughter even as I drifted off to sleep the previous night. It had been good to hear my sister laugh, for there had been a time when I thought I would never hear that sound again.

"It looks like they have become friends," Epaminondas said, picking up on my thoughts as he adjusted his tunic. "It pleases me."

Meli's green eyes locked on mine for an instant. She whispered something to Althaia and the two of them shared a private smile. "I worry that my sister may be a corrupting influence," I said.

Epaminondas was doubtful. "I fear the opposite is more likely."

Epaminondas strode to one side of the courtyard and launched into his own odd but rigorous ritual of calisthenics, which involved a great deal of jumping. He told me it was to increase his agility and endurance. I glanced over at Althaia, who was observing us impassively. My sister's green eyes danced with mischief.

"Please continue," Meli said. "We will be as invisible as shades."

But Althaia was not invisible. I felt her eyes on me. It stole my concentration. My cuts were sloppy and my thrusts off-target. Had they been real, my phantom opponents would have had bested me that day. I finished my routine with a vertical snap of the rhomphaia. Meli applauded loudly. I felt myself redden.

Epaminondas rescued me from my embarrassment. "Shall we spar? I am eager to prove to my sister that my time in Athens was not wasted!"

"Just be sure to put on a good show, or your sister will think me a poor teacher!" I said. Epaminondas grinned and went to fetch our gear. I returned Whisper to her scabbard. I was about to lay her down at the edge of the courtyard, but another thought seized me. I approached Althaia and Meli. Althaia rose to her feet. I could smell the delicate scent of her jasmine perfume. Althaia looked at me warily, unsure of my purpose. I held out Whisper to her. "I entrust her to your care, O Althaia."

Blinking in surprise, she let me place the rhomphaia across her outstretched palms. Her eyebrows rose. "It is not as heavy as I expected!" It was the first thing she had said to me not laced with scorn

"Heavy enough when I'm practicing!" I said. With a nod, I began to turn away.

But if I had caught Althaia off guard with my approach, it was her turn to do the same. "Do you like being a warrior, O Daimon?" she asked suddenly.

I stopped, turning back to face her. It was innocent enough, but her serious gaze suggested there was hidden purpose to her inquiry. Did I like being a warrior? On the battlefield, when the *aresteia* surged through me, I felt as if I had stolen some power from the gods. My skill had given me reputation and my enemies feared me. But the men I had sent to the Underworld haunted my nights, and a dreamless sleep was as precious to me as any treasure. Sometimes I wished for the idyllic rustic life that Mnasyllus praised so highly, knowing that it would never be mine. I answered her question as honestly as I could.

"It is my nature," I said more quietly than I had intended. Her features softened.

Whatever reply she intended to give was thwarted by her brother's return. Epaminondas swung his wooden sword. "I feel confident today! Perhaps being back in Thebes has given me strength!" he said handing me an old helmet. As we slipped on the gear, the house was coming to life. The slaves Manus and Bulis shuffled from their room to set about their day's chores. The stout woman Kore put in a brief appearance before disappearing into the pantry. The clumsy girl slave came down the stairs, carrying a chamber pot to be emptied on the street. The corners of her mouth curled upwards in the briefest of smiles when she scurried past me towards the entrance of the house.

Epaminondas tapped his shield with his wooden sword. "Are you ready?" I nodded and we stepped apart.

In Athens, Epaminondas had been an enthusiastic pupil. His drive made up for deficiencies in his form. He was not bloodthirsty by nature but logical and relentless. He approached fighting like a game of draughts. He was not my equal, but his attacks had grown enough in skill that I could no longer afford to let down my guard. For the time being, at least, Althaia's gaze was forgotten, if only for my own safety.

After feeling each other out, the contest grew more heated. Sometimes I would roar and charge, but the young Theban had learned to hold his ground against such ferocity. A successful feint on my part left Epaminondas turned away from me and I swept his feet from under him, sending him heavily to the ground. Once he would have let the failure frustrate him, but now he rolled away, lashing out from his knees. As wild and desperate as the swing was, it was also effective, for it drove me back, giving Epaminondas the opportunity to scrabble to his feet. I raised my wooden sword in salute and the young Theban grinned.

"Come again!" I shouted and Epaminondas fell upon me with renewed vigour.

The audience had grown. Polymnis and his wife stood behind the altar. Even the head slave Manus had taken up a spot at the edge of the courtyard. Between warding off strikes from Epaminondas, I glimpsed Meli and Althaia exchanging whispers. When I looked back at Epaminondas, the young Theban was gone.

Dazzling light flooded my vision as a resounding blow rapped off the side of my helmet. When the brightness faded and my eyesight returned, I was met by the sight of an open-mouthed Epaminondas.

"Are you hurt?" he asked, his concern evident.

I gave my head a shake. "My ears are ringing, but it will pass." I took off my helmet and grinned in defeat.

"It was a lucky hit," Epaminondas said modestly.

I waved his protest off. "It was a fair blow. Your skill has improved, Pammo."

The young Theban beamed like a child receiving praise from his father. "Then I should quit now!" he joked. Suddenly his exuberance overcame him and he broke out in a chant of war. A chant of victory. Polymnis was moved to add his voice to his son's, the two of them concluding with a rousing shout.

"What was that?" I asked.

"The *paean* of Thebes," Epaminondas said, his face flushed. Every army has its own war chant to heat the blood of its warriors before battle.

Polymnis looked on his son proudly. "I have never seen you fight like that, *pai!*"

"It was Daimon and the other *peripoli*. They beat their lessons into me!"

Polymnis looked at me appreciatively. "Then I thank you, O Daimon!"

"If all Thebans are as ferocious as your son, then Sparta has much to fear!" I said.

Iokaste called for some water. The slave girl with the short hair returned with a jug and some cups. Althaia hastily relieved the clumsy girl of the jug and poured water for me and her brother. When she handed me the cup, my fingers brushed hers. I became conscious of my sweaty, helmet-matted hair. My throat was suddenly very dry and I drained the cup in two great gulps. Water dribbled down my chin and I wiped it away with the back of my hand. Iokaste frowned with disapproval. My sister saved me.

"I learned to fight in Thrace, Dammo. The *hurisa* taught me," she said, naming the Thracian female warriors.

I glanced at Epaminondas and his family, who were listening with fascination. "You will have to show me when we return to Athens," I said.

Meli, not to be dissuaded, threw down her challenge. "Test me now, Brother." All eyes turned to me expectantly.

I hesitated. "We are guests in this house, Sister. It can wait for another time." Althaia's and Epaminondas' faces fell.

It became clear that the decision fell to Polymnis. He sighed. "I do not object if you wish to proceed. And I must confess that I am curious, for I have never seen a woman fight, if you would forgive me for saying so," he said, addressing my sister.

"You are a gracious host, O Polymnis," I said. I turned to Meli. "Are you sure, Sister?"

Her only answer was a vulpine smile. I shrugged and indicated that Epaminondas should give Meli his training sword, but Meli shook her head.

"I am used to fighting with real blades," she said with a dismissive sniff at the wooden weapon.

I narrowed my eyes. Meli's stubbornness would put a mule to shame. It would not do to squabble in front of our hosts. But I would not go easy on her. She knew it.

"Do you have some old blades?" I asked Epaminondas. He nodded. "Then go and fetch them. We will see what skills my sister has brought with her from Thrace."

Epaminondas returned with an assortment of battered swords. "I used to train with them as a youth," he explained.

Meli elected to fight in the Thracian fashion with her pair of hooked *sica* swords. I took a tarnished *xiphos* sword and the small shield I had been using with Epaminondas. The leaf-bladed *xiphos* had seen better days, but it would suffice.

We took our positions. Meli held her weapons loosely, almost casually, but the tips quivered with energy. My sister was as tall as most men, with a slim, hard figure. Without her cloak she was as lean as a hound, and I am sure that the sight of her flaming red hair and emerald eyes would have planted fear in the heart of many men. But I knew her better. I raised my shield and settled into a defensive crouch, inviting her to attack.

Meli threw herself at me with a flurry of shrieking, grunting cuts. I gave ground, taking in her strengths and weaknesses. Her form was sloppy. Her footwork left her unbalanced. There was much wasted movement. But there was a wild, unpredictable savagery to it that made her dangerous. Fending off the strikes of her twin blades was like fighting a two-headed serpent.

I found myself smiling, for there was challenge where I had been expecting none. The ring of sparking blades filled the courtyard. A low stab came from behind a well-executed feint and I had to leap and roll away to avoid it. Like a wolf going for its quarry's throat, Meli followed hard, trying to catch me before I recovered. She paid for her carelessness. I lunged inside her defences. My weight behind the shield was like a battering ram. The impact sent her flying, and her swords skittered across the flagstones. With animal instinct, she rolled over so that she was crouched on all fours like a beast ready to leap. My sword tip was a hand's breadth from her face. Her incipient snarl transformed into a broad smile. She rose to her feet, becoming human once again.

"What do you think, Dammo?" she asked.

I was proud of her. "A match for a Spartiate, I should think!"

"Good enough to be one of the *peripoli*?"

So that was what she was fishing for. "We will see," I said. "But I promise nothing." My sister bowed, knowing she had won a small victory by wringing such a concession from me. Still breathing hard from our exertions we turned towards our hosts. Althaia gasped, staring at us wide-eyed. The rest of our audience regarded us in stunned silence. I had done nothing to quell our reputation as savage barbarians.

Polymnis coughed and Epaminondas found his tongue. "That was astounding! Such ferocity!"

My gaze shifted from Epaminondas to Althaia as I spoke.

"It is our nature."

CHAPTER 23

Morning training became our routine. Epaminondas and I would drill first. Afterwards I would spar with my sister. I fought her with spear and sword and rhomphaia. I spared her no pain, for an enemy would show no mercy. Her body was bruised and sore, but the next day her zeal would be undiminished. I was proud of her, though I did not tell her so.

Every day, too, Althaia would attend our sessions, observing intently from her spot on the stairway. She offered supportive words for her brother and Meli. For me, her heretofore frosty demeanour had thawed into a kind of cool formality. She offered polite greetings but little more. I should have liked to speak to her, but propriety prevented it. I could not help stealing furtive glances at her, for I was drawn to her beauty as mindless sea creatures are attracted to the flame of the night fishermen's lanterns. If she saw me, she gave no notice of it. I thought myself discreet.

Such matters of propriety did not concern my sister. Althaia and Meli spent most of their waking hours together, often hidden away in the women's quarters but more often than not in quiet conversation in the salon or a corner of the courtyard. My sister brushed aside my inquiries about their discussions. She was discreet as well.

Following a morning meal, Epaminondas would show me around the city and its environs. Any distraction was welcome, for it spared me the distraction of Althaia. That she would marry the arrogant shit-eater Eurymachus in a few days stoked flames of jealousy within my heart. I swallowed my bitter feelings and wounded pride. The Fates are imaginative in their cruelty.

At least I was not accosted by angry Thebans on the street. Looks of wariness and even curiosity replaced those of naked hostility. "Word of your victory over Thaletos has spread," Epaminondas explained. "It's worth some respect if nothing else."

The beginning of the great festival of the Dionysia no doubt contributed to the improved mood of the locals. The first day had been subdued and solemn, with the aroma of burning olive leaves pervading the air as the people of Thebes purified their homes. Today, the second day, the agora of Thebes thrummed with commerce and a palpable air of excitement. "It's because the final day of the Dionysia is tomorrow," Epaminondas explained as we manoeuvred our way through the milling crowds. The wine merchants in particular were doing brisk business. Suddenly we found ourselves in front of a raised wooden platform, on which stood an assortment of men, women, and children.

"This is —"

I cut him off. "I know what it is," I said more harshly than I needed to.

A slave market in any large settlement looks much the same, though this one was larger than most, even larger than the one in the Athenian agora. The yellow-robed dealer ran through his patter as he advertised his wares. Beside him, another man sat at a small table with a strong-box and a ledger to keep track of the day's sales. My eye wandered over the ill-fated souls on display, those the gods had cursed with servitude. The red-haired Thracians were easy enough to recognize, as were the Skythians with their high cheekbones and almond-shaped eyes. There were some paler-skinned women with large, dark eyes who might have been from Kolchis, and some others whom I could not place. No matter their origin, all the slaves were manacled, even the children. Whatever defiance they might have harboured had long been beaten out of them. Only fearful resignation remained.

An unwelcome realisation came to me. "These slaves belong to Leontiades?" I asked, gesturing at the luckless people.

"Most likely," Epaminondas said. "But other slave dealers also pay a fee to him to sell their wares here. Leontiades makes money from every slave sold in Thebes." My frown deepened. Leontiades thrived on the misery of others.

A voice called out from behind us. "You shouldn't stand so close, Athenian, or you'll be mistaken for merchandise!"

We turned to see the grinning Eurymachus approaching in the company of his fork-bearded captain Kepheos and four more bodyguards. In contrast to the grubby, threadbare clothes of the slaves, Eurymachus wore a fine knee-length tunic edged with silver thread. "Are you considering a purchase, or just looking for some relatives?" Eurymachus asked with a sniff. Kepheos smirked as the others sniggered dutifully at their leader's jibe. I advanced on Eurymachus, my fist tightening. Only the firm grip of Epaminondas stopped me from smashing the aristocrat's haughty face in. Eurymachus acknowledged Epaminondas with a grateful nod. "It's gratifying to see you have some control over your barbarian friend, Epaminondas. Such obedient dogs do not come cheaply."

"Your curse is to believe everything has a price, Theban," I said.

"Loyalty is a commodity like any other," Eurymachus countered, waving towards the slaves.

Epaminondas pulled at my shoulder. "Let's be on our way, Daimon."

Eurymachus smiled with all the warmth of a crocodile. "I know we haven't always seen eye to eye, Epaminondas, but in a few days I will be marrying your sister after all. It is neither my wish nor yours but our fathers'. For the sake of our families, we should try to get along, wouldn't you say?" He extended his hand towards Epaminondas.

Warily, Epaminondas shook hands with his sister's future husband. "I agree."

Eurymachus held on to Epaminondas' hand. The aristocrat's lip curled in distaste. "Think of me, will you? Do you think I want to wed a worn-out old boot like your sister? Is she even capable of having children any longer?" Epaminondas stiffened. Eurymachus continued. "There are some benefits, I suppose. Althaia may be old, but by the gods she still looks like Aphrodite! I won't mind ploughing her field! And if she fights back, that will only heighten the pleasure." Epaminondas wrenched his hand free of Eurymachus' grip. The aristocrat laughed and gave his captain a sly wink. "Maybe I'll even lend her to you when I tire of her, Kepheos!" As Eurymachus grinned lasciviously at Epaminondas, he did not see the baleful look of Kepheos at his back. I saw it though.

I pounced on the chance to sow discord between Eurymachus and his captain. "I've heard, O Kepheos, that Polymnis rejected your offer to marry his daughter because he was waiting for a better man," I said, rubbing salt into the mercenary's wounded pride.

The barb struck deeply, for Kepheos' gaze was filled with murder. "You know nothing of me, Athenian."

"I know that Polymnis failed in his search for a better man," I said.

Eurymachus bristled. "Meaning what, Athenian?" His fingers played with the pommel of the dagger at his hip.

I shrugged. "It's just that I'm surprised Polymnis agreed to a proposal from a shit-eater like you, what with your traitorous family's long history of Mede-izing."

"Who is the Mede-izer, Athenian? You just arrived with a hundred talents worth of Persian coins!" Eurymachus sneered.

I brushed aside his fair point and pressed on. There was a suspicion I wanted to air. "I think your entire traitor family is plotting with the Spartans right now. In fact I would be surprised if you weren't behind the attack on your fellow Thebans on their way back from Athens." Eurymachus stiffened. Kepheos snarled.

"I will give you one chance to take back your slander, Athenian," Eurymachus said in a voice like cold iron. Kepheos and his companions fixed us with threatening stares. It was six against two, and Epaminondas and I were weaponless. But I was not going to back down to some perfumed turd-sniffing aristocrat. I could only hope that Epaminondas would stand by me. I raised my fists. Out of the corner of my eye I noticed with a flicker of satisfaction that Epaminondas did the same.

A voice like thunder boomed behind us. "Is there a problem here, Eurymachus?" The brawny figure of Thaletos stepped past me and placed himself between our two hostile parties. Kepheos and his men took a step back.

With the ease of an oily politician, Eurymachus slipped into artificial cordiality. "I didn't expect to see you here, O Thaletos!" he said pleasantly. "We were just having a friendly chat with our Athenian visitor."

"Ah, I misunderstood. It seemed to be otherwise," Thaletos said flatly. "It was foolish of me to think that the son of a leading citizen like Leontiades had forgotten that it is sacrilege to commit violence during the Dionysia."

Eurymachus held his false smile. "As you said, a misunderstanding."

Thaletos scratched his crooked nose. "And what was the subject of your 'friendly chat', if I may ask?"

Eurymachus spread his arms wide. "My upcoming nuptials with the beautiful Althaia, of course! I invited Daimon to attend the celebration at my home, his being the friend of my dear Epaminondas and all. I wanted to show him that we are not all bumpkins and swineherds here in Thebes! I even mentioned how you would be a guest as well, O Thaletos. But Daimon was resistant to my invitation and words became a little heated, I confess," he finished with an apologetic bow.

Thaletos raised a doubtful eyebrow but played along. "I don't know about Athens, but in Thebes a gracious man accepts such an invitation, even if he is disinclined to do so," the imposing Theban said to me. Eurymachus could not hide his delight at my awkward silence.

My plan had been to leave before the wedding, but now I was trapped. I could not give a steaming turd about Eurymachus' honour. But to refuse the invitation, as spurious as it was, would cause Epaminondas and Thaletos to lose face. With a defeated breath, I relented. "I will attend."

Eurymachus clapped his hands. "Then it is settled! But I have business to attend to, I'm afraid. Preparations for your sister's wedding night and all," he said, giving Epaminondas another sly wink. Eurymachus placed his hand on my shoulder and looked up at me. "My guests will be eager to meet you, Daimon of Athens. You are such a ... curiosity." He gestured for his companions to follow him. Kepheos made a point to bump into me as he passed.

Thaletos watched them go with a sceptical eye. "That one has his father's arrogance but lacks his discretion. But I expected better of you, Epaminondas, son of Polymnis," he said, raising an admonishing finger.

"Eurymachus insulted us," Epaminondas said.

Thaletos considered it. "That may be so, but there should be no violence during the Dionysia." The Theban champion pointed at the crudely carved horn amulet at my chest, which had popped out from under my tunic. "I thought an acolyte of the God would know that, Athenian?" He did not need to say which god.

"I wear it as a promise to someone, nothing more." I answered.

Thaletos pulled back his own robe to reveal a golden horn hanging at his own chest. "The God always chooses his instruments for a reason, O Daimon."

"I am no god's instrument, O Thaletos."

Thaletos smiled like a parent amused by a child's foolish innocence. The expression seemed odd on the hulking fighter's scarred and disfigured face "The God's purpose is known only to Him. Perhaps that is why he let you beat me," he said, arching a playful eyebrow. He became more serious. "I will see you at the wedding, O Daimon," Thaletos said, giving me a steady look. It was as much an order as it was a statement.

"I will be there, O Thaletos." Satisfied, the Theban champion bid us farewell, leaving us standing before the slave market. "I am surprised that Thaletos was invited to the wedding," I observed.

"He comes from an old Theban family," Epaminondas said. "They are much respected in the city. Even Leontiades would think twice about snubbing him."

I looked at the receding figure of Thaletos in a more appreciative light. "I thought he was just a common man by his dress."

"He is modest, despite his standing and achievements."

I looked back at the slaves on the platform. They had been an audience for the entire drama. Whatever they might have thought, the incident would soon be forgotten as they were sold and taken away to their new lives of drudgery or worse. We departed, leaving the slaves to their fates.

I did not speak. Epaminondas misunderstood the source of my brooding. "Don't be so gloomy, Dammo," Epaminondas said, squeezing my shoulder. It was the first time the younger man had addressed me so informally.

"Why not? What is there to be happy about?"

Epaminondas grinned. "Tomorrow is the final day of the Dionysia!"

A celebration of the god of wine. The god of madness.

The god of chaos.

CHAPTER 24

The population of Thebes thronged the agora for the last day of the Dionysia. Men and women, young and old, slave and citizen, all mingled and celebrated their city's patron god, their jubilation fuelled by the wares of the busy wine-sellers.

"They've been drinking since this morning!" Epaminondas confirmed, clearing a path through the sea of people. "It is the first wine of the season from last year's harvest!"

"A good vintage, by the look of it!" I said, observing the drunken smiles around me.

Epaminondas laughed. "Come with me. I know where there's a good view!"

We shoved our way to a vantage point atop the steps of the main stoa. In vain I scanned the teeming agora for Althaia or my sister. Meli had coyly suggested they would be present but had said no more. I had little time to dwell on their absence, for we had hardly claimed our spots when the sound of drums beating in unison floated over the marketplace.

The crowd parted to clear a path for an astounding sight. At one end of the agora, a gleaming life-sized statue of a bronze bull stood atop a wheeled platform. Garlands of spring blossoms hung from the metal beast's neck and its broad horns were gilded with gold. Six men gripped two thick ropes and pulled the statue forward, their muscles straining against the great weight. A train of beflowered oxen tramped obediently in the wake of their metallic leader.

"It is Bromius!" Epaminondas shouted over the cacophony of celebration. My hand drifted towards the bull-horn charm at my neck, for Bromius is one of the many epithets of Dionysus.

The men towed the divine image until they reached the base of the broad stairway that ascended the slopes of the Kadmeia to the temple complex at its peak. A stone ramp split the steps leading up to the first of several terraces, and it was up this ramp that the men hauled the god's image. The crowd cheered as the bronze bull crested the ramp's upper edge, and the roar grew louder as the exhausted men raised their arms in victory. Yellow-robed priests placed wreaths of laurel on their bowed heads. Still basking in the adulation of their countrymen, the bull-haulers descended the temple steps to join their fellows.

A grey-beard in a brilliant blue robe came to the fore. He lifted his hands high, his right hand grasping a thick staff around which was entwined a leafy vine. The din of the spectators diminished to a low thrum.

"Who is that?" I asked.

"It is Heremos, the head priest," Epaminondas said. "His family has held the position since the time of Cadmus!"

"What is that in his hand?" I asked.

"A *thyrsis* staff," Epaminondas replied, his attention fixed on the spectacle. "The symbol of Dionysus!"

The priest Heremos stepped aside, and a huge, bare-chested man came forward bearing an enormous jug precariously balanced on his shoulder. "It is Thaletos!" I exclaimed as the crowd cheered.

"It is a great honour to bear the sacred wine," Epaminondas shouted. Thaletos halted, holding the plugged mouth of the jar over the bronze bull. Even from our distant vantage point, I could see the Theban champion's muscles straining with the effort of holding the massive container aloft.

The thrum of the crowd dropped even further. Among the spectators I was perhaps the only one who was ignorant of the ceremony, but I was enthralled nevertheless. There was a collective intake of breath as the blue-robed priest cocked his staff as though he were wielding a club. Then, with a vigorous swing, he knocked off the top of the wine jar. The crowd roared its approval. The priest Hemeros stepped aside and Thaletos hefted the massive jug, tipping the vessel over the golden-horned bull. The dark purple wine gushed out and splashed over the bronze behemoth's shoulders and back like a spring stream cascading over boulders. The citizens of Thebes went mad with joy.

The ritual was only beginning. The first in the line of oxen, a lumbering bull with the broadest set of horns I had ever seen, was led up the ramp to platform. Thaletos bent down to retrieve something and arose wielding a *labrys*, a double-bladed axe of ancient times. The burnished blades were bronze, not iron, and the fiery metal gleamed in the morning sun.

"The Axe of Herakles!" Epaminondas exclaimed, a touch of awe in his voice.

The priest Heremos extended his arms high, his right hand clutching his *thyrsis* staff. The throngs settled into hushed anticipation. A pair of bare-torsoed men yanked the bull's lead taut. The bull, resisting the sudden tension, attempted to back away, bellowing in protest. The beast's neck stretched in front of Thaletos like the thick trunk of an oak tree. The Theban champion, his two hands spread widely along the long haft of the ancient *labrys*, swung a mighty stroke. The axe bit deep into the bull's beck, severing the beast's spine. The bull collapsed in a heap.

A cheer erupted as the next animal was led to its doom. The earlier solemnity of the event took on a more bloodthirsty air. One by one, Thaletos dispatched the beasts, his chest and face now dripping with sacrificial blood. A small army of men had ascended to the terrace to drag the carcasses off to the side to be butchered. The men's axes and long-bladed knives made short work of the animals. Thigh bones wrapped in fat would be burned for Dionysus — the god's share. But the rest of the meat would be for the people of Thebes. Already many were clambering to claim their portion. Some Thebans were already descending with glistening chunks of flesh held up triumphantly in their blood-soaked hands.

Epaminondas tugged at my shoulder, distracting me from the spectacle. "Let's go and find a drink!" he shouted.

The celebration had begun in earnest. People sang and danced and toasted each other. Couples embraced each other amorously, not a few of them men. One would not see such things in Athens, not openly at least, but the Thebans had a reputation for such things, I reminded myself.

The copious amounts of wine helped relax my offended sense of Athenian modesty. The liquid gift of Dionysus flowed like rivers and matters of the Thebans' bawdy nature disappeared into the bottom of sloshing cups of wine. "To Thebes!" Epaminondas cried and we drained our wine in a few gulps. No sooner had our cups been emptied than they were refilled by some generous passerby. Music filled the air, and suddenly the thoughts of the impending war with Sparta were distant concerns, like the lean times of winter on a radiant spring day. I was happy.

With the music came another novelty I had never witnessed in Athens. Scores of cloaked women appeared, dancing and twirling through the crowd. The dancers' faces were hidden behind gruesome masks with womens' features in contorted, maniacal expressions. "They are fearsome! What are they?" I shouted in Epaminondas' ear.

"Maenads!" Epaminondas yelled back. "Bacchae! The servants of Dionysus!"

The masked women began to grab men from the crowd, pulling them away and forcing them to dance. Some men resisted, but most, their sense of propriety already weakened by wine, let themselves be led away, half-dancing with, half-pursuing the women. I looked over at Epaminondas, who took another swig of wine and shrugged. "It is the madness of Bacchus!" he shouted, throwing his empty cup to the ground. I laughed.

Epaminondas, staring at me, seemed to struggle with a decision before resolve quickly settled over his face. He reached up and cupped his hand around my neck. His meaning was clear.

I slapped his arm free and shoved him away more forcefully than I meant to. "My tastes do not stray in that direction," I said coldly. We stood like two statues while the revelry of the Dionysia swirled around us.

Epaminondas' face was a mask of shocked embarrassment. "I thought —" he stammered, blinking hard.

I cut him off. "I do not seek a lover," I said too harshly, discomposed by the young Theban's unexpected advances.

"Daimon, I'm —"

If he had more to say, the opportunity vanished, for one of the masked women seized his wrists. His face still marred by pain, the dancer pulled at him with renewed insistence. The crowd surged around me. When it subsided, Epaminondas was gone, snatched away by the Maenad. I was adrift on my own in a sea of revellers.

Another one of the Maenads swept close and grasped my hand. I tried to free myself but the stranger's grip tightened. The masked woman leaned in close. "Don't be a fool, Daimon of Athens!" I blinked like a wool-headed farm boy. The Maenad was Althaia.

"COME WITH ME!" Althaia ordered.

Her grip still firm, she led me through the cavorting crowd towards the edge of the agora. We wended and twisted through the wine stalls and the celebrating citizens of Thebes. The boisterous din ebbed as we ducked into a gap between two stone buildings and out behind them.

Onward past homes, workshops, and pens of pigs and goats we went, slipping through deserted lanes and paths. Our route left me disoriented and only a distant hum told me the direction of the agora. "Where are we going?" I asked. Althaia remained silent behind her grotesque Maenad mask.

A few more turns brought us before a small temple. Fresh offerings of fruit and wine sat on a circular tripod at the entrance, along with a smattering of other objects left for the temple's god by the pious citizens of Thebes. "Come!" Althaia commanded, leading me past the tripod and into the dark sanctum within.

Narrow sunbeams passed through the screens above and dappled the floor with spots of light. The redolent scent of incense was underlain by a faint acrid tang from a few flickering lamps in the corners of the chamber. The odour of the place was momentarily eclipsed as Althaia brushed past me and fragrant jasmine filled my senses. She stood away from me and removed her mask. My eyes began to adjust to the dim space. Althaia's intense gaze followed me as I explored the small chamber.

It was evident that the inner sanctum was more ancient than the exterior. The floor was not leveled tiles but the original uneven rock of the place. At the rear of the chamber the banded rock rose up into a natural altar that was roughly square and as tall as a man. Sundry offerings were heaped at the base of the rock. In a niche chiselled in the centre of the stone stood a crudely carved wooden statue, the object of the suppliants' devotion. I bent down and peered closely at the idol. I could not guess at its age. The black wood was so old that it had cracked in many places. Countless pious hands had rubbed the features so smooth as to make the god unrecognizable.

"Whose temple is this?" I asked. The sound of my voice seemed to offend the tranquility of the place.

"*The* God's," Althaia said.

"Dionysus?"

"That is one of his names. He has another name — a secret name — known to his true followers."

"Like you?"

Althaia evaded my question. "Do you worship the God?" she asked, glancing at the horn on my chest.

"I pray to no gods," I said.

"Because you do not believe in them?"

"Because they are bastards," I said.

Althaia smiled. "Then why do you wear the God's symbol?" she asked. I explained how the Thracian slave-woman Erta had come to give me the amulet. Althaia laughed when I told her how the freed slave had berated me in front of the *peripoli* for having removed the charm. "She sounds like a fierce woman!"

"She is, but I have met many fiercer."

"Your sister?"

"Among others. Even the men of the *peripoli* dare not provoke her!"

"I have come to like her. She is wise in many things. But she frightens me a little. You both do."

"Because we are Thracian barbarians?" I asked, recalling the vehemence in her voice when she spoke of the Thracians who had ravaged Boeotia during the war.

She shook her head. "No. Do you remember the day when you two first fought in the courtyard? When you looked at us afterwards?"

"I remember," I said, recalling her fearful expression. "You looked as though a pair of wolves were about to devour you."

She shook her head again. "No. Not wolves. Standing there, both of you, with your green eyes upon me and your hair like fire. You looked like something more like mortals."

My laughter echoed in the ancient stone of the sanctum. "I have been called many things, but not immortal!"

Althaia flushed. "I did not say it was so, only that the sight took me by surprise!"

I changed the topic. "Why have you brought me to this place?"

"I wished to speak to you."

"I thought you disliked me, though I do not know what offense I have caused you."

Althaia scoffed. "Dislike you? I hated you!"

I was taken aback. "What had I done to make you my enemy?"

"How could I not hate you?" she said with an exasperated laugh. "You were all Pammo talked about when he returned from Athens! 'Daimon said this. Daimon once did that.' I was sick of you before I ever met you!" At the mention of Epaminondas, I winced inside, the incident in the agora still fresh in my mind. Althaia continued. "But there are other tales about you as well. That you and your men ravage farmsteads. That you slaughter innocents and desecrate the dead."

"Is that all?"

"No. There are whispers of even worse things."

"Such as?"

"There are rumors that you murdered the Pythia in Delphi."

The lamps guttered and the sanctum grew darker. "And you believe these rumours?" I asked.

"People say many things. Do you know what they call you in Thebes?"

I am known by many epithets. Tyrant-Slayer. The Godless One. The Demon. "No," I said.

"'Daimon the Slaughterer,'" she said. "When I saw you for the first time, standing in our home with that great sword across your back, I could believe it. There is a menace about you."

"But you have changed your opinion of me?"

"Yes."

"Why?"

"Your sister told me your story," she said.

Her words blew through my soul like a cold wind. "Everything?"

"Your parents. Lykos. Phaia. The boy Sosias," she said. It was not my story. It was a list of the dead.

I regarded her grimly. I would rather people believe the worse of me than know of the people who died because I failed to protect them. I would rather people fear me than pity me. Althaia regarded me with pity now. "I avenged them," was all I could say.

Althaia nodded. "I know," she said softly. "But your sister told me something else."

"More of my secrets?" I said, inwardly cursing my sister's indiscretion.

"She said that you are a good man," she said. The words hung in the air.

"She is wrong," I said at last.

Althaia shook her head. "Epaminondas says the same. My brother has many faults. He is wont to let his passions lead him most of all. But he is a just man and a good judge of character. I should have trusted his opinion of you."

Epaminondas might say otherwise now, I thought. "He is wrong too."

Althaia smiled gently. "I have watched you closely. I think they are right."

"You brought me here to tell me this?" I asked. "Why?"

Althaia looked embarrassed. She stepped towards the altar and lay her hand softly on the wooden statue. "I don't know." She cocked her head towards the image of Dionysus. "I think the God has brought you here for a reason."

"No god brought me. I came at your *brother's* invitation."

"That is not what your sister said," Althaia said. "She said the God has some purpose for you here."

The hairs on the back of my neck rose. "My sister?"

"She said the God spoke to her in a dream."

"You should not put too much faith in my sister's words. But even if you are correct and the God has whispered to my sister in her dreams, why have you brought me to this place?" I asked, glancing around the gloomy sanctum.

Even in the low light of the temple, I could see her face redden. "I don't know. The God put some madness in me. But I felt a desire to talk to you. So I brought you here."

"With my sister's help," I said, understanding.

Althaia cringed slightly. "She had the idea when I told her about the dancers of the Dionysia," she said, looking at the maenad mask in her hand. Suddenly she laughed at the memory of it. It was like a cascade of light in that dim place. "I'm afraid she has led my brother on a merry dance far away from here!" she said, confirming my suspicions of the identity of the other dancer.

I sighed. Perhaps the Fates had willed it. But I had my own curiosity to satisfy. "You have said what you want to say, but I would ask questions of my own."

Althaia gave a nod of permission. "It is only fair. Ask me what you will."

"You know much of me, but I cannot say the same about you. Your brother was reluctant to tell me much."

"You asked him?" she said casually. She seemed faintly pleased.

"He was evasive. He told me you were a widow but not much more."

"Perhaps because there is not much to tell. I was married to a man named Onomakles. He was from a respected Theban family. My father was pleased with the match."

"Were you?"

Althaia gave a bitter laugh. "Do you think my opinion mattered, Daimon, son of Nikodromos? In Athens do girls choose who they wed?"

I shrugged. "I thought Theban women had more say in matters."

Althaia snorted. "Then you are mistaken. During the Dionysia, perhaps, we can escape the confines of our lives, but otherwise we are not free from the restrictions our families place on us, especially when we are young. I was fourteen years old when I was told whom I would wed, hardly past the age of playing with my toys. I did what my father told me like a good daughter should."

"Did your father choose well?"

Althaia chose her words carefully. "Onomakles was not a bad man. He was forty years old when he took me into his household. He was an influential man and had little time for domestic life. But he was generous in his way and did not beat me. For seven years I did my best to be a dutiful wife." It was a respectful if not overly affectionate description of the man. Many girls found themselves the wives of much worse men than this Onomakles.

"What happened?" I asked.

"Onomakles became ill with a wasting illness. I nursed him as best I could but he died. So I moved back to my father's household." This was normal for widows in Athens as well.

Seven years was not a short time. An obvious question occurred to me. "Were there children?" I asked abruptly. Pain washed over Althaia's features and I regretted my inquisitiveness. "Forgive me," I said. "It is not my place to ask.".

"No," she said with a small wave of her hand. "It was I who brought you here. And there is no malice in your question." She took a deep breath. "We had a son, Idaios. He died in his third winter. The God did not bless us with more children before Onomakles died. After I mourned my husband for three years, my father began to hear the petitions of new suitors."

"You are not a mere girl now," I said, angling towards my true question.

Althaia considered her words before speaking. "Do you think that changes anything? I am older, yes, and wiser than that foolish fourteen-year-old girl who was sent off to marry a man three times her age. I understand a woman's power but also the limits of that power. And I understand my duty to my family and how my actions can bring to my family honour or disgrace, hardship or prosperity. And so I will marry Eurymachus because that is what my father wishes." Althaia noted my disapproving frown. "You do not care for him, do you?"

"There are many people I do not like," I said.

"It is a beneficial match," she said, sounding unconvinced by her own words. "My father's business interests will prosper with the help of Leontiades."

"And your family's good name will help wash away the treacherous stink that clings to Leontiades and his kin," I said, repeating what Epaminondas had revealed to me.

The comment pricked a sensitive point. "You still think I have a choice in the matter, Daimon of Athens?"

I thought of the choices I had made in my life, some good, many bad. But they were mine. "We all have choices, even if they are woven by the Fates."

"But does not honour dictate our choices? How many times have you fought, risked your life, to defend your honour? Your family? Or Athens?"

"I fight for my own reasons," I said evasively.

She dismissed my weak answer with a short laugh. "Then why did you fight for the slave women?" she said, her tone incisive. "Why do you fight for Thrasybulus? Why do you avenge others who have been wronged? For fame? For reputation? For wealth? No. It is because you feel a sense of duty and to do otherwise would make you feel shame in the eyes of others. Why should I be any different?"

"So you are marrying Eurymachus for honour?" I asked flatly.

My distaste must have shown on my face, for Althaia scowled in frustration at my obtuseness. She composed herself with a deep breath. "It is easy for a man to go and die on the battlefield, and he will be praised for it. A woman will give her life for her family in a different way for no glory at all because it is expected of her. I will never bring disgrace to my family. You must understand that, Daimon."

We stared at each other for some time. She was startlingly beautiful, her face full of resolution and vulnerability all at once. She was right of course. I knew nothing of her burdens. I made a shallow bow towards her. "My feelings have clouded my thoughts, O Althaia. Forgive me."

"Like you said, I am no longer a girl, fearful and weak. I understand my duty and accept it." She turned her gaze to the ground. "Even if I might choose otherwise were I free to do so," she said more softly.

My heart sang at her quiet words. For an instant I might have swept her up and stolen her all the way back to Athens. I desired to reach out to her. But the thought faded as quickly as it had appeared and brightened the dark corners of my soul. My heart fell once more for the loss of something I had never had in the first place. "I know our destinies are not our own," I said awkwardly.

She smiled sadly. "Not in this life," she said cryptically, glancing at the idol in its niche. I knew of what she spoke, for it was not the first time a woman had shared such secrets with me.

The featureless face of the statue seemed to watch me in silent judgment. I turned to Althaia. "My wife, Phaia, believed much as you did," I said.

"Believed what?"

"That there can be happiness after death. That there is a secret place for those who choose to look for it, a place of light and plenty."

"And you do not?"

I believe that when our allotted span of life reaches its end, our shades descend to the Underworld where our memories fade until we are but shadows of shadows. The phantom dead will languish there until the last star vanishes from the sky and even the gods are no more. But I admit I will not know until I myself have taken the Dark Road. "I hope it is so, but I do not believe it."

Althaia smiled in the mysterious way that women sometimes do. "Then perhaps I can yet make you the God's acolyte, Daimon of Athens. Come with me." She swept past me in a swirl of perfume and exited the temple.

When I stepped outside into the bright light of the world of the living, we were not alone. Iokaste's handmaiden Kore stood with her hands held in front of her, a cloth sack slung across her back. How long the stout slave woman had been waiting outside the temple I did not know. Althaia touched me lightly on the shoulder. "Go with Kore," she instructed.

"Go where?" I asked.

Althaia repeated her directions. "Go with Kore and do what she tells you, if you don't mind taking orders from a slave." While I stood dumbly, countless questions racing through my mind, Althaia slipped on her mask and once again took on the form of a fearsome maenad, a servant of Dionysus. She touched my arm and left me with one more command before she hurried away from the temple.

"Believe."

CHAPTER 25

I was alone with the Kore. The middle-aged slave-woman's expression of practiced neutrality could not completely hide a trace of disapproval. "Follow me," she said tersely. She turned on her heel and strode away without another word.

And I followed. Not only because Althaia had asked it of me. Wherever the slave Kore was leading me, it was a more attractive destination than the home of Epaminondas and the awkward encounter that waited therein. So like an obedient hound accompanying its master, I let the slave woman lead me on.

Kore guided me with determined purpose. She stuck to the smaller streets and lanes, avoiding the main festivities of the agora. Not that it seemed to matter. The entire population of the city was deep in their cups. Only the lonely guards at the city gates noticed our passing.

Seeing us striding towards the gate, a burly Theban soldier hastened to block our path. "Oi! Where do you think you're going?" he demanded.

"My business is my own, Theban," I said. It was easier than saying I myself had no idea of my destination.

The guard's partner narrowed his eyes at me. "You're that Athenian I heard about. The Thracian Demon."

"I am Daimon, guest-friend of Epaminondas, son of Polymnis," I confirmed.

"Then why aren't you at the festival with your host?" he asked suspiciously.

"I am not accustomed to the strong wine of Thebes. I needed a walk to clear my head," I said.

The guard looked at Kore. "So you're just going for *a walk*?" he said with a slow nod of understanding. Kore herself stood impassively, letting the guard's appraising gaze run over her.

Better to let the man's prurient assumptions ease our journey. "Let's just say I prefer wine that has mellowed with aging," I said.

The guard grunted and stepped aside. "Every man has his own tastes. You're free to go on *your walk*, Athenian," he said with a lascivious grin. "But the gates shut at sunset. You won't be let in later than that."

"That would be a welcome outcome at this point, Theban," I said pushing past him.

When we were out of earshot, Kore muttered, "Theban pig." I glanced at her but her eyes were fixed on the road ahead. Neither of us was in the mood for conversation.

Our journey took us through the countryside beyond the city walls. A few people still lingered in the outlying villages and farms, most likely slaves charged with guarding homes and granaries while their masters partook in the celebration inside the city walls. We tramped along a well-used path into the range of forested hills that extend west from the city, breathing hard as we ascended. Kore took a side path off the main route that led deeper into the forest. The path branched occasionally, but the slave-woman chose her route without hesitation, not bothering to check if I was keeping up.

At last Kore came to a stop atop a rock face. I peered through the scrub to see what lay down below. It was a surprising sight. The ledge looked down onto a near-perfect circular clearing some twenty strides in diameter. A large stone-ringed fire pit full of brush and sticks was slightly off-centre. Somewhere beyond the clearing a spring or stream gurgled. The slave unslung the cloth sac from her back and tossed it at my feet. She pointed at the ground. "You will wait *here*," she ordered in her accented Greek, the first words she had uttered since her muttered curse at the city gate.

"Wait for what?" I asked.

"You will know." Without another word, the brusque slave turned and tramped off the way we had come. I considered calling out after her but decided it would be useless. With a resigned sigh I stooped to pick up the sack. The bundle contained a water-skin as well as some bread, figs, sausages, and a hunk of hard cheese. I would be waiting a long time it seemed. My stomach rumbled at the scent of the food. I sat down and began to eat. Whatever was coming, it was better to face it on a full stomach.

And I waited.

I waited as the shadows lengthened and the sky darkened. I waited as the light of the rising full moon washed out the stars that peeped through the forest canopy above. I waited as the mice and foxes crept around me, playing out their nightly contest between hunter and hunted. I waited because Kore had told me to wait. But nothing happened.

With a rising sense of ridiculousness I sat alone in the nighttime forest to the west of Thebes. I rose to leave. I hesitated. Where would I go? The city gates would be shut until the morning. The appearance of a soft glow among the trees to the east solved my dilemma for me. I squatted back down in my place of concealment, the sound of my heart beating in my ears. The light grew in strength until the bright flame of a torch suddenly crested a rise. One by one a line of torches blinked into existence as the flame-bearers advanced towards me. The cloaked intruders entered the clearing. Some bore sacks on their backs. Each of them carried a rod wrapped in vines like the *thyrsis* staff the head priest in Thebes had wielded during the sacrifice earlier that day. The newcomers' faces bore contorted, gruesome expressions. They were Maenads.

From my hiding place, I spied on the procession of masked women in amazement. I had heard of such secret rituals in Athens, midnight gatherings of female worshippers of Dionysus in secluded groves in the hills. They were rumours mostly, something to be mocked by the elites as the beliefs of the ignorant and the superstitious. But in my patrols in the countryside, I had come across too many isolated clearings to dismiss the whispers out of hand.

I looked on in fascination. A young bull was led into the clearing by one of the Maenads. She was unusually tall with familiar flaming red hair erupting from behind her mask. I suppressed a curse, withstanding the urge to reveal myself and scold my sister. I huddled back down as Meli let the rope fall from her hand and moved back to the edge of the clearing. The bull made no attempt to flee. The creature was as docile as a sheep. One of the women, her patterned cloak more elaborate than the others', stepped forward. From within the folds of her cloak she pulled out a long object and held it aloft. The butcher's dagger glinted in the torchlight. With practiced confidence, the woman drew a powerful stroke across the bull's throat. The animal let out a low groan and collapsed on its haunches. The woman held the beast's horn while its lifeblood pumped out onto the forest floor.

What happened next was terrible yet enthralling to behold. The clearing transformed into a hive of activity. Some of the masked women revealed their own butchering tools, and then, shedding their cloaks and other clothes, the naked women, still in their masks, fell upon the bull carcass like a mob of long-taloned harpies. Their blades flashed and sliced in the torchlight as they gutted the animal and carved off chunks of meat which they tossed into a glistening heap. At the same time, other women set about lighting the wood in the enormous fire pit. Soon great dancing fingers of flame were leaping up towards the sky. Above all this, floating in the air, was the haunting melody of an *aulos* flute accompanied by a drum that pulsed like a heartbeat.

Blood-splattered women tossed bones and entrails into the blazing fire. Some chunks of meat were dumped into canvas sacks while others were spitted and placed on the edges of the bonfire to cook. The aroma of roasting meat reached my hiding spot before wafting ever upwards to where the winds would carry the savoury scent to the gods. My stomach complained to me in a fit of rumbling.

From the women's belongings there appeared wineskins and drinking vessels. Streams of wine as dark as blood filled the cups and women tipped back their masks to drink in hearty gulps on par with any man. I squinted at their faces. My sister was there, of course. The apparent leader, who had slaughtered the bull, was revealed to be Iokaste. One of the blood-spattered butchers was the slave-woman Kore, who took a full cup from her mistress and downed it in one gulp. There were other women of varying ages that I did not recognize. I did not see Althaia. My heart sank.

Another *aulos* player had joined the first. The melody became more complex, more lively. Many of the Maenad women abandoned their empty cups, picked up their *thyrsis* rods, and began to dance. The women moved around the fire as though in a trance, swaying and tumbling like drunkards, yet their bare feet always sure. Their gently-smiling faces radiated quiet bliss. Meli was among them, her eyes closed as she twirled and twisted. The effect was hypnotic.

So entranced was I by the spectacle that I did not hear the intruder at first. Soft footsteps approached from the darkness behind me, each step careful, like those of a stalking leopard. I remained motionless. The scent of jasmine perfume told me who approached even before I felt the tip of the dagger pricking the skin between my shoulder blades.

A soul-deep weariness, long held at bay, welled up inside me. "You know my story, O Althaia," I said quietly. "You would be bestowing upon me a mercy if you plunged the dagger deep."

The pressure of the point grew, but then the dagger withdrew. I felt a drop of blood trickling down my back. "Turn around," ordered Althaia.

I did so. She wore the same contorted mask as in the morning. The Maenad's mouth was frozen agape in a scream of fury. Althaia's face was hidden, but her long unbound hair spilled over her shoulders. Her pale cloak was unblemished by the blood of the sacrifice. The dagger tip crept up my chest until it rested under the crudely carved horn beneath my throat. "You are fortunate, Athenian. The God's token puts you under his protection."

I remained motionless, the dagger tip still at my throat. "And if I removed it now and cast it into the forest, would you kill me then?

"If you believe I brought you here to kill you, then you truly are a fool, Daimon of Athens." With her free hand she lifted her mask and dropped it on the ground. In the cold moonlight, she seemed not to belong to either this world or the next. Her wide dark eyes stared up at me. She took a step closer. "I told you that I watched you at our home. Do you know what I saw?" she asked.

"A good man?" I said.

One corner of her mouth arched in amusement. "Perhaps. But I noticed that you always avoid looking at me. Why is that?"

Without realizing it, I found her hands in mine. The dagger tumbled to the earth. "If you do not know the answer to that, then it is you who are a fool."

The moonlight glinted in her eyes. "Then I am a fool. Tell me."

"It is because I feared you."

She pulled back a little, her sculpted eyebrows raised in surprise. "You feared me?"

"I feared you for what you made me feel. It was something I thought I had lost long ago."

Althaia squeezed my hands more tightly. "Desire?" There was a hint of sweet wine on her breath.

Now it was I who smiled. "That too. But something more. Something I fear to lose again."

"It is better not to say."

For many years there had been armour around my heart. I thought it protected me. But it did not. It was imprisonment. It was loneliness. Now the armour cracked and I gave voice to what I kept hidden. "Come with me to Athens," I said, for that is what I truly desired. Yet

I knew her answer before the words finished tumbling from my lips. My rational soul scolded me for my weakness.

Althaia looked at me sadly. "If I told you that is what I wished, would it change anything? Not all women can be free to choose their lovers like your sister. Tomorrow I will do my duty and wed. But tonight I belong to no one but the God. Tonight I am free." She reached up and pulled my head down to hers. Our lips met and I forgot who I was. I pulled the pin at Althaia's shoulder and her robes fell free.

Dionysus is the god of ecstasy. Of madness. Most of all he is the god of change. He gave us the gift of all those things for one night.

But one thing is always true of gifts from the gods.

There is always a price.

CHAPTER 26

I was in no hurry to return to the home of Epaminondas. The home of Althaia. *Only until she is wed,* a persistent voice in my mind reminded me. I growled to myself as I trudged eastwards through the forest towards Thebes. If I had any choice, I would have stayed away. I had no desire to witness the marriage of Althaia to the loathsome scion of a family of wealthy slave merchants. I could have collected my gear and headed back to Athens with or without my sister, my oath to Thaletos be damned. But I had no choice. Althaia had seen to that. The memory lingered, a seed of happiness encased in a bitter shell.

"Promise me something," she had said as we lay on the forest floor wrapped in her cloak. She nestled deeper into my shoulder as I caressed her hair with my free hand. The moon had gone behind the trees long ago and the revels of the maenads were beginning to ebb, judging by the distant noise. Soon the first hints of dawn would start to intrude on our secret refuge.

"I cannot refuse you," I said.

She raised her head and stared at me intently. "Swear to me that you will attend the wedding."

It was a long time before I answered. "Why?"

She smiled sadly. "Do you not fight more bravely when your friends are at your side?"

How many times had it been so? "Yes."

"Then tell me you will be there, for I need a friend to give me courage."

"I will be there."

"Swear it to the God!"

"I swear it."

Althaia sighed happily and put her head back on my shoulder. "Thank you, *Dammo,*" she said, trying the familiar address that my sister used. We laughed gently at the sound of it before settling down into a peaceful silence for our last moments together.

An oath to the gods is a serious matter. Even I, despising the gods as I do, do not take such things lightly. But I would violate an oath to the gods to help my friends, the gods could damn me to Tartarus for all I cared. But I would not break my promise to Althaia, as much as it pained me.

Thus my mood was grim by the time I arrived back at Thebes. The city gates were open for the day. The weary soldiers on duty had the dark-ringed eyes of the hungover. The burly guard from the previous day was there as well.

"That was a long walk, Athenian," he observed. I scowled at him. The guard frowned. "Where is the woman?" he asked.

I had no idea how or when the cult members had exited or reentered the city. "I am not her keeper," I growled.

The Theban held up an appeasing hand. "Don't take it out on me if things didn't go as planned! Should have just stayed in the city and gotten drunk." Shaking his head, the guard waved me through. The fading laughter of the other guards burned my ears.

I took a meandering path through the city, spending the last of my coins on a breakfast of day-old sausages and barley porridge. Munching on the food beside the stall, I scanned the agora. The remnants of the previous day's festivities were hard to miss. Broken amphorae and wine cups lay about, as did more than a few drunkards sleeping off the excesses of the blessings of Dionysus. It was past midday when I finally returned to the home of my hosts.

As I had hoped, ongoing preparations for the wedding meant my return drew less attention than it might have. The slave Bulis was busy decorating the doorway with boughs of olive and laurel and I had to step around his ladder to get past him. The courtyard had been swept and Manus was setting up some chairs under the direction of Polymnis. Atop the altar sat a bronze platter flanked by arrangements of laurel. Epaminondas, standing beside the altar, heard my footsteps and turned around. His face tightened as I approached him.

"I apologize for my harshness yesterday," I said. "I meant no offence."

"None taken," he said stiffly. "The wine brought some madness upon me. It was my error to have been so presumptuous. Now you must excuse me, for there are matters I must attend to." He turned on his heel and went to discuss something with his father. If anything, the rift between us had widened even further.

An arm looped through mine. "Is something bothering you, Brother?" Meli asked, watching Epaminondas with her fox-like eyes.

I sighed. "Is there ever a time when it isn't so?" We spoke in Thracian to avoid prying ears.

Meli gave me a sympathetic smile. "He will forgive you in time," she said, glancing at Epaminondas. "But he will drive you farther away before he realizes where his true loyalties lie." I acknowledged her with a vague grunt. I wondered how much my sister knew, but then again she was perspicacious when it came to seeing into the hearts of others.

I changed the subject. "Where were you last night, Sister?"

Meli suppressed a small laugh. "I could ask the same of you, Brother, but sometimes it is better to leave things unsaid, even when they are known."

I glanced around the courtyard. "Did I miss anything?"

"Only the sacred bath at dawn."

I sniffed. In Athens brides underwent a purifying bath before the wedding. It seemed the custom here in Thebes as well. That was not what surprised me. "She was here at dawn?" I asked.

"She was here all night as far as I know," Meli said innocently.

"Where is Althaia now?" I asked as naturally as possible.

Meli arched an eyebrow. "She is upstairs with Iokaste. Many rituals must be observed."

My sister's coyness tried my tired patience. "Did you undergo such rituals for Lykos?" I asked but instantly regretted my words.

Meli retreated into herself for a heartbeat before coming back to me. "No."

"Nor did Phaia for me," I said. Each in our own thoughts, we observed the preparations around us.

Meli broke the silence. "They will never see you as a Greek, Dammo, no matter how hard you try. To them, you and I will always be curiosities." She leaned in close. "*Barbarians,*" she whispered, switching to Greek.

"Is that what Althaia thinks too?"

Meli shrugged. "Perhaps. But she did keep asking me if you had returned."

My guts felt like I had been stabbed with a dagger of pure gold. "I'm sure she has other concerns."

"She was worried that you would not attend."

"I swore I would," I said.

"To her?" Meli pried.

I had but was not willing to admit it. "To Thaletos the Theban," I said, which was also true. "And what role will you play, Sister?" I asked, throwing the question back at her.

"I think one Thracian at the wedding will be quite enough. I will stay out of sight as much as possible."

THE GUESTS TRICKLED IN a little before sunset. I stayed off to the side of the courtyard, trying to remain inconspicuous. Epaminondas was still being standoffish and made no effort to make introductions. I could only assume they were mostly members of Polymnis' extended clan. The arrivals threw curious glances my way. The women especially, quickly segregating themselves to the far side of the courtyard, were less discreet in their interest, some even pointing at me. With resignation I accepted that my effort to remain unobtrusive was doomed to failure.

Theban notables were also among the guests, as was to be expected for so important a union. Their arrival drew attention away from me, for which I was grateful. Ismenias acknowledged me with a friendly nod before going to greet his host. The imposing Thaletos was one of the last guests to arrive. The brawny Theban champion was clad in a simple white robe trimmed with a pattern of winding blue lines. Were he to limp, the ugly Thaletos could easily have been mistaken for the god Hephaestus. Seeing me, Thaletos, smiling, made to approach but was immediately surrounded by other guests eager to greet him.

The guests chatted while I remained alone. Eventually Thaletos broke away from a knot of Thebans and made a second attempt to reach me. But a cymbal began to chime from the front porch, signalling the arrival of the bridegroom. Thaletos gave me an apologetic shrug. All eyes turned towards the front of the courtyard as Eurymachus strode in.

He was almost Persian in his opulence. Gold threads embroidered into his deep blue robe glinted in the evening light. Thick necklaces of gold and silver hung in concentric rings across his chest and bejewelled rings decorated his fingers. His immaculate oiled curls were restrained by a golden headband and his beard was waxed to a fine point. He was a handsome man and he knew it.

One step behind him, a dim moon to Eurymachus' sun, was Kepheos. The mercenary captain was serving as the bridegroom's traditional companion, I presumed. Most attention was on Eurymachus, who was accepting greetings from the various guests, but it was the grim-faced Kepheos whom I watched. The fork-bearded warrior wore the expression of one attending a funeral rather than his friend's wedding. Like me, I noticed, no one was in a rush to talk to him.

In my case, the exception was Thaletos, who finally found a moment to share words with me. "It's good to see you, Athenian! I wasn't certain I you would stick to your oath!"

"I had nowhere else to go."

Thaletos chuckled, but my unhappy tone did not escape his notice. "Cheer up, *pai*. I wouldn't be here either if I had a choice, but Polymnis invited me."

"He has been a gracious host," I said. "But I'm looking forward to getting back to Athens."

"When are you leaving?"

"My sister and I will leave tomorrow," I said. "We would already be gone if it weren't for this wedding."

"You are so eager to leave our fair Thebes? Is it to get back to something or to get away from something?"

I thought of Althaia and the wall that had come between me and Epaminondas. "Both," I said vaguely.

"Hmm." Thaletos scratched at the fading bruise on his cheek. "Have you fallen out with young Epaminondas?" Thaletos asked, nodding towards the young Theban. "The lad would hardly leave your side before, but now he acts as if he hardly knows you." The fighter's brutish appearance concealed an observant, thoughtful mind, I was discovering.

"He has learned the hard lesson that our heroes are never all that we imagine them to be."

Thaletos regarded me seriously. "It is a lesson that all young men need to learn, no? But," he said, "That is a subject to discuss over a pot of wine some other time. I think the wedding is starting," he said, nodding towards Polymnis, who was encouraging his male guests to take their seats. Eurymachus and Kepheos seated themselves in the front row along with Epaminondas. Thaletos and I found places at the back. The women remained standing around a pair of chairs near the family altar.

The guests settled, Polymnis raised his hand. At the signal, one of the hired musicians began to play his double *aulos* flute. Althaia appeared at the top of the stairs, Iokaste standing behind her. There was a collective intake of breath. "By the gods!" Thaletos muttered under his breath. I would have said the same, but my voice had been stolen from me. Before us was no thin young maiden of fourteen or fifteen years, like most brides, but a woman in the full prime of her strength and beauty, truly an incarnation of Aphrodite herself. A dress of purest white cascaded over her body, its pinned folds accentuating her curves rather than hiding them. Her hair was a glorious crown of coiled braids, but a thin veil of translucent gauze hid her face from view. As the pair descended the stairs, Althaia moved with a restrained sensuality. Behind the veil I thought I saw her gaze flit my way, but perhaps it was only my desire that made me imagine it so. She filled my soul with fire.

From the bottom of the stairs, she glided across the courtyard, the solemn figure of Iokaste behind her. Mother and daughter sat down in the two empty chairs near the altar. The music ceased and Polymnis nodded to Manus, who disappeared into the kitchen. The slave returned promptly, struggling to hold a squirming, squealing piglet. The piglet fought for life more fiercely than the docile oxen I had seen the day before. But a piglet is no match for a man. Polymnis, chanting a prayer to Zeus, cut the creature's throat as Manus restrained it on the bronze platter and soon it was lying in a shallow pool of blood. Polymnis then raised the wide cup and tipped it so that a stream of wine splattered on the altar while he intoned a prayer to Hera asking her to bless the marriage of his daughter. All the while, Althaia sat as motionless as a statue, her thoughts hidden behind her veil.

The prayers went on, imploring Apollo, Artemis, and to protect the marriage, but not Dionysus. Perhaps the god of change and chaos was unwelcome within the bond of marriage. Polymnis completed his invocations to the gods, The *aulos* player raised his instrument to his lips and began to trill a joyful melody. On cue, the guests rose from their seats, smiling and clapping. While the music played and the troupe of hired slaves droned on behind the altar. The men gathered on one side of the courtyard, congratulating Polymnis and the new groom on their good fortune. Thaletos moved forward to pay his respects. He glanced my way. I gave a small shake of my head and he shrugged, leaving me on my own.

I stood awkwardly at the fringes of the celebration, wishing I were anywhere else. On the far side of the courtyard, a gaggle of women and maidens formed a chattering crowd around the seated Althaia. Her face remained veiled, so I could not see her expression as her mother whispered something in her ear.

My gaze wandered over the crowd. I was not the only outcast. The fork-bearded Kepheos stood alone, occasionally casting an occasional tight-faced glance towards Althaia. It was clear that Polymnis' rejection of his proposal still stung. He was a slaver mercenary whom I would have happily gutted, but for a moment I pitied him for the humiliation he must be feeling. My own jealously whispered insistently in my mind. Swallowing my resentment, I continued to scan the courtyard. A figure lurked in the shadows near the stairs. From her hiding place, Meli smiled at me sympathetically.

Slaves with platters were distributing small honeyed cakes covered in sesame seeds to all the guests except for the veiled Althaia, who still sat in silence next to her mother. I sniffed at my cake with mild distaste. A nearby guest, an older man with friendly eyes, noticed my reluctance to take a bite. "They are Hera cakes. They are said to make the bride fertile," he explained with a wink, gesturing that I should take a bite. I glared at him and he hastened to find someone more receptive to his conversation. I surreptitiously tossed the cake behind a column.

The chanting of the prayers came to a halt and the conversation dropped to a low murmur. In front of the altar, Polymnis stood before Eurymachus bearing a single Hera cake on a silver dish. "O Eurymachus," Polymnis announced formally. "I give you my daughter so that you can sow her and produce legitimate children."

With none of Polymnis' solemnity, Eurymachus casually snatched the cake and took a bite. He glanced towards his seated, silent bride. "I accept," he said through a mouthful of Hera cake. It was a signal that this part of the wedding was over. Althaia would now become part of Eurymachus' household in the home of Leontiades. Eurymachus extended his hand towards Althaia. She rose and stepped away from her mother. Eurymachus took his new wife by the arm to applause and cheers.

The guests parted to open a path to the front door. Eurymachus led his bride at a measured pace, accepting congratulations with an impatient smile. Althaia remained facing straight ahead. But as the two of them approached, Althaia turned her head towards me, her face still hidden behind the diaphanous veil. Eurymachus, following her gaze, saw me watching grimly. His frown vanished behind a wolfish, lecherous grin. I could only glower helplessly as he exited the house, laughing, with Althaia at his side. The family and guests began to follow. The ceremony, despite appearances, was not finished. A procession would now pass through the streets of Thebes to deliver the bride to her new home, where the celebration would continue. Epaminondas, studiously ignoring me, was among the first to follow his sister outside. As the guests trickled out onto the street, my sister emerged from the shadows to join me in the almost deserted courtyard.

"You are not going?" I asked.

Meli shook her head. "I fear I would attract unwanted attention," she said, gesturing towards her tattooed face and Thracian cloak. "I will remain here with Iokaste."

"Perhaps I should do the same."

Meli's eyes flashed. "And break your promise to Thaletos? To *Althaia*?" she said, fixing me with a hard, flinty stare. She pushed me towards the door. "You must go!" With great reluctance, I followed my sister's command.

The road outside the house was filling with guests. Each guest was handed a lit torch by a small contingent of well-dressed slaves. A torch-lit procession would accompany Althaia to her new home. A slave offered me a torch but retreated under my murderous stare.

I had no choice but to pass the sturdy cart with two oxen waiting outside the doors. Althaia, staring straight ahead, sat atop the wagon with a chest containing her dowry behind her. If she saw me, she gave no indication of it. Beside her was Eurymachus, who was bent over to chat with one of the guests. At the bridegroom's side sat Kepheos. Like the bride, his expression suggested the event was a grim rite of passage to be endured rather than celebrated. I shifted towards the shadows away from the crowd.

A meaty hand fell on my shoulder. "I thought you had slipped away."

"The thought had occurred to me."

Thaletos chuckled. "You don't like celebrations?"

"I would rather stand in the front rank of a phalanx facing ten thousand Spartiates."

Thaletos scratched at his disfigured nose. "I share your sentiments if not their intensity. Take my advice: drink the fine wine, eat the rich food, and it will be over soon enough." He slapped my back. "We will face Leontiades and his fashionable hordes together, Athenian."

The slaves pulled at the oxen's leads. With a groan the cart lurched into motion.

Thaletos and I trailed the chanting torchlight procession. In my heart I was treading not the shadowy streets of Thebes but the dark road to the Underworld.

CHAPTER 27

The house of Leontiades was a monument to his wealth.

Admission past the high stone walls was through a double gate of panelled oak. Two guards with swords on their belt scrutinized the stream of wedding guests as they passed through the imposing entrance. The interior was even more impressive, with tasteful trellised porticoes surrounding a large stone house. It was more like the residence in the palace of Pharnabazus than the home of a private citizen.

Somewhere within, someone played a lyre and the gentle twang drifted over the garden, accompanied by the buzzing undertone of the guests. Thaletos and I were among the final members of the torch-lit procession to arrive. I followed the Theban champion through gardens adorned with statues of animals and nymphs to whatever trials lay within.

A slave guided us through brightly painted salons to the crowded central courtyard. My gaze was drawn to Althaia first of all. She stood at the far side of the space. She had removed her veil. She looked like an immortal. She looked sad. Her eyes found me too and suddenly I felt the distance between us was as wide as the sea. She looked away, leaving me stranded once more.

She was not alone, of course. She was flanked by Eurymachus and his father Leontiades, who, along with Polymnis and Epaminondas, were accepting congratulations from a steady stream of well-wishers. For his part, Polymnis was already benefitting from his daughter's marriage due to the social opportunities it was affording him. His daughter, the price of admission into Leontiades' circle of the Theban elite, remained silent, as did the stern-faced Kepheos, who stood off to one side, out of place and ignored.

"Will you not offer congratulations?" Thaletos asked, nodding towards the wedding party.

"I will do so later," I said.

Thaletos accepted the lie graciously. "As you wish," he said. He left me to brood by myself.

There was little to do but observe. Men stood in clusters or sat together, chatting with animated gestures. Not a few women were present as well, ranging from older to younger, but all with fashionable hairstyles and abundant jewelry. At least two of them had been among the maenads in the forest the night before, I realized. In one corner of the courtyard, a group of musicians played. The soft, complex melody of the *aulos* player drifted above the hum of conversation. Slaves dressed in simple tunics flitted among the guests, replenishing wine cups and offering dainty snacks.

I recognized one of the slaves. The short-haired slave girl focused all her attention as she poured the last of some wine into the ornate cup of one of the guests. The clumsy girl must have returned with Althaia to the service of Leontiades. Surprisingly, there was an aura of energetic happiness about her. Curious, I moved to the edge of the courtyard to watch her as she scurried off to fetch more wine

I discovered the source of her newfound contentment. He was handsome and young, not past his twentieth year by the look of him. His wide eyes and gently-curved nose suggested an eastern origin, but little more than that. They stopped for a moment as they passed each other in the corridor. He placed his hand on her shoulder and leaned down to whisper something in her ear. She giggled and flashed a radiant smile. She was pretty, I realized, when she wasn't cowering. The handsome slave gave a small wave as he hurried off to his duties. The slave girl watched him go with adoration. No wonder she had been so miserable in the home of Epaminondas, away from her lover.

I did not have much time to reflect on the secret romance. The formal greetings done, Leontiades and his son were now circulating about the courtyard. While Leontiades and his wife moved off to converse with other guests, Eurymachus made the rounds with his coterie of brutish companions. Althaia remained dutifully behind her new husband.

Large and crowded as the courtyard was, there was nowhere to hide. Spotting me among the guests, Eurymachus made his way towards me.

The Theban aristocrat greeted me with artificial warmth. "Welcome to my home, Athenian." I could smell the wine on his breath.

I could not bring myself to congratulate him on his marriage. "It is a fine celebration," I managed, trying to ignore the cloying scent of his perfume.

Eurymachus sniffed at my grudging compliment. "Do you often attend such parties in Athens?" he asked, taking in the sight of his chatting, drinking guests. "Or perhaps one of the *symposia* for which Athens is so renowned?"

"No," I said flatly.

Eurymachus smirked. "Why would you? I don't suppose poetry and philosophy are among your interests."

I ignored his baiting. "I'm just a soldier," I said with a shrug. "But perhaps someday I will pay someone to write a poem about my exploits and have it recited here for your father's enjoyment." From her place behind Eurymachus, Althaia regarded me with dancing eyes.

A scowl flickered across his face but was quickly masked by another condescending smile. He took one of the dainty morsels from the tray of a nearby slave and popped it in his mouth. He smacked his lips with appreciation. "I suppose, then, that you are not used to such fine food? What does someone of your position eat every day?"

"Barley porridge with onions. Hard cheese. Harder bread. Mutton, if I'm lucky."

Eurymachus nodded knowingly. "The nourishing food of the working man." He indicated the slave's tray. "Try one of these. Our cook once prepared food for the Great King himself! Some of the ingredients cost more than a labourer earns in a year." I took one and ate it, chewing reflectively. "So what do you think?" he asked.

"Salty," I said. Althaia bowed her head to hide her smile.

Eurymachus' eyes flashed with anger. He took a long sip of wine, regarding me over the edge of the cup. His free hand reached out to pinch my newly-purchased robe. "I hardly recognized you in this. One could almost mistake you for a Greek!" He leaned towards me and sniffed. "Though I can still smell the barbarian!" I narrowed my eyes at Eurymachus. Althaia gave a tiny shake of her head.

I had borne such insults my entire life. In my youth, I was a slave to my pride. I would let someone like Eurymachus goad me to violence. Pride still had its place, but the barbs of spoiled shit-eaters like Eurymachus meant little to me. I would rein in my urge to lay him low, if only for the sake of Althaia and her family.

"I confess that I find a simple tunic more agreeable." Epaminondas, perhaps sensing the growing tension, made his way towards us. He took his place with Eurymachus and his companions. He would not meet my eye.

The presence of Epaminondas only spurred Eurymachus on to further insults. His eyes drifted to the bull-horn amulet at my chest. He held it between two fingers and peered at it. "And you are superstitious?" He let go of the pendant and sneered at me. "Simple beliefs for simple minds!"

"You do not believe in the gods, Theban?" I asked.

Eurymachus scoffed. "The gods? The gods of our forefathers are a lie. Zeus, Apollo, Dionysus, the lot of them. What are they now? Just an excuse to have a festival and get drunk. Men of ambition do not need the gods to succeed!"

"I once knew a man who denied the gods as you did. He became the most powerful man in Athens."

"You see!" Eurymachys exclaimed, pleased. "And what happened to him? I suppose you will say that Zeus struck him with a thunderbolt or Apollo inflicted some illness upon him for his impiety," Eurymachus said with a snort.

"No. I cut him in half on the slopes of Munychia"

Eurymachus, considering a retort, raised his cup to his lips but found it empty. Irritated, he scanned the courtyard. He beckoned the nearest slave with a wine jug. It was the short-haired girl. She came over to refill her master's cup.

I often wonder about the Fates. Sometimes I believe we are powerless as the three Moirai manipulate the fabric of our lives under their hands, interweaving our threads with those of others as they create the grand pattern known only to them. Other times I believe differently, that our lives are our own choices and the Fates only spin our threads as we force them to. Whatever is true, the Weavers' fingers were busy that night.

The bulky wine jug was shaped like a ram's head, one of those bits of ostentatious frippery so loved by the rich. The freshly-filled jug was too heavy for the waifish girl. With some awkwardness she lifted the vessel and tipped it towards Eurymachus' cup. Then she noticed me. Her eyes glinted with recognition and she shared a shy smile with me. The foolish distraction was enough. She tipped the jug too far. The wine gushed out of the ram's mouth in a flood, spattering the deep purple liquid over the Theban aristocrat's fine wedding robes. The jewelled cup slipped from Eurymachus' hand and fell to the floor with a clang, splashing wine on the feet of those nearby. Guests turned their attention to the small commotion.

The girl cringed, not daring to meet her master's eye. "Forgive me, *despote*!" she said quickly, blinking at the floor.

An angry blush climbed up the Theban aristocrat's face. "Clumsy slave!" Without warning, he struck the girl. She tried to avoid the blow and his open hand glanced off the top of her head. Her resistance, meagre as it was, infuriated Eurymachus. The girl cowered in fear. He raised his hand to hit her again.

I caught his wrist before the blow could fall. Eurymachus glared at me with a mixture of astonishment and rage.

I do not know why I did it. I was a guest not only in Thebes but in the home of Leontiades. It was not my place to interfere with a man disciplining his own slaves. Epaminondas had stood for me as his guest-friend in Thebes, and I was violating the trust he had placed in me for an insignificant slave.

Yet it made me angry. Perhaps I did it to protect the thin, clumsy girl. After all, my mother had been a slave, and it would have shamed me to stand by and see her treated thus. But Eurymachus was an arrogant brute who had gone out of his way to belittle me. I would have welcomed the opportunity to lay him low. Perhaps I acted only because Althaia was present. I do not know. But the Moirai smiled.

Kepheos and his companions took a threatening step towards me, but Eurymachus found his tongue. "Stop!" he commanded. The men held back. Eurymachus glared at me. "You dare!"

The scrutiny of the crowd was like heat on my body. "It is not necessary to strike her," I said, releasing his wrist. The musicians had stopped playing. The quarrel was the entertainment now. I kept my eyes fixed on Eurymachus.

"She is my property! This is my home! It is not the place of a shit-eating Athenian mercenary to tell me what is necessary!" He raised his hand again. I shoved him away and stepped in front of the terrified slave-girl.

"You will not touch her." I was aware of the stares of the other guests. Polymnis looked horrified. Epaminondas stared at me grim-faced. Thaletos was frowning. At the edge I glimpsed the face of the slave-girl's lover, his handsome face tight with apprehension.

"And what will you do? Stay here all night?" He shifted to look at the girl cowering behind me. "I promise you that I will beat her bloody tonight. Who knows? I might even take my pleasure of her after I have consummated my wedding," he said with a casual wave towards Althaia. "It will not be pleasant, I promise you."

I was trapped. By my rash action I had led the girl to greater harm than if I had done nothing. "I am taking her," I said. From behind Eurymachus, Althaia's gaze never left me.

Eurymachus' eyes became as round as shields. "You're *stealing* a slave from my house? During my wedding party?"

"You will be compensated."

"I don't want your silver, Athenian! I want my property!"

Kepheos and his men awaited their employer's command. I was unarmed. If they fell upon me, I could not win. But I would fight nevertheless. "Then you will have to come and take her," I said, meeting the eyes of each of them. I could not help but look towards Althaia, for in the entire courtyard, hers was the only opinion that mattered to me. I feared I would see anger or shame or embarrassment. But I something else. Althaia looked upon me with pride. With renewed resolve, I returned my gaze to Eurymachus. Uncertainty rippled across his face. The men hesitated. They knew who I was. Perhaps the reputation of Daimon the Slaughterer would be enough.

Or perhaps not. Eurymachus made a signal and the two bodyguards joined detached themselves from their posts and lined up with their employer. Their scarred and weathered faces bore no trace of fear. No aristocrats these, but professional fighting men used to putting their bodies in danger. They would not be intimidated.

A firm voice filled the silence. "You will have to face me as well." It was Epaminondas. He stepped away from Eurymachus to take his place at my side.

Polymnis pushed his way forward and grabbed his son's shoulder. "*Pai*! Don't be a fool!" A hint desperation lurked under his angry voice. But Epaminondas shook him off. Althaia's pride radiated from her like sunlight. Kepheos and his mercenaries shifted, ready to fall upon us at the command of Eurymachus.

A voice of authority came down like a clap of thunder. "Enough!" Leontiades strode forward and put himself between the opposing lines. He glared at his son. "This is not a tavern of brawling drunks! And," he said, turning on me. "In Thebes, it is not usual for a guest to attack his hosts!"

Leontiades was in the right. But I was proud and would not give him the satisfaction of an apology. I glanced at Althaia. I reckoned it would be the last time I saw her. "I will be leaving," I said, grabbing the wrist of the slave-girl. "I am taking this slave. I will see you are compensated."

Leontiades dismissed my offer with a wave. "Take her. I have a thousand slaves on my estates. She is worthless."

Eurymachus spoke up. "Behold the Athenian thief!" he said to the guests.

Polymnis made a desperate attempt to salvage the evening and his newfound status. "Epaminondas, stand down!" he said in a tone that was equal measures fatherly anger and powerless pleading. Epaminondas' resolve wavered.

"Listen to your father," I said. My words had the opposite effect as Epaminondas, his frown deepening, ignored his father's plea. His misguided loyalty moved me. I was not the only one, for pride infused Althaia's face as she looked upon her brother. Polymnis seemed stunned by his son's recalcitrance.

"Enough!" Leontiades repeated. "Be gone!" He turned his implacable stare on Polymnis. "All of you."

Polymnis' shoulders fell. He pointed at me. "He is not one of us!" he protested

"When you associate with beasts, you end up smelling like dung," Leontiades answered coldly.

With whispers and stares at our backs, we departed. Eurymachus and his mercenaries hounded our heels. In the torchlight, the gardens crept with shadows and silent eyes. At the gate, Eurymachus seized a handful of my robe.

"I do not like the way you look at my *wife*, Athenian!" He leaned in close. "More to the point, I do not like the way she looks at *you*!" he hissed in my ear.

I shook him off. I wanted to tell him. Of our night in the forest during the rites to Dionysus. That I would take her away from him. But I said nothing. And by the change in Eurymachus' expression, I realized that my silence was as damning as if I had confessed to everything.

We fumbled through the black streets of Thebes without even a torch to light our way, Epaminondas, Polymnis, myself, and a clumsy slave-girl who could not properly pour a cup of wine. I cursed the Fates. I swore at the gods.

I had only myself to blame.

CHAPTER 28

Polymnis was livid with rage. "You have brought shame down upon us!" The furrows and creases in the Theban's face were deepened by the light of the torch held by his slave Manus.

The slave was not the only witness to Polymnis' fury. Iokaste and my sister had come down to greet us in the courtyard, no doubt surprised by our early return from the wedding feast. I kept my focus on the irate Theban. "I am sorry, O Polymnis," I said. "I did not think."

He stepped close to me, a move that forced him to look up at me. "And if you had thought, would you have acted differently?" I remained silent. Polymnis' lips parted to reveal his clenched teeth and I heard a low growl building in his chest. For a moment I thought he would strike me. I would not have resisted. His fury was justified.

Instead, his gaze shifted to the slave girl, who trembled behind me. The rumbling in Polymnis' throat grew louder and exploded in a roar of frustration. He spun away and strode towards the stairs at the edge of the courtyard. One the first step he came to a halt and twisted his upper body to look back at me. "You are not welcome in my home!" he spat, pointing an accusing finger at me. "But I will not cast you out, though you deserve it, for I swore an oath to the gods to protect you as my guest. I, for one, respect my obligations!" He marched up to the second floor to brood in his bed-chamber. Iokaste cast a last, unreadable look my way before hurrying after her husband.

I was left to explain myself to Epaminondas, a task no less daunting than facing his father's wrath. Before I could speak, Epaminondas turned on me. "You should not have interfered!" he said bitterly.

I kept my voice level. "She only spilled some wine. Eurymachus should not have struck her."

He shot a disgusted glance at the slave-girl, who cowered beneath his gaze. "Did you act to protect *her*? Or was it only to impress my sister?"

"I don't know what you mean."

Epaminondas snorted. "You think I have not noticed how you look at each other?" He stabbed a finger into my chest. "*You* were *my* guest, not *hers*!" His wrath did not completely conceal his pain. There was nothing I could say. He turned his back to me and leaned on the family altar with both hands. The offerings of fruit and wine from the wedding had attracted flies. At least the sacrificed piglet had been removed.

Whatever Epaminondas thought of me, there was something I needed to say. "Thank you for standing with me."

He spun around. "It is a decision I regret more and more with each passing moment!" he snapped.

"We cannot always choose what battles we fight," I said. "Only how we choose to fight them."

"People warned me about you, but I chose not to listen. Yet I see now they were right. You care not for those around you. As long as you win, the lives of others are a fair price. You are selfish," he said coldly. My soul flinched, for the sharp accusation had stabbed at a place deep within me.

"Nevertheless, I am grateful for your friendship." It was all I could offer.

Epaminondas flicked my gratitude away with a sneer. He pulled himself up straight and bowed stiffly towards me. "I understand my obligations," he said sardonically, echoing his father's words. "But I will be glad to see the back of you."

"My sister and I will return to Athens tomorrow," I said.

"That will be best." Without another word, he trudged up the steps, leaving us in the courtyard.

An embarrassed cough to my right broke through the awkward silence. The house-slave Manus was still standing with us holding his flickering torch. "Is there anything you need?" he asked.

My stomach rumbled. I had eaten nothing at the wedding feast besides the tidbit Eurymachus had offered with such pride. I was sure the slave-girl was hungry as well. "Some food for me and the girl, if you have any."

"I'll see what I can do." He lit two lamps for us before disappearing to the larder. While he scraped something together for our late meal, I turned my attention on the slave.

I towered over her. It was like a wolf looking down on a quavering fawn. A silly girl. The cause of so much trouble. "What is your name, girl?" I said brusquely. I had not bothered to learn it earlier.

She flinched at my harsh tone. "Keaera, *despote*," she whispered.

Meli shot me an angry look. "For the love of Bendis! You're scaring her!" She turned to the slave Keaera. "Come here, child," she said, opening her arms. *Child.* It was odd to hear my sister use that word. In my eyes, she was little more than a child herself. I realized how much older she was now. How much older we both were. The girl Keaera glanced nervously between me and my sister, like a mouse caught between a predator and the safety of its hole. Finally she scurried into Meli's protective embrace.

The house-slave Manus returned with a platter with bread, hard cheese, oil, a jug of wine, and three cups.

"This is very generous, Manus. Thank you," I said.

Manus scratched reflectively behind his ear. "I reckon there's no problem that isn't made worse by an empty stomach." It was a sound observation. "The same goes for sleep," he added. We thanked him again and he shuffled off to his room.

The three of us sat on the ground beside the household altar, our meal dimly illuminated by a lamp Manus had left us. Keaera, hesitant at first, fell upon her food like a ravenous dog. She watched me nervously, as if I might snatch the food from her at any moment. When she was sated, her wariness abated somewhat and she peered at my sister's tattooed face with fascination.

"You're a wise-woman! Touched by the gods!" Keaera declared in a voice tinged with awe. Meli's silence served to confirm her observation, and she gave a satisfied chirp before grabbing another hunk of bread.

"Where are you from?" I asked.

She squinted at me as though looking for some kind of trap. "Far away," she said. "From across the sea." It was not very helpful.

"When were you enslaved?" I pressed.

She paused to consider this. "Three or four years ago?" she said uncertainly. "They came to my village and killed my father and the other men. They put the rest of us in ships. I was separated from my mother and my brother. I don't know where they are." She recounted her tale with little emotion.

"And you were sold to the household of Leontiades?"

She shook her head. "Someone else bought me from a slave-market by the sea. There were twenty of us. They made us walk for many days with chains on our hands. But we were attacked. They killed the —" She dug for an unfamiliar word. "The merchants of slaves! They killed the merchants of slaves. They brought us to Thebes."

"Who killed the merchants?" I said, using her word.

She hesitated. "The *despote*'s guard. He was at the party. You saw him."

"Kepheos?" I asked. Keaera made a sign to ward off the evil eye. Attica was not the only place Kepheos and his mercenaries had been raiding then. "And he brought you to Eurymachus?"

The name made the girl close in on herself. "He likes to beat us, especially the girls. And he does worse things when no one else is around." She stared at the ground. "I hate him," she finished in a voice barely louder than a whisper.

My sister laid a hand tenderly on the girl's shoulder. "You do not need to fear him anymore," Meli reassured her. "You will not go back there again. My brother will protect you." Without warning, Keaera burst into tears. Meli and I exchanged a confused glance. "You do not need to be afraid!" Meli repeated

Keaera shook her head. "It is Donax!" she managed between sobs.

"Who is Donax?" I asked, already suspecting the answer.

She smeared her tears across her cheek with the back of her hand. "We love each other!"

I nodded. The handsome youth. Meli looked to me for explanation. "The other slave. I saw him talking to you."

Keaera sniffed. "How can we see each other again?" Then her tears spilled forth once more.

Meli, grasping the situation, held the slave girl close. "Do not worry about that, child. The gods will see that you are reunited."

My sister's words calmed the girl, but only for an instant, as fear returned to her eyes. "What if the *despote* comes for me? He will punish me!"

"My brother will kill him before he ever touches you," my sister promised on my behalf.

Keaera blinked away her tears. "Do you promise?" she asked with a child's sincerity.

I scowled at Meli, whose expression, in turn, dared me to contradict her. I sighed in defeat. "You have my word." I leaned close and whispered, "I am fiercer than any watchdog!" A smile broke through the girl's tears. She laid her head on Meli's lap. My sister stroked her light-brown hair and soon the slave was asleep.

"So what dung-heap have you landed yourself in this time, Brother?"

"It's a long story," I said snappishly.

She looked around the dark, empty courtyard. "I don't think anyone will disturb us." She looked at me patiently. In the dim light, her green eyes had become as black as charcoal. I told her what had transpired at the wedding feast.

"It was stupid," I said. "I was wrong. I should have done nothing."

Meli considered this. "Wrong, perhaps, but it was the just thing to do."

I snorted. "Just! I have made myself the most hated man in Thebes!"

"'The just man who is not hated is not just!'" she said.

"You sound like that shit-eater Plato," I said. The sudden intrusion of the blathering Plato into my thoughts only served to pollute my already foul mood. I had driven the turd-spouting wind-bag from Athens more than a year earlier, threatening to hang him by his own guts if he returned. Where he had gone, I had no inkling. Perhaps in his exile he had been captured and enslaved, and was now chained to the oar in the fetid bowels of a Phoenician war-galley. The image lifted the corners of my mouth into a smile. Another concern made me forget the happy thought of Plato in misery. "I have made Epaminondas my enemy."

"Epaminondas will understand. Give him time."

"Why in Hades would you say that?"

"Because Epaminondas is a just man," she said.

"That may be so, but it is possible for two just men to hate each other," I retorted. "You need look no farther than Lykos and Thrasybulus to know the truth of that." The mention of my sister's former lover left her silent.

Lykos, ten years dead, was the younger brother of Thrasybulus. He had been my mentor and friend. The two brothers had not hated one another — that was too strong a word — but I had never seen an encounter between them that had not ended in bitter words. In contrast to the staid, measured Thrasybulus, Lykos was restless and passionate by nature, energy he had focused to hunt down the enemies of Athens with ruthless efficiency. Unlike Thrasybulus, he had shied away from public leadership, preferring to stay in his brother's shadow, a fact that irked Thrasybulus to no end. They were both good men, yet still found each other as adversaries more often than not.

"I'm sorry, Meli. I didn't mean to…" I groped for words.

She smiled sadly. "I know. I miss him. But I have Tibetos now." Now it was Meli who looked embarrassed, for she knew I had no one as she had Tibetos. But my sister saw the deepest concern that lay within my own heart. "There is something else that vexes you, Brother." It was a declaration, not a question.

For all the repercussions my actions would have, one was more immediate, more personal. "Althaia. I fear Eurymachus will harm her to punish me."

"So what are you going to do, Brother?"

For a long time I said nothing. That was the question, indeed. I had been playing with different scenarios since I left the home of Leontiades. I imagined abducting Althaia in the night. But I was in a hostile city with only Meli to help me. And, with its high walls and small army of guards and slaves, the house was more akin to a small fortress. Every plan I could think of ended up with my head on a pole outside the gates of Thebes, to say nothing of how such an act would strain the alliance between Athens and Thebes. But Althaia, whatever her feelings, had made it clear she would do nothing to dishonour her family.

At last I spoke. "I don't know," I said, rubbing my temples. I looked at my sister. Having found no escape from my dilemma, I did something I was loath to do in normal circumstances. "What do the gods tell you, Sister?"

Meli peered at me. She knew that I must have been desperate indeed to ask for guidance from the gods. But my moment of weakness bought me no reward. "Bendis is silent. This land belongs to Dionysus."

"And he said nothing to you?"

She furrowed her brow in thought. "I have been having strange dreams. It is Dionysus, I am sure! But I don't understand. He is chaos! Madness!"

"That is not helpful," I observed.

"But I think he favours you," she said.

I snorted. "A god favours me? That seems unlikely!" I hated the gods and they hated me.

Meli shook her head. "No. Remember, Dionysus is not from here. He comes from across the sea, from the land of our ancestors. He is an outsider in this place, like you. But he made Thebes his own. He wants you to do the same."

I struggled to recall the stories of Dionysus from my childhood. There were so many, some from my mother, some from Neleus, some from my older brother Heliodoros. In my mind the pieces of various tales all blended together like a pot of stew. "Didn't he die first?" I asked

"In some stories, yes," Meli confirmed.

"That doesn't sound promising," I said. "But I will die to free Althaia, if I must."

A sphinx-like smile appeared on her lips. "I know you would, Brother, but don't be rash."

"Like tonight?" I asked, glancing at the sleeping Keaera.

Meli stroked the slave's hair. "Althaia is strong. If the gods wish it, they will provide you a path to be with her."

"I'd rather make my own path," I said.

Meli shrugged. "They are one and the same."

The flame of the lamp flickered, waned, and extinguished itself with a small pop. "That is a sign from the gods if I ever saw one," I said. "Get some rest, Sister. It's a long way back to Athens and I want to set out early."

CHAPTER 29

I did not sleep.

I remained on guard while mulling over the events of the previous day. I thought Epaminondas, having had time to consider things, might seek me out. He did not.

In the grey-blue world between night and day, I packed our few belongings. I wanted to depart as soon as the city gates opened. I donned my horse-hoof corselet and armoured skirt, thankful for their familiar weight and odor. Meli still slept, her protective arm still draped over the frail figure of Keaera. I sensed someone's gaze upon me. Keaera observed me, her wide eyes wary.

I held up my hands to show I meant her no harm. "I won't hurt you," I said.

"I know," she said with a timid smile.

"Wake my sister," I said, nodding towards Meli. "Help her prepare her things. We'll be leaving soon. Away from this place." Keaera gave Meli a gentle prod. My sister sat up and stretched and yawned like a fox after a nap.

It would have been too much to hope to have slipped away unnoticed. Polymnis and Epaminondas descended into the courtyard bleary-eyed and sullen. Iokaste followed a few steps behind, her dignified bearing unruffled by the events of the previous night.

"You sought to slink back to Athens before we woke?" Polymnis asked icily.

It was exactly what I had been doing. I glanced at Epaminondas. "I admit my error, O Polymnis. I have betrayed your hospitality. But I cannot change my decision."

"Cannot or will not?" he snapped. He pointed at Keaera. "Take the slave back to Leontiades. She is his property. Apologize to Leontiades and his son for your behaviour. Perhaps some honour remains to be salvaged!"

Keaera, watching like us like a prisoner awaiting a verdict in the law courts, moaned softly and took shelter behind Meli's imposing figure. My sister, with her swirling tattoos and patterned Thracian cloak, radiated all of her barbarian glory. Keaera peered out at me, awaiting my judgment.

If Polymnis believed I would beg forgiveness from Leontiades and Eurymachus, he was poor judge of character. Epaminondas knew me better. "You are mistaken to think he will abase himself for our family's sake," he said.

I faced his accusing stare before turning away. "Sister. Keaera. We're leaving." I slung Whisper over my shoulder. Meli and Keaera, following my lead, picked up their satchels. Under the gaze of our newly estranged host, we headed across the courtyard for the door.

"So it is true!" Epaminondas said bitterly at my back. "The great Daimon of Athens is nothing but a sneak-thief!"

I turned to face him one last time. The contempt in his voice did not match the pain on his face. "I am what I am," I said, repeating what I had told Althaia. "I have never claimed anything more than that. You only deceived yourself if you thought I was anything different, Theban." Epaminondas opened his mouth to respond, but his words abandoned him. His shoulders slumped. I opened the door to the street. A curious sight thwarted my efforts to put the home of Epaminondas behind me.

A wooden box waited just beyond the raised threshold stone across the doorway, blocking the way. It must have been delivered in the night, but I had heard nothing. The container was neither large nor small, an almost perfectly cubic box with each side the length of a man's forearm. The erratic lines of the olive wood's grain kinked and jerked across the highly polished surface. The seam between the lid and the bottom was almost invisible except for the bronze hinges and latch. It was an exquisite piece of craftsmanship. I stared at it with a growing sense of unease. Meli's cold silence matched my own.

"What is it?" Keaera asked. She received no answer.

Our apparent reluctance to depart brought Epaminondas striding towards us. "Is it not enough to have dishonoured us? Why do you tarry? Be gone!" I stepped aside. Epaminondas' eyes fell on the box for the first time. The sight cut off his tirade. He looked at me in confusion. I said nothing.

Epaminondas, frowning, squatted down and examined the chest, running a finger along its top edge. His hand moved to the bronze latch. He lifted the bronze pin holding the box shut and pulled back the lid.

Keaera let out a pitiful wail.

The features were unmistakable. Tight ringlets of black hair. An aquiline nose. Wide, handsome eyes that looked up at now with the dullness of death. My sister's prediction had come true. The gods had reunited Keaera with her lover Donax.

Just not in the way she had hoped.

EPAMINONDAS AND I NEARLY CAME TO BLOWS, so heated did our argument become.

I said, unreasonably and perhaps selfishly, that he and Polymnis should demand the return of Althaia. Did he need a clearer indication of Eurymachus' cruelty and vindictiveness than the murder of the slave Donax? Who could say what Eurymachus would do to Althaia, if only to spite me?

The head of Donax was convincing evidence, and I could see Epaminondas wavering. But Polymnis was having none of it. He clung to the hope that the relationship with Leontiades could be mended once I was gone. I called him a fool for believing this, and doing so was my undoing, for it drove Epaminondas to his father's defence.

With Epaminondas won over to his cause, Polymnis grew bolder. "And I will give Leontiades your horses as compensation for the girl!" he shouted, pointing a shaking finger at Keaera. The value of two good horses far exceeded the price of a mousy slave-girl.

"And you dare to call *me* thief!" I sneered. Polymnis, red with fury, spat and hurled curses at me. The quarrel was intense enough to draw neighbours from their homes. The spectators sided with their fellow Thebans by default, and I felt their growing antagonism towards me like heat on my back.

Beyond Epaminondas and his father, in the courtyard, Iokaste looked on, her face pale. Our eyes met, and Iokaste gave me an imploring look. I sensed she was my ally in the cause of reclaiming her daughter, though she could not openly declare it so.

I appealed to Epaminondas once more. "You must help Althaia!"

But the combined weight of loyalty to his father and the heavy stares of his fellow Thebans crushed any lingering sympathy Epaminondas might have had for me. His expression hardened. "Go back to Athens. I am your *xenos* no longer."

I stared at him in disbelief. Then my frustration erupted. I accused him of selling out his sister. I called him a pig-headed, horse-humping

Theban and worse. His face reddened under the barrage of insults, but he did not budge.

Then came my most foolish utterance. I seized his tunic and pulled him close. For the first time, there was a ripple of fear in his eyes. "If you are too much of a coward to free your sister, then I will do it myself!" I shouted, shoving him back.

Meli pulled gently at my sleeve. "Brother." Her voice was calm, as though she were merely asking me for a cup of wine. "I think we should leave." The hostile Theban horde surrounded me. The anonymity born of numbers gave courage to some, who hurled abuse our way. The mob would tear us apart like a pack of hounds if we remained.

My sister began spinning complex gestures with her hands, spitting Thracian curses at the crowd. Fear of her arcane spells quelled their ardour for our demise, and they stepped back a step as though my sister had the plague. How long it would be before they regained their courage I did not know.

I grabbed Keaera's hand, casting one last look at Epaminondas. "Come!"

We pushed our way through a gap in the onlookers. The crowd at our backs picked up followers as we strode through the streets of Thebes. The urge to run was strong, but I would not give them satisfaction. By the time the city walls loomed before us, a noisy mob of more than a hundred people dogged our steps. Only the sparse crowds at the early hour let us reach the city gates without being torn to pieces.

Outside the city, The Boeotian plain stretched before us. It was going to be a long walk to Athens.

ONLY WHEN WE HAD REACHED THE MOUNTAINS that separated Boeotia and Attica did I begin to feel safe. I had half expected Eurymachus to set Kepheos and his men on us like hunting hounds on the trail of their quarry. But there had been no pursuit. We ascended into the hills.

Spring might have arrived in the plains, but the ghost of winter still haunted the mountains. On the first night we sheltered in a shallow cave, one of the many such refuges known to the *peripoli*. The cave protected us from the wind and the fire fought off the worst of the cold. I had endured worse for longer, but some food would not have been unwelcome.

Keaera huddled with my sister, the two of them enveloped in Meli's thick Thracian cloak. From within the warmth of the woolen folds, the slave girl stared at the dancing flames of the fire.

"I hate him," she said suddenly. She did not have to say whom. A gust of wind penetrated the cave, battering the fire for a spell.

Meli leaned forward and whispered into the girl's ear. "And what would you do to him if you could?"

"I would kill him!" Keaera hissed with unexpected vehemence. "I would cut off his head!"

A smile played on Meli's lips. "Pray to the gods and they will hear your plea for vengeance," Meli said.

I gave Meli an angry look, but she studiously ignored me. My sister should not have been putting such thoughts into the foolish girl's head. Vengeance! It was just the impossible fantasy of the powerless. Keaera twisted around to peer at my sister. Meli nodded towards the fire. "Pray, Keaera," she repeated.

Keaera closed her eyes. Her lips moved in a silent prayer, her brow furrowed in concentration. As the gullible girl implored the uncaring gods with her whispered invocation, my sister's hand emerged from her cloak. With a flick of her wrist she scattered a sprinkling of dust towards the fire. Green flames flared up, hissing and crackling. My sister, connected to the gods though she might have been, was not above using the cheap tricks of the more mundane type of soothsayers, it seemed. Keaera's eyes flicked open and she gasped as the green flames dissipated back into nothingness.

"The gods have heard you," my sister said, staring at me as though daring me to call her out.

I glowered at her as I rose to my feet. "Get some sleep. I'll keep watch."

Keaera's hand snaked out to grab my own thin cloak as I moved to the front of the cave. She flinched under my gaze but held my stare. "Thank you, *despote*,"

"I'm not your master, girl," I said harshly, yanking my cloak from her weak grasp.

I hunkered down at the cave entrance, brooding. The ill will I had stirred up in Thebes would follow me to Athens, I knew. My enemies would seize on the incident to attack me and undermine the authority of Thrasybulus. But I had endured worse. The matter would blow itself out just as the howling winds swirling around me would ebb by morning.

Like so many other things, I was wrong.

AN ARMY ON A FORCED MARCH could cover the distance from Athens to Thebes in a day and a half. Our journey took three days. Part of the reason was Keaera, who was unaccustomed to such walking, but our route through the mountains also hindered our progress. We arrived in Piraeus dirty, tired, and with empty bellies.

Tibetos was among the first to welcome us back to the *peripoli* compound. He took in our road-weary appearance and grim faces, his eyes coming to rest on the haggard-looking Keaera. "I'm sure there's a good story to this," he said dryly.

"We are no longer welcome in Thebes," I said.

"Why am I not surprised?"

More *peripoli* trickled into the courtyard as news of our return spread. Neon came as well, standing apart from the crowd. At least Iollas had kept his promise not to murder the Spartan. At the front of the throng was Taras, who was gawping at the slave girl Keaera.

"What are you staring at, Boy?" I said irritably.

Taras snapped to attention. "Sorry, *lochagos*," he sputtered.

Keaera bore the brunt of the men's scrutiny. She cowered under the curious stares of the hard-faced veteran warriors. It was better to get her out of the crowded courtyard, I decided. My gaze settled on the smooth-faced Taras, who was by far the least threatening. I jerked a thumb towards Keaera. "Taras! Make yourself useful and take her to the women's quarters," I snapped.

"Yes, *lochagos*!" He coughed softly and gestured at Keaera. "Come with me," he said a touch shyly. Keaera looked uncertainly at my sister. Meli nodded and the slave girl reluctantly followed Taras, who spoke quietly as he led her away. I shook my head and forgot about them.

"And what about that story?" Tibetos prompted.

My rumbling stomach reminded me of my priorities. "Get us something to eat and I'll tell you all about it."

AFTER A FEW DAYS OF SLEEPING ON ROCKS, roots, and hard-packed earth, the pallet bed in the disused storeroom that was my bedroom was a luxury. Many days of little rest and food caught up with me and I slept like the dead. When I awoke, brilliant, late-morning light outlined the cloth curtain of the storeroom entrance like a rectangle of fire. My mind cleared as I sat on the edge of the bed and blinked away the remnants of sleep. For a moment, Thebes was a distant worry, like a fading dream. But if I expected my troubles to be over, I was mistaken.

The curtain was thrust aside. I squinted at the figure silhouetted against the blinding light pouring in from the doorway. The shadow spoke. "Thrasybulus is here," came the voice of Tibetos.

"Thrasybulus?" I said, cracking my neck and shoulders.

Tibetos lowered his voice. "He's unhappy."

"That's nothing unusual," I said, rising to my feet.

"*Very* unhappy," Tibetos warned.

"Then we'd better see what he wants," I said, emerging into the harsh light of the mortal world.

Entering my administration chamber, I was brought up short by the scowling face of Thrasybulus. The *strategos* was a serious man at the best of times. What emotions he showed, whether in private or on the battlefield, were deliberate and controlled, just another tool to be used. His passions ran deep, to be sure, but it was rare for him to let his feelings get the better of him. But this was one of those rare times.

"Is it true?" he demanded, his booming voice almost shaking the dirty plaster walls.

I held his angry stare for an uncomfortably long time before I responded. "I don't know what you're talking about," I said with a straight face. It was a lie.

Thrasybulus was having none of it. He knew me too well. "The girl, you pig-headed fool! The girl!" he said through gritted teeth.

So it was about Keaera. Of course Leontiades and Eurymachus had seized the chance to further sully my reputation and undermine the fragile alliance between Thebes and Athens. But the deed was done. The girl was under my protection and would remain so.

"He would have harmed her," I said in an even voice.

The *strategos* could rein in his anger no longer. "What were you thinking?" he exploded. "Your actions jeopardize everything!" His voice might have shaken the dust off of the walls in Athens.

"He would have harmed her," I repeated. "Perhaps even killed her," I said.

"It was not your affair!"

I recalled the wedding banquet. Eurymachus' violent outburst had only occurred because of my presence. It was very much my affair. "You would let a man beat an innocent girl in front of you?" I asked.

Thrasybulus' face tightened. The question had hit the mark. I knew him to be a just man. But the flicker of sympathy vanished as his sense of practical politics reasserted itself. "Where is she?" he demanded, already looking past me at the door.

I knew where this was leading. I stepped between Thrasybulus and the door. "He wants her back?" I asked, preparing for a fight.

"Of course he wants her back!" Thrasybulus boomed. "What kind of man would not demand his wife be returned to him?"

The words struck me like a thunderbolt. For a moment I was stunned to silence as Thrasybulus' words rang like hammer blows in my mind. "His *wife*?" I uttered, still not certain that I had heard correctly.

"Don't play me for a fool, Daimon! I know you abducted Eurymachus' wife from her room in the night! Two house guards were killed! Do you deny it was you?"

I was as mute as a statue. He was not talking about stealing some insignificant slave-girl.

He was talking about Althaia.

Althaia was gone.

PART THREE

ΛΑΚΕΔΑΙΜΟΝΙΟΙ SPARTANS

CHAPTER 30

Thrasybulus listened patiently as I explained what had happened at the wedding banquet. I also related how Eurymachus had sent the head of the slave Donax to the home of Epaminondas. The explanation dulled the sharp edge of his anger, but only barely.

"It is hardly better that you stole one of Leontiades' slaves," he said. "In any case, Leontiades has lodged a complaint against you. He has demanded that his daughter-in-law be returned to him and that you be sent to Thebes to face justice."

"I have committed no crime," I said grimly.

Thrasybulus let the matter of the stolen slave pass for the moment. "Did you not, in front of witnesses, threaten to take the woman by force from the home of Leontiades?"

I had no good answer for that. "Yes," I admitted. Thrasybulus regarded me through narrowed eyes as he weighed his options. "You can't be considering giving in to their demands!" I said, my voice rising in disbelief.

He hesitated long enough that I was certain that he had been. But he waved off my accusation. "Don't be absurd, Daimon. But I cannot do nothing. And there is something else," he said gravely.

Another hammer blow was coming. "What?"

"The Thebans' share of the Persian gold is missing."

I thought I had misheard him. "Missing?"

"After you left, someone had the idea to check on the gold. It was gone."

"All of it?" I asked in disbelief.

"The chests were all empty, so the herald from Thebes has informed me."

I scoffed. "Surely this is the doing of Leontiades and Eurymachus! I'd wager the gold never even made it to the Theban treasury!" Thrasybulus remained silent. My eyes grew wide. "I am being blamed for that as well? Even after I delivered the gold to Thebes myself?"

"You were seen leaving the city during their festival and only returning the next day," Thrasybulus reported.

This accusation was even more ridiculous. "Was I carrying one hundred talents of Persian gold on my back?" I asked in exasperation.

"Of course not," Thrasybulus said, his voice suddenly tired.

"Then it is mere slander!" I said.

Thrasybulus sighed. "I do not doubt it, but suspicious enough for the Thebans, especially given the other accusations against you." He found a stool and sat down. "But where did you go during the festival?" he added, almost as an afterthought.

I felt my face turning red. "My business is my own!" I said sharply.

Thrasybulus did not press the issue. "All that matters is that the money is gone and the Thebans are saying you stole it."

Leontiades had done well to drive a wedge between Athens and Thebes. I pushed the heel of my palm against the sudden pain in my forehead. "Will the alliance hold?"

"Ismenias still wields great influence in Thebes. He will be able to keep Leontiades and his faction in check for now. In a way, it is too late for Leontiades to do anything at all. The Thebans have been provoking the Spartans all winter. We have reports that Sparta is preparing for war." Thrasybulus leaned forward. "We are committed to this path now, Daimon, whether we like it or not. We cannot squander this opportunity. Thebes is strong. Athens is not. We have no walls. We have no ships. Without Thebes, we cannot stand against Sparta."

I knew what his tone of voice portended. "I have a feeling you have some request of me."

"I have been considering it. Given the Thebans' suspicion of you, I think that it is best that you leave Athens for a time," he said.

I frowned. "You want me to go into exile?"

Thrasybulus held up an appeasing hand. "No, but if the Thebans believe that, it is no bad thing. Rather, I have a mission for you."

I resisted the urge to refuse him outright. Sending me away from Athens was a reasonable suggestion, as much as I hated to admit it. "Where?"

Thrasybulus scratched his beard. "I want you to go to Phokis."

"Phokis?" Phokis lay to the west of Boeotia. It was not what I had been expecting Thrasybulus to say, but it made sense. The Phokians had long been allies of Sparta and hostile to Thebes. But Phokis was a backwater and hardly a threat. "Why Phokis?"

"I have received reports that a Spartan general has arrived there with instructions to muster an army from among the Phokians, Aetolians, disaffected Boeotian cities... Anyone who opposes the growing power of Thebes. I need someone to find him and keep me informed of his progress."

Something made the hairs on my neck stand on end. "Spartan commander? Who?"

Thrasybulus smiled grimly. "An old friend of yours."

And I knew of whom he spoke.

Lysander.

THAT IS HOW I FOUND MYSELF sitting atop a horse in the backwaters of Phokis.

Ten *peripoli* accompanied me. Neon had wished to join us, and I saw no reason to turn the Spartan down. Iollas, upon learning of my decision, had demanded to come as well, "To stab that Spartan bastard in the back before he does the same to you," Iollas had warned me ominously. One woman was among our number as well. No one questioned Meli's presence. By her nature and because of her time in Thrace, she was the best rider among us. She was as inured to the hardships of a warrior's life as the most stalwart veteran, suffering hungry days on horseback and long nights on cold, hard ground under an open sky without complaint.

Our mission was simple. We were to find Lysander, monitor his efforts to raise an army, and dispatch riders back to Thrasybulus in Athens to report on what we had observed. For more than ten days we had roamed the rugged lands of Phokis, moving farther and farther west. So far we had found no trace of Lysander and his nascent army.

The long, fruitless days afforded me plenty of time to think. For once I would have welcomed the distraction of tending to the day-to-day administration of the *peripoli*, vexing as it was, for my thoughts were not happy ones. Most of all, thoughts of Althaia plagued me. That Eurymachus had been behind her disappearance I had no doubt. By taking her he could revenge himself on me and serve his father's ambition of driving a wedge between Athens and Thebes. Whether Althaia was alive or dead, I did not know. Reason told me the latter, for it would be dangerous to let her live. My silent promises of vengeance did little to change the glaring truth that my actions had sealed Althaia's fate. All for an insignificant slave girl.

I let out a tired breath. The girl Keaera was not insignificant to all, I corrected myself. I glanced over at Taras. In the time before our departure, the lad had been spending much time with the girl, though he sought to keep their meetings secret. He was besotted with her. I would have warned him off, but the girl did not seem to object to his attentions. Now the boy had a faraway look in his eyes. I knew he was thinking of her.

"Taras!" I called out.

"Yes, *lochagos*!"

"Quit your daydreaming or you'll fall off your horse!"

Taras reddened as the others laughed, for they were well aware of the young man's affections. "Yes, *lochagos*!"

I could have well rebuked myself in the same way. I delved in my pack for a water skin. Taking a long swig, I wondered if Thrasybulus' information had been wrong. It was also early in the year. Thrasybulus did not expect the Spartans to attack until early summer, but snow still capped many mountain peaks. It could have been that Thrasybulus just wanted me as far away from Athens as possible. I would not have put such a ploy below him. I wiped my mouth and shoved the skin back into my pack. There was nothing to do but keep searching.

We remained out of sight, as was the manner of the *peripoli*. Our mission was to scout and report, not to draw attention to ourselves. We foraged when we could, but when need arose, we raided isolated farms, for we needed grain for our gruel and to feed the ever-hungry horses. I forbade the needless slaughter of the inhabitants or destruction of their buildings, for farmers and their families were not our enemies. But our predations still left our ill-fated victims short on livestock and grain. Their futures would be a struggle if they survived at all. In Attica, we hunted bandits. Now we were the raiders.

The sight of our party of armed men was enough to frighten most farmers into handing over the supplies without a fight. Most but not all. One farmer, lying in wait in an outbuilding, ambushed me with a spear. His blow was a good one and would have skewered me had my black scale armour not turned away the thrust. A second attack never came, for Meli cut him down with a twin stroke of her Thracian swords. She shrugged apologetically as she wiped her blades on the man's tunic, leaving a crimson streak on the farmer's threadbare garment. I stood over the dying man as his blood soaked into the earth. Blinking in disbelief, I cursed him for his stupidity as his wife and children wailed with despair. What would impel a man to take on so many single-handed? Why die protecting some hardscrabble farm in the wilds of Phokia? As we departed, our provisions restocked, the man's daughter, not more than ten years old, cursed our backs through her tears as she hunched protectively over the body of her father. One more face to haunt my dreams. One more rumour of the evil deeds of the red-haired Demon. Daimon the Slaughterer.

The memory of the screaming girl clung to me as we sought our quarry. Farther and farther west we ranged without success. When we finally found Lysander, it was a surprise. Having no success in one area, we located a pass to the next valley north. Night was coming fast. We emerged from the pass tired and hungry.

Stachys, taking in the view of the valley below, spoke for us all. "By the gods!" he whispered.

Campfires dotted the plain like stars in the sky.

We had found Lysander.

Thrasybulus had been wrong. Armies of such size did not gather without reason.

The Spartans would not attack in the summer.

Lysander was coming now.

CHAPTER 31

The light of day afforded us a better view.

"How many now do you reckon?" Tibetos asked. From our vantage point high in the hills, we peered down at the sprawling army below. Lysander's forces trailed through the wide valley plain below like a great snake.

"Twelve thousand, maybe?" I said, making my best estimate.

Stachys leaned forward. "And how many of those are soldiers?" he asked.

I scratched at the several weeks' worth of beard growth on my cheeks. "Seven thousand hoplites, five hundred skirmishers, and maybe the same number of cavalry." The remaining slaves, porters, and various camp followers did not bear mentioning. Stachys nodded in agreement at my assessment.

I sent a rider back to Athens. With a change of horses in Eleusis, it would take a few days for him to reach Thrasybulus. In the meantime, we would shadow Lysander's army.

Every day was the same process. In the morning, the camp would pack up and the army would set out. The cavalry ranged ahead but could not go far from the lumbering army it led. Ranks of hoplites and light troops formed a loose, snake-like column nearly a mile long. The tail of the snake was more diffuse, being made up of the carts and slaves of the supply train.

It was clearly not a Spartan army. To be certain, a contingent of red-cloaked Spartans marched at the front of the column in good order. But the bulk of the army consisted of allies gathered by Lysander. In addition to Phokians and mercenaries, I reckoned there were many disaffected Boeotians among their number, for many Boeotian cities resented the growing power of Thebes.

By the late afternoon, the snake would coil up in a great camp for the night. The next day the process would begin anew. "Let's get ahead of them and set up camp," I said. My horse nickered as I gave its flanks a small kick.

I cast one last look down at Lysander's army. I foolishly hoped to catch a glimpse of Lysander standing proudly in his snow-white cloak. My eyesight was sharper than that of most men, but not that sharp. But I saw something else. I turned my horse around to face west. Motionless, I peered towards Lysander's army. The others, taking their cue from me, pulled up their mounts.

"What is it, Dammo?" Tibetos asked.

The sharp-sighted Sabas answered for me. "A rider. He's headed east." Sabas gave me one of his mad grins. "And he's a Spartan!"

"It's likely," I said. The distant rider flashed with the tell-tale scarlet cloak of a Spartan warrior. All eyes turned to me in anticipation of my decision.

Over the past few days, we had observed lone riders coming and going from the main body of the army. There was no chance to intercept them, though the temptation to pursue them was great. Any knowledge of the wily Lysander's intentions would be invaluable.

And now just such a messenger was galloping in our direction. It was an opportunity that could not be missed. The broad plain on which Lysander had encamped his army narrowed to a choke-point at the eastern end of the valley. It was the messenger's likely route.

I gave the order. "Let's cut the bastard off," I said, kicking my horse into motion.

Intercepting the messenger was no sure thing. We would lose sight of the Spartan horseman as we descended into the valley. The messenger himself was travelling fast and there was a good chance we would simply miss him.

As the slope levelled out, we picked up the pace. Branches lashed our faces as we pushed through the woods. Suddenly the trees thinned out and we found ourselves among the rocky scrub at the edge of the road through the pass. It was hardly more than a beaten path just wide enough for two carts to pass each other.

"Sabas, take three men farther up the road in case he gets by us," I said. The Cretan flashed a mad grin and galloped off, leaving me the remaining *peripoli* and Meli. "Tie up the horses out of sight and take your positions, three on either side," I commanded the others, taking out a coil of rope from my horse's pack. "Mnasyllus, with me."

It was not a sophisticated plan. I handed one end of the rope to Mnasyllus and trotted to the other side of the road. I secured the rope around the trunk of an ash tree and hurried back across the road, kicking dirt on the exposed rope to make it as inconspicuous as possible. The rope snaked down the opposite ditch, taking a sudden turn around the base of an oak tree, and ended wrapped around the meaty fists of Mnasyllus. The others returned from concealing the horses. Taras joined Mnasyllus and me, while Meli and Tibetos found cover on the other side of the road with Neon and Iollas.

There was no sign of the messenger. I wondered if he had taken another route through the pass. Or worse, we had been too slow coming down from the hills and the Spartan was already miles ahead of us. Just as I began cursing inwardly at the lost opportunity, we heard it. The unmistakable rhythm of a galloping horse.

We crouched lower in our hiding places. The Spartan messenger appeared around a distant bend, his crimson cloak flapping around him. The beating of hooves grew louder.

"Now!" I hissed.

The thick muscles in Mnasyllus' arms bulged as he jerked the rope taut. The rope jumped off the ground with a twanging snap to form a spear-straight line two feet above the surface of the road. The Spartan's horse hit the cord mid-stride. Its front legs folded under it as its momentum took it hurtling past us. The beast twisted to one side before crashing to the ground and tossing its rider from its back. The Spartan bounced along the ground like a tumbling boulder. We burst from concealment and swarmed towards the unmoving Spartan.

Lysander's messenger moaned as we bound his hands and relieved him of his sword and the leather satchel around his shoulder. I undid the bag's ties and pulled open the flap. Tucked inside like eggs in a nest were two leather cylinders. We jerked the dazed Spartan to his feet. Sabas and his men came riding towards us from farther up the road. The Cretan was leading the Spartan's horse. "I assumed you'd been successful when this fellow appeared without his owner," he said with a small jerk of his head towards the Spartan's horse. "And him?" he asked, glancing at the dazed Spartan.

I displayed the leather bag. "Success!"

The dazed Spartan was recovering. I took out one of the message tubes and held it out for our prisoner to see. "Why does Lysander send a full-blooded Spartiate on a messenger's errand?" I asked.

His face fell as he beheld the leather cylinder in my hand. "Eat shit, Athenian!" he spat, glaring at me. His baleful eyes darted from man to man, widening in recognition as they fell on Neon. "Traitor!" he barked. He spat and the gob of saliva splattered on Neon's chest. Neon met the insult with a stony stare.

"There is no time for this," I said, popping open the cap of the message tube and sliding out the scroll within. Unrolling the papyrus, I squinted at the missive. I swore at my naivete. The Spartan messenger smirked as I regarded the meaningless string of letters with perplexity. The Spartan's amusement faded as Neon extended his hand towards me.

"Let me see," Neon said.

The messenger bared his teeth in rage, "You will die —" His threat was cut short as Mnasyllus hooked the Spartan's neck in the crook of his arm and squeezed. The Spartan's face turned from red to purple. Mnasyllus let off some pressure and the Spartan gasped for breath.

I handed Neon the scroll. Neon's gaze tracked back and forth across the papyrus, pausing at times as he deciphered the Spartan code. "It says that Lysander will arrive in three days' time and tells them to prepare a market and provisions. It also instructs the recipient to have the shipment ready so that Lysander can take it into his possession as soon as he arrives."

"Shipment? Shipment of what?" I asked.

"It only says 'shipment,'" Neon said.

"And arrive where?" I asked.

Neon shrugged. "It says no more than that."

I slid the second message from its leather cylinder and handed it to Neon, who cracked the wax seal and unrolled the scroll. As he began to read, his brows rose slightly. He glanced at the messenger, whose shoulders sagged in defeat.

"'O King Pausanias,'" Neon began. "'Meet us at Haliartos in four days' time as reckoned before.'"

"Haliartos?" Now we knew Lysander's destination. Haliartos was a small city in western Boeotia. It lay on the southern shore of the marshy lake called Copais. We had passed it on our journey west. Epaminondas had told me Haliartos was one of the wavering Boeotian cities likely to defect to the Spartans. From the captured message, it seemed that it already had. Another thought struck me. "The second message said 'four days'?" I asked. Neon acknowledged this with a grunt. "But in his first message Lysander stated that he would be in Haliartos in three days' time?"

"That is correct," Neon confirmed.

I stepped close to our captive. He was of average height and I towered over him. "Why is it so important that Lysander arrive in

Haliartos before King Pausanias, Spartan?" I demanded. The Spartan clenched his jaw and stared at my chest. His defiance was answer enough, for it confirmed my suspicion that Lysander had some purpose in Haliartos that he wanted to conceal from Pausanias. Our prisoner's silence did not halt my interrogation. "And where is Pausanias now? Where were you taking the second message?"

Neon spoke. "Kithairon. Pausanias will be coming north through the pass at Kithairon and past Plataea." The messenger's eyelid twitched. Once again his face betrayed him though his tongue had remained loyal.

I turned to Neon. "You are certain of this?"

"It is the preferred route into Boeotia. I have taken it myself many times."

Our captive could hold his tongue no longer. "You will be flayed for your treachery!" he shouted, twisting furiously to escape the grasp of Mnasyllus.

Neon regarded him with cold disdain. "You betrayed the ways of our forefathers long ago, Dorieus."

The Spartan Dorieus cursed and spat at us. I barely heard him, for my thoughts had cast themselves elsewhere. The seeds of an idea began to grow in my mind. It was a mad plan with failure being the likely outcome. But with the capture of the Spartan messenger, the Fates, for once, had favoured me, even if time did not.

Fate and luck, however, had deserted the man Dorieus. I drew the sword at my waist. Dorieus, seeing the blade in my hand, halted the stream of abuse he had been hurling at his erstwhile comrade. His eyes locked on mine. "Your death will be swift, O Spartan," I said flatly. The Spartan was an enemy and we could not risk him escaping and getting word back to Lysander. "Mnasyllus, hold him." I raised my sword. A quick cut across the throat would be a mercy. The Spartan glowered at me. He hid his fear well. My muscles tensed as I readied the blow.

"Wait!"

It was Neon who had called out.

"You object to this man's death?" I asked.

Neon extended his hand towards my raised sword. "He is my countryman. It is my duty."

Silence descended on our forest execution ground. Neon's expression was unreadable. Suddenly I doubted the Spartan's loyalty.

It would be mad to try and free his fellow Spartan, for he was heavily outnumbered. But Neon had proven himself a dangerous man and loyalty can drive a man to mad acts. Iollas shared my suspicions, I reckoned, for the former helot's hand drifted to the hilt of the dagger at his hip.

"It is my duty," Neon repeated. My hesitation lasted a few more heartbeats before I flipped my grip and handed the sword to Neon.

He tested the blade's weight and turned to Dorieus. "I will give you a Spartan death, if you wish it."

Dorieus suppressed his fury at his countryman's betrayal enough to nod. "I wish it, by the twin gods."

Neon looked at Mnasyllus. "Release him, O Mnasyllus." Mnasyllus glanced at me. I nodded and the big farmer reluctantly stepped away from the captive Spartan. The rest of the *peripoli* had stood in a loose circle around us, their hands on their weapons, alert for any sudden moves from Dorieus or Neon. Iollas watched Neon with a predator's intensity.

Dorieus fell to his knees and stared ahead with eyes that had already accepted death. "Do it," he said flatly.

Neon circled behind the kneeling prisoner. He reversed the sword and gripped the handle with both hands. Finding the gap between the front and rear plates of the condemned man's armour, Neon thrust the blade down through the Spartan's shoulder and into his heart. Dorieus stiffened. A last breath rattled in his throat and his face slackened as his shade left him. Neon jerked the blade free and the Spartiate's corpse flopped forward onto the forest floor.

The *peripoli* were hard men inured to violence and death, but it is a different matter to witness the murder of a kneeling man, enemy or not. The equanimity with which the Spartan had taken his death and the calm with Neon had delivered the stroke made the event even more shocking. But as I have said, the *peripoli* were hard men, and soon turned away to tend their horses and gear, their thoughts shielded from the others. Only Iollas remained. The freed helot stared at the dead Spartan as though struggling against some internal enemy. He shot Neon a final hostile look before stomping off after the others.

Neon knelt and wiped the sword on the dead man's crimson cloak. He stood up and returned the weapon to me.

"He died bravely," I said, taking the sword.

Neon considered this. "He was a good Spartan," he said finally. "But not a good man."

The interception of the messenger was invaluable. That he was a Spartiate was even better. "Take his armour and cloak," I told him. "You're going to need them." Neon raised an eyebrow, shrugged, and set about methodically stripping the armor from his countryman's corpse.

The messenger. The Spartiate. The Fates had presented me with the gift of opportunity. Now they would watch what I did with it, their eager hands on the loom of destiny. But there was no time. I found Meli. Her emerald eyes watched me expectantly as I approached. "Sister," I said. "I have a task for you." A knowing smile crept up her face. My sister was the lightest and the fastest rider, and speed was essential if we dared hope to thwart Lysander. I explained to Meli what I needed her to do. Her expression danced with Hekate's malice. Had I not known her better, she would have frightened me.

Meli hurried to prepare her horse for the difficult journey ahead. Her hand reached out to untie the beast but then paused. She turned and jogged over to Tibetos, who had been observing her with anxious eyes. The two embraced and exchanged some whispered words. I looked away as they shared a deep kiss. When I looked back, Meli was already atop her horse. She flashed one last grin at me, flicked her reins, and was off in a flurry of hoof beats.

Tibetos sidled over to me and we watched Meli's horse shrink in the distance. She disappeared around a bend in the road and was gone.

"She will be safe," I said, not entirely certain if it were true.

Tibetos sighed. "I know," he said. "It's more us that I'm worried about. What do we do now?"

Instead of answering, I smiled. Then I began to laugh. I turned my face to the darkening sky and continued laughing until tears threatened to stain my cheeks. I could not help myself. I wondered if Dionysus had infected me with his madness. I regained some control and wiped the wetness from my eyes.

Perhaps I was mad, but it was madness born of opportunity. The Fates had delivered the messenger into our hands. We knew where Lysander would be in three days' time, a day before Pausanias arrived with his own army of Spartans and Peloponnesian allies. What Lysander wanted to hide from Pausanias was a mystery, but it was not my concern. I just wanted to crush him.

The others had gathered round, looking upon me with a mix of concern and curiosity, as if I were one of the mad beggars in the agora.

I took a deep breath. "Prepare your mounts. We have a long journey and we need to push ourselves hard." The *peripoli* leaned a little closer, eager to hear my instructions.

I looked to the east. To defeat Lysander, I would have to walk into a nest of vipers.

"We're going to Thebes."

CHAPTER 32

The burly Theban's spear-point pressed against my sternum. It was the same guard who had let me leave the city during the festival of Dionysus. He was markedly less amiable now than on that occasion.

"I have important information for your leaders," I repeated for the third time. "Bring Epaminondas, son of Polymnis. He is my *proxenos*. And find Ismenias."

The Theban sneered. "You do not give orders here, Athenian!" The pointed pressure on my chest grew stronger. A dozen of his comrades surrounded me, their spears levelled and ready to strike.

I stared down at him. "I am an ambassador from the *strategos* Thrasybulus of Athens," I lied. "Ismenias would be displeased if you killed me before I delivered my message." The soldier's face tightened as his desire to drive his spear through my breastbone grappled with his sense of duty to his city. The latter won out, barely, and with a growl he ordered two of the guards to go in search of anyone with more authority.

The Thebans' spears barely wavered. I met the guards' inimical stares with bored indifference. It was a good thing I had left Tibetos and the others hiding out in the hills outside the city. The sight of Neon alone would likely have provoked the Thebans to violence. The silent standoff continued until there was some commotion as the two guards returned. They were not alone.

I was heartened to see Epaminondas and Ismenias were among the new arrivals, as was the hulking Thaletos. My sense of relief dissipated as close behind them I saw Leontiades and his son Eurymachus. Our ring of guards opened up to let the delegation pass. Ismenias gave me a wary smile. Epaminondas pointedly would not meet my gaze.

I nodded to Ismenias. "O Ismenias! I bring critical information…" My gaze flicked to Leontiades and Eurymachus. "…That I would share with you in private."

Before Ismenias could respond, Eurymachus pointed an accusing finger at me. "Why should we trust this *Thracian* mercenary? He abducted my wife and stole my slave. And it was he and his band of thieves who somehow stole the Persian gold from our vaults! We should kill him now and be done with it!"

I felt the Thebans' ill will towards me hardening. I appealed to Ismenias. "I stole no man's wife and the missing gold is not my doing," I said, casting a glance at Leontiades and Eurymachus. "Hear what I have to say. If you do not believe me, then do with me as you will."

Ismenias was in a difficult position. Many of the Thebans were suspicious of me, while those siding with Leontiades were outright hostile. Yet he knew that I represented Thrasybulus and that their goals were aligned.

"I wish to hear what the Athenian has to say," Thaletos said evenly. His firm stare made me uncertain as to whether the Theban champion was hostile to me or an ally. But Thaletos' opinion carried some weight, giving Ismenias room to act.

"You will be given the chance to speak to the generals," Ismenias declared. "I think everyone will agree that there is no harm in hearing you out." Leontiades and Eurymachus could not hide their fury.

I would survive a little longer at least. "And I request Epaminondas be present as my *proxenos*." Epaminondas looked directly at me for the first time, surprise on his face. "If he wishes to do so," I added.

Epaminondas quickly collected himself. "I wish it," he said.

"That is acceptable," Ismenias said.

I accompanied the Theban delegation towards the Kadmeia with a contingent of guards. As we ascended the wide path to the top of the citadel, Epaminondas interrogated me in a low voice.

"It was not you who abducted my sister?" he asked.

"Don't be a fool!" I growled.

Epaminondas flushed at the rebuke. "I knew it wasn't you, but I needed to hear it from you."

"You know who's responsible, then," I said, scowling at the back of Eurymachus, who was engaged in hushed conversation with his father farther up the path. Epaminondas mulled over this hard truth.

"Where do you think my sister is now?" he asked finally.

I thought she was dead, or perhaps sold into slavery by her greedy husband, the latter perhaps being the worse fate. "She is safe somewhere," I said.

Epaminondas bobbed his head as though to reassure himself. "I think you're right," he said. "May Apollo protect her!" I thought back to the forest rites I had witnessed. If any god protected Althaia, it was

Dionysus, not Apollo. Epaminondas spoke again. "What information do you bring?"

We were passing through the gateway of the Kadmeia. "A chance to hobble the Spartans before the war has even started," I said. "If you Thebans are smart enough to see it," I added. "But I need your support."

"I'm too young," he protested. "I'm only here because you requested it!"

"That piece of weasel-shit Eurymachus is here, so that says enough. Just speak for me if you can. That is all I ask."

His face tightened with resolve. "I will stand by you, Dammo," he promised. With his informal address, I knew the wall between us had begun to crumble.

There was no more time to converse, for we had arrived at our destination. "Our council building," Epaminondas explained as he led me inside. Two rows of benches surrounded the central floor of the square chamber. Ismenias and the other Thebans took their seats, leaving me standing in the centre of the chamber. A row of soldiers stood behind me.

One of the Thebans rose. "I am Androkleidas, a general of Thebes. You are not a popular figure here, Athenian. You have been accused of crimes by our citizens," he said, gesturing towards Leontiades and his son. It was not an auspicious start. "Yet," he continued, "You return here claiming to have crucial information about our enemies."

"I do, O Androkleidas," I answer.

Eurymachus leapt to his feet. "I demand justice! This man stole the Persians' gold! He abducted my wife! He is not to be trusted!"

Androkleidas regarded the aggrieved young aristocrat as though he were a particularly annoying fly buzzing in his ear. "If the information is as important as the Athenian claims, do you not think we should at least hear him out?"

"He is here to mislead us!" Eurymachus declared.

Androkleidas massaged his eyebrows. "Sit down, Boy, or I shall throw you out of this chamber myself." Eurymachus looked about for support but was met with impatient stares. Apparently Androkleidas was a man of some authority. Reluctantly, Eurymachus sat down beside his father. Androkleidas waved a hand at me. "Speak, Athenian."

So I spoke. I related how we had shadowed Lysander's growing army for many days and how we had intercepted the Spartan messenger. "He was headed to Haliartos," I said.

Ismenias and Androkleidas exchanged a knowing look. Ismenias cleared his throat. "We already believed Haliartos had sided with Sparta. This only confirms our suspicions." A rumble of surprise and anger filled the room as the Thebans absorbed the report of treachery from what they regarded as a subject city.

I sensed the mood of the room shifting in my favour. I raised my voice above the din. "March an army to Haliartos immediately. Ambush Lysander before Pausanias arrives to reinforce them. You can defeat half of the Spartans' forces right now. You must not miss this opportunity."

With some effort, Ismenias calmed the agitated Thebans. "We must consider the Athenian's words," he proclaimed, taking up my cause.

"We must attack now," seconded Androkleidas.

Leontiades, having held his silence until now, sprang to his feet. "You are asking us to send the bulk of our army and cavalry to Haliartos and leave Thebes virtually undefended? What if Pausanias brings his army here?" he challenged. Sympathetic shouts of support showed his sentiment was shared by at least a few in the room. Only Thaletos remained seated and above the fray, watching me intently through narrowed eyes.

"The Athenian is correct," Ismenias said. "We must take our army to Haliartos at once!"

Leontiades pounced. "Shall we trust the word of a Thracian bandit? He is likely a Spartan spy sent to misdirect us! Perhaps Pausanias is leading his army to Thebes as we speak! It would be convenient if he found the city defenceless!"

"A small contingent is enough to man the walls," Ismenias countered.

"It takes only one man to open the gates and let them in," said one of Leontiades' supporters.

Another Theban sympathetic to the views of Leontiades made his voice heard. "And what of Haliartos itself? If Haliartos has turned, Lysander can find refuge behind its walls. Pausanias will arrive and we will be trapped between a hammer and an anvil."

Until then I had let the Thebans argue, but I could no longer afford to stay silent. My voice cut through the din. "Not if we take Haliartos before Lysander arrives." A stunned silence filled the chamber. "I can capture the city," I declared to the disbelieving Thebans.

Leontiades snorted at the suggestion. "You see?" he said, waving a dismissive hand at me. "Just like an Athenian to make such an outrageous boast!" His supporters rewarded him with laughter at my naivete. Leontiades smirked. "And what will you do when you find the gates of Haliartos shut, *pai*?"

"Locked gates do not concern me," I said, pulling the Spartan message tube from under my armour. "I have a key."

SOME GUARDS ESCORTED ME to a prison down in the city. There I would wait while the Theban leadership debated the merits of my plan. The cell was small, but the Thebans gave me some barley porridge and water. I had suffered worse imprisonments.

Night fell and still no one came. My frustration grew. At last some approaching footsteps and the glow of torchlight heralded the arrival of some news.

"It's me!" came the voice of Epaminondas. There was a grating thud as the outer bar was lifted. The door swung open to reveal the young Theban.

"What did they say?" I asked. His glum expression told me all I needed to know before his lips even parted. "They're not going?" I asked.

Epaminondas shook his head. "You have the support of Ismenias and Androkleidas of course. Thaletos spoke strongly for you as well. It made the vote close."

That Thaletos had come out in favour of my proposal pleased me. "But not by enough?" I asked.

"The others aren't willing to leave the city undefended."

I let out a roar. I cursed the gods and the timidity of Thebans. "A hundred women and old men could defend this city!" I seized Epaminondas by the cloak "It's no wonder your people choose the bull as your symbol: stupid and obstinate!" I pushed him back and turned away. It was unfair to him, but he was the only Theban in sight upon whom I could loose my frustration.

"I spoke in favour of your plan!" Epaminondas protested behind me.

I kneaded my brow with my thumb and forefinger, collecting myself. I let out a deep breath and turned back to Epaminondas. "I know you tried, my friend," I said, cracking a weak smile. "And me?" I asked. Epaminondas hesitated. "I'm to remain a prisoner?" I exclaimed, guessing the meaning of his reticence.

Epaminondas winced. "Ismenias said it was for your own safety. If it's any consolation, no one can leave the city."

That caught me by surprise. "What do you mean 'no one'?"

Epaminondas allowed himself a thin smile. "Ismenias and Androkleidas are in charge of the city guard. They have had all the gates to the city locked. No one may leave or enter."

It was a spark of good news, for I knew why Ismenias had given such an order. He was afraid of spies leaving the city to contact Lysander. That he took such a step meant that he still hoped to convince his fellow Thebans to adopt my plan before Lysander arrived in Haliartos. But the time to act was slipping away quickly.

Epaminondas promised to see me freed as soon as possible. But the following morning brought no news from Epaminondas. My hope of some action was fraying. By late afternoon that hope was suspended by the finest of threads. The opportunity was gone. Lysander would evade me once more.

But then the storeroom brightened as the door swung open. Epaminondas was there, but it was the figure beside him that made my heart surge.

Meli's face was haggard. Her hair was matted and heavy with dust. Exhausted, she tottered slightly and leaned on a grinning Epaminondas for support. Yet her eyes still sparked with energy.

I leapt to my feet and seized my sister by the shoulders. "Is he here?"

And her smile told me all I needed to know. I let out a whoop of joy. Meli had travelled to Athens and back to Thebes. More importantly, she had not returned alone.

Thrasybulus and the Athenian army had arrived.

CHAPTER 33

With Thrasybulus and the tired Athenian army left to protect Thebes, the Thebans were willing to attempt my plan. All I needed to do was capture Haliartos as I had promised.

Capturing a city is difficult.

City walls, provided they are manned by a sufficient number of defenders, can thwart the efforts of even a large army. The walls of Athens had kept the Spartans and their allies at bay for more than thirty years. Haliartos was hardly more than a village compared to Athens but decades of war had taught even small cities the wisdom of possessing formidable defences.

The stout walls of Haliartos were the height of five men, even higher if one included the depth of the ditch that encircled the city on three sides. No ditch was needed beside the north wall, for Haliartos sat upon the edge of vast muddy, mosquito-infested marshes that prevented any attack from the north. From the crenellated ramparts defenders could rain down javelins or other missiles on the enemy. The massive wooden gates on the southern wall were hardly less daunting, reinforced as they were by a lattice of iron bands as broad as a man's hand. Even if the outer gate was breached, the inner gates were an equally solid obstacle, and beyond that lay the fortified acropolis. In short, Haliartos was unassailable.

I had promised to capture the city with ten soldiers in the time it takes a man to eat his morning meal. Or, if we failed, we would be dead in less than half that time.

Our paltry force of *peripoli* galloped across the plain towards the closed gates of Haliartos. I looked over my shoulder at the only Theban among our number. Thaletos had insisted on joining us. "I have staked my reputation on your success, Athenian. Better to die with you than return to Thebes in shame," he had explained. Iollas had demanded to be present as well, though for his own reasons. "To keep an eye on the Spartan," he had told me bluntly.

Our band had looped unseen south of Haliartos during the night. Now we approached openly from the west, as if we were coming from Lysander's army. A few hundred paces from the walls we pulled up, slowing our horses to a trot and then to an easy walk. When we were within shouting distance, our leader, Neon, held up a hand and we came to a halt.

Neon, dressed in the gear of the dead messenger Dorieus, blazed in all his Spartan glory. The crimson cloak flowed down his back and over the haunches of his mount like a cascade of blood. His black braids, shiny with oil, hung down over his bronze breastplate. The morning sun glinted off his burnished greaves and helmet. It was a contrast to the plain borrowed armour and weapons the rest of us bore. Our helmets were down, but otherwise presented a picture of ordinary soldiers escorting a Spartan of some importance.

Neon flicked his reins and his horse took a few steps forward. Our lives were in the Spartan's hands. "Open the gates!" he bellowed at the soldiers above.

There was a pause. One of them cupped his hand to his mouth and leaned over the wall. "Password!" he shouted.

Neon took out the cylindrical leather message case and pointed it at the soldier, somehow making the gesture appear menacing. "Open the damn gates, or by the twin gods, I'll cut your balls off!" he shouted back.

Neon stared up at the intransigent guard for what seemed like an age. My heart sat in my chest like a lump of stone. The others, too, could not help fidgeting as they awaited the response. Tibetos' horse pawed at the stony ground. Stachys' mount nickered and tossed its head, and the aristocrat reassured the beast with a pat on its neck. I glanced up at the soldier who was speaking inaudibly to his fellow guard. The second man disappeared from view and the leader scowled down at us. Behind me, Mnasyllus coughed.

Suddenly muffled clicks and bangs penetrated the thick wood of the iron-banded gates. There was one final thud and then the gates began to swing inward with a creaking groan. The inner gates beyond were still closed. Neon, kicking his horse into a walk, barked a command and we urged our mounts to follow slowly behind him.

Neon's natural Spartan authority had not completely assuaged the guards' suspicion One of them extended his hand towards Neon.

"The dispatch," the soldier demanded. Neon glared down at the Boeotian from behind his helmet before finally handing him Lysander's coded message. The Boeotian, rather than returning through the door, walked to the inner gate and thumped his fist on the wood three times. A small square of light appeared beside the man's head, and I could now see that there was an opening in the gate with a sliding wooden cover. The guard passed the tube through to a waiting hand, which promptly vanished. The Boeotians' gaze wandered over us, but their cursory inspection found nothing amiss. We waited in an awkward silence broken only by the snorting breaths and stamping hooves of the horses.

"What is the delay, Boeotian?" Neon demanded. The disdain in his voice was so natural that I suddenly wondered how much he had truly distanced himself from his Spartan upbringing.

The guard stood his ground. "No one is admitted into the city without the commander's permission."

Neon grunted. He dismounted from his horse and stood in front of the soldier. Like me, Neon was a tall man. He glared down at the Boeotian. "You will not let us in now?" said threateningly.

The Boeotian did not flinch. "You have to wait," he said, raising his chin.

Neon exhaled with a low rumble before exploding into harsh laughter. He slapped the Boeotian's shoulder. "You are a good soldier. Perhaps you will make worthy allies after all!" Neon turned and grinned at us and we chuckled at his forced humour. The Boeotian relaxed, breaking into an uneasy smile.

We dismounted and made a show of inspecting our horses or looking bored. I was conscious of Whisper's absence at my back, but the rhomphaia would only have drawn unwanted attention. I had to be satisfied with Soul-Thief. Meli had brought the spear-blade from Athens, newly affixed to an ash-wood shaft. I glanced at Thaletos, who stood near the rear of the company. The Theban fingered the war-axe at his hip, a smaller version of the double-bladed *labrys* he had used to dispatch the oxen during the sacrifice to Dionysus.

A dull thud in front of us saved us from further testing our acting skills. The passage brightened as the inner gates opened with agonizing slowness. Beyond the gate, a few dozen soldiers milled about with an unsuspecting air. Two other men stood apart, examining the dispatch from Lysander.

My breath stopped in my throat, for I knew them.

The first was the mercenary Kepheos.

The scarred face of the second man had haunted my dreams since I was a boy.

Orchus.

The Andrian mercenary had eschewed the Spartan armour he had been wearing in the palace of Pharnabazos. His current gear had been chosen with an experienced soldier's eye for practicality. Under an unremarkable green cloak he wore a scaled leather cuirass and plain bronze greaves dulled by years of use. His left hand sat easily on the sword hilt at his waist. In his right hand he held Lysander's message.

Suddenly I feared for the success of our ruse. Orchus raised his hand to greet Neon. The Andrian mercenary knew Neon, but for the moment Neon's identity was hidden behind his helmet. It is fortunate that in dress and hair one Spartiate looks much like another, at least from a distance. Neon acknowledged Orchus with a curt nod and turned to adjust his horse's halter, giving me a knowing look as he did so.

My men knew what to do. Still in the gate passage, the *peripoli* were unslinging their shields and spears in an unhurried, casual manner, making a show of stretching out their kinks as if they had just completed a long journey. Taking off my shield, I kept the contingent of Boeotian soldiers in view. Kepheos was giving instructions to his men. Orchus listened half-heartedly, a bored expression on his face. I could not help but look at the Andrian mercenary one more time.

As if sensing my eyes upon him, the scar-faced veteran turned his disinterested gaze our way. Our eyes met. He paused, his forehead creasing into a deep frown that lasted for but a heartbeat before his eyes widened in recognition.

"Close the gate!" he shouted. "Close the fucking gate!" Beside him, Kepheos looked at us and then back at Orchus in startled confusion. Orchus drew his sword and stabbed it in our direction. "They're Athenians! Kill them! Kill them now!"

I cursed at my stupidity. There was nothing to be done. "Attack!" I shouted, but the *peripoli* were already rushing to action.

Suddenly there was pandemonium. My men knew their jobs. Behind me, three long peals of a horn rang out in succession as Mnasyllus gave the signal that the gates were open. The Boeotian guards in the tunnel fell under a flurry of spears and swords before they knew what was happening. We slapped the horses' rumps and drove them towards the stunned defenders. Some of the enemy hurled their spears, but a confused wall of horse-flesh shielded us from harm. We ran to fill the gap of the open inner gate. Our shields overlapped like a snake's scales to form the most miserable phalanx ever witnessed by the gods. But we did not need to win. We just needed to hold.

Belatedly, the soldiers of Haliartos reacted to Orchus' frantic commands. The Andrian was no fool and perceived our aim. "Close the gate!" he screamed. Instead of engaging us, the bulk of the defenders broke off to the left and right, heading to the rear of the gates to push them shut. Against their strength we would be helpless. If they pushed us back into the passage and locked the gate, our ruse would be in vain.

My mind raced. A wild-eyed horse with a spear buried deep in its flank trotted back in our direction. As the panicked beast came past me I threw down my shield and spear and leapt from the line, seizing the animal's halter.

I shouted at Thaletos, who was closest to me. "Thaletos!" Somehow the Theban heard me in the fray and looked my way. "Kill the horse!" I shouted, straining to hold onto the frantic horse.

Thaletos looked at me as if I were mad.

"For the gate!" I screamed. "Like the sacrifice! Block the gate!"

The Theban's expression changed as he grasped my meaning. I was close to the open gate as I would get. A glance over my shoulder told me the defenders of Haliartos had not seized the initiative to engage our line of shields. Instead they were waiting for their comrades to push us out with the closing gates.

I pulled the reins down but the horse reared up. The fear-maddened beast attacked me with a flurry of kicking forelegs. A hoof deflected off my helmet. Stunned, I stumbled back, somehow managing to keep hold of the reins. Thaletos stood with his axe raised, looking for his chance to strike.

The beast's actions were its end. As it landed back on its front legs, the weight of my reeling body added to its momentum. For an instant the line of the horse's neck was nearly horizontal. Thaletos did not miss his opportunity. His axe swung down, biting deep into the animal's spine. The horse gave a violent spasm and collapsed just as the gate reached it. The heavy door stopped as it met the unexpected resistance.

I found myself lying on my back on the ground beside the dead horse, my head still ringing from the blow from the horse's hoof. Thaletos seized my wrist and began to drag me towards the safety of the *peripoli* line. Suddenly his boots slid on the spreading pool of the slain horse's blood. With a curse he skidded and fell on his backside. Recovering too slowly from my daze, I saw Orchus screaming orders and pointing his sword at us, directing any nearby soldiers to attack us. Thaletos and I were dead men.

A figure stepped out from the *peripoli* line and bounded over us in a swirl of red. Neon. The advancing Thebans balked at the sight of the crimson-cloaked Spartiate. Their hesitation was brief, however, and a spear-wielding Boeotian mustered the courage to take on the Spartan.

The spear-point snapped towards Neon's face. The Spartan stepped into the attack, jerking his shield up to neatly deflect the blow as he countered with an underhanded spear thrust up into the Theban's groin. The man screamed and fell back. The man's bowels held fast to the spear-point, forcing Neon to abandon his spear and draw his sword. Another Boeotian spear lanced forward. Neon dropped low and the olive-leaf blade of the spear scraped over the Spartan's shoulder. Neon charged before his attacker could pull his spear back for a second thrust. The Spartan's recurved *kopis* blade chopped into the spearman's neck. Neon ripped the blade back, nearly severing the man's head in a plume of crimson blood.

A forest of bronze-clad legs surrounded us as the advancing *peripoli* stepped over us, blocking my view of Neon. A brawny hand seized my wrist and I was yanked to my feet by a grinning Mnasyllus. The big man cuffed the side of my helmet before turning back with a roar to shore up the line.

Over the shoulders of the *peripoli*, I could see that more defenders were scurrying to form their own line opposite our own. Neon held his place between our ragged formation and the advancing Boeotians. "Neon! Back in line!" I shouted.

But a ferocious blood lust had taken hold of the Spartiate. The bodies of three Boeotians at his feet, Neon screamed his challenge at the wary Boeotians. Reluctant to engage the howling Spartan directly, an anonymous enemy hurled a chunk of stone that deflected hard off of Neon's helmet.

The stunned Spartan staggered two steps in a valiant effort to stay on his feet before toppling into the ground like a felled stag. The suddenly confident Boeotians advanced to finish off their helpless quarry. From behind the *peripoli* lines, I could only look on at the prone figure of Neon helplessly.

A small, wiry figure burst from the *peripoli* line and in three strides was among the Boeotians, skewering one of Neon's would-be killers with a spear-thrust through the guts. It was Iollas. The Messenian drove his shield into the chest of another Boeotian, shoving him back. Iollas pressed a foot against the impaled man's chest and pushed, ripping his spear free. Screaming a challenge, Iollas stood astride the unmoving Neon. The unexpected sight of the howling Iollas had startled the Boeotians and once more their advance faltered. Before they could regain their nerve, the *peripoli* surged again to reabsorb their comrade into the line, stepping over the inert figure of Neon as they did so.

I grabbed Neon's wrists and dragged the unconscious Spartan to the side of the tunnel passage. It was the best I could do for him. A growing mass of Boeotians were assembling opposite the *peripoli*. I seized a spear from the ground and shoved my way into the line, knowing it would do little against such numbers.

But amidst the screams and clamour of battle, I became aware of a growing rumble to my rear. I glanced over my shoulder just in time to see the new but welcome danger bearing down on us. "Clear the way! Clear the way!" I shouted. The *peripoli* pressed themselves flat against the gates and let out a cheer as horsemen galloped through the narrow gap between the gates.

The Theban cavalry had arrived.

CHAPTER 34

The men of Haliartos had no stomach for a fight.

The defenders broke at the sight of the Theban horsemen and fled into the streets of the city. Other fighters threw down their arms and fell to their knees, putting their faith in the mercy of their fellow Boeotians. I scanned the chaotic scene in search of Orchus and Kepheos with no luck. They would not get far, for Ismenias had sent riders to blockade the other gates of the city.

Theban cavalry and hoplites crowded the open area just inside the city gates. To my eye, one Theban horseman looked much like any other. But one slight, fire-haired rider stood out. "Meli!" I shouted, raising my spear high. Somehow she heard my voice among the din and manoeuvred her mount my way through the sea of horseflesh.

Meli stared down from atop her horse. Grinning, she unslung something from her back. "I have something for you, Brother," she said, tossing the long object my way. I grabbed Whisper out of the air and pulled the weapon close to me like a long-absent lover.

I checked my men. Wounds, there were many, but all had survived the onslaught. Tibetos limped towards me, wincing with each step. He raised his hand from his thigh, showing me his bloody palm. "One of the turd-sniffing bastards got me in the leg, but it's nothing" he said, forcing a wan smile. His face was pale. Meli alighted from her horse's back and ran to her wounded lover. "You see, Dammo?" Tibetos said. "Meli will take care of me." He winced again as my sister examined his injury.

I leaned close to my sister, squeezing her arm. "Orchus is here," I said quietly. "He is trapped. We will find him," I said, feeling less confident than I sounded. Meli nodded, but I saw her uncertainty. We both knew the Andrian mercenary enjoyed the protection of some god, for he always eluded the death he deserved.

I patted my friend on the shoulder and left him to my sister's ministrations. There were others whose condition concerned me. I found Neon where I had left him. The Spartan had managed to pull himself to his feet but was leaning on Iollas for support. His helmet hung from his left hand and his face was clenched in discomfort as he rubbed the side of his head. "I always knew Spartans had thick skulls," I said, tapping Neon's dented helmet with the hilt of my rhomphaia.

Neon allowed himself a weak smile. "I could say the same about Athenians," he said, his eyes flicking upwards to my helmet. I rubbed my crown and felt where the horse's kick had bent the bronze inward. My chuckle infected Neon and soon the two of us were laughing like two drunks deep in their cups. It was the mad laughter of warriors who knew they had cheated death one more time. It was too much for Neon, who bent over and vomited.

When Neon's guts were empty, Iollas helped the weak-kneed Spartan straighten up. I put a hand on the Messenian's shoulder. "Brother," I said. "Today you have won great reputation. The *peripoli* will still tell this tale long after our shades have journeyed to the Underworld."

Iollas bared his teeth in a jagged smile. "I saw the chance to show him who was the better man," he said, still propping up the woozy Spartan.

Upon hearing these words, Neon, shrugging off Iollas' supporting arm, straightened up with a grimace and gave the Messenian an unreadable look. The diminutive Iollas, raising his chin ever so little, matched the tall Spartan's stare. Then Neon extended his hand towards the former helot. "And you have done so," he said in his flat Spartan voice.

For a moment, Iollas regarded the outstretched hand like it was a baited trap, and I thought he would reject the Spartan's gesture. But then he grasped Neon's hand warmly. "Welcome to the *peripoli*, Brother."

I left the two men, for there was someone else I wished to speak to. I found him with a knot of Thebans in conversation with Thaletos. "Pammo!" I shouted.

Epaminondas looked my way. His helmet was tipped back over his sweat-matted black hair, and his sphinx-emblazoned shield was slung across his back. He raised his spear in a salute. "Your plan worked, by the gods!"

"We have more work to do," I responded. Lysander's army might appear at any time but the celebrating Thebans seemed in no rush to prepare for his arrival, I noted with annoyance.

Epaminondas waved off my concern. "Androkleides is already assembling the troops at the ambush point," he reassured me.

"And Leontiades?"

Thaletos smiled coldly. "The matter is under control, Athenian. Ismenias has given special instruction that Androkleides keep Leontiades and his men close. If there's even a whiff of treachery, Leontiades will find a spear in his back."

Epaminondas pointed at my borrowed breastplate. "You have done battle today," he said.

I glanced down at the darkened blood splattered across my armour. I scoffed. "Horse," I said, indicating the dead animal blocking the gate. The gathered Thebans frowned in confusion. I jerked a thumb at Thaletos. "He made another sacrifice to Dionysus."

Thaletos laughed. "That was quick thinking, Athenian." He related the tale of how the horse met its end. "Otherwise we'd still be shut outside the city." The Thebans commented appreciatively.

But I had more pressing concerns. "Where are the prisoners?" I asked.

"Ismenias ordered that all the men in the city be rounded up and held in the agora," Epaminondas informed me.

"I need to see them," I said.

We made our way to the agora. A section of the marketplace had been cleared of its flimsy stalls to make space for the captives. Hundreds of men sat glumly on the ground, while Thebans brought even more prisoners who had been captured trying to flee the city only to find the exits well-guarded.

"Who are you looking for?" Epaminondas asked.

"Kepheos was here," I said. "He was with one of Lysander's captains, a mercenary named Orchus." If the Fates continued with their generous allotment of good fortune, Orchus and Kepheos would be among the prisoners.

"Kepheos!" Epaminondas exclaimed. His brow knotted at the implication. It would not reflect well on Leontiades were his man to be discovered conspiring with the Haliartans. He turned to Thaletos. "Is it true?"

The big warrior shrugged. "It may be so. My sight fails me at a distance, but I accept the Athenian's word."

I scanned the hundreds of seated prisoners. Citizen and slave both had been rounded up without distinction. The citizens were easy to recognize, distinguished by their broken and frightened faces. Their fates lay in the Thebans' hands. The leaders would undoubtedly be executed in reprisals for their treachery. Other ardent supporters of the oligarchic faction might be sold into slavery of the worst kind, working in mines and quarries until they dropped dead from exhaustion. The lucky ones might return to their lives under Theban-approved leaders. But I cared not for the men of Haliartos. My only wish was to locate Orchus and Kepheos, neither of whom I could see among the captives.

"Perhaps you were mistaken?" Epaminondas ventured.

"I know I saw them!" I said loudly, slamming the butt of my spear on the ground in frustration. I held out hope that the wily Andrian was hiding somewhere in the city. Still, it would take time to flush him out.

A light hand touched my shoulder. I turned to see my sister. She had brought some of the *peripoli* with her, including the wounded Tibetos, his leg tightly bound. "He's not here," Meli said. There was a hint of desperation in her voice. I know of whom she spoke.

"Orchus won't get far," I said.

We were not alone in scrutinizing the horde of prisoners. "Eurymachus!" I shouted, striding towards the Theban aristocrat, who was peering at the captured men. Eurymachus grinned coldly at my approach, his confidence no doubt bolstered by the cluster of hardened warriors at his back. I stopped chest to chest, forcing him to take a step back. Epaminondas and Thaletos were behind me. "Looking for someone?" I asked.

Eurymachus smirked. "Just estimating how much money this lot will be worth on the slave market," he answered smoothly.

"I think you are looking for Kepheos," I said bluntly.

Eurymachus deflected the accusation with a scoff. "Don't be absurd."

"I saw your man Kepheos here when the Haliartans first opened the city gates," I insisted.

"That's impossible. Kepheos accompanied us from Thebes. My men will swear to that," he said, indicating the dead-eyed brutes at his back. The blatant lie only confirmed that Leontiades had been conspiring with Lysander.

"Then where is he?" I challenged.

Eurymachus shrugged. "I expect he's here somewhere. Probably off shagging a slave girl. The spoils of war and all that."

"You're a liar."

There was little I could do and Eurymachus knew it. "Accuse me all you want, Athenian. I think you'll find the word of a known thief and murderer like yourself will carry little weight in Thebes," he said confidently.

"*Despote*," came a voice from among the seated prisoners. Eurymachus turned, scowling at the source of the unwanted interruption. A kneeling captive rose slowly to his feet, his hands raised in supplication. The light-haired man was young, probably not much older than his twentieth year. A slave, judging by his manner and accent. He had tough, wiry muscles from whatever labours his master had set for him.

"Sit down, slave!" Eurymachus snarled.

But the slave remained standing. The young man glanced nervously at Eurymachus and his men before addressing me. "*Despote*, I may have information for you regarding the man you seek," he said, dipping his head. The slave's intelligent eyes darted between me and Eurymachus.

The aristocrat advanced on the slave. "You dare speak, slave? You will taste my blade!" he said, his hand moving to the sword at his waist.

I put my palm on Eurymachus' shining breastplate and shoved him back towards his men. Eurymachus' eyes widened in anger. "We should hear what the man has to say," I said.

Eurymachus' fury radiated from him like heat from a fire. "You would listen to a slave! Only a slave would value a slave's words!" he sneered. Beneath the contempt in his voice, there was an edge of worry.

I turned to the slave. "Speak."

The slave's throat bobbed as he swallowed his fear, like a man about to leap into the swirling sea from a great height. "I will tell you what I know for my freedom, *despote*," he said.

I almost laughed out loud. The powerless slave surrounded by armed men, many of whom would cut him down without compunction, was trying to extort me. The audacity of it endeared him to me. "You think your information is worth your freedom?" I asked.

"I believe so, *despote*," he said, not budging from his price.

"What is your name, slave?"

"Pibos, *despote*," he said with a nervous bow.

"Then I will grant you your freedom, Pibos," I said. "*If* your information proves worthy of such a reward."

Eurymachus blinked in disbelief. Whatever information the slave possessed, the Theban aristocrat feared it. He pointed at the slave Pibos. "Kill him!" he barked at his men. Eurymachus' henchmen drew their weapons. There was a hiss of daggers and swords being unsheathed as the *peripoli* prepared to meet them.

Only Thaletos prevented an eruption of violence. The Theban champion placed himself between the two sides, his hands on his hips. Eurymachus' men checked themselves, reluctant to attack their respected, and fearsome, countryman. Thaletos spoke. "I wish to hear what the slave has to say." Eurymachus gritted his teeth but did not move, torn between his desire to silence the slave and the fear of defying the imposing figure of Thaletos. The two sides glared at each other, neither side willing to back down.

An embarrassed cough from the slave Pibos interrupted the standoff. "*Despote?*"

"Tell me what you know, slave," I said, my eyes not leaving Eurymachus.

"I must show you, *despote,*" he said apologetically. "There is a house."

"A house?"

"I will take you there, *despote,*" he said, bowing his head.

"Do it," I said.

The slave Pibos led us through the convoluted lanes of Haliartos with Eurymachus and his men at our heels, and Tibetos limping hard in an effort to keep up. Soon Pibos halted in front of a run-down home near the eastern wall of the city. "What you seek is in there, *despote.*"

The house was in a state of some dilapidation. But the walls were high and the door appeared solid enough. I pulled at the door but it was locked. I stepped aside and Mnasyllus stepped forward and remedied the situation with a mighty kick. I charged in with Whisper in my hands.

Kepheos stood in the small courtyard, a sword in his hand. The look of desperation on the mercenary's face grew as more men poured into the home. His gaze fell on Eurymachus. whose eyes were locked on his captain.

I levelled my rhomphaia at him. "Surrender," I said flatly. I wanted the mercenary alive, if only to reveal the treachery of Eurymachus

276

and his father. Kepheos's gaze flitted around the courtyard, looking for some escape. There was none.

Before Kepheos could respond to my demand, Eurymachus stepped forwards, his arms held wide. "Kepheos! I wondered where you had disappeared to. Ignore this Athenian *pig*," he said, looking my way with a sneer. "Come with us." Kepheos glanced my way uncertainly.

The mercenary opened his mouth to speak but was interrupted by a dull thud. Kepheos froze, panic on his face. There was another thud and a muffled voice. A woman's voice.

"It came from over there," Tibetos said, pointing. In the far corner, partially hidden by the overhead stairs, was one more room that stood out because it was behind a barred door. I glanced at Eurymachus. The aristocrat seemed as surprised as the rest of us.

I strode towards the door. Kepheos belatedly moved to intercept me but suddenly found himself in the iron grip of Mnasyllus. The mercenary struggled in vain against the *peripoli*'s massive strength before going still, defeat etched on his face.

"Keep them back!" I barked, pointing at Eurymachus and his men. The remaining *peripoli,* joined by Epaminondas, put themselves between the Thebans and the mysterious door. Eurymachus and his men surged forward but were checked by the raised hand of Thaletos.

"Hold!" he boomed. It was enough.

Stachys and I stood before the barred door. I nodded at Stachys, and he lifted the wooden beam and jerked the door open.

The chamber was small and dark, a simple storeroom, thick with the musty odor of stale grain. Knee-high pots and stacked amphorae covered the greater part of the rough floor. But in the remaining space stood a figure, bound and gagged, squinting against the sudden intrusion of light. My heart leapt.

"Althaia!" I exclaimed. In an instant I was at her side, freeing her from her bonds. No sooner had her hands been untied than she embraced me, her body shaking with sobs of relief. We separated and we took each other in. "You are unharmed?" I asked. She nodded, her face tight as she fought back a tide of emotions. I held out my hand.

She took a deep breath and let her natural dignity reassert itself. "I'm ready," she said. She put her hand in mine and together we emerged back into the courtyard.

A stir of confused muttering greeted our appearance. Epaminondas' jaw dropped. "Sister!" he exclaimed. He ran forward and the siblings embraced each other. My gaze fell upon Eurymachus. Rather than the fear or panic I had expected, the aristocrat's face was a knot of rage. But his fury was not directed at me or Althaia. His anger was focused on Kepheos, who was still held fast by Mnasyllus.

In a swift movement, Eurymachus unsheathed his sword and lunged at the immobilized Kepheos. The aristocrat plunged the blade into his captain's chest with a calm, upward thrust, grasping Kepheos's shoulder with his other hand and pulling the mercenary forward until the blade was driven in up to the hilt. The mercenary's eyes widened in shock. Eurymachus tore the blade free and stepped back towards the protection of his men. Kepheos' body spasmed and then his face slackened as his shade left his body. Mnasyllus released the dead man and Kepheos collapsed in an unnatural heap on the ground.

A shocked silence filled the courtyard. And I suddenly understood. Kepheos had disobeyed his employer. The presence of Kepheos in Haliartos had been no surprise to Eurymachus, but the sight of Althaia had thrown him into a rage. Because Althaia should have been dead. Kepheos had been ordered to abduct her and kill her so that the blame could be placed on me. But instead, the spurned mercenary had merely taken her for himself. His desire for Althaia had saved her but doomed himself. Dionysus had infected him with madness.

Eurymachus turned to his men, pointing his bloody blade at the body of the man he had just murdered. "This is the fate of traitors to Thebes!" he proclaimed. The aristocrat's eyes flashed with victory as his gaze met mine. Whatever Kepheos' purpose in Haliartos had been, the link between Leontiades and Lysander was now lying in a pool of blood before me. I could slander and accuse all I wished, but my word would be worth less than a cartload of dung to the prickly Thebans.

Eurymachus extended his hand towards Althaia. "Now come to me, Wife," he said sternly. Althaia did not move. A note of irritation crept into Eurymachus' voice. "Wife, I said come to me." Althaia leaned in closer to me. The rage began to build on Eurymachus' face, but there was little he could do.

Beside me, Epaminondas spoke. "My sister will not be returning to your household, Eurymachus." Resolution and authority infused the young man's voice.

Before Eurymachus could protest, Thaletos stepped forward. "Son of Leontiades," he said. "Take your men and report to Ismenias and Androkleidas. Lysander's army will be here soon. It is time to assemble for battle. I will accompany you to ensure you do not get lost," he added.

Eurymachus lips moved as if to protest, but he checked himself. He looked past us towards the storage room where Althaia had been held. Reluctantly, he acknowledged his countryman's command. "Of course, O Thaletos," he said. He pointed at us. "And the Athenians?"

"They have won us the city. Their part is done. Now go," Thaletos said, impatience creeping into his voice.

There was nothing to be done. Eurymachus glared at me. "*We* are not done, Athenian!" The aristocrat spun on his heel and barked at his men, the lot of them leaving us in the decrepit courtyard, the warm body of Kepheos before us.

Thaletos addressed us. "I am pleased to see you still live, Althaia, daughter of Polymnis," he said, dipping his head towards Althaia with a deference at odds with his hulking, armoured body.

"You honour Thebes with your service, O Thaletos," she responded.

Thaletos looked abashed. "I must be off to ensure that your husband does not get lost on his way to join the army," he said in a deadpan tone.

"A wise idea," Althaia said. Thaletos cast a curious glance my way before leaving us.

Althaia stared at the body of Kepheos and shuddered. "Eurymachus ordered him to kill me, but he killed his own companions when they tried to…" she said, her voice trailing off. "He killed them to protect me. And then he brought me to this place. He begged me to accept him. He never harmed me when I refused," she said sadly. I put my arm around her and she leaned in close, not caring that her brother and others were present.

"But he wanted you for himself," I said. I did not know if I were speaking of Kepheos or myself.

There was a small cough behind us. Althaia left my embrace as though suddenly recovering her sense of propriety. The fleeting moment gone, I turned towards the anxious Pibos. "You have more than fulfilled your promise to me, Pibos. I will guarantee your freedom, for what it's worth."

The slave gave a small bow of acknowledgment. "I am grateful, *despote*. But there is more here than this man," he said, looking distastefully at the corpse of Kepheos.

Before the newly-freed slave could explain, Tibetos interrupted. "Dammo," he said. He was looking around the courtyard, anxious eyes burning through his haggard face.

"What is it?"

"Where's Meli?"

An icy worm of fear slithered into my heart. Tibetos was right.

My sister had vanished.

CHAPTER 35

The windbag philosophers who debate in the agora argue that reason and logic are superior to instinct. They are wrong.

My reason told me that my sister could handle herself. But my instinct told me she was in danger.

"Stay here! Take care of Althaia!" I ordered, already dashing for the door.

I burst out onto the street with Tibetos limping behind me. "Where did she go?" he asked.

"To find Orchus," I said, looking in all directions. There was no sign of Meli. My mind was racing. Orchus could be hiding anywhere. If so, it would take time to flush him out, even for Meli. But if he were not concealing himself? Escape from the city would be difficult, for Ismenias had secured the city gates. I looked northward to the acropolis. Perhaps escape was not the Andrian mercenary's goal.

The ramparts of the citadel merged with the city walls on the north side where they overlooked the great marshy lake on whose shores Haliartos lay. At the centre of the north wall was a watchtower, atop of which was visible a raised platform. It was a fire beacon. If Orchus could not escape, he might seek to warn Lysander and his approaching army that something was amiss in Haliartos.

The acropolis walls were clear of defenders, for the men of Haliartos were now prisoners in the agora and the Thebans were mustering for the battle ahead. Relief that my instincts were wrong washed through me. Just then a figure appeared on the south rampart of the keep. He was too distant to see clearly, but I knew it was Orchus.

I cursed. "He's going to light the signal fire!" All our efforts would be for naught if he succeeded. Meli would have to wait.

I sprinted north. Tibetos called out behind me but I could only abandon him. Preventing Orchus from warning Lysander was my only thought as I barreled through the streets of Haliartos.

I found the gates to the acropolis open, their only sentries the corpses of two Theban soldiers lying in the dirt. Another one of Orchus' victims lay at the base of the steps leading up to the ramparts. The dead man's unseeing eyes watched as I bound past him.

I flew up the narrow steps. At the top of the wall I spotted Orchus approaching the north tower. I could make out a thick coil of rope slung over his shoulder. I was too far away. I could not stop him from lighting the fire beacon and escaping over the wall.

There was no one between Orchus and his goal. And then there was. A slight figure appeared from the doorway of the tower. "No!" I hissed.

Orchus came to a sudden halt to assess his foe. Meli raised her pair of short, curved *sica* swords. I feared for her. Orchus was a cunning, experienced fighter, with tricks and instincts honed by the harsh lessons of a thousand battles. She was not his match.

I pulled up and cupped my hands to my mouth. "Orchus!" I bellowed, trying to distract him. The Andrian glanced back towards me. The wily veteran knew I would soon be upon him. He needed to deal with Meli quickly.

His guile showed itself immediately as he lashed out at my sister not with his sword but the coil of rope on his shoulder. The heavy cord extended out from the mercenary's hand and struck Meli on the side. The jarring impact sent her stumbling into the parapet, nearly throwing her over the top. In an instant Orchus had his sword in his hand and loomed over the stunned form of my sister. She was defenceless,

In desperation, I pulled back Whisper over my head in a two-handed grip. With all my strength, I hurled the rhomphaia at Orchus just as he raised his blade to hack down on Meli. Whisper spun end over end towards its target. The hilt of the weapon struck the mercenary's shoulder, defecting the rhomphaia harmlessly over the wall to plunge into the marsh below. But the distraction delayed the mercenary's killing blow as Meli twisted desperately to avoid the falling blade. The delayed ring of metal on stone reached my ears an eye-blink after the mercenary's sword bit into empty wall where Meli had been. Orchus gave his opponent no respite, pushing off the wall and charging the off-balance Meli like a wild boar. His shoulder slammed into my sister's chest.

The impact sent her reeling backwards, but instead of resisting she let herself tumble back, curling her body as she did so. She rolled in a backwards somersault and up onto the balls of her feet, her twin swords brandished like a lion's claws. Orchus had no time to collect himself before my sister launched herself at her ancient enemy with an eerie keening howl.

Orchus retreated under a flurry of attacks from the swirling *sica* swords. He dealt with my sister's wild fury, deflecting each blow with practiced efficiency. Suddenly the Andrian's blade snaked out, slashing deep into Meli's thigh.

A normal man would have crumpled under such a wound. But my sister was not a warrior trained in the *peripoli* drilling yard or the Spartan *agoge*. A pure, primal instinct drove her, and she burned with the spark of older, wilder gods. Like a cornered, wounded beast, she did not retreat but stumbled at her tormentor with a feral scream.

They clashed together in a tangle of weapons and limbs. For a heartbeat they were locked together like two grappling wrestlers, their faces inches apart. Orchus grunted and snapped a vicious head-butt to my sister's face, sending her flying towards me. She landed in heap as a *sica* sword clattered on the stone and off the edge of the wall. She lay unmoving. Orchus loomed over her crumpled form, his sword raised.

Meli was at his mercy. I was still too far to save her. I cried out. "Orchus!" I shouted again in desperation. "Orchus! Fight me!" I challenged him, closing the last of the distance between us. I was weaponless. "Take me!" I implored.

Orchus ignored me. He turned and walked away with odd, shuffling steps. I reached my sister and stood over her motionless body, my chest heaving. I raised my empty hands, waiting for Orchus to spin and attack. But no attack came. Orchus, swaying like a stalk of barley in a gentle breeze, shifted to face me. "You're too late, my Thracian whoreson!" He looked down. The hilt of the *sica* sword protruded from under the lower lip of his leather breastplate. His own sword dropped to the ground with a clang. He gripped the handle of the weapon buried in his belly and winced. He leaned back against the parapet and stared at the sky. "Bitch Oracle!" he laughed. "She told me a woman would be my end! I thought it would be an angry whore knifing me in the back." With a look of contempt, he spat a gob of bloody phlegm and wiped his mouth with the back of his hand. He turned his head to look at me. "Should have throttled you both when I had the chance, and by the gods I had chances!" He shook his head to himself in regret. He pulled himself up straight. "I told you so many times, Boy," he said through a smile of blood-lined teeth. "A corpse don't bite!" Without another word, the Andrian mercenary leaned back and let himself topple over the edge of the wall.

Beneath me, Meli moaned. I sat down and cradled her in my lap. Sticky blood from her broken nose covered her lower face, and a swollen, purple hue was already ringing her green eyes. Tibetos appeared at the far end of the parapet. With a limping gait he ran towards us, wincing with every stride. He fell to his knees beside us. "Meli!"

Meli's eyes flicked open at the sound of her lover's voice. "Help me up," she mumbled through her split lip. We lifted her between us onto her wounded leg. Then, without another word, she pulled us close. Our embrace dampened the heavy sobs that wracked her body.

I knew the sorrow that had seized her. The ancient revenge we had sought was ours. But I knew from bitter experience faithless vengeance, however just, does not heal the heart that tended hatred like a fire for so long. The deed done, the flame goes out, leaving nothing but ashes.

MNASYLLUS AND THE OTHER *PERIPOLI* greeted us with both relief at our return and concern for my sister's injuries.

"I will take care of her," said Althaia. Her tone was confident as she directed us to make a comfortable spot for Meli in what must have served as the salon of the run-down house. We prepared a makeshift bed on the floor and set my sister down.

Meli closed her swollen eyes and breathed deeply. Tibetos knelt beside her, stroking her hair. I was not accustomed to seeing her so helpless, her strength having given way to a child-like vulnerability. I hesitated to leave her.

Althaia sensed my reluctance. "We need some privacy while I treat her injuries," Althaia said.

Meli, her eyes still shut, reached out to touch my foot. "Althaia will be here and Tibo will be guarding me. We'll both be fine, Brother," she said, smiling weakly. I knelt down and kissed her forehead and she sighed into unconsciousness.

Tibetos looked at me. "I'll stay a little longer, Dammo."

I nodded and rose to my feet. Althaia led me out of the salon, giving Tibetos a moment alone with my sister. At the doorway, she put her hand gently on my arm.

"Your sister will recover. She is strong," she reassured me.

My sister, for all her injuries, was not the only one I feared for. "And you?"

She squeezed my arm more firmly. "I am fine now." The lingering shock in her eyes belied her brave smile.

We looked at each other, saying nothing. I wished to take her in my arms and hold her. I wished to tell her I was sorry. But there were others present. It would not have been proper to embarrass her so. And the day was not done. "Where is your brother?" I asked. Epaminondas had been absent when we returned to the house.

"He went to join Thaletos for battle," Althaia said. She gave me a knowing look. "And you wish to join him, I think."

"What makes you say that?"

Althaia smiled sadly, her hand dropping to take mine. "Because it is your nature."

"I will be back," I said.

"And I will be waiting," she replied softly. Althaia had more courage than me. She stood on her toes and her lips brushed mine as lightly as a butterfly's wings. She hurried away back into the salon, leaving me momentarily speechless.

I turned to find the *peripoli* waiting patiently. Mnasyllus and Taras, conservative farmers at their core, studied the floor while fidgeting with embarrassment at Althaia's open display of affection, Stachys maintained the practiced neutrality of the educated aristocrat that he was, while Sabas, being a hedonistic Cretan, was grinning from ear to ear. I cleared my throat. "Did anything else happen while we were gone?" I asked.

Mnasyllus, relieved to put what he had seen behind him, answered. "Pibos showed us something else," he said, indicating the slave. "You need to see it, Dammo," he said anxiously, pointing to the storeroom where Althaia had been held.

"What?"

"Take a look," Sabas said, still grinning broadly.

The others followed me to the storeroom. One of the clay pots had been smashed open. I took a sharp intake of breath, for it was neither wine nor oil nor any other commodity that had spilled out onto the floor. I squatted down and lifted a handful of gold coins. And I knew why Lysander was in such a rush to arrive in Haliartos before King Pausanias.

Not believing my good fortune, I smashed the top of another sealed pot. A stream of golden Persian darics trickled to the ground. Stunned to silence, I took in the stacks of pots and amphorae. Doing a rough calculation. I reckoned they would hold close to all the Persian gold I had delivered to Thebes. All awaiting Lysander, a gift from Leontiades to the ambitious Spartan general. A small price to pay to win the favour of the future king of Sparta. No wonder Eurymachus had been reluctant to leave.

For a moment, I was speechless.

"I've done well for you, *despote*?" the slave Pibos asked.

I laughed. "More than well, friend Pibos. Never again will you call another man 'Master!'" I said, shaking my head in amazement.

"Is this gold not worth the freedom of more of my fellow slaves?" he asked hopefully.

The man did not lack for boldness. But there was no time. For even then, the Theban army was assembling to face the approaching forces of Lysander. The matter of Pibos' request would have to wait. "Talk to Tibetos," I said, impatiently delegating the matter to my friend. Yet at the same time, I had come to a decision about the gold.

I instructed Mnasyllus and the *peripoli* what to do.

The day was not done. I grabbed Soul-Thief from where I had left her leaning against a wall, I would be needing her.

I was going to battle.

CHAPTER 36

We waited.

Lysander's march to Haliartos from Phokis would be along a narrow corridor between the great marshy lake to the north and a ridge of low mountains to the south. The mountains ran close to the lakeshore until Haliartos, where the gaping maw of a valley interrupted the ridge for a spell before the mountains resumed their eastward course. It was in this valley that the restless Theban army lay hidden.

Midday had passed, yet there was still no sign of Lysander. Standing in the front rank of Theban phalanx, my fears revolved more around being made a fool of than the knee-weakening carnage of battle. I fought back a creeping dread that my assertions had been wrong or that Lysander had been alerted to our presence.

As if sensing my misgivings, a Theban a few ranks behind me called out. "Where are your Spartans, Athenian?" His comrades jeered at me.

I turned to eye the offender, a tough-looking type in battered armour. I shrugged. "Patience, friend. They'll be here," I said with false confidence. "Or are you just eager to get back to humping your sheep, Theban?" The man's yellow-toothed smile froze as his companions hooted and hollered until he started laughing too.

Men blunt their fear in different ways. Some, like the Thebans behind me, masked their secret dread with bluster and jests. Even more find courage in the bottom of a wineskin. I reckoned more than half the men in the valley were well on their way to drunkenness. I was sober. Drink bolsters valour but weakens prowess, my former arms-master Neleus had warned me. I trusted in my weapons and skill. By habit, I reached out to touch the reassuring shape of Whisper only to find her absent. The rhomphaia was still lying submerged somewhere in the marsh outside the walls of Haliartos. I gripped the shaft of Soul-Thief more tightly.

Beside me, Epaminondas wrestled the god Phobos in silence. He had never faced the churning terror of battle, I knew. Now, like countless young men before him, he was discovering that talking of strategy and tactics around a fire was a very different beast from the reality of the battlefield. Despite his fear, he had insisted on standing beside me in the front rank and would not be dissuaded. Thaletos stood on his opposite side. Between us, I thought, Epaminondas just might survive.

Epaminondas saw me studying him. He swallowed nervously. "The sacrifice was propitious," he said, as if to reassure himself.

"Yes," I responded noncommittally. Ismenias had overseen a sacrifice of a sheep. His personal seer had proclaimed the animal's entrails augured success for the coming battle. I put little stock in such things, for such seers tend to see only what their paymasters want them to see.

Epaminondas, being of a more pious nature, still sought signs from the gods to assuage his fear. "Look!" he said, pointing at the sky. An eagle was circling high above the valley. "I've been watching him. Soothsayers can see the future in the flight of birds," he said. *Mantises* often spout such nonsense, though their pronouncements are as worthless as a dribble of piss from an old man's cock. I turned my gaze upward, spying the eagle. The enormous bird abruptly veered northward towards Haliartos. I inhaled sharply. "What is it?" Epaminondas asked anxiously.

"A omen!" I said, adding a touch of awe to my voice.

"Good or bad?" Epaminondas asked, leaning closer in anticipation.

"The eagle's northward flight means we will have victory this day," I lied. Thaletos, no fool himself, snorted lightly but held his tongue.

"You are sure?" Epaminondas pressed.

I sniffed. "Do you think that my sister is the only one in our family with the gift of foresight?"

Epaminondas shook his head. "I didn't mean to suggest..."

Just then, for its own unknowable reasons, the eagle did an about-face. The bird soared back towards us, passing over the gathered Thebans before continuing its southward journey. Epaminondas frowned. "Does that augur well?" he asked.

A commotion behind us prevented the need for another lie. Someone was pushing their way to the front rank. I turned to find the handsome face of young Taras peering at me from within his borrowed helmet. "What are you doing here?" I snapped. The boy should have been with the rest of the *peripoli* behind the walls of Haliartos.

"I want to prove myself, *lochagos*," he said, trying to push forward into the front rank.

I shoved him back. "Don't be a fool! Get to the rear lines!"

Taras raised his chin defiantly. Epaminondas called out before Taras could give voice to his disobedience. "Look!" Epaminondas said, pointing north.

A horseman was racing down the valley towards us. Berating Taras would have to wait, for the scout's return could only mean one thing.

Lysander had arrived.

IT WAS TOO LATE TO DO ANYTHING ABOUT TARAS. "Stay behind me!" I snarled. Taras did not budge. "Don't disobey me, Boy, or I'll kill you myself!" For a heartbeat I thought the lad would defy me further but he nodded and took his place behind me.

The head of Lysander's army was visible now. My hatred for the man penetrated my very bones, but it was tempered by a wary respect. He was no fool. Expecting to be welcome at Haliartos, he had nevertheless exercised caution, for the glint of distant armour and spear-points meant that he had approached the city under arms. The head of the Spartan-led army was already in front of the city wall. Inexplicably, they had found the gates of Haliartos shut tight. And only a blind man would fail to see the army of Thebans filling the valley to the south.

Murmurs of doubt rippled through the Theban ranks. Even at a distance it was clear that Lysander's army was half as large again as our own. Confidence in the venture was wavering. Not a few angry looks were directed my way, for it was no secret whose intelligence had brought them to the city of Haliartos this day.

Activity rippled across the distant enemy ranks. Horsemen galloped up and down the column, their shouted commands just whispers in the air. I did not need to hear them to know what was happening. Lysander, with the sealed city of Haliartos to his rear and our army of Thebans arrayed against him, was realizing the nature of the trap he had found himself in. And he was preparing to fight.

We should have fallen on them like wolves on a pack of sheep. Lysander's army greatly outnumbered us, it was true, but his loose coalition of Spartans, Phokians, and sundry other allies were in some disorder. If we had closed the distance at a run, we would have smashed their ranks like a line of triremes ramming a fleet of merchant ships. Instead, the Theban army balked at Lysander's superior numbers. Under my helmet, I seethed with frustration, for every moment of delay gave Lysander more time to solidify his phalanx and broaden his lines so that they outflanked our own.

Lysander knew it too. A line of enemy cavalry advanced, putting itself between us and Lysander's still porous lines. The Theban cavalry, at least, knew their duty. A wedge of more than a hundred Theban horsemen charged out. The horses kicked up a great cloud of dust, hiding the cavalry battle from our eyes, but the result of the skirmish was never in doubt. The motley cavalry from Lysander's allies were of poor quality, and his Spartan horsemen not much better. They were no match for the Thebans and their strong animals bred on the broad plains of Boeotia. Among the Greeks, only the Thessalians were their superiors. Soon the enemy horsemen were scattered with the Thebans in pursuit.

A few dead lay on the field while their riderless horses trotted aimlessly, but in truth the enemy horsemen had suffered few casualties. The cavalry feint was only a delaying tactic while Lysander firmed up his lines. When the dust settled, I could see that he had not wasted the precious opportunity. The line stretched almost as wide as the city wall no gaps visible.

The delay had not been Lysander's only goal. His fleeing horsemen had drawn off the Theban cavalry, giving Lysander the chance to bring his light troops into play. A few hundred skirmishers ran towards our lines. The poorly-armoured fighters let fly a hail of stones, arrows, and heavier javelins.

Volley after volley rained down on us, harmlessly clattering off of raised shields for the most part. Sling-stones cracked off my shield with their crisp percussion sound. But even in the most compact phalanx with men huddled behind their shields, some missiles will find a gap. Soon there were cries and grunts of pain as bullets cracked bones and arrows and javelins pierced exposed flesh. The Thebans, scornful of such light troops, had none of their own to match those of Lysander. Lysander was whittling down our already inferior numbers with the pestering missile fire.

Some of the Theban cavalry had broken off their pursuit of the enemy horsemen and returned to the field. Lysander's skirmishers sprinted back to their lines, but a few stragglers who had tarried to loose a few final shots paid the price for their foolhardy courage when the Theban riders cut them down.

Still the Thebans dawdled while Lysander's army broadened his lines even further. It would not do. We were under no obligation to wait. I leaned over to Epaminondas. "Start the paean," I growled.

"It is not my place!" Epaminondas protested.

"Start the bloody paean!"

Epamimondas swallowed, and then, in his loudest voice, he began to sing the Theban paean that he had sung so often. My own voice joined his, and Thaletos picked up the song, his own booming voice joining our small chorus. The paean spread outward among the mass of armoured men. Shouting now, I began to march forward, quickening my pace with each step. To my side Epaminondas hurried to match my speed, as did the man beside him and so until the entire Theban army surged into a run. My armour chafed my skin with each stride, but I felt none of it, for I felt the *aristeia* welling up inside me. The battle-lust beat down the fear in my guts. My war-cry spread and the Theban paean was washed away by the screams of five thousand charging hoplites. A hundred paces now separated the two armies. Then fifty. Then only twenty.

Suddenly, amidst the ranks of helmeted faces arrayed against it, I saw it. The reflection of gold among the duller hues of tarnished bronze. It was like a glimpse of a brilliant songbird in the forest, a flash of colour out of the corner of your eye that disappears in an instant. And I knew. Lysander was among the mass of men in front of me. A greed for glory filled me, like a hunger. I felt the gods' eyes upon this place. We hit them.

It is the *othismos*, the instant of collision between two armies. The weight of the Theban hoplites slammed into the stagnant lines of Lysander's forces. The enemy's serried ranks buckled under the impact of flesh and bone and metal. And the killing began.

In the *othismos*, an underhanded spear-thrust carries the most power and is most likely to penetrate the defenses of the man facing you, a lesson my arms-master Neleus beat into me as youth. A man facing a charging enemy cannot help but raise his shield in anticipation of the impact to come. So it was now. I dropped low, Soul-Thief to knee height, driving the spear up under my shield just as the jarring shock of the collision thudded through my body.

The spear found the absorbing resistance of flesh rather than the unyielding barrier of wood and bronze as the blade skewered my opponent's groin. His scream was lost in the storm of noise around me, like a shout in a tempest. He dropped his weapon and collapsed, his free hand groping the fatal wound. The momentum of our charge pushed Lysander's ranks back and I stomped my foot into the wounded man's back before stepping over him to let the men behind me finish him off with the sharpened butts of their spears. I never saw his face.

I sensed Epaminondas to my left, stabbing furiously with his spear as my shield protected his exposed right side. Beyond him Thaletos matched me attack for attack. From behind me, Taras' spear darted back and forth over my shoulder like a serpents' tongue, flicking at the throats and faces of the enemy in front of me. Iron death sought me out as well, and many times blades grated past my helmet or deflected off the top of my shield. I roared in defiance at the hungry spears, returning each attack with one in kind.

I jerked my shield up to deflect an incoming spear from a few ranks back in the enemy line. I answered the blow as Soul-Thief reached deep into the enemy phalanx to murder my attacker with a jab to the neck. No sooner had the death occurred than it vanished from my consciousness. There was no time for thought, only a mindless need to push forward.

In the chaos of battle, being crushed by screaming bodies on all sides, his vision limited by his helmet, a man knows nothing. There is only the enemy in front of him, and whether the battle is being won or lost is a mystery. Only survival matters. I do not know how many men I sent to the Underworld that day. Soul-Thief proved her worth. Her ever-sharp point pierced and tore flesh and bone. One nameless enemy would fall only to be replaced by another. Stab, thrust, grab, claw, scream. Stomp on a fallen enemy or crash the edge of your shield down upon his neck before he rises to skewer your groin. That is the limit of the senses in battle.

And yet. For an experienced fighter, the phalanx is a body. He can sense whether it is strong or weak. Healthy or injured. Its parts coordinated as one, or its limbs working at cross-purposes. I felt it then. We were losing. Lysander's centre was holding while his flanks wrapped around our own.

The initial clash had been in our favour. Lysander's forces, in a battle they had not expected, could easily have crumpled under the vigour of the Theban assault. But they did not. Instead the enemy tightened their lines and the centre had held firm. With each passing moment, the advantage of the surprise attack dripped away. The Thebans were flagging and Lysander's superior numbers were beginning to assert themselves.

The fingers of Phobos, the god of Fear, reached into my chest. The sealed gates of Haliartos beckoned, whispering of refuge. But with Lysander's army between the Thebans and the city, our only path of escape was blocked. A vision of my sister and Tibetos flashed through my mind. My son. And Althaia.

The man in front of me pulled his shield in and stepped back. It was a simple trick, one that any experienced hoplite knew and that Neleus had beaten into me and I now drilled into the young fighters of the *peripoli*. But doubt had made my attention lapse and I suddenly found myself stumbling forward into the empty gap like a youth at his first lesson in arms. My shield dropped. My face and neck were exposed. I was a dead man.

A howl came from my left. With graceless haste I regained my balance, only to see that Epaminondas had thrown himself at the man opposite me and wrestling for control of the man's shield with his right hand. The man screamed at the thief who had stolen his victory over me. Taras' spear shot over me, its tip punching through my would-be killer's exposed cheek and out the other, shattering teeth and ripping flesh. The man shrieked through his ruined face. Epaminondas let go of the shield and the man stumbled back, his burst of courage suddenly snuffed out. Taras yanked me back into our line once more.

For a few ragged breaths, there was a gap between the two armies. It happens at times, after the initial clash, this lull in the battle. Two armies, as if by tacit agreement, step back from each other to recover and reassess the enemy before beginning the slaughter anew. The bloody-faced man glared at me over his shield, having recovered his courage despite his terrifying wound. My gaze rose to the walls of Haliartos that loomed a short distance behind him. My heart sank at what I saw.

I am taller than most men, and I could glimpse what was happening over the bristling field of spears of Lysander's army. The southern gate of Haliartos was open and armed men were pouring out. Where had they come from? Only a few Thebans had been left to garrison the city along with the few remaining *peripoli*. Had the numerous traitors of Haliartos somehow freed themselves to come to the aid Lysander and his army? If it were so, it would tip the scales so heavily in Lysander's favour that we were doomed to defeat. My hope wavered, for I feared that the Thebans, already sensing the tide of battle shifting against them, would break and run.

But the Thebans did not break. The pressure of shields at my back renewed itself. The same was not true of the enemy. Growing shouts of alarm drifted from the rear of the enemy ranks. The hoplite in front of me turned his mangled face to look over his shoulder, aware that something was amiss. It was a poor decision, for Taras' spear shot over my shoulder and pierced his exposed neck. He let out a gurgled scream and clamped a hand to the fatal wound. He dropped to his knees as his life pumped out through his fingers I was already stepping over him before he died.

The Thebans, on the verge of collapse only a few moments before, were sundering the enemy ranks. The weak bonds that had held Lysander's coalition together frayed and snapped as the enemy backed away from the death promised by our stabbing spears and slashing swords. My spear arm shot forward and retracted with the steady rhythm of a rower at his oar. More space opened before us as the enemy either died on our blades or fled before them. And then I saw him. Lysander.

Lysander had not fled, even as his allies abandoned him. As much as I hated him, the Spartan commander was no coward. And he was not alone. A wall of ten or more crimson-cloaked Spartiates blocked our path to their besieged leader. Their overlapping shields formed a half-ring of impenetrable scales coiled around the snake's head. There would be no grace or elegance to our attack. The Thebans, their blood inflamed by the tantalizing prospect of victory, fell upon their Spartan foes.

I drew my arm back and snapped my spear forward at the sword-wielding Spartan in front of me. The execution was perfect. The thrust flowed up through my planted feet and my pivoting hips and shoulder until the power of my entire body was concentrated in the tip that now flew at the Spartan's face like a thunderbolt. And it failed.

The Spartan jerked his shield to meet the spear blade, timing his movement perfectly. The blessing of Bendis was no match for the shield's reinforced centre. The ash shaft that held Soul-Thief splintered, and the spear blade now dangled uselessly by a few fibres of wood and leather cord. The Spartan let out a roar of victory as he launched himself at me. Seeing me weaponless, he hazarded a heavier attack, swinging his *kopis* sword in a high overhand blow meant to cleave my skull. In desperation, I dropped to one knee while flinging my shield up over my body. The movement caught the Spartan by surprise. The power of his overextended blow took him forward and suddenly I felt the weight of his body on the shield above me. With a great heave, I surged to my feet, propelling the Spartan up and over me. He grasped the edges of my shield, twisting my shoulder. The desperate tactic forced me to release the grip on the shield to stop my arm from being torn off. The Spartan fell to earth like a rock and landed flat on his back, the impact driving the air from his lungs. My broken spear was still in my hand, with Soul-Thief dangling from a few frayed fibres of wood. I tore the spear head free, and before the Spartan could recover, I dropped to my knees and stabbed the supine Spartan through the side of his neck.

Behind me I heard a war-cry. I scrabbled to my feet just in time to see Taras skewer a Spartan who had been about to attack my exposed back. With a scream Taras placed his foot on the Spartan's chest and ripped the spear free. The young warrior's face, spattered with blood and with bared teeth, was all but unrecognizable. Another Spartan advanced on the boy. Taras side-stepped his new opponent's spear lunge with casual ease before sending the stunned Spartan stumbling back under a flurry of ferocious stabs and thrusts. I glanced away and when I looked back the boy was lost in the chaotic melee that enveloped me. On all sides, Thebans and Spartans battered and hacked at each other in desperate combat. I spun, looking for another opponent. And then he was before me.

Lysander.

CHAPTER 37

Age had not diminished the Spartan leader's skills. The golden-armoured Lysander drove his spear through a Theban's breastplate, burying the blade deep in the man's guts. The weapon lodged in the Theban's body and Lysander abandoned the spear, his hand moving to the *kopis* sword at his waist. His darting gaze met mine and stopped as recognition flashed in his sword-sharp eyes. I wielded only Soul-Thief and bore no shield. Lysander, his teeth bared, launched himself at me.

I leapt straight up, bringing my knees up to my chest and kicking out both legs. My feet slammed into the centre of Lysander's shield. I twisted in the air and landed hard on my shoulder. The jarring impact of the kick stopped Lysander in his tracks, but that was all. Lysander recovered and found me lying helpless before him. My desperate tactic had only served to forestall my doom.

Defenceless as I was, lying on the ground made it awkward for Lysander to strike me with his sword. Instead he raised his broad shield high and drove it down towards my head. I rolled away and the shield slammed into the hard earth where my head had been. The shield cracked and shattered, so strong was the attack. Lysander tried to shuck off the flopping remnants of his shield. From my side, I kicked out my right leg and the sole of my boot punched into Lysander's gut. His gilded armour took the kick, but he gasped with the force of the blow, staggering back and dropping his sword. I clambered to my feet, wielding the still-pristine Soul-Thief like a dagger. Lysander had recovered from the kick and now, weaponless himself, saw the danger. He was a good warrior. Without hesitation, he threw himself at me as though we were in a wrestling contest and I leapt to meet him.

We collided like two rams. The crown of his golden helmet caught me hard on my cheek plate and my vision vanished in a flash of blinding light. Instinctively I wrapped my left arm around his back and pulled him close. With my right hand I stabbed at him with the broken spear-head. The tip caught a furrow of golden musculature. Soul-Thief's unbreakable point bit into the softer gilded bronze. Before I could wrench the blade free and strike again, Lysander seized my right wrist with his left hand, preventing the second attack that surely would have found his flesh. His right arm snaked around my back to hold me tight.

Like two lovers, we were locked in a rigid embrace. The foreheads of our helmets ground together, our eyes barely a hand's breadth apart in the midst of a sea of life and death struggles. Up and down I ground the broken spear-tip against the molded abdomen of the breastplate, working the blade deeper. Lysander's grip on my wrist tightened as we fought for control of the blade, oblivious to the chaos engulfing us.

I was the larger man, but Lysander had the better position. With his iron grip he was twisting my hand away slowly but surely. "You die today!" he hissed.

My gaze locked on his. I felt my grimace of effort twist into a mad smile. Through gritted teeth I mocked him. "I have stolen your gold!" I said, grunting as we shifted our weight. "Your army is dying around you!" And something sparked in his eyes, something I had never beheld in the man before: fear. Not a fear of death, but of failure. Suddenly, it was as if the rest of the world had gone silent. I whispered what he feared the most. "You will never be king of Sparta!" With my last reserves of strength I pushed the relentless blade forward.

Lysander's breastplate resisted valiantly but with a groan it yielded to the adamantine metal of the spear-tip. Lysander's jet-black eyes, so close to my own, widened as Soul-Thief bit hungrily into his skin beneath the armour. A desperate strength surged through him. His free hand pounded on my back and neck, seeking a vulnerable point. But Lysander's swell of power ebbed. No gods came to help him. The spear blade crept forward, its edges grating on the widening gap in the armour. The Spartan let out a groan through clenched teeth as the weapon penetrated metal and flesh up to its haft.

Lysander gasped from the shock of the insolent wound. His body shuddered in protest at the obscenity being done to it. The god-man went limp and the weight of him did what Lysander could not do in life as the earth pulled him from my arms.

I spun about, seeking another opponent. But there was no need. Lysander's army had broken and fled. Some of the Thebans, inflamed with blood-lust, pursued the enemy and hacked them down without mercy. More, however, put self-interest above vengeance and were already stripping the broken, ruined enemy bodies of valuable armour and weapons.

Close to me were Epaminondas and Taras, standing in a daze with battered shields and bloody swords. Relief flooded my heart. They had fought bravely against Sparta's best and survived. Farther away was the sturdy Thaletos, who was now dispatching any wounded Spartans with cold thrusts of his spear. There was a madness in his eyes that had yet to be sated.

I looked back at Epaminondas. Drops of blood covered his face and chest. A deep tear in his shoulder was oozing blood through a mess of congealing gore."Epaminondas!" I called. "See to your wound!" Epaminondas looked down at his arm, frowning at the indignity done to his flesh. When he returned his gaze to me, his eyes had a hardness to them. The gruesome reality of battle had burned away his friendly, studious innocence. Battle was not arranging men like they were pieces on a gameboard. It was where men shat themselves with fear and pissed their armour. It was where men held onto their spilled guts as they cried out for their mothers. It was where the *keres*, daughters of the night, gorged themselves on fresh corpses left to rot in the sun. Battle transformed men into something little better than savage beasts.

And battle had altered something deep in Epaminondas. I could feel his new aura like heat on my skin. He had become something greater, something more unyielding. A shiver passed through me. It might have been a premonition that the young man before me would one day bend all of Greece to his will. Perhaps it was hint of future sorrow, as if I knew that one day on the plain of Mantinea I would cradle him in my arms as his stubborn shade clung to his dying body. I shook off my unease. "Go to your sister," I ordered him. "She will tend to your injury."

Epaminondas blinked away his delirium. "And what shall I tell her of you?"

Tell her what indeed? That to see her now was the only thing I craved? That the distraction of her in my mind had nearly ended in my death on the battlefield? "Tell her I will return to her soon." Epaminondas let out the barest shake of his head before following my command to depart.

I turned my attention to Taras. "Taras!" The boy did not respond. "Taras! You did well!" The lad's empty eyes regarded me as if I were a stranger. Only then did I take in the number of slain enemies that lay near him, some with the long braids of Spartiate warriors. Had Taras not been my protector, I surely would have perished to a spear in the back while I struggled with Lysander. Like Achilles of old, Taras stood there among the dead, whose flesh he had torn and pierced, whose guts he had spilled on the ground before Haliartos. Such had been his terrible skill that though crimson glistened on every part of him, I perceived no wounds marring his body. Rivulets of tears trickled down his face, carving tiny tracks through the blood and dripping onto his stained armour. And I saw his soul was rent and torn even if his body was not. For Taras was not a murderer in his heart. Not a soulless monster who kills as if he were born to it. Not like me.

Thaletos saw it too. "You fought bravely, Boy. A testament to your teacher's skill," he said with a glance my way. My face tightened. Thaletos laid his arm across the young man's shoulders. "Come with me. A drink is needed!"

Taras blinked at him. Thaletos gently guided him towards the gates of Haliartos. I moved to follow them.

A hand gripped my ankle."Daimon!"

The ashen face of Lysander stared up at me. The erstwhile god of Sparta lay on his back, his shade still clinging to this world. Soul-Thief's base protruded from the golden armour. He had been my adversary for so long. He was ruthless and cunning. He had taken so much away from me, and there were many more who had suffered greater losses than me because of his ambition. I should have cut his throat. Instead I knelt down and propped up the dying Spartan.

Lysander winced. He gathered his strength with a few rasping breaths. "I should have killed you," he said through gritted teeth. He spoke without anger and only as a statement of fact. "At Ephesus. I should have killed you then."

Ephesus. It had been many years earlier when I was hardly more than a boy. It was my first battle and Lysander had smashed us. I had gone to Lysander after the slaughter to request permission to collect our dead. He had frightened me then. "You remember?" I asked, surprised.

Lysander smiled through his pain. "The boy who came to claim the dead while better men cowered by their ships? Yes, I remember, Daimon of Athens." His face twisted in discomfort as he fought against his dying body. When the pain had passed, he surprised me again. "I granted your request at that time and now I have a request of you, Athenian."

I scoffed. "Even in death, you are bold, Spartan!" But somehow he had intrigued me. "Speak, Spartan, so that I can deny you one last time!"

His eyes blazed with the harsh light of old. "Avenge me!"

It was the madness of a dying man. "Avenge you? I don't understand."

Disappointment washed across the god-man's face. "Against those who have forsaken me! Against Sparta!"

I saw the bitterness that rotted his soul. I saw too that it was like peering at my own distorted reflection in a rippling pool of water. A man, an outsider, who, despite his achievements, was never truly accepted by his own people. "Is that all?" I asked coldly.

Lysander managed a weak laugh. "I know you will find a way! Vengeance is your nature!" His laugh turned into a cough, speckling my face with blood. His sword-sharp eyes dulled.

And then, in my arms, a god died.

I PUSHED OFF LYSANDER'S CORPSE and rose to my feet. I was left surveying the plain before the walls of Haliartos. Hundreds of dead lay scattered about while the living stripped their fallen enemies of their valuable armour and weapons. We were victorious. But I still did not know why.

The answer to my question came in the form of some familiar figures tramping towards me. One of the armoured figures limped my way, raising a hand in greeting. "Dammo!"

I embraced Tibetos before stepping back. "You saved me again," I said wearily, exhaustion suddenly catching up with me.

"You looked like you needed help," Tibetos said, not a little smugly.

The rest of the small force of *peripoli* stood behind Tibetos. Ferocious fighters all, but hardly enough to turn the tide of battle by themselves. There was a new face as well. I pointed at Pibos. The freed slave held a bloodied spear and was equipped with an odd assortment of armour. "What is he doing here?"

Tibetos put an arm around Pibos' shoulders. "Pibos here reminded me that there were hundreds of able men sitting in the agora along with armour and weapons confiscated from the Haliartans. They just needed the right incentive."

"Incentive?"

"I promised the male slaves their freedom if they took up arms against Lysander."

I frowned. "The Thebans aren't going to be happy about that."

Tibetos shrugged. "A small price to pay for victory."

I turned to Pibos. "Once again, Pibos, it seems I owe you a great debt. For now tell your fellow freedmen that they should identify themselves as *peripoli* of Athens. Let it be known they are under my protection."

Pibos gave a small bow. "I will do so," he said before hurrying away to spread the news.

"*Peripoli?*" Stachys said, watching Pibos go. "All of them?"

I waved the question away with a tired hand. "We'll worry about it later." For now, I had questions of a more urgent nature. "How is Meli?"

A cloud passed over Tibetos' face. "She is strong. She will recover."

I put a hand on my friend's shoulder. "There is no one stronger. And Althaia?" The mention of Epaminondas' sister made Mnasyllus shuffle embarrassedly.

"She is taking care of Meli."

"And the other matter?" I asked. "With the gold?"

Mnasyllus spoke up. "Taken care of as you instructed, Dammo!" A glimpse of sun on a dark day.

Sabas pointed at the golden-armoured corpse of Lysander. "Your doing?" he asked. I nodded. The Cretan gave an exasperated shake of his head. "'Tyrant-Slayer' is bad enough, but don't tell me we'll have to call you 'God-Slayer' now!" he moaned. The *peripoli* laughed.

The respite of levity was brief, overshadowed by the approach of a group of Thebans with Ismenias at their head. A few paces behind were the cunning Leontiades and the odious Eurymachus. The grime of battle covered their armour. They had made a good show of loyalty, then. The *peripoli* fell silent as the Thebans drew near. Their leader, Ismenias, raised a hand in greeting. "Your timely reports have brought us victory this day, Daimon! Thebes is grateful! And

Lysander dead, at your hand, I believe," he said with a disdainful glance at the dead Spartan general. "A great victory indeed!" The other Thebans offered none of Ismenias' gracious praise. Leontiades and his son regarded me with undisguised loathing

I swept my arm towards Tibetos and the *peripoli*. "It was my comrades who won the day." I briefly explained how the *peripoli* and the freed slaves of Haliartos had turned the battle.

Eurymachus broke his scowling silence. He pointed an accusing finger at me. "Just like an Athenian to steal undeserved honour from others! Look at him trying to claim victory for himself!" This elicited a sympathetic rumble where Ismenias' praise had met only resentment. "And he has freed the slaves? He has no right to do so!"

"I also found your gold, Theban," I said casually. Eurymachus flinched, his tirade suddenly cut short by the revelation. Leontiades glared at me but wisely held his tongue. Alerted by his son of the gold's likely discovery, it was clear that he had steeled himself for just such an outcome. Ismenias listened with interest as I described the pots of gold darics we had found hidden in the rundown house with the mercenary Kepheos.

Leontiades, wilier than his son, stepped in to minimize the political damage. "It was clearly that scoundrel Kepheos' doing!" Leontiades shook his head sadly in a poor attempt at looking contrite. "It shames me that a man *formerly* in my employ is responsible for such acts."

I was having none of it. "Everyone here knows you have conspired with Sparta, Theban," I said.

Leontiades curled his lip. "You dare accuse us of treachery?" He stepped forward, rising to the moment. "Look at our battered shields and bloodied armour! Look at our shattered spears and blunted swords! You accuse us of cowardice and treason, but these things are witnesses to our fidelity to Thebes! We fought the forces of Lysander and the rebels of Haliartos as much as any man today! Look at these things and call me a traitor again, Athenian!"

Eurymachus sneered at my frustration. With a roar I lunged at him. As we grappled amid the uproar, our heads ground together and we exchanged words that only we could hear.

"Do you think you can protect her from me, Athenian?" Eurymachus whispered.

"Touch her and you are a dead man!" I said through clenched teeth.

Eurymachus snorted at my threat. "You and your false god are powerless to touch me!"

Before I could respond, strong arms tore us apart. Ismenias shoved his way between us. "Battle inflames the blood and clouds judgment!" the Theban leader said loudly. I glared at the Eurymachus, who was readjusting his armour. Ismenias raised his arms. "Let us depart and discuss matters later when cooler heads prevail." The Thebans began to depart.

I was frustrated. Leontiades had read the situation well. His actions on the battlefield and subsequent disavowal of Kepheos had blunted any accusations I could throw at him. The aristocrat had failed this time but was still a poison in the heart of Thebes. The victorious smirk he allowed himself as he tramped by with his sneering son was proof enough of his duplicity. And there was nothing I could do.

Ismenias took up the rear of the departing Thebans. As he passed, I seized his arm and pulled him close. "Sleeping with scorpions is a bad idea. You would do well to crush them now before they come back to sting you, Theban!" I whispered in his ear. Leontiades and Eurymachus, out of earshot, were watching me closely. They knew well enough what I was saying to Ismenias.

Ismenias gently freed his arm from my grip. "You are still young, Athenian, ruled by passion rather than good sense. They fought well today. There is nothing I can do." Powerless, I watched him go. He was wrong. A scorpion can lie concealed under a rock for months, biding its time. And I knew Leontiades had the patience of a scorpion. But that was a matter for the future. Now there was a more imminent threat than the thwarted Leontiades.

I looked to the east. Lysander's was just the first Spartan army we would have to face. Pausanias and his even larger force would arrive the next day.

We would need a miracle from the gods to win.

As usual, the gods were silent.

But our salvation, when it came the next morning, was in the form of a man.

CHAPTER 38

Pausanias, the elder of the two Spartan kings, frowned at the distant army arrayed before the walls of Haliartos. He had expected to join up with Lysander's forces but it could be an enemy army. But if it were Lysander, why had he arranged his soldiers on the plain? Pausanias squinted. It could be anywhere from four to six thousand troops, he reckoned, depending on how deep their ranks were. He had nine thousand fighting men at his command, including his personal bodyguard of three hundred Spartiates. On the flat plain, he felt confident of victory, were it to come to that.

But if they were the enemy, they were behaving in an odd fashion. An army chattered and shuffled to push down the growing fear of the battle to come. Soldiers bragged of the feats they would do that day, or checked the straps of their armour for the hundredth time. This army was so still and silent that it could have been an army of statues. His gaze fixed on the eerily quiet ranks in the distance, Pausanias addressed the *polemarch* at his side. "Kleagoras, form a line to match theirs."

"Yes, O *basileus*!" the general said with a snap in his voice. Pausanias, still facing Haliartos, listened to Kleagoras as the *polemarch* relayed his orders with confident efficiency. Kleagoras had done well for himself after the war with Athens, Pausanias thought. He was one of a new breed of Spartiates following the lead of Lysander, ambitious and ruthless. There had been some scandal when he had inherited his father's considerable wealth instead of his elder brother. It had gone against the laws of their forefathers, but then again many traditions were falling by the wayside. Wealthy Spartans! Wills and legal disputes! They were hardly better than the Athenians now. Pausanias sighed inwardly. He would have to keep an eye on Kleagoras at the very least.

Kleagoras returned, pulling his horse up beside the mounted Pausanias. "The army awaits your command!" he reported briskly.

Pausanias glanced over his shoulder. Indeed the soldiers had already consolidated themselves into a solid line of metal and flesh. His Spartiate bodyguard held the position of honour on the right flank. His cavalry was arrayed in three loose lines in front of the allied hoplites, ready to drive off any Boeotian horsemen that they might face. The Spartan king felt his confidence rise. The enemy would be foolish to face him this day!

But still... He squinted once more towards the distant army. Was that a flash of Spartan red among them? Pausanias knew his eyesight was not what it had once been. There was some movement at the centre of the mysterious army. The King leaned forward, straining to make out what was happening. The ripple of movement resolved itself into a modest contingent of horsemen advancing at a trot.

"They're sending a delegation of some sort," Kleagoras observed, confirming what Pausanias was seeing. "Should we ride out to meet them?"

If Kleagoras had a shortcoming, it was that he sometimes let his impatience get the better of him. "No need to be hasty," Pausanias said dryly. His *polemarch*'s face tightened at the mild rebuke, the king noted with satisfaction. "Let us see who it is we're dealing with first."

The aging king's eyes had not deceived him. The crimson of the Spartan cloaks flashed against the landscape like a spatter of blood on burnished armour. The line of red-clad horsemen made the unmistakable white cloak at their centre stand out all the more. Only one person dressed so. Pausanias spat out an unkingly curse, drawing a curious stare from Kleagoras, who had the tact to stay silent. Lysander! The half-breed upstart had arrived first and claimed the city!

Damn him to Hades! Pausanias thought, glaring across the plain. It was just like the arrogant prick to put on such a display. He still had pretensions of power! *I should have had him killed long ago.* But Lysander had stayed out of his reach in Asia for more than a year. Word was that the former hegemon had squandered what little goodwill King Agesilaus still had for his former mentor and lover. If Lysander thought he would find haven in Greece, he was sorely mistaken.

Suddenly he swore again. Lysander and his retinue had come to a halt halfway between the two armies. It was clear he wanted Pausanias to ride out to meet him as equals. Kleagoras looked at Pausanias, awaiting his king's command. Pausanias ground his teeth.

In his six decades, Pausanias had seen many battles. He was no great strategist — something he was all too well aware of — but he was no coward either. He had stood alongside his fellow Spartans in the phalanx, and his sculpted breastplate bore the dents and scratches to prove it. One thing his experience had taught him, though, was to adapt when the Fates conspired against him. He was a survivor.

At least I can make that bastard half-breed wait, Pausanias thought spitefully. "With me, Kleagoras. And do not speak until I have." He flicked his reins and his black horse advanced at a plodding walk. Kleagoras brought up the rear, bringing with him a dozen cavalry to match the number Lysander had with him.

With deliberate slowness, the Spartan king led his retinue forward. He could see Lysander clearly now, his damn gilded armour glinting brilliantly in the late morning sun. Even his greaves had ridiculous lion heads at the knees! The love of ornamentation and ostentation that had infected Sparta stemmed from this man, Pausanias knew. Once Lysander was dead, Pausanias would enforce the code of frugality and simple living that had made Sparta great. Some, like Kleagoras, would object, he knew. But he was the king and they would fall in line soon enough For the moment, though, Lysander was still alive with an army at his back. He would be a useful ally in the war to come. Once the horse-shagging Thebans and the restless Athenians were put in their place, there would be plenty of time to deal with Lysander. For now, though, Pausanias would have to bide his time. The king took a deep breath and came to a halt half a dozen spear-lengths from the former hegemon.

On either side Lysander was flanked by five red-cloaked Spartans, stalwart soldiers who had probably been with their leader for their entire military lives. In his heart, Pausanias envied the loyalty Lysander aroused in his men. He wondered if he would be able to count on them once their commander was dead. If not, they would soon follow him to the Underworld, Spartan or not. But first Pausanias would wait for Lysander to acknowledge his king.

The strange silence drew out to the point of awkwardness as the two parties regarded each other across the patch of sun-beaten Boeotian plain. A few horses pawed at the ground restlessly. Pausanias waited, as still as a statue. Lysander truly was a fool if he thought he, Pausanias, King of Sparta, would address him first!

Lysander's patience broke first. The former hegemon of Greece placed his hands on the sides of his head to remove his ornate helmet. *Thank the Twin Gods!* Pausanias thought to himself, relieved to have won the battle of wills.

Then the thin smile died on the king's lips, transforming into a look of slack-jawed, furiously-blinking confusion as Lysander revealed himself.

For it was not the hateful Lysander that grinned back at him now. It was me.

I TUCKED LYSANDER'S GOLDEN HELM under my arm and raised my free hand in salutation. "Hail, King Pausanias!"

The Spartan king's mouth flapped open and closed like that of a gasping fish. I half-expected the old man to drop dead from shock. His bodyguards tensed at the sight of me. Their sudden agitation infected their horses, which began to shuffle and toss their heads. My own party, to their credit, barely twitched a muscle.

The king managed to bring his wayward jaw to heel. "And what of Lysander?" he demanded, biting each word.

My hand drifted to the rent in the breastplate's flank. "Dead," I said. "At my hand." A glimmer of satisfaction flickered across the Spartan king's face and was gone. It was no wonder. Pausanias was certainly pleased that his rival was dead. But Spartan honour had been stained, something that could not go unchallenged.

The king's eyelids twitched as his mind grappled with this new reality. He mustered back some composure and gave me a calculating stare. Perhaps something could be salvaged. "Do you have his body?" he asked, forcing a haughty tone.

I gave a slight jerk of my head towards Haliartos. "His corpse still lies before the walls, along with those of many of your countrymen." I paused. "Hundreds of them, in fact."

The king's guards drew their swords, shouting and cursing us as they did so, but were silenced by the raised hand of Pausanias. "You will return them to us," he declared.

I frowned in mock confusion and scratched at my helmet-matted hair. "You approach me as a supplicant, requesting access to your dead, Pausanias?" I asked, addressing the king in a familiar fashion.

A red glow began creeping up the king's face like a growing fire. "You dare ask this of me?" he asked, fighting to keep his composure.

I shrugged innocently. "We are the victors, Spartan. We hold the field. It is not *our* place to request truces, only to grant them."

The king scoffed. "Your boldness is without foundation. We outnumber you by thousands. My men are fresh. We will crush you if you come to battle. You should retreat while you have the chance."

But I had one more surprise for Pausanias and his army. "You are wrong, Spartan." I made a small wave, and at the cue, Stachys, disguised in his Spartan cloak, took out a *salpynx,* raised the horn to his lips, and blew three sharp notes.

I did not need to look at what was happening behind me. The look of growing dread on the king's face told me Thrasybulus had heard the trumpet blast and was moving his forces into position. The *strategos* had arrived in the morning after an all-night march. More importantly, he had brought with him more than five thousand Athenian hoplites, who were now spreading out on the plain in front of Haliartos. Now it was Pausanias who was outnumbered.

"Perhaps you wish to reconsider my terms, Spartan," I said coldly, letting my words stab deep. I twisted the knife further. "I guarantee your men safe passage to collect your dead Spartiates, otherwise they will be food for crows and foxes. You only need to ask."

Pausanias winced as if in pain as he struggled with the dilemma. For a heartbeat I thought I had pushed him too far and he would abandon the corpses of his countrymen. But duty to the dead won out, and the king's shoulders dropped a fraction as his spirit broke. "I agree to your terms," he said, spitting the words out as if they were poison.

"You may send three hundred men, unarmed. Swear your good faith to whatever gods you wish," I said.

"By the twin gods, I swear it!" he hissed. His bodyguards glared at us, but they were bound by their king's oath.

With his bitter humiliation still strong, the king's gaze moved across my companions, noting too late that all lacked the long oiled braids common among Spartan warriors. Except one. Pausanias fixed an icy stare upon the man beside me. "Who are you, Spartan?"

The horse beside me advanced a few steps and stopped. The rider removed his helmet. "I am Neon, son of Heitor."

The Spartans could contain their rage no longer. Shouting and hurling curses, they brandished their spears at Neon, their advance only checked by the levelled spears of my own men. Neon and I had not moved, nor had Pausanias. With a raised hand, the king held back his soldiers' rage, frayed though his authority was. Like a pack of dogs restrained by their master's command, the Spartans growled and bristled but did not attack.

The Spartan beside Pausanias kicked his horse forward a few steps. By his striped, transverse crest, I knew him to be a *polemarch*. The Spartan general pointed at Neon. "You are a traitor to Sparta! I will flay you myself!"

Neon turned his head a touch to regard the Spartan general. For such a small movement, it echoed with disdain. "Brother," he said simply.

The *polemarch* lifted his helmet to reveal the glowering face of Neon's brother. The likeness to Neon was striking. "I would sooner call a pig my brother than you," he sneered.

Neon was unmoved. "I see you are a *polemarch* now, Kleagoras. I know it is a reward not earned on merit." Neon addressed Pausanias. "How much silver did it cost him?"

Pausanias reddened at the insult. "A man with no honour dares cast such an accusation?" he huffed.

"Honour abandoned Sparta long ago," Neon said in his flat voice. His gaze shifted to his brother. "As it did my own family."

The king's vaunted Spartan self-control deserted him. "You are exiled, Neon, son of Heitor," Pausanias exploded. "If you return to Sparta, you will be killed on sight!"

I barked a laugh. "I should worry more about your own fate, Pausanias," I observed. "I have slain a Spartan *polemarch* and a Spartan hegemon, and I would gladly display a Spartan king's armour among my trophies." I bared my teeth at him. "And I owe you a death from Thrace," I hissed.

Pausanias' eye twitched, for he knew of whom I spoke. The death of the boy Sosias on the order of Pausanias was one that weighed heavy on my heart. The Spartan king collected himself and responded with a threat of his own. Pulling himself straight, he returned my stare. "I protected Athens from destruction when your newfound Theban allies would have razed it to the ground and turned it into pasture for their horses. No such mercy will be extended by Sparta this time."

I gave the king a wicked smile and glanced at the army at my back. "Only if you defeat us, Spartan."

Pausanias growled and wheeled his horse around. His bodyguard followed suit. Kleagoras shot his brother one last baleful stare before riding after his king.

For a moment, we reflected on the backs of the receding Spartans. I looked over at Neon. "You are welcome among the *peripoli*, Neon of Sparta," I said. There was a murmur of agreement from my comrades.

Neon was still staring at the dwindling figure of his brother. At last he spoke. "We should return to the army," was all he said. I shrugged and flicked the reins of my horse. Our party of false Spartans galloped back towards the walls of Haliartos.

Thrasybulus awaited us. The *strategos* was dressed in his hoplite panoply, ready for battle should it come. His was not the ostentatious armour of a king or an aristocrat, but practical gear not dissimilar to that of the men around him. I had no doubt that Thrasybulus would fight ferociously in the front rank if battle came. His courage was not in doubt. But Thrasybulus was above all a shrewd politician; always a man of the people, at least in public, I thought. I dismounted and approached the First Man of Athens.

 Will he fight?" Thrasybulus asked.

"Pausanias is a coward," I said.

Thrasybulus was unconvinced. "You have shamed him in front of his men. Do not underestimate a man whose honour has been challenged."

But I had looked into the Spartan king's eyes. I knew. "A coward," I repeated.

A growing cheer rose from the combined forces of Athens and Thebes. The distant Spartan army was beginning to break up.

Like the coward he was, Pausanias was running away.

PART FOUR

BAKXAI BACCHAE

CHAPTER 39

I wiped a dusty forearm across my dripping brow. Perspiration had long since soaked through the leather strap I had tied to keep my hair back. Blinking away a rogue drop of sweat, I took the moment of respite to take in the scene.

As far as the eye could see, men toiled at their tasks like an army of slaves, the tang of their sweat and clamour of their shouts and grunts filling the air. To be sure, many of them were slaves, but most were free men of Athens. There were not a few women as well; modesty was no excuse for absence. From sunrise to sunset we pushed ourselves with enthusiasm born of urgency, for we knew what would happen should we fail at our task. The very survival of Athens itself was at stake. We were rebuilding the walls of Athens. All of them.

I gave a tired smile. Nearly ten years earlier, I had endured Spartan whips and taunts as we had been forced to tear down the walls that had protected Athens for so long. Now I was helping rebuild the defences from the rubble of the old walls and any other stone that could be salvaged.

The walls were only half-completed, but already offered a fair measure of defence. I shielded my eyes from the sun to inspect progress to the west. The twin lines of the growing Long Walls stretched back towards the rocky hills of Athens in the distance. Closer to where I was, the walls of Piraeus and the harbour construction were farther along. When completed, Athens would once again become an island of sorts and almost invulnerable to a land army.

A young boy appeared at the top of the wall, a dozen or more water-skins strapped around his person. He was breathing heavily from the effort of hauling the heavy load. Seeing me, he unburdened himself of one skin and offered it to me. "*Pater*," Niko said. I took the water from my son gratefully and drank deeply. Niko watched me silently as he caught his breath.

The boy was adjusting to life in the *peripoli* compound better than I had expected. He missed his tutor Iasos, but still had the company of the dour slave Xanthias. Sometimes the two of them would visit Iasos' tomb outside the city walls.

A booming voice jerked me from my ruminations. "*Archos*! Are you shirking your duties? You will set a poor example for your men!" Thrasybulus, his bare torso as grimy and sun-darkened as that of any man present, strode towards me. I glanced back at Niko, but the boy had already scurried away to deliver refreshment to other thirsty labourers atop the wall.

I extended the water-skin towards Thrasybulus. He took it gratefully and slaked his thirst with mouth-filling glugs. *Archos*. Commander. I did not contradict Thrasybulus any longer. The weight of the responsibility that came with the rank was heavy. But I had given in and accepted the burden of authority. Reluctantly. I shook my head to myself.

The gesture did not go unnoticed by Thrasybulus. "Is there a problem, *archos*?" he asked, frowning. He insisted on addressing me by my new title, only resorting to calling me by my name when we butted heads over strategy, which was often enough.

"Nothing, *strategos*," I replied. "Just recalling the last time I stood atop these walls."

Thrasybulus nodded knowingly. "They were good men," he said, as if reading my thoughts. "They are not forgotten." For a moment, there was nothing more to say, and we watched the industry around us. Thrasybulus had initiated the wall-building project and set about mobilizing the people of Athens to undertake the monumental task. Given his position, he could have stayed in Athens to coordinate the work of others, but chose to haul rocks with the rest of us. He moved to a different work site each day to check progress and be seen by the people. It was shrewd politicking but sincere for all that, for he was a good man.

He took another deep swig from the water-skin and wiped his mouth. "With the war coming, I will be able to convince the assembly to free more funds for the *peripoli*," he said, abruptly changing topics. Thrasybulus was always more interested in looking to future possibilities than dwelling on past tragedies. "Then we can talk about those plans of yours."

"That would be appreciated, *strategos*," I said. More money was always welcome. Especially for the ambitious proposal I had broached to Thrasybulus. There were hundreds of new *peripoli* from Pibos and the other freed slaves of Haliartos. I had a plan to use them in the war ahead.

The most influential man in Athens cleared his throat. "It might be some time. I would be willing to loan you a talent or two in the meantime," he offered casually. Thrasybulus was a very wealthy man for all his conspicuous modesty.

"That is unnecessary, *strategos*," I said. "But I might hold you to your offer in the future."

He raised an eyebrow, for above all things Thrasybulus had a keen ear for what was left unsaid. "You have money?" he asked.

I was not to be drawn out. "As I said, *strategos*, you might regret your promise, but not today," I replied a touch curtly. Thrasybulus narrowed his eyes before surrendering with a shrug.

It was true that I did not need money. The Persian gold had been returned to the Thebans. Most of it at least. Leontiades, like all greedy men, had likely skimmed a few talents for himself as payment for his services to Lysander. There was also the matter of the five talents now hidden away in the *peripoli* compound. Not stolen, of course. Just fair compensation for my services. As we had returned from Haliartos a few months earlier, Stachys, his panniers laden with Persian coins, had laughed at my sophistry all the way back to Athens. Let him laugh, for it was enough to pay my debts and keep the *peripoli* in the field for years.

Thrasybulus had been right about setting an example. The *peripoli,* observing that Thrasybulus had stopped working, took that as their cue to grab a moment's rest.

We watched as Niko picked his way over the uneven surface to the next section of wall where Neon was labouring. The Spartan rubbed a hand through his closely-cropped hair and flicked away the sweat. He had shorn his Spartan braids upon his return to Athens. His meaning was clear and the *peripoli* had welcomed him with open arms. He was one of us now.

Neon accepted a water-skin from Niko, who scampered away to the workers farther along. Neon did not drink himself, instead handing the bulging leather bag to his work companion Iollas. The two men were an odd pair. The tall soldier of Sparta dwarfed the wiry figure of the former helot, but more strange was that the two had become close friends. Neon said something, and Iollas bared his jagged, yellow teeth in a barking laugh.

My gaze drifted to where Tibetos was working. My friend listened intently as Stachys explained something or other, while beside him

Mnasyllus swigged mightily from a water-skin. The big man had practically built their section of wall himself. Another among their number noticed me watching. Young Taras waved at me, a broad smile across his face.

I nodded at the boy, a wave of sadness passing through me. Soon he would be gone. I would miss him. But I could not blame anyone but myself, for his imminent departure was my doing.

I had summoned the lad to my office a few days earlier. When he entered, I rose from my chair, glowering at him. He cringed under my glare.

"Why have you called me, *lochagos*?" he asked, no doubt wondering what he had done now to spark my anger.

"I have heard," I said, scowling, "that you intend to wed the slave girl Keaera." Keaera had confided such to my sister, who in turn had let slip the news to me.

Taras flushed. "She is a slave no longer," he said, pointedly not denying my charge.

"I think you are too young to wed. Would you not agree?"

Taras stuck out his chest in defiance and I had to struggle not to crack a smile. "I have fought in battle, so I think I am old enough."

I snorted. "And where did you plan to live, Boy? You and this young wife of yours?"

Taras winced. "I thought I could live here, with the *peripoli*. There are some men who have wives here."

I shook my head. "It will not do! This is not a village, Boy!" I growled, ignoring for the moment that the *peripoli* compound was in fact very much a small village.

Taras, his plan fraying before his eyes, looked desperate. "Then what are we to do, *lochagos*?"

I gave him an ultimatum. "If you wed, you will have to leave the *peripoli.*"

"But I have no money!"

"What of your gains from Haliartos?" I asked. Like all who had fought, Taras had his share of the booty stripped from the dead and vanquished."

"It will not sustain us for long!"

I shrugged. "Can you not return to your father's farm?"

Taras bristled at the suggestion. "You know I cannot." As the fourth and youngest son, Taras would inherit little. It was one of the things that had driven the lad to seek out the *peripoli* in the first place. Taras looked at me imploringly. "Can you not reconsider, *lochagos*?"

I made an exaggerated sigh. "I would not throw you out completely destitute, Boy." I directed his attention to the numerous sacks on the table. "Open one," I said.

Taras picked up a bag, frowning at its unexpected weight. He undid the cord and gasped, dropping the bag on the table. Silver drachmae spilled out. He stared at the coins in confusion. "I don't understand, *lochagos*."

I folded my arms across my chest. "What's to understand, you fool? The money is yours. Take it."

Taras squinted in perplexity as though I were speaking Persian to him. "*Lochagos*?"

"Keaera has no father to offer a dowry. So I will provide one. It is enough to buy a good piece of land, I think," I said, waving my hand at the bags. "After that you're on your own."

Taras' gaze drifted over the other bulging sacs. "They are all filled with drachmae?" he asked.

"Yes," I said. I had converted a good sum of the Persian gold I had claimed into less suspicious drachmae. The money-changers took their cut, but they would have been very brave men indeed if they sought to cheat me.

"I could never repay this debt, *lochagos*," Taras had sputtered finally, blinking at the bags of silver coins.

"It is your bride's dowry," I said, brushing aside his protest. "If you wish to repay me, you can do so by cultivating your land and having many children and raising them well." I had no doubt Thrasybulus could be persuaded to part with one of his many parcels of land at a fair price.

Taras seemed to struggle with indecision. "But what of the *peripoli, lochagos*?"

"We are going nowhere. You can return when you are older." I hoped that he never would. It was not the life for a kind boy like Taras, despite his skill. But he had a chance for a life that I would never have. A better life.

The silent force of my will must have swayed him, for he suddenly broke out in a broad smile as he finally saw the potential future that lay before him. "Thank you, *lochagos*!"

"Now go, before I change my mind, Boy!" I barked.

Taras snapped to attention. "Yes, *lochagos*!" He spun and marched out of the building. At the door, he stopped and turned towards me, joy and excitement in his eyes. "You are a good man, *lochagos*!" he said before hurrying off to share his good fortune with his future bride. I frowned at his words. He did not know me well enough.

Taras had insisted on remaining until the Long Walls between Athens and Piraeus were rebuilt. Now, under the morning sun, he turned to accept a water skin from one of his comrades. I looked at the lad and smiled to myself. I would miss his wool-headed innocence.

But in Athens, for every man that departs, two more arrive to take their place. As if to prove my point, I caught sight of just such a recent arrival approaching the base of the wall where Thrasybulus and I were taking our rest. The newcomer climbed the ladder with an agility that belied his age. I extended a hand to pull him up the last step. "I did not expect to see you here today, Admiral," I said.

The normally serious Konon allowed himself a smile. "I heard the *strategos* was in the area and came to have a word," he said. Thrasybulus came forward and the two men shook hands warmly.

Thrasybulus stepped back and gave Konon a critical stare. "I can see that you didn't come to get your hands dirty," he said wryly, gesturing at the admiral's fine patterned tunic and heavy silver necklace.

"I leave that to more worthy men!" Konon conceded with a bow. The two men laughed and moved off to discuss their business.

I appraised Konon. The admiral had only recently returned to Athens, openly this time. The manner of the former *strategos'* return more than earned him the right to absent himself from toiling at the walls with the rest of the population; he had his own duties to attend to.

A few months earlier, he had been across the sea in Ionia serving his master Pharnabazus. Under Konon's command, the Persian navy had trapped the Spartan fleet at Knidos and smashed it, sending Sparta's Asian ambitions to the bottom of the sea once and for all. A grateful Pharnabazus had released Konon from his service, permitting the admiral to return home to Athens to join in the war against Sparta.

Konon had not come alone. With him he had brought more than a hundred warships, a gift to Athens from the Great King of the Persians and guaranteed to keep Athens and Sparta tearing at each other's throats for years to come. I peered towards the sea. A dozen triremes were practicing manoeuvres. With the Spartan forces abandoning Asia, all of Ionia would fall under Persian rule once more. A hundred warships was a small price to pay for such a prize. In the looming war between Athens and Sparta, Persia and the cunning Pharnabazus would be the true victors.

Yet with walls and ships, Athens was once more a power to be reckoned with. She was reborn, rising from the ashes of ruin and servitude. But Sparta would not yield power willingly. The war was just beginning.

But before that I had one more thing to do. A secret mission of my own.

I had been summoned to Thebes.

CHAPTER 40

I was just another shadow lurking in the laneways of Thebes.

The shroud of darkness gave me comfort, for it shielded me from the curious stares and other unwanted attention. There were still those in Thebes who wished me harm, so it was better that my presence remain secret, even from Epaminondas. Any attacker would find me well-armed. I felt the reassuring familiar weight of Whisper slung across my back. The rhomphaia was no worse for wear from having spent a few days submerged in the marsh outside the walls of Haliartos, retrieved by some local boys who were thrilled by the gold daric I paid them for their efforts.

Like any nighttime in Athens, there were a few drunken revellers returning home after an evening of wine and games, as well as the occasional bored sentry patrolling the streets, but they were simple enough to avoid. Holding to the shadows, I made my way to my destination with the stealth of a fox, my footsteps almost as soft. Though my movement was silent, my mind was not, and my heart thudded in my ear like a war-drum. For I was afraid. Not afraid that I would be detected, but that my summoner would not be there.

The temple was a black silhouette against the midnight blue of the sky. A weak glow leaking from the patterned screens showed that at least one lamp burned within. I paused before the paired doors of the sanctum, listening for the slightest hint of noise. Hearing nothing, I slipped inside.

She was there, standing with her back to me as she gazed upon the ancient wooden statue of Dionysus. An oil lamp at the god's feet flickered."I knew you would come," she said.

Althaia turned to face me. The sight of her was like water on a parched tongue. She was beautiful. I had last seen her in Haliartos. After the battle, we had no time alone. She had returned to Thebes with Epaminondas, a parting gaze her only farewell. Back in Athens I had waited for months, hearing nothing from either Althaia or her brother. I had almost given up hope when the mysterious, short message arrived, bidding me to "stand before the oldest god" at midnight on this day.

Now that she was here before me, I steeled myself to say what I must say. For we cannot hide trembling behind the high walls we build in our hearts. That is not life. We must risk ourselves to gain anything. I would ask her to be my wife and to let me be the shield against her fears and let her be the shield against mine. Propriety could go to Hades.

"I have missed you," I said, stepping towards her. She stiffened as I drew near. I stopped. "What is it?" I asked. I was so close I could have reached out and caressed her marble-smooth cheek.

Althaia hesitated, as though afraid. But she collected herself and spoke the words she had come to say. "Thaletos has asked my father for permission to marry me. My father has agreed. We are to wed next month."

My heart was a cold stone in my chest. I withdrew a step. "He is a good man," I forced myself to say, my face tight. I stared at the ground. "I would do nothing to dishonour him."

"Nor I," she said. I found the strength to look at her. The wet trails left by her tears glistened in the lamplight.

"It is a good match. I am happy for you," I managed to say, heart-scarred though I was. It was true. Althaia would marry a good man from an esteemed Theban family. The union would only enhance the reputations of both families. They would, gods willing, have strong children together. My soul wept.

Althaia wiped the tears from her cheeks. "That is not all, Daimon." Her hands moved protectively to cover her belly. "I am with child."

Many thoughts raced through my mind. There were many implications. "Thaletos is aware of this?" I asked.

"He is. He believes it to belong to Eurymachus." There was something in her tone that suggested otherwise.

"It does not?" Hope and fear swirled within me.

Joy sparked through the sadness in Althaia's eyes, and the corner of her mouth curled upward. "There was an incident on my wedding day, if you recall. The marriage was never consummated before Eurymachus sought to make me disappear. For that I am grateful at least."

"You carry my child?" I asked, not daring to believe it.

Althaia tipped her head towards the ancient carving of Dionysus. "The God has blessed us."

Like all blessings from the gods, the price was steep. Though I stood but steps away from Althaia, there was an uncrossable gulf between me and the future I would never have with her. "What will happen now?" I asked.

"Thaletos has said he will raise the child as his own, if..."

"If?"

"If Eurymachus does not claim him," she said, blinking away tears.

By law, in Thebes as it was in Athens, the child would belong to the household of Eurymachus, even after the divorced wife returned to her own family. I recalled Eurymachus' whispered threat in Haliartos, that I would not be able to protect Althaia. The Theban aristocrat, for all his vileness, was no fool. He would surmise whose child it was and use it to strike back at us. Of this I had no doubt. The dark part of my being, the demon that is my namesake, stirred within me. "That will not happen," I said.

"But how?"

"I will do what is necessary," I said.

Althaia nodded. She glanced at the worn statue in its niche. "No," she said, her voice filled with resolve. "By the God, we will share this burden together."

THE FOREST OPENED UP INTO A CLEARING. In the moonlight the space seemed smaller than it was, with the ring of trees pressing in like a cordon of soldiers. I shrugged the body off my shoulders. There was a muffled explosion of breath through the canvas sack I had tied over my prisoner's head as he hit the ground with a heavy thud.

The bound figure gasped to regain his wind, finally sputtering, "Where have you taken me, Athenian?"

I kicked him in the gut. "Shut up."

"At least take off this hood." I kicked him again. He moaned weakly but wisely held his tongue.

The heavy breathing of the hooded captive was the only sound that disturbed the night. But we were not alone. Not for long. The glow of approaching torches grew brighter to the east. Soon their bearers reached the grove. The masked procession filed into the clearing and formed a menacing ring around us.

"Release me!" the hooded captive demanded. "Return me to my men at once!"

I had tracked Eurymachus while he was on a hunting expedition with his bodyguards. Hunting is a pastime of the wealthy. The rich are so predictable, like the game they like to pursue. Being predictable is as dangerous for men as it is for the beasts they hunt. Especially when I am the hunter.

"You'll be joining them soon, Theban," I said.

Eurymachus mustered enough courage to challenge me. "Why haven't you killed me?"

"It is not my place," I said. I knelt and removed his hood.

Eurymachus sucked in the cool night air, glaring at me. He opened his mouth to speak once more, but the words caught in his throat as he belatedly became aware of the torch-wielding masked figures around the perimeter of the grove. "What is this madness?" he finally croaked, his eyes flicking from one grotesque mask to the next. I ignored him and rose to my feet.

The sputtering crackle of the torches filled the grove. At last, one of the acolytes spoke, raising a dagger from the folds in her cloak and pointing it at me. "It is forbidden for men to profane this sacred place!" Iokaste declared from behind her mask.

Another of the maenads broke from the ring, putting herself between me and Iokaste. The second maenad extended her own wicked dagger and lifted the bull-horn amulet from my chest. From behind the mask, Althaia's eyes glinted in the torchlight. "No! See the token at his throat. He is a servant of the God!" A murmur of acknowledgment rippled among the masked acolytes of Dionysus.

Iokaste grunted with reluctant acceptance. "Then we shall forgive his trespass. *This time*." Her dagger point moved away from me to aim at the prone Eurymachus. "And what of the other?"

"He bears no such token," Althaia said.

Eurymachus found his voice. "Iokaste! Althaia! Do you think I do not recognize you? Free me now and you will be spared my wrath!"

"Silence!" Iokaste boomed. The mask amplified her voice so that it filled the natural theatre formed by the surrounding trees. Eurymachus' protest was stifled by my foot on his neck. Iokaste made a slow turn, appealing to the other members of her sisterhood. "What price shall be paid for this one's blasphemy?"

A maenad with a profuse tangle of flaming red hair stepped into the circle. "Blood," Meli said. The utterance had barely fallen from her lips when blades revealed themselves in the hands of every maenad. Eurymachus squirmed in vain under my boot.

"And who among us shall deliver the first blow?" Iokaste demanded of her sister.

"Let the newest initiate be the first to strike!" Meli answered. She gestured at the slight woman beside her.

The masked figure, taking my sister's cue, advanced. I backed away. She was slight of build, and the dagger in her hand seemed unwieldy in the thin arm that held it. The weight of the weapon made it tremble in her hand, but I do not know whether it was fear or anticipation that caused the blade to quiver. The girl's free hand reached up to grasp her mask. The contorted features slipped away to reveal the face beneath.

The wide eyes of Keaera the slave girl trapped her former tormentor in their icy grip. A slave's vengeance on a cruel master was my wedding gift to Keaera. Eurymachus quailed under the freed slave's merciless stare.

The maenad Iokaste pointed her dagger at me. "Daimon of Athens. The God thanks you for this offering. But now you must leave. It is forbidden for a man to witness the Mysteries of the God." The maenads parted, offering me an exit. As I slipped into the night, I hazarded one last glance at the secret rites. The robed figures began to encircle the kneeling Eurymachus. Desperate, he cast a terrified look my way. "Athenian! Save me!" But he had offended the god. And the god would have his revenge.

I picked my way through the moonlit forest. A distant scream fractured the stillness of the night. It ended with unmistakable abruptness, leaving only the sound of my breathing to disturb the night. Eurymachus would threaten Althaia no more. My unborn child would be safe.

I tread lightly on the trail down the mountain, eager to put Thebes and thoughts of Althaia behind me. That I believed such things were possible only proves what a fool I am, for the threads of two lives are not easily separated once they become entwined. How could I have known what pattern the Fates would spin? How could I have foreseen what that child would become? But that sadness lay far in the future, concealed even from the most far-sighted of the gods.

Before me now was only the path beneath my feet. I picked up my pace.

With luck I would be at the borders of Attica before dawn.

Shadow of Thebes

AUTHOR'S NOTE

To a certain extent, when people speak of the history of Classical Greece, what they are really talking about is the history of Athens. Our main historical sources for the period, Thucydides and Xenophon, were Athenians. All extant classical Greek tragedies and comedies, from which so much cultural and historical information can be gleaned, were written by Athenians. Plato, perhaps the most influential philosopher in history, very much had his home city of Athens in mind when he composed his dialogues. So, we have to remind ourselves on occasion that Ancient Greece was much more than just Athens.

We only have to look at Sparta to understand how different two Greek cities could be in their customs and politics. As for the other great city of the period, Thebes, we know relatively little, even compared to the unhelpfully silent Spartans. It was very fortunate, then, that *Thebes: The Forgotten City of Ancient Greece* by renowned historian Paul Cartledge came out just as I was writing this book. Pulling together information from a wide variety of sources, Cartledge shows how Thebes was both similar to and different from the more familiar Athens.

Though the cultured Athenians often looked down their noses at the Thebans, the city was renowned for its poets, musicians, and artists, something I tried to touch on here and there, but did not have the space to explore further. Perhaps more important for Daimon's story were the historical figures of the time as well as Thebans' attitudes towards gender and sexuality.

There are indications that women in Thebes, though by no means equal to men, had more freedom than their Athenian counterparts. Whereas Athenian women (more well-born ones, at least) would have been largely confined to the private spaces of their homes, it is thought that women in Thebes enjoyed some degree of liberty in public in both speech and visibility, something I have tried show through characters like Althaia and Iokaste. This is not to say, however, that even Theban women did not suffer from the restrictions and expectations placed on them because of their sex, as Althaia stated so plainly.

Another area where Theban mores seemed to have differed from those of Athens were their attitudes towards homosexuality. In addition to Cartledge's book, my main source regarding homosexuality in Ancient Greece was *Bisexuality in the Ancient World* by Eva Cantarella. Like any culture, Greek attitudes towards homosexuality were not static but varied from place to place and over time (just think about how much attitudes towards sexuality have changed over the decades in our own time.) In Athens, older men might have sex regularly with their wives or female prostitutes while also having a male lover, usually quite young. There are indications, however, that in Athens, open, exclusive homosexual relationships between adult men were increasingly frowned upon as the late 5th century BCE progressed.

Thebans, however, seemed to be more tolerant of homosexual relationships. This is best evidenced by the famous Sacred Band, an elite group of three hundred Theban soldiers made up exclusively of pairs of male lovers (the Sacred Band came into existence in the decades following the events of Shadow of Thebes.) More importantly for this story, there is quite suggestive evidence that Epaminondas was a homosexual. Through Epaminondas and other characters, I have tried to touch on how homosexuality and bisexuality were ever-present in Ancient Greek society.

For those who may not know, Epaminondas, son of Polymnis, is not a fictional character. Like Thrasybulus, Epaminondas is a Very Important Person in the 4th century BC. The Theban general will shape Greek history for the next three decades, not to give any spoilers. Given the central role of Thebes in this story, it would have been remiss of me to have Daimon running around Thebes while not having some influence on the slightly-younger Epaminodas, perhaps even nudging him on his path to greatness.

Ultimately, I wanted to write an exciting adventure story with plenty of action and battles, but I cannot ignore the cultural setting in which Daimon's story takes place, including aspects such as the status of women and the sexual attitudes of the time. As such, slavery, though present in the previous two books, is much more front and centre in Shadow of Thebes.

If we were to travel back in time to Ancient Greece, the omnipresent institution of slavery is likely what we would find most shocking. It is difficult to overstate how pervasive slavery was in the ancient world. So many times, ancient writers reduce the sacking of a city into a single, all-too-familiar sentence: "The men were killed and the women and children were sold into slavery." A slave's fortune could vary considerably. Among the worst fates was to end up in a mine or quarry, where life expectancy could be a matter of months. Many slaves ended up as house-servant or labourers for farmers or craftsmen. Slaves who proved their intelligence sometimes ended up with a certain amount of freedom or authority. Slaves in Athens even had nominal rights (although how strictly these rights were enforced is a matter of debate.) In Persia, slaves like Tolmides could rise to positions of power and influence, but were still slaves nevertheless.But knowing what people are, there is little doubt that slaves were subject to all kinds of humiliations, especially female slaves, who must have suffered from the sexual predations of their masters on a regular basis. Daimon, as the son of a slave himself, is more sympathetic to the plight of slaves himself, but he is also a man of his time who accepts slavery as a fact of life. It is important to remember how different the Greeks were from us, no matter how temptingly familiar they must seem at times.

Besides social and cultural details, there is also the matter of historical events. What I love the most about Greek military and political history is how crazily unlikely it is. The events described in the previous pages are no exception, as I largely adhere to what ancient historians have passed down to us. The Persians did send money with Timocrates of Rhodes to fund Athens and her allies and force a withdrawal of Spartan forces from Asia Minor. Spartan messages were intercepted, revealing that Lysander was bringing an army to Haliartus. The Thebans were reluctant to leave their city until Thrasybulus miraculously appeared at Thebes with the Athenian army. The Thebans, after a night-long march, arrived in Haliartus before Lysander, setting up an ambush and trapping Lysander up against the city walls, where the Spartan general was killed. It was said that pro-Spartan Thebans such as Leontiades, fought with extra effort in order to lessen the suspicion against them. Thrasybulus arrived in Haliartus the next day, just in time to face off against the second Spartan army led by Pausanias, who, seeing the numbers not being in his favour, left the field without a fight (Why Pausanias arrived a day later is a matter of speculation. Many believe that it was merely the result of a miscommunication. Others, however, suggest that for some reason Lysander wanted to be in Haliartus before the Spartan king. If this is true, then Lysander's secret purpose died with him.) And finally, after decisively beating the Spartans at sea, the Athenian exile Konon did bring an entire fleet of warships to Athens, a gift of the Great King. In a historical instant, Athens had regained much of the strength it lost at the end off the Peloponnesian War. As I said, history can be stranger than fiction.

Where history leaves gaps, the writer of historical fiction can exercise some imagination. Daimon's ploy to take Haliartus is one such creative interpretation but is not as far-fetched as you might guess. The Greeks, in general, were not good at dealing with city walls. More often than not, successfully taking a city in war involved getting the enemy to open their city gates, either through betrayal from within or through some other tricks. Many such schemes and ruses are described in my Loeb edition of *Siege Defence* by Aeneas Tacticus (Aeneas the Tactician), a near contemporary of Daimon's.

The Dionysian cult in Thebes is another aspect of Daimon's story which though fabulous is based on fact. A wide array of such mystery cults were flourishing in Greece during this period. It is thought that Euripides' play The Bacchae, was in part a response to the popularity such cults in Athens at the time, and I could not help but riff on some scenes from what many consider the greatest Greek tragedy (Read it if you haven't!) Though many may picture Dionysus as a slightly overweight deity lounging about eating grapes and drinking wine, the god was much more than that. It is generally agreed that Dionysus was originally an eastern god (perhaps even Thracian), and his is one of the earliest appearing deity names in the archaeological record. In one version of the god's story, Dionysus is killed, mankind arises from his flesh, and the god is born again. As such, the cult of Dionysus is associated with the idea of secret knowledge and eternal afterlife for his initiates in a heaven-like realm. Over the next few centuries, the cult of Dionysus only grew in importance. In short, Dionysus is ancient, powerful, and dangerous.

Finally, some of you may be asking, "Where's Plato?" Alas, Plato is exile, and as much as I tried, I couldn't fit him into the story. But don't worry! Daimon, gods willing, still has many adventures ahead of him, in which Plato certainly has a role to play…

ACKNOWLEDGMENTS

I don't get many emails from readers, but I do get some. I can't express how encouraging it is to hear from people who have been enjoying Daimon's adventures. In particular, when people ask me, "When is the next book coming out?" it really gives me the motivation to keep going. Daimon might have stopped after Book 1 if I didn't know that there were at least a few of you out there who like what I'm doing, so thank you. And for others, please reach out to me through the contact email on my website. I would love to hear from you. Cheers.

A REQUEST...

I hope you enjoyed this story. If you did, I would really appreciate it if you could leave a review on Amazon or Goodreads. It is really important for the Amazon algorithm-y things, and it is also good for the author's fragile ego. A tweet on Twitter, a post on your Facebook book club page, anything is appreciated! Thank you!

M.S.

ABOUT THE AUTHOR

Martin Sulev graduated from the University of Toronto with a degree in Palaeontology but now wishes he had studied Classics. He has worked as a freelance writer in the ESL industry and has contributed translations of Chinese short stories to two anthologies published by Cornell University. He currently lives in Toronto with his wife and son.

More information on upcoming Demon of Athens novels can be found at:

www.martinsulev.com

Follow on Twitter @MSulev

Facebook: @MartinSulevAuthor

COMING IN 2024

EXILE OF CORINTH
Demon of Athens Book 4

Shadow of Thebes

338

Printed in Great Britain
by Amazon

25718510R00199